Please feel free to send me an email. Just know that my publisher filters these emails. Good news is always welcome.

Shreya Pandey - shreya_pandey@awesomeauthors.org

Sign up for my blog for updates and freebies!
shreya-pandey.awesomeauthors.org

I0666733

About the Publisher

BLVNP Incorporated, A Nevada Corporation, 340 S. Lemon #6200, Walnut CA 91789, info@blvnp.com / legal@blvnp.com

DISCLAIMER

This book is a work of FICTION. It is fiction and not to be confused with reality. Neither the author nor the publisher or its associates assume any responsibility for any loss, injury, death or legal consequences resulting from acting on the contents in this book. The author's opinions are not to be construed as the opinions of the publisher. The material in this book is for entertainment purposes ONLY. Cover image from Shutterstock com.

Praise for A Flirtationship

This book was so entertaining, it kept me on the edge of my seat throughout the whole book. I loved it!
-Katie, *Goodreads*

I loved this book, I read so many times and never got bored of it.
-Jaskiran, *Goodreads*

A Flirtationship is probably by far one of the most addicting books I have read, and for some good reason. Pandey puts so much effort and detail into Scarlett and Aiden that it makes me want to meet the pair in real life. Scarlett with her passionate thinking on every subject matter and her decisions kept me turning pages throughout the late nights. Aiden with his not-so-perfect lifestyle once he realizes his flaws are what make this book appear to be real to me as a reader. The character dynamics are well planned, the plot isn't cliche driven, and overall the book kept me on the edge of my seat the whole time!
-Melissa, *Goodreads*

A Flirtationship is an achingly beautiful tale. Readers will swoon over Aiden and Scarlett.
-Emma, *Goodreads*

This book is so well written, that when you read it, it feels like you're with the characters, experiencing what they're experiencing. The plot is great too, with just enough bumps along the way, to make the reader want to read on. All in all, it's one of THE best teen fiction books I've read, and I've read a LOT.
-Chaitrali, *Goodreads*

A Flirtationship

By: Shreya Pandey

ISBN: 978-1-68030-967-6

Table of Contents

To all the girls who feel invisible
To all the girls who believe they aren't good enough
To all the girls who have so much to give, but love always evades them

FREE DOWNLOAD

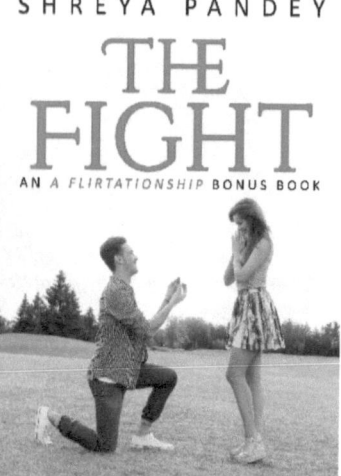

Get these freebies and MORE when you sign up for the author's mailing list!

shreya-pandey.awesomeauthors.org

Prologue

Some things never change. My best friend Aiden Walkers barging into my room every Friday night to convince me to go to some stupid high school party is one of them.

Today is no different.

I am pretty sure he'll be making an appearance tonight. *Especially* tonight. School is out, and summer has officially begun, which is why I'm not wearing my favorite tee.

It's all faded now, with a couple of holes here and there. My mom keeps pestering me to throw it away. I refuse to though. I always wear it before the weekend and two days straight after that. That's gross, I know. But it's also *so* comfortable. And considering that I won't be leaving my room during the weekend anyway, it doesn't really matter. I'm not wearing the tee right now, for obvious reasons. I don't want Aiden to see me in it.

My bedroom door bangs open at exactly 7 PM, and in strolls Aiden. That's another thing that never changes—that precise time. He can be the most unpunctual creature on this earth, but he always stomps into my room at the same time every week, without fail.

"And here you are," I mutter, sounding decidedly unexcited.

"And here I am!" he announces. *Honestly, if he expects me to be surprised...*

"I know you missed me, but I'm here now," he says, plopping down on my bed.

I snort. "Missed you? We were together like four hours ago."

"Details-shmetails, don't matter." He brushes it off.

It's not like I go out every week, you know? Most of the times I stay in, refusing Aiden's invitation. That never stops him though. He makes it a point to come over anyway.

"So, are you ready?" he inquires.

"For what? Another party?" I roll my eyes.

"Exactly!" He *does* look ready to party. He's changed out of the plaid shirt he'd worn to school today, exchanging it for a tight-fitting black tee. He's also styled his dark brown hair so it appeared effortlessly messy. He looks hot.

"No Aiden, not again. I'm *done*. We've been going to a different party almost *every* week. I'm so sick of this. I don't want to do this anymore. Plus, sophomore year has just ended. So I'm going to—"

"Exactly! Another school year is over. Summer has begun." He's unfazed by my lack of interest. "You can't just miss the start-of-summer party! *Everybody's* going."

"Well, that's just great then. You'll have loads of people to keep you company. You should go without me." I turn back to what I was doing earlier: watching the latest episode of *Pretty Little Liars*.

"Never!"

"I don't understand why you do this every week Aiden." I sigh. "You have *so* many friends, why don't you just go out with them?"

"Because they are not *you*."

My heart flutters just a little. Aiden smiles down at me, his milk chocolate eyes twinkling.

"Now chop chop! Get dressed. Wear something sexy, okay? It's going to be fun."

It's going to be fun. That's what he *always* says. Then when we get to the party, he gets swarmed by all these people and I'm left to fend for myself. We hardly spend more than an hour together. He always leaves with some random girl. *Totally not fun.*

If given the chance, I'd spend my weekend cooped up in my bedroom, binge-watching TV shows or reading books. Aiden doesn't let me do that though. He just has this way of coaxing me out of my shell.

So that's how I find myself at yet another party.

I encounter the same thing I always do at these parties: the house filled with the stench of sweat and the thrum of bass; teenagers dancing to obnoxious hip-hop music; red plastic cups littering the floor; and couples occupying the couch, making out.

Aiden gets swarmed by people as soon as we arrive. They either greet him from afar or come up to him, offering him a drink. Why did I have to be friends with someone as popular as him? It's so tiring.

He's talking to some of the boys from the football team, when this girl pushes past the guys and plants herself right in front of him. It's Brittany, the girl he hooked up with last week.

Oh dear Lord, here we go.

"Hello Aiden," she coos, running her fingers through her strawberry blonde tresses. I stare at her face, her lips in particular. *How are they so pouty and pink? And how is her hair so bouncy? What's her secret? What products does she use?* I can't help but glance down at my own hair—dark and wavy, tangled at the tips, just a little limp.

She takes Aiden's hands in hers, tracing soft patterns on his wrist. "I've been looking *all* over for you." She flutters her eyelashes. "I noticed one of the bedrooms upstairs is empty. What do you say, we get out of here and . . .?" She smiles suggestively at him.

Ugh. Kill me already.

Of course, he'll concede and then they'll go off to some secluded corner of the house and get it on. And I'll be left to stare around awkwardly, feeling dejected and miserable just like always.

"No, not today Brittany. I'm kind of busy."

Wait, what?

She gapes at him. "Busy? With what?" she demands, sounding extremely vexed.

"As you can see, I'm here with my best friend." He gently wraps his arms around my shoulder. "So you'll just have to find some other guy to mess around with."

Brittany is momentarily taken aback. My gaze flits between Aiden and her, feeling awkward. She glares at me and then walks away. I instantly turn to Aiden.

"Wow, what was *that?* Brittany's going to be really pissed about this."

"A hundred Brittanys will come and go, but there's only ever going to be one of you," he quips, pulling me closer to him. I open and close my mouth like a fish, unable to formulate a response. "I'm not going to abandon you tonight, Scar. I promised you we'll have fun, and I'm planning to keep my promise. Tonight, we're going to party *together.*"

"Uh . . . I don't know if—"

"C'mon." He leads me through the throng of people. "Dance with me."

We push our way through the crowd and stop at a relatively uncongested area. Aiden starts swaying his body to the music. He rolls his arms in the air, beckoning me to join him. I can't help laughing. He looks ridiculous.

I chuckle. I know he's deliberately dancing like this to lighten my mood. "Aiden, you're such a dork!"

"Shh, come here." He takes my hand and twirls me around as the speakers blast a popular number by Rihanna. Aiden and I have our arms wrapped around each other, and every time he exhales, I can feel it on my cheek. I feel laughter bubble up on the tip of my tongue. My hair bounces wildly, going all over. We continue dancing, moving our bodies to the lively beat of the music.

Suddenly, my gaze falls on this girl. She's really pretty— long auburn hair, sharp hazel eyes, and warm honey brown skin. She's the kind of girl Aiden hooks up with in empty bedrooms. She's just sitting there on the couch with a friend of hers, ogling Aiden. She realizes I'm observing her and looks away, embarrassed.

I turn back to Aiden. My heart stops for a moment, hit by the sheer intensity of his gaze. He's breathing heavily, his chest rising and falling rapidly with every breath he takes. The air in the room suddenly feels electric. My insides twist and my breath comes out in short spurts.

Why is he looking at me like that?

He takes a step closer. My breath quickens.

His lips hover over mine. His eyes burn with a silent question. He starts leaning towards me ever so slowly . . .

"Uh, I feel *really* thirsty. I think I'm going to go get a drink," I interject.

"Oh, uh sure." He massages the back of his neck awkwardly. "I'll come with you."

I shake my head furiously. "No, no, it's okay. I'll be back in a few. Do you want me to get anything for you?" He refuses. "Cool, I'll be right back. Till then, why don't you go talk to *her*." I gesture towards that girl I'd noticed looking at him earlier.

Her face flames up when I suddenly point towards her. She's been checking him out for the past hour. Her eyes have been practically glued on Aiden. "She has been looking at you for a while. She's *definitely* interested."

Before he can protest, I turn around and walk away, heading straight to the bowl of punch in the kitchen. I grab a cup and start pouring myself some.

I really *am* thirsty, and I *genuinely* need a drink. But even the dumbest person in the room can figure out that that's not the reason why I practically ran away from Aiden.

I needed to get away from him. It was too much. *He* was too much.

He just . . . he caught me off guard. *What was he thinking!?* He can't really expect us to kiss! I mean we're friends. We've never seen each other like that. Whatever we have is purely platonic. It wouldn't feel right.

Or would it?

I wrap my arms around myself, suddenly feeling cold.

Think about it Scarlett, would it really be so bad for you two to kiss?

I shake my head in refusal, trying to convince myself. I can't just...kiss him. I can't.

Oh c'mon. Don't be a chicken. Go back in there and do it. You know you want to.

I . . . I *want* to?

Yes. Go.

My heart jumps in my chest. With newfound fervor, I take a huge swig from the cup that's clutched in my hand and then stomp back where I'd come from.

Yes, I should totally kiss him. Maybe I always secretly wanted to. What's the worst that could happen?

And so, I head back to do what I should have done the first time—kiss my best friend.

But of course, Aiden listened to me. He always does. He listened to me and now he's talking to that girl just like I suggested him to. They both are laughing about something. He's playing with his hair. He *always* plays with his hair when he's talking to someone he finds attractive.

I can't really go and kiss him now, can I?

I dump the empty cup in the nearest trashcan, and then head outside. I know Aiden and I were supposed to hang out tonight but I just can't anymore. It's all so weird now. I quickly shoot him a text. I could have said it in person, but I know he would have insisted on driving me home.

I'm heading home, I feel queasy. I think I'm about to get my period. You stay and have fun. Bye x

My head flashes back to when we'd almost kissed. For just a second, I contemplate going back and kissing him; consequences be damned. But then I think about that really hot girl he's talking to right now. Why would he want me when he can have someone like her?

You know what? This is probably for the best. It would have probably changed everything.

Little did I know that things had already started changing.

Chapter One

Scarlett

"Is she here yet?" I ask impatiently.

There are a dozen things I could be doing right now. Dozens. I'm not even kidding. I could be working on that article I need to submit to our school newspaper this Friday. It's about the deplorable condition of the chemistry lab equipment. I could be huddled up in my friend Sharon's car right now, jamming to the songs of our favorite boy-band. Or the best: curled up on my bed, reading a book.

But here I am instead, on the roof-top of the dilapidated brick building that I call school, waiting for Aiden's girlfriend-to-be.

Yes, you heard that right.

I still have difficulty using the words 'Aiden' and 'girlfriend' in the same sentence. It's certainly strange. For starters, he's never had a girlfriend before. Never. He's had plenty of opportunities, of course. What with girls throwing themselves at him left and right. But he never felt the urge to take things further with any of them. It never went beyond casual.

But suddenly one day Aiden's telling me about this girl he met at this party, and how they had this instant connection—as if that ever happens in real life—and how they've been hanging out all summer.

So what? I'd asked. *You've dated plenty of girls before.*

But it's different this time, he'd retorted.

Different how? Are her boobs bigger? I'd laughed, brushing it off.

I guess he'd taken that jest to heart, because he never mentioned her again. Of course, I'd assumed his silence as confirmation for what I'd known all along: that this was just another fling. Maybe it had lasted a little longer than most, but it was a fling all the same.

Turns out, I was wrong. A week ago, Aiden came up to me, demanding my help. Apparently, he was going to ask this girl to be his girlfriend. *Girlfriend!* God, can you believe it? I knew I couldn't.

"Okay, okay, stop!" I'd exclaimed. "You almost got me there for a second. You're going exclusive? As if!" I start laughing. "But honestly, drop it. It's not that funny."

"It's *not* supposed to be funny. I'm being serious here, alright? I like Hailey and I'm going to ask her to be my girlfriend. I came to you because you're my best friend. But *that* was obviously a mistake."

My eyes had widened. So he was serious. *Wow.* "No! It wasn't," I'd protested. "You just took me by surprise, that's all. So tell me, who is this special girl?" I'd looked at him with curiosity burning my insides.

"You'll find out soon enough. What I need you to do right now is to help me surprise her on her birthday next week."

Aiden had wasted no time telling me his plan. The detail and precision with which he'd related it made me realize that he had spent a lot of time thinking it through. And that was saying something. Aiden's not a planner. This Hailey girl must be really special to him.

And turns out she is. Because here was Aiden Walkers, a week later—cool and confident Aiden Walkers, hyperventilating over a *girl*. I'd never thought I'd see this day.

He's leaning against the railing. I think I've told him to not do that at least *five* times already. It's prohibited to come up here. This place is always kept locked for safety reasons. But Aiden being his reckless self refuses to budge. I keep worrying someone will spot us here and then it'll be detention for a week.

Aiden's genius little birthday plan had been this: us stealing the janitor's extra key, sneaking to the school's roof and giving Hailey a surprise here. We'd cut the last two classes of the day and spent time blowing purple and pink balloons and spreading confetti on the floor of the roof. Of course, since it was a little windy here, that had back fired. The balloons were still here. The confetti? Not so much.

Of course, we could have done all this at his house. Or hers. Or he could have taken her out like normal people do. But oh no, why go with the easier and the normal when you can break a dozen rules and make your life harder? Aiden's justification: "it's more fun this way."

Boys.

I'd be giving him a hard time right now if I couldn't see how obviously nervous he was. His cheeks are tinged with a pinch of pink. He's running his fingers through his wavy hair. *Holy shit. Aiden is actually nervous!* I still can't believe it.

"Hey! Chill out, will you? Why are you so tense? You're Aiden fucking Walkers for God's sake! No girl in her right mind would turn *you* down," I say. I know I'm going a little overboard with this and it'll probably go straight to his head but I don't care. He needs this right now.

"You sure she won't?" he asks, sounding doubtful.

"I *know* she won't. It'll be okay, I promise." I give his shoulders a gentle squeeze.

He smiles his beautiful smile at me. "Thank you so much Scar. You *really* helped me out."

"Honestly? You're thanking me? I thought we were past these formalities."

He steps forward. His arms wrap around my body, pulling me in for a hug. I gently collide against his chest. My heart reacts violently, thudding hard and fast. It's still in a state of chaos when Aiden steps back. I smile at him, as if my heart hadn't almost shot up my throat a few seconds ago. It has been happening for a while now. I have no idea why.

"You're sure about this, aren't you? You're sure about her?" I ask him rather seriously. It shouldn't be a big deal. Teenagers get into relationships all the time. It's normal. It's fun, even. But for just a few seconds I get this strange sensation that everything's happening too fast. For a few seconds, it all feels wrong. That if he doesn't stop and think, it'll be too late.

Too late for what?

I don't know.

He looks at me, and I see something flicker in the dark pools of his eyes. Some strange, unnamed emotion I can't quite put a finger on. It comes and it goes.

His lips part. He's going to say something. He's . . . going to answer his phone. It's her.

"Yes." He nods. He's smiling, but it looks a little strained. "Yeah, come upstairs. We're—I mean, *I'm* at the roof. See you!"

He hangs up, and then turns to me.

"I'm sure."

I feel something change; a sense of loss. Like we've crossed a threshold and can never go back now. I don't know what I'd wanted to hear. But somehow, this wasn't it.

I nod. "I should go now. She'll be here any minute. Don't want to be the third wheel! Tell me how it went tomorrow, okay?" I'm about to head downstairs when I hear footsteps. Aiden and my eyes meet at the same time. He mouths the word 'hide' at me. I head towards the water tanks at the back and hide behind them.

About two seconds later a black high heel emerges through the doorway. She's here.

Wait, I know her . . .

I carefully look at her face, trying to commit it to memory. *Where have I seen her before?*

And then it hits me. Aiden had mentioned that he'd met her at a party. Well that wasn't just *any* party. It was that party we attended together, Aiden and I, right before summer started. The one where we almost…

Oh but it's her! It's that same girl who'd been staring at him throughout the evening. There's no mistaking it.

Who would have thought, right?

She starts walking towards him. This is my cue—I need to leave. But for some unknown reason, my legs stay frozen to the spot.

She's looking at the balloons. Then she buries her face in the palm of her hands, blushing. She's actually surprised.

Okay, okay, can we please get on with it?

He clears his throat, glancing at a box we'd carefully set on a spare desk lying on the roof: the cake.

He's going to go ahead with the surprise. Finally.

Now would be a good time to leave.

"So, I got something for you." He gestures towards the box. They both step towards the desk, and he opens up the box to reveal the cake. I can't see it but I know it's red velvet. I ordered it after all. Aiden quickly sets up the candles and lights them.

She giggles, not able to help herself. "Wow, is this for me?"

I roll my eyes. *Of course, it's for you! Can you get any more stupid? I don't recall anyone else here who has a birthday today.*

She blows the candle, shutting her eyes closed for just a few seconds. She grabs the plastic knife that came with the cake and cuts out a small piece of cake. She brings it up to Aiden's mouth, letting him take the first bite. He takes a bite, making her eat what remained. "Happy birthday," he says softly, staring deep into her eyes.

Great, he's working his Aiden charm on her. Soon enough she'll be weak in the knees, kissing him like there's no tomorrow.

Oh wait, I don't want to be here when that happens.

"I . . . uh . . . also brought you something." He extracts a tiny box from his pocket and takes out a necklace. I can't see it very well from here. But she obviously likes it because she claps her hands excitedly like a child.

He didn't mention this part of the surprise to me...

She turns around, removing her hair to expose her neck, gesturing Aiden to put it around her neck. He takes this opportunity to look in my direction. He silently asks me what he should do next. He's still a little nervous. 'Ask her,' I mouth, nodding my head fervently to emphasize my point.

He takes in a long breath, licking his lips.

"Hailey . . . I . . . uh wanted to ask you something," he mumbles.

She gestures for him to go on, while her fingers play with the pendant dangling down her neck.

"I like you, Hailey. I-I really do. The last few months have been almost dream-like. I've loved all the time we've spent together. I've loved hanging out with you. I don't think I've ever been this happy before." He pauses for a second, trying to compose himself. "I don't want us to stop doing this. As much as going out on random dates has been fun, I want *more*. I want to *be* with you. Will you be my girlfriend?"

She gapes at him. Her cheeks pop, her eyes twinkle. She's blushing. For a few seconds, there's nothing but silence. Then she nods, ever so slowly.

"Yes Aiden, I'd love to."

"Wait, really?" he asks, shocked.

She nods, then starts chuckling. He pumps his fist in the air, victoriously. His shoulders relax. He doesn't look stressed anymore. Everything has gone exactly as he'd wanted it to, maybe even better. He is happy.

I smile to myself. Maybe this is a good thing. Maybe this is *exactly* what Aiden needed . . .

They are doing that thing, that thing couples do. They are looking into each other's eyes, smiling like a bunch of fools and slowly, oh so slowly, leaning towards each other.

Oh god, they are going to kiss.

I suddenly feel nauseous. My insides were in knots, until it got hard to breathe. My chest hurts just a little. It's not a nice feeling.

I need to get out of here.

I finally gather the courage to leave. I stealthily head towards the door. Once out of sight, I rush down the stairs. I can finally breathe again.

Chapter Two

Scarlett

The bell rings for a full minute, indicating that class was over. Everyone immediately hurries out, grabbing their bags and books. I was more than happy to follow them out of here. The past hour has been nothing but torture. There's something about history lectures that make you want to sleep. Five more minutes and I would have happily joined the group of students who were deep onto the path to slumber, snoring gently at the back of the class, unnoticed by the teacher.

Lunch hour has begun, which means I'm supposed to meet my friends at the lockers. We'll spend the next fifteen minutes there talking about anything and everything. I trudge down the tiled hallway, trying my best not to bump into people.

I notice Aiden a few meters away, leaning against a locker with his girlfriend standing next to him, both of them laughing about something. My eyes automatically look away. It's been happening for a while now. It's like a natural reflex. Whenever I see them both together, I automatically avert my gaze, feeling uncomfortable.

It's been a little over a month since they both became official. When he's not with me, he's with her (which is most of the time). She's not a junior like us, so he's only able to spend time with her in between classes and after school. Nevertheless, they've been dating exclusively and now everyone at school knows about them.

I spot my friends Sharon, Andrea, and Kayla perched against the locker next to mine. Andrea is jabbering away and Kayla is clutching her stomach, laughing. Sharon meanwhile is flipping through a fat textbook. "Hey guys, what's up?" I greet, pulling open my locker after putting in the combination. I stuff my books inside and turn to my friends.

"Same old, same old. Andrea tell her what happened today in the physics lab." Kayla insists, her choppy platinum colored hair bouncing. She had it dyed recently. She loves experimenting with her hair. Last year, she'd gotten hot pink highlights. She'd looked like a wannabe emo.

Andrea immediately repeats the story. Apparently, a guy named Joshua pushed the pendulum so hard during the experiment they were performing that the string holding the bob came loose. The very next second, the bob came flying through the air and struck the skinny lab assistant square on his forehead. He passed out on the spot. I join them in laughter, imagining the scene unfurl in my head.

As I stand there, laughing with my friends I wonder how I got so lucky. I'm *really* shy. I have a hard time befriending people, not because people don't like me or anything. It's just . . . I'm just really awkward with strangers. I can't make small talk for the life of me. I always question every word that comes out of my mouth, wondering if I'm boring the other person. It's too much stress and so I mess up. It takes me a while to get comfortable, after which I never shut up. But good luck getting to that stage with me. There are layers of social anxiety you'll have to deal with first.

I still don't know how I befriended these awesome girls. We're not the best of friends, but we enjoy each other's company.

Out of the three of them, I'm the closest to Sharon. She's the prettiest girl I know, with long chestnut brown hair that curl at the tips and mischievous brown eyes. She always has this lazy smile playing on her lips like she's up to no good. She always appears to be all calm and serene, but that's an obvious façade. She'll open her mouth and you'll figure out pretty quickly how hyper she can get. I'm not even sure how we get along since we are polar opposites. But somehow, we always have fun together. I bring the much needed calm and peace in her life and she brings the touch of crazy in mine.

Five minutes later, after dumping our books in our lockers, we head towards the cafeteria. This is our routine: we all meet for her when the bell rings for lunch. Then we gossip near the lockers for some time before making our way to the cafeteria. We have a fixed table there. It's near one of the large windows that looks out into the garden. I sit there every day; or well, the days I don't sit with Aiden. We have a system. I get to sit with my girl squad every other day and with Aiden on the rest of those days.

Or at least, that's how it used to be. But he spends lunch with his girlfriend now.

I smile faintly to myself as I take my usual seat. There was a time when I'd felt like a loner and had nowhere to sit. I used to wander from place to place, usually ending up spending my lunch hour in the library. That was in the beginning of ninth grade.

But that changed a few weeks later.

"Hey, mind if I sit here?" I had asked her during lunch one day. I had been very nervous, but at the same time, I was sick of being all by myself.

Kayla was the first person who hadn't been turned off by my tendency to be overly quiet. "Oh, sure!" She had smiled enthusiastically at me and had moved over to give me some space. Everyone else had been busy talking among themselves, while I just sat there, munching my food silently.

"So Scarlett, you're Scarlett, right?" Kayla had spoken up. I'd nodded in response. "Let me introduce you to everyone." She has no idea how much I'd appreciated her doing that. If it hadn't been for her, I would have never interacted with all these people. Kayla had pointed to everyone sitting around the table one by one and had told me their names. I'd honestly not remembered a single name—except one.

"And this is Aiden," Kayla had said. Weirdly, his name had stuck in my mind long after. We'd awkwardly smiled at each other then and shook hands. And it's been over a year and I remember every tiny detail of that scene: how his hands had been slightly rough when I'd held it, how he had looked a little distracted when he smiled at me. How I'd felt this strange *click* somewhere deep in my chest and had sat there frozen for a couple of seconds, trying to figure out what I'd just felt. It had felt like a sign, a sign telling me that my life was going to change forever.

It still hasn't.

"Oh my god, look who's here!" Andrea exclaims, bringing me back to the present. Our eyes immediately snap in the direction of her gaze. The very next second, my friends dissolve in a fit of giggles. I, on the other hand, try really hard not to blush.

William Hayden has just entered through the cafeteria doors and is making his way towards his usual table. Four pair of eyes follow his every move.

Why the sudden excitement due to this William, you ask? Well, during a certain game of spin the bottle that we played *ages* ago, I mentioned that I found William, now a senior, *really* hot. My friends refuse to forget this insignificant detail. They think I have a *huge* crush on him when really, I just find him attractive. And why wouldn't I? With his beautiful mop of honey colored curls and bright blue eyes he's the definition of gorgeous.

Popularity has its consequences. Nasty rumors are one of them. Rumor is that he's a womanizer. He dumps girls right and left and is absolutely heartless. Of course, I've heard all of this from people, so I can't be sure. It's not like I personally know him, and I probably never will. He's *way* out of my league.

"Oh, here he comes again!" Andrea nudges me. William gets up from his seat and starts walking towards our table. I don't get alarmed. As usual, he's not stopping by; he doesn't even know us for god's sake! He's just heading towards the lunch line. Kayla nods in appreciation as he passes us. And then she and Andrea dissolve in a fit of giggles again. Sharon rolls her eyes at their childishness. I choose to glare instead.

"God, shut up! If he hears you—"

"Oh cmon, he won't. Besides didn't you say so yourself that he *knows* you have a crush on him?" Andrea says dismissively.

"For the last time, I *don't* have a crush on him. Plus, I'm not sure what he knows. Maybe he has a slight idea of how attractive I find him. But then, that would be no surprise, he knows *every* girl does."

"But you said he's *always* looking at you, what about that?"

"Not *always*! But yeah, I did catch him looking at me a few times. Maybe he finds me weird and knows about my obsession with his hair."

"*Or* he finds you really cute," Kayla says, shrugging.

This time I join Sharon in her eye rolling. It takes Andrea and Kayla so little to get all worked up, it's kinda ridiculous.

"Oh my god, he just looked at you!" Andrea and Kayla gush at the same time.

I quickly slap both of my hands over their mouths. "Shut up you morons! I bet he heard you." I feel so nervous and scared. What if he *actually* heard them? How embarrassing would it be if he walked over to our table or something and asked us why we're always ogling him?!

They remove my hands almost immediately and look at me.

"Who cares? The bottom line is that he *looked* at you. And guys just don't randomly stare at the same girl every day!" Andrea protests. "Maybe he's interested in you."

"Hello, he as a girlfriend, remember?"

I don't really see a lot of him except during lunch or sometimes in the hallways. But when I do, he's *always* with this girl. She's his latest 'catch', or so everyone says.

"His girlfriend's name is Angelina and let me tell you, she's also his best friend. I bet he's in love with her or something," Sharon states seriously.

"That doesn't mean anything. You know how he's with girls. They come and go so fast out of his life," Kayla pipes in.

"See? He could be interested in you. You should totally talk to him." Andrea encourages me.

I shake my head in refusal. "Now why would I do that? He dumps girls like they're dirty tissue papers. It doesn't matter if he's interested or not. Because it always ends in the same ugly way for all of them."

I continue to stare at William. His girlfriend has joined him now. His hands are intertwined with hers. I silently wonder what he's like. Is he really as amazing as certain people believe? Or is he exactly like those nasty rumors suggest?

Either way, it shouldn't matter. He doesn't even know I exist.

Someone suddenly stops by our table, interrupting our collective ogle-fest. "Close your mouth girls. You're drooling too much. You look so thirsty, it's ridiculous."

It's Darren, my elder brother. He's a senior just like William. They aren't friends though.

I glare at him. "Go away, will you? We do *not* look thirsty."

"You did. At least be a little subtle. I don't want everyone to think my baby sister has a crush on that douchebag."

"But I *don't* have a crush on him!" I protest.

"Whatever." He saunters off, leaving me exasperated.

I turn to look at my friends, ready to rant about my brother. He can be such a pain in the ass sometimes. Instead, I see their attention has shifted. They are looking at my brother's receding figure now.

Oh God no.

"You know . . . Darren's really hot too," Andrea murmurs.

"I know right! He's got that whole rock star vibe going on for him," Kayla remarks.

"Ew gross! He's my brother. Can you guys not?"

"Whatever, just stating a fact." Kayla shrugs. "But really, he's always lobbing around that guitar of his, wearing those cool band t-shirts. He's *hot.*"

"But William's hotter, don't you think?" Andrea inquires.

"I don't know. I prefer guys with darker hair and look at Darren's long brown locks. He's sexy."

I groan, getting up. "Oh, I'm outta here. I'm not having this discussion, especially since it involves my *brother.*" With that said, I bid them goodbye. Lunch's almost over anyway.

* * *

"Today, I'll be assigning you all partners for the semester project. I want you to submit the final report by the end of next month." Miss Summers, our homeroom teacher instructs us. A ripple of whispers travels through the classroom. She turns around and starts writing 'Semester Project' on the board in bold letters.

Ah yes, I'd heard about this. This is a cross disciplinary project all juniors are forced to do. A small percentage of the final grade is determined by our performance in this project.

We wait curiously, trying to see what she's writing. Everyone's wondering what this project is about. Is it something absolutely boring? Will we spend hours locked up in the library, or on the internet, researching?

A couple of minutes later she steps aside so we can get a good look at the board. There are about ten things written there.

"I'll be assigning you what you have to do. Each task will be accompanied by a written report." Several groans are heard at the same time.

"I wish we get the fourth one," Sharon whispers to me.

My eyes flutter towards the board. '*Grow different vegetables in your garden. Take care of them and write a detailed report describing your experience (about 1500 words)*' I read the first topic. I silently pray I don't get this. I'm not really a fan of the outdoors. As I read through the different project options written on the board, I realize most of them aren't really the kind where you need to study and research a lot. In fact, it could even be fun. Well only if you're partnered with someone cool.

"Um, excuse me, but what's the point of doing all this?" A boy at the far end of the class quips.

The rest of us gawk at him.

Well, he does have a point…

"Hmm, I was wondering when you'd ask that," Miss Summers responds. "Well, we're trying to encourage learning that isn't facilitated by textbooks alone. So we've compiled a list of activities that aren't necessarily related to the academic disciplines you're studying. You're expected to participate enthusiastically in this project that constitutes of fifteen percent of your overall grade."

With that explained, she heads back to her seat.

"Sharon Hawthorne," Mrs. Summers call out, signaling Sharon to come over to her table. Sharon gets up, wondering why on earth the teacher is calling her. Everyone stares at her, as if she has two heads. A minute later, Sharon returns with a frown on her face and a paper in her hand.

"What is it?" I ask.

She looks up at me, annoyance clear on her face. "The project guidelines for the semester project and oh, I'm stuck with Dean." She makes a face as she says his name.

Well, this is called bad luck.

"Sucks to be you. But at least you will get an A." Dean is one of the most studious people in our class. Being partnered with him guarantees an A, but it also guarantees hours and hours of utter boredom.

"What is your project?" I ask her.

She frowns deeply. "We have to go around the neighborhood, instructing people about energy conservation and then write a report about it." She sounds really annoyed. Damn, she really got one of the boring projects.

One by one everyone walks up to the table as their name is called and return with a paper in their hands. All of my friends go off to their partners and get busy discussing their projects, while I just sit there all by myself.

Suddenly, I see a hand on my table, tapping it. I look up, only to see it's Aiden.

"What?" I ask.

"Don't you want to discuss the project?" he replies, looking at me incredulously.

"I don't know what my project is or who I'm partnered with," I explain.

"You're *my* partner, and our project is to dance."

I stare blankly at him, not able to comprehend what he's just said. But it slowly sinks in and then:

"Wait, our project is to what!?"

"Our project is to dance." He repeats.

I visibly freeze; my eyes widen with bewilderment. This has to his idea of a joke. I am partnered with *him*? And what's more, we have to dance?! He can't be serious.

"Whoa, there has been a mistake. We're supposed to dance? What kind of a project is that anyway?"

He shrugs indifferently like it doesn't matter and thrusts the paper towards me. I read it wide-eyed.

You have to prepare a small dance routine with your partner. It should be an internationally renowned dance form. Also enclose a short report that briefly discusses the dance form, its origins and growth, and summarizes your experience. You must also perform the dance in front of the student body on the final day of submission.

I read the whole thing at least five times, not able to wrap my head around it. We have to *perform* in front of *people*?!

"*Please* tell me you're kidding," I mumble, searching his eyes for that little flicker that would give him away; that would reveal he is, after all, joking. But I don't see it. He stands in front of me looking completely serious.

"For the last time: I'm serious!" he roars. "So we better decide what we're going to do about it. Because sadly, it's not some boring shit we can get off the internet. We'll have to work *hard*."

This is nothing less than a horrible nightmare. I have to perform a dance routine with him? Hell, I don't even *know* how to dance, and they expect me to do *this*? And with Aiden of all people?! No way, I'm *so* not doing this. I mean, it'll be weird and—

Oh god, kill me now.

Just then Miss Summers calls out my name and I stand up, excusing myself to head to her table. There had been a little hope in my heart that maybe Aiden really *was* joking, but that fades when I see Miss Summer hand me over the same project guidelines that Aiden had with him.

This seals the deal then. Aiden and I really *are* partners—and oh, we have to dance *together*. Maybe it's good that I'm partnered with him. It'll probably be less awkward since we're best friends. It might even be fun.

Oh, who am I kidding? This is going to go horribly.

"So what dance form should we do?" I ask him, once I return to my seat.

"I'm not going to do ballet dance with you or well, *anyone*. And honestly, I don't know if we'll be able to do hip-hop. What about tango? I wouldn't mind doing the tango with you," he says, wiggling his eyebrows suggestively. I roll my eyes. No matter how serious the situation is Aiden can never stop flirting, can he?

"No, we're not doing the tango, okay? Actually, give me some time, let me think about it. Till then, you think of some dance forms too. We'll make a decision soon."

Aiden nods and leaves. I sit there and spend the rest of the time thinking about this godforsaken project and how it would go. I think of the various dance forms we could do. But somehow, the scene of Aiden and I pressed up against each other—chest to chest, hand in hand keeps entering my mind. I *don't* want to get excited but somehow even thinking about all this sends a thrill up my spine. I can't believe it but I might actually be *excited* about this.

After the bell rings, Sharon and I walk to our next class; she's complaining about how much work we have to do at school these days. I, on the other hand, feel stressed. I want to tell her I'm nervous that I have to dance with Aiden. But I just can't seem to. Instead, I feel excessively drained. I can't help shutting her out, getting lost in my own thoughts. I silently hope she won't ask me any questions and I won't have to give any response.

I'm still lost in my own thoughts and unaware of what Sharon is saying when I see something that makes me stop in my tracks. I pause for only a second, but that second is more than enough. I start walking again, faster this time, but the image is already plastered in my head. The image of Aiden and Hailey is etched in my mind, and no matter how hard I try, I'm not able to shake it off. The image of her slim fingers knotted through his wavy black-brown hair, his arms tight around her waist. They were kissing.

A sick feeling makes its way up my stomach. I feel like throwing up. It's not a very good feeling, to be honest. I just want to sit down and take a long breath.

Sharon doesn't notice how pale my face has gotten, or how stiff I suddenly am. She doesn't notice how quiet I've suddenly become. She doesn't notice these things but I do. I notice these things for exactly what they are: symptoms of jealousy. This weird, sick feeling in the pit of my stomach, this sudden shift in my mood—they all are symptoms of jealousy.

Chapter Three

Scarlett

I put in the combination and try opening my locker. Nope, no chance; it doesn't even budge. I try to pull it, and then bang it a bit. But it makes no difference. My locker is really stuck. Feeling frustrated, I decide to report this to the student services. But that will have to wait, I'm getting late for class right now. Clearly annoyed, I try putting in the combination once last time, and voila, it opens!

I sigh. I'd put in the wrong combination before, of course. But how is that even possible? My locker combination is something I *never forget.* This clearly shows how preoccupied my mind has been with *other* things. Things like why seeing Aiden kissing his girlfriend made me feel jealous with a capital J.

Why am I jealous, though? I shouldn't be jealous. I should be happy that he has finally found someone he genuinely likes. In fact, I *am* happy. I can't help but feel happy when I see how happy *he* looks. He looks absolutely adorable when his face lights up when he's talking about her. His eyes literally sparkle and he practically exudes happiness. It's just how he is. Seeing him like that makes my heart beat fast, and I can't help but smile right back at him.

I just don't understand why I don't feel happy when I see *her* with him. *Why am I jealous of her?* It makes no sense.

Maybe it's because I'm scared he'll forget about me. It happened once. It can happen again.

It happened during this summer. After that party, Aiden's presence in my life visibly reduced. Initially we spent hours texting each other just like we always did. Then his responses started coming in later than usual. I'd be sitting on my bed every Friday, staring eagerly at my bedroom door, waiting for it to burst open and for Aiden to pop in. That didn't happen much. He came over the first few weeks, then he stopped. His texts that used to bombard my cell at every possible hour, stopped. He'd maybe message twice or thrice a week. We hung out a few times and then that stopped too. Really, we barely spent much time together.

By the time summer came to an end, I'd long given up hope and accepted that our friendship, or whatever it was, was over. His behavior had obviously hurt me and for some unknown reason, he wasn't so inclined to be around me anymore.

But then school started and he started talking to me like we'd never stopped. I didn't have the heart to ask him *why* he had been MIA the whole summer. I just...took him back, forgave him without him apologizing for what he did, or rather, didn't do.

Then I came to know that he'd spent the *whole* summer with Hailey. They'd gone on numerous dates and gotten close. He'd been with her all the time while I'd spent my holidays being sad over the fact we weren't in touch. It hurt.

I think I'm scared of having to go through that all over again. It already feels like I've been replaced in some ways. But to completely lose this thing we have . . .

I head to class after grabbing my books and enter it exactly when the bell rings. Mrs. Levine, our history teacher, narrows her eyes at me.

"Turn to page seventy-five of your textbooks," she instructs us. I absentmindedly start flipping the pages as the teacher reads out from the book. A couple of minutes later, I realize that I've actually brought the wrong book to class.

Great, that's exactly what I needed!

"Crap!" I curse under my breath, realizing my mistake. If only my mind hadn't been preoccupied with Aiden, this wouldn't be happening right now.

A second later, I see a book slide across my desk. I look up, surprised, only to see the boy who has been on my mind since morning.

Aiden shifts his desk closer to mine so that our desks are situated alongside each other's. How surprising that I didn't notice I was sitting next to him of all people. He chuckles. "You're so forgetful Scar," he says. "But I'm glad to be of service. Whatever would you do without me?"

I resist the urge to glare at him. Whatever would I do without *him*? *He's* the reason I don't have my book with me. *He's* the reason I was late to class. *He's* the reason my locker won't open. *He's* the reason I wasn't able to sleep last night.

I press my eyes shut and take in a deep breath to calm myself. The sudden realization that he is sitting really close to me dawns upon me at the same time. Our bodies are almost touching. I can feel the heat radiate from his skin.

Our eyes meet and he gives me a reassuring smile. And that's when it happens. My heart flip-flops inside my chest. All the air rushes out of my lungs and I feel a little pain inside my stomach. But it's a good pain, a weird pain—butterflies.

I try to focus on what Mrs. Levine is teaching. But it's all in vain. I'm aware of one thing and one thing alone: Aiden sitting close to me, really close. I notice each and everything he does; how he shifts in his seat, how he absentmindedly shakes his legs and how he plays with the pen—everything. It sucks because I don't know why all of a sudden, I'm finding all these things interesting. It's not like this is the first time we've sat together.

The teacher finishes reading the paragraph and turns the page. Aiden and I reach forward to flip the page of the book in front of us at the same time, causing our fingers to brush against each other's. A small tingle travels through the tip of my fingers. Its effect vanishes almost immediately.

We both lean towards the book to get a better look, and again I notice our proximity. It never bothered me before. Why is it bothering me now? He doesn't look bothered at all though. His gaze is locked onto the book like it's the most interesting thing ever, and mine? It's locked on him.

As I sit there, trying to focus on the lesson, I wonder if it's possible that I like Aiden—more than a friend, I mean. We're really good friends. I won't say best friends because best friends aren't supposed to flirt with each other, but we do. I know it's just harmless banter though. He has a girlfriend after all.

I glance at Aiden who's sitting beside me and feel my heart give an unfamiliar flutter.

What is up with me?

* * *

I'm curled up on my bed, looking at memes when I hear a familiar ping, someone's just texted me. I resist the urge to ignore the message, and instead check the notification bar.

My heart does a little somersault in my chest as I read Aiden's name there.

What does he want to talk about? It has to be something important. He doesn't text me much these days. Maybe it's about the project. But what if it's something totally random and unexpected? What if . . .

Okay, I should stop thinking and just read the damn message.

I take in a huge breath and click on the chat box.

Hi.

My heart immediately starts beating rapidly against my chest. Why am I getting so damn excited? It's just a two-lettered word—a minuscule greeting.

Me: Hey

Him: Sup?

Me: Nm Just Bored...

Him: Oh...

Me: So what's up with u?

Him: Missing someone...

I actually sit there for a whole minute not knowing how to reply to that. That 'someone' has to be Hailey, right? But then why is he telling *me* that he is missing *her*? I feel really confused but after sitting there idly for a few seconds I reply—

Me: lol get a life

Him: lmao look whose speaking

Me: EXCUSE ME?

Him: Let me guess, you're listening to crappy pop music and reading a book?

Me: No, I was actually just looking at memes.

Him: What did I say? ha-ha :3 Get a life.

Me: Whatever -_-

Him: Damn, I really miss her

So finally he reveals that he's missing *her*.

Of course he's missing *her!* Then why is it annoying *me?*
Because you like him.

I stare at the screen for some more time. What should I say? What does he want me to reply to something like this? And why do I feel so pissed?

God, I'm pathetic.

Me: Well go and talk to her if you miss her. Why waste your time chatting with me?

Him: I'm already talking to her.

Me: Good. I won't disturb you then. Goodbye.

I throw my phone across my bed, not able to take it anymore. I feel really frustrated. But I *shouldn't* be feeling like this. Why should I care who he's missing or not? How is that any of my business? Why is it even affecting me?

I realize that the only way to stop thinking about all this is to go to sleep. So that's what I try to do

* * *

Don't think about Aiden. Don't think about Aiden.

I chant this inside my head as walk through the school hallway the next morning. He was the first person I thought of today as I woke up this morning. I seriously don't know what is happening to me. I mean, it's just a tiny crush for god's sake!

I'm so tired of convincing myself that I shouldn't be thinking of him. Maybe it's time to accept reality.

I'm falling.

With this new discovery fresh in my mind I slowly take out the books I needed for the first few classes and stuff them in my bag. As I'm about to leave I see Sharon walk up to her own locker, which is beside mine and pull it open. We greet each other.

Then I wait for her so that we can walk off to our next class together.

Two minutes later we're walking at a moderate speed and talking. She's telling me about the latest guy who asked her out, and how she broke his heart. You see, Sharon is *really* pretty. It's no surprise guys are always asking her out. And then there's me. I'm not saying I'm ugly. But compared to the other girls out there…well, I'm non-existent.

And so I'm walking through the tiled hallway with Sharon next to me when suddenly Aiden walks up to me. Yes, *Aiden.*

He's standing right in front of me. Up close I notice the dark brown of his eyes and his intense cologne. He looks really good, I gotta admit. His jeans hug his hips perfectly, and his torso looks taut and lean. His hair looks unkempt and messy but it only makes him look sexier. I see him almost every day but only now do I realize how insanely hot he actually is. No wonder he's got girls lining up for him.

"Hey Scar, can I talk to you?" he says.

I freeze. I realize I'm not ready to talk to him just yet. Not after just realizing I have feelings for him. Something about the way my heart starts beating erratically as soon as I see him, proves it. I just stare at him, not sure what to do.

"No, you can't. She's getting late for class," Sharon replies before I can. My eyes snap to her. She's in her protective best friend mode. I don't care about class though, I just want to talk to him.

"Uh, it's okay Sharon. I'll talk to him," I say, hoping Sharon will let go.

"But Scar, we'll be late—" she protests.

"No, it's okay really. You go ahead, I'll catch up." I assure her.

She sighs, finally giving up, and then walks away. I stare at Aiden, not knowing what to say. What does he want to talk about? I'm still slightly annoyed because of our conversation from last night. I mean, first *he* messaged *me* and then, when I hoped he would talk, he started blabbering about how much he misses *her*. Who does that?!

"What do you want?" I ask. My voice comes out sounding a little harsher than I intended it to.

"Um I just wanted to talk about our project—the dance."

So he's here to discuss the project. He probably wants to tell me he doesn't want to do it. Why else would he be here anyway? Maybe he realized dancing with me is a bad idea. "You don't want to do it, do you? I get it. I don't want to do it either." I lie. I sound so calm and collected as I say this. But on the inside, I am anything but.

"No, I *want* to do it. Why would I not? I just wanted to ask you how we're going to go about it. But wait, *you* don't want to do it?" he asks, perplexed.

"Oh . . . I don't know. I'm not sure," I mutter nonchalantly, feeling surprised to know Aiden wants to dance with me, even if it's only because of a project. "We'll think about it later. Why are you so keen on discussing it now anyway? We have a lot of time to prepare for it."

"I-I don't know . . . I think we should start practicing," he mumbles hesitantly.

"Don't you have better things to do, like maybe hang out with your girlfriend?" I say sardonically, remembering what happened last night. "Besides, you don't usually care about projects." I point out.

"I just think we should start. I mean it's a dance we're talking about here, and it's not our cup of tea."

"Why are you being so persistent? We can discuss this later, okay?"

"Yes we can, but I'd rather do it now."

"Why now? We have ages to prepare for it. You never care about school related stuff. *I'm* the one who does all the worrying." I point out, annoyed.

"Because I get to do it with *you*."

"Huh?"

He smirks and my heart explodes inside my chest. "I get to dance with you, what's better than that?" he leans closer and my heart skips a beat. His warm breath caresses my face. My hands tremble from the proximity and surprisingly, I want him to come even closer. "I'll meet you at your house after school today, okay? For practice," he whispers. "Bye beautiful!" Saying this he walks off, leaving me standing dumbstruck, thinking: *Oh my god, he just called me 'beautiful.'*

Chapter Four

Scarlett

"I like him," I say.

It feels strange to finally admit this to someone, even if it is through the phone. I hear my best friend Susan gasp.

"Finally! I was just *waiting* for you to figure it out."

Susan and I have known each other since forever. She's like my non-biological sister. We used to live in the same neighborhood, but I shifted two years back. After which, we were forced to go to different schools. Now we meet up occasionally. Even though I've become good friends with Sharon, Kayla, and Andrea, I don't share everything with them. Susan's the one who knows me inside and out.

"Wait, you *knew* I had a thing for him?!"

"Duh! I'm your best friend. Of course, I did. So tell me, when did you figure it out?"

"Today I mean, I had my doubts earlier. But it just sort of became clearer today," I say. "It's really weird because I *do not* want to like him. I feel it's not right."

"Why not?"

"Because Aiden's my friend. That's it. We're just friends. He doesn't think of me as anything more. It just feels *so* wrong having these feelings for him when he feels absolutely nothing for me. How can I like him?"

"Of course, you can. It's common for friends to start liking each other."

"Except there *is* no 'each other'. He likes *her*, not me." I point out. "I sort of regret realizing this—that I like him. It makes everything ten times more awkward. And we had to be partnered up for this project out of all things!"

"Wait, what project?"

"Yeah, Aiden and I have to perform a dance routine."

"What kind of project is that?!"

"I know right! I can't believe I'm supposed to dance with Aiden, *dance*! I think I'd rather plant dirty saplings or grow bugs in my room then dance with him. It will be so awkward."

"Awkward, but oh-so-worth it; you are just being dramatic. Deep inside you're super thrilled, aren't you?"

I chuckle. "Ugh, you know me *so* well. Anyway, I have to go and get ready. Aiden will be here anytime now. We're going to have our first dance practice!"

She squeals. "Awesome! I won't keep you up then. But just want to remind you—don't end up doing something you're not supposed to, okay?"

I roll my eyes. "Yes *Mom*, now shoo!" She laughs on the other end. After mumbling a goodbye, I hang up.

I sigh and flop down on my bed, relishing the feel of the soft sheets against my skin. I wonder how our dance practice will go. I can't imagine I'm supposed to dance with *him*; what dance form will we perform? I hope it's something intimate like salsa or tango. I can already imagine us dancing . . . I sigh with delight.

God, I need to stop. I need to stop imagining myself with him. It's just a silly project.

Aiden must be on his way here, I should start preparing for his arrival. I brush my hair as much as I can so that it looks presentable and then tie it up into a bun. I change into a pair of comfortable track pants and wear a lose tee. Yes, I'm aware I don't exactly look the definition of glamorous, but I need to wear something comfortable so I can dance properly.

Then I start cleaning my room. It's so messy; I can't remember the last time I cleaned it. I fluff the pillows and change the bed sheet. I clean up the floor too and move some of the furniture so there's space to dance. By the time I'm done, I feel mildly tired but somehow, I'm still buzzing with energy; just knowing that in a couple of minutes I'll be dancing with my crush wipes off my lethargy.

The bell rings twice—Aiden is here. I stand up so suddenly that I knock off the pillow beside me and it falls down on the floor. I pick it up and rush out of my room; I stub my toe against the door in my hurry and let out a muffled scream. But I don't have time to focus on the pain. I rush down the stairs and almost slip.

Get a grip Scarlett!

I pause at the foot of the staircase and lean against it to catch my breath. The doorbell rings once more, so I will myself to walk towards it. My heart's in my mouth and my stomach hurts due to all the anticipation and nervousness. Composing myself, I open the door.

Aiden's sweet smile greets me. He's wearing a pair of faded blue jeans and a grey colored hoodie over it.

"Hey," he says; his eyes linger on mine before they look elsewhere. I mumble a 'hi' back, suddenly feeling shy and unsure. I shift away from the doorway so that he can step inside the house.

"So…um…what do you want to do?" I ask. The question apparently comes out sounding wrong, because the very next second Aiden smirks.

"We can do *whatever* you want to," he says, winking at me.

I roll my eyes at him. "God Aiden, can you *ever* be serious?!"

"I was being serious."

I ignore him. "So, I was thinking maybe we could see some dance tutorials on YouTube and try to choreograph our song based on them."

"Sounds like a plan. But which dance form are we going to do?" he asks.

Now *that's* the big question: which dance form? Immediately, my mind throws at me all these intimate dance forms—salsa, tango, ballroom dance. I quickly put that thought to rest. There is *no* way I'm suggesting any of those dance styles to him.

"What about salsa? Do you want to do that?" He suggests.

I want to refuse. I know I *should* refuse. But I don't. "Uh . . . uhm . . . sure!" I quickly turn around before he can notice how flustered I look.

We head upstairs to my room. He flops down on my bed like he owns it, while I head to my laptop and switch it on. I select some dance videos on YouTube and then let them buffer.

"Do you want a soda or something? And maybe some snacks?" I ask him.

Aiden chuckles, his eyes twinkling as he looks at me. "Why are you being so formal?"

"I'm not being formal, I'm being courteous. So do you want something or not? I'm not allowing you any snack breaks during the dance practice."

He laughs. "Okay, I'd like a soda," he says.

I nod and turn around after subtly warning him to not sneak around my room in my absence.

"*Okay* Scar, I *won't* go through your underwear drawer." He mocks. I turn around to glare at him before heading out of the room, closing the door behind me.

I take my time getting the soda from the kitchen. I need to clear my head. I know that as soon as I'm back in that room, my heart will start beating erratically again. I'll be in Aiden's arms and we'll be dancing.

Aiden's arms . . .

As I reenter my room I see Aiden sitting right where he was, staring at the wall directly in front of him. He's looking at my photographs. He doesn't notice my presence in the room. A soft smile is playing on his lips.

I just stand there and stare at him like a creep. I feel completely blissful for those few seconds, just silently appreciating his beautiful form. But it doesn't last for long. The very next second my body doubles up and I let out a big, heavy sneeze. "Aaachoo!"

He immediately turns around to look at me. I mentally curse myself.

"Bless you." He beams, then takes the can of soda from my hand.

"So . . ." I trail off.

"The videos?" He prompts.

I nod and head to the laptop. By now the videos have finished buffering and we can start our practice straight away. In the very first video, there's a woman and a man demonstrating the most basic salsa step. Aiden and I simply stare at the screen in awe. When the video's over there's nothing to shatter the silence except our soft breathing.

"We're supposed to do *this*?" Aiden murmurs.

My head snaps to look in his direction. *What does he mean? Does he not want to do this?* "So…you don't want to do salsa?" I ask.

He immediately shakes his head in refusal. "No, of course not. It's just dancing like this would be…"

Awkward.

Neither of us says it out loud but we both have this fact established: there's going to be a hell lot of awkwardness involved. And I am not looking forward to it. Well, maybe I am. God, I don't know. When did I become such a confused little mess?

We both decide to check out another video after this. Our hands reach for the laptop at the same time. We both lean towards it simultaneously, causing our heads to bump. *Oof!*

We turn to look at each other at the same time. All the air gets knocked out of my lungs as I notice how close we suddenly are. His warm breath fans my face. *Oh god, I've never been this close to a guy.* Our eyes meet and for a second and I can't look away; I'm so fixated.

I suddenly realize *what* I'm doing. I quickly avert my gaze and clear my throat awkwardly. He stiffens too and shifts away. I feel slightly disappointed when he does that. We watch the video in silence, not giving any indication of what happened a couple of minutes ago.

When the videos finish, I glance at Aiden and see that he's already looking at me. I quickly look away, already feeling my heart beating faster. "Uhm . . . shall we?" I prompt.

He shrugs and gets up; I do too. At first, we both simply stand to face each other, not knowing what to do. Then we take a step closer and I extend my hands to put it on his shoulder while he puts his arms around my waist. His other hand takes mine and we both stand still. None of us are looking at each other.

"Uhm . . . so I'll put my right leg back and you'll extend your left leg forward, then you'll put your left leg back and I'll extend my right leg forward. I will do the exact opposite." I explain.

His right hand clasps mine, while his left hand plants itself a little above my butt. He pulls me closer, our chests gently collide. I gasp. "*Now* that's better." He smirks.

I don't know what to do anymore. I don't know how *not* to lose my cool with Aiden so close to me—his warm hands pressed against my skin. How do I show I'm completely in control of my emotions when I'm clearly not?

"One . . . two . . . one-two-three. One . . . two . . . one-two-three." I count as we try to practice. The first couple of times, we feel awkward doing it. But soon enough, we get used to the weirdness.

After some time, we both get tired of doing the same steps over and over, so we decide to try a complicated one for a change. We start with the same old basic step after which Aiden and I step away from each other. We continue doing the cha-cha-cha after which Aiden extends his hand towards me. I grab it and then start twirling round and round, simultaneously making my way towards him. Now the final part, he has to pull me towards him, and then we have to freeze.

So that's what we set out to do. I lightly grab his arm and twirl round and round, making my way to him. Within seconds I come closer which is when he has to pull me towards him. And so he does just that. He pulls me towards him, I crash against his chest and then we both tumble down on the bed which stands right behind us.

Somehow, I end up pressed against the mattress while Aiden lands up on top of me. We're both panting for breath. He tries to lift himself up but our tangled legs make it difficult. His warm breath fans my face. The tips of our noses are practically touching. Unable to move, I can't do anything but stare straight into his deep brown eyes.

This isn't a very comfortable position. Aiden is quite heavy and I'm basically crushed under his body. Yet even during all this discomfort, I can feel my heart beating faster than before and my breath coming short. For reasons unknown to me Aiden has stopped squirming. He's just bent over me in this awkward position and staring right back into my eyes.

Oh my god, why is he looking at me like that?

I quickly look away, not able to handle the intensity of his gaze.

"What?" I prompt, shattering the silence.

"Huh?" He's finally out of his trancelike state.

"Why're you looking at me like that?" I ask, feeling awkward.

"Oh, nothing," he mumbles quickly.

We both realize at that exact moment that he's still on top of me and how . . . how close we really are. His eyes widen and his body freezes for a fraction of a second before he quickly gets off me, as if his body's suddenly on fire.

I slowly get off the bed and pretend to smooth out the wrinkles on my tee so that I don't have to meet his eyes. I can feel his gaze burning a hole through my head.

"Uhm . . . shall we continue this some other time?" He suggests hesitantly.

I look up and see he's running his fingers through his tousled hair.

"Uh . . . sure, yeah. That'll be good," I mumble, not knowing what else to say.

I bite my lip in frustration. Oh god, how did things end up like *this*? He exits the room without saying another word. As his footsteps fade away, I groan, burying my head in my hands.

Well, that was awkward.

Chapter Five

Scarlett

"Hey Marion, would you mind sitting over there?"

"Sure Aiden, no problem!" she chirps, flashing him a smile and then heading over to the empty seat in the first row. Normally, I would have rolled my eyes at how flirtatiously Marion had smiled at him, not even asking him *why* he wanted to shift seats. But I didn't feel normal—not at all.

The bench next to me creaks a bit and Aiden sits down.

Why is he sitting here? Shouldn't he be avoiding me after what happened that day, during our practice?

Maybe he doesn't want to sit in the first row—yeah that's probably it. Why else would he choose to sit next to *me* after what happened?

First period has just started. I was *not* looking forward to coming to school today. It's a boring Monday morning and the absolute certainty that I would come across Aiden today was a major factor in my reluctance to get out of bed today.

I'd spent the whole weekend replaying what had happened at the dance practice—replaying how his taut torso had felt against my own, replaying how his soft breath had fanned my face and our eyes had meaninglessly stared into each other's. It had just been an awkward act of clumsiness. It didn't mean anything. At least, that's what I'd been trying to convince myself.

My train of thought is rudely interrupted when Aiden shifts his seat closer to mine—so close in fact that when he sits down, his left leg touches my right.

"Hey Scar," he says casually.

My head instantly snaps in his direction. My eyes widen in astonishment. I'm at a loss for words. He smiles at me; then frowns, probably noticing my expression.

"You okay?" he asks, worry lines creasing his forehead.

"Uh . . . yeah, I'm okay. What would happen to me?!" I exclaim a little too chirpily. I hope I don't sound as nervous as I feel. *Why do I feel nervous anyway?*

"Okay, whatever you say . . ." He shrugs, smiling at me again, before turning to look at the blackboard. The teacher tells us to note whatever's being written on the board, and like the diligent student I am, I start doing so.

Aiden as usual is *not* doing what the teacher has instructed everyone to do. He's tapping his feet and humming a tune I don't recognize. He's bobbing his head from time to time. How is the teacher *not* noticing the ruckus he's making? I want to tell him to stop, but I don't. I try to focus on my work instead.

I soon realize it's futile. No matter how hard I try, all I can do is notice Aiden and all that he's doing. I can't help but notice every time he shifts in his seat or taps his toes or runs his finger through his wavy locks. There's something particularly serene about how lost Aiden is in his own world, not knowing what's going on beyond it.

When the teacher pauses to explain what she's written on the board, Aiden stops. I stare at the teacher as she explains everything. I nod at all the right moments and try to look as focused as I can, even though I've not understood a single word she's said. Hell, I've not even *heard* a single half of the things she's been explaining. It's like they're floating past me. I know I can understand if I really focus myself. But that's what I cannot do, especially not when Aiden keeps looking at me.

Yes, instead of looking at the teacher he's looking in my direction. I can practically *feel* his hot gaze. This . . . this is slightly annoying because it's not allowing me to do what I want, yet at the same time it's . . . different. *I* feel different. My stomach is churning. I feel so nervous.

Finally, after I can't take it anymore I turn to look at him. A lazy smile graces his lips almost immediately.

"You're such a nerd Scarlett," he remarks.

His words catch me off guard. "Wh-what?! I'm not." I protest.

"Let me see. You score straight As on *all* the tests, you never miss a deadline, you don't break curfew or skip classes, and you've never been in detention. You're always reading some book and you have no social life. You're not even dating anyone."

"So?!"

"So nothing. I just think you should live a little, that's all."

"If living means failing in all my classes and getting detention then I *don't* want to live. And what's wrong with books? I mean, books are awesome! They have this whole new world inside of them. They're *perfect!*"

"Hey, don't get so defensive. I'm not saying scoring straight As is bad or that reading books is boring. I mean it *is*, but to me I just . . . never see you doing anything fun, and *that's* bad."

"I do fun things," I blurt out. Which is partly a lie, and Aiden knows that.

"Right . . . that's why you spend all your Friday nights huddled in front of your laptop, reading fan-fiction and eating junk food? If *that* is your definition of fun . . ."

"Hey, don't judge it before you try it! But seriously, my life's not as boring as you think. Yeah, I read books, because I love reading them. I do my homework on time and I'm punctual but that's only because I don't want to get in trouble. And I don't have a boyfriend because I don't really think I need one," I explain.

"Why not?"

"Why not what?"

"Why don't you want a boyfriend?"

"Because I just don't..."

Except, I wouldn't mind if it was you.

"But wouldn't it be nice having someone to adore you and hangout with—someone to have endless conversations with and not get tired?" he asks me.

"Well yeah, it'd be nice but . . . I haven't really met a person like that so..."

"You sure you haven't?"

"No . . . but when I will . . ."

"Are you sure? Is there *no* guy you know, who you'd want to date? Not one?"

I glance at him. Is he implying what I think he's implying? Well, I don't know. I can't just assume something like that and risk humiliation.

"No, I'm positive I haven't," I declare firmly.

He frowns, almost looking hurt. Our conversation morphs into silence.

I get back to taking notes. Surprisingly he starts writing too. When the teacher starts explaining again, I put down the pen and rest my hand on the desk. Except I accidently rest it on his hand. I inwardly gasp as I realize my blunder.

Why do these little touches matter so much? We've hugged for god's sake!

I realize his skin is really soft and . . . warm—really warm. I glance at our hands and wonder why he isn't removing his. *Has he not noticed or doesn't he care at all?*

He shifts his hand so that now it lies on top of mine. My eyes widen with surprise. He *knows* and he *doesn't* care.

I turn to look at him, and realize he's already watching me. We both just look at each other. No words are spoken. My heart starts thudding dangerously fast. I stealthily slip my hands from under his and put it on my notebook before I can feel any more uncomfortable.

I want to focus on what's going on in class, but I can't because I notice him observing me again. I wait for him to look away but he just doesn't. Slightly annoyed and a little confused, I snap my head in his direction. Our eyes lock.

"What!?" I hiss.

"Does my touch make you *this* uncomfortable?" he whispers, sounding hurt?

"What? No!"

"Yes, it does. Like now . . . and Friday too . . ."

I can't believe he brought up that up!

"No, it doesn't."

"*Yes*, it does," he retorts.

"No!" I exclaim, exasperated.

"You don't like being so close to me."

You're right. I don't like being so close to you. I love it.

"No," I respond firmly.

"Well then, you wouldn't mind holding my hand." He challenges me.

"Of course, I wouldn't." Saying this, I confidently clasp his hand.

This? This is no big deal.

I can feel my heart beating fast. I realize how good it feels—holding his hands. His hands are soft and warm as I said before, but there is this firmness to them. They are strong.

"Let's play a game." He suggests.

"What? Seriously?"

"Yes. The staring game. We have to look into each other's eyes without blinking. Whoever blinks first loses."

"We're in a *class*, Aiden. What if the teacher spots us?"

"Oh Scarlett, live a little."

"Fine. What does the winner get?"

"Anything he or she wants."

"*No*, I mean 'anything' means practically everything and what if I lose and you make me do your homework for a month?"

"*C'mon*, don't be such a spoil sport. It'll be fun. Think about it this way: if *you* win you can make me do anything you want, *anything*." There's so much promise in his tone when he says that, my temptation wins. So before I can convince myself otherwise, I agree.

"There's a catch."

"What catch?" I narrow my eyes at him suspiciously.

"You cannot let go of my hand. You have to hold it all the way through when you look into my eyes."

Confusion lines crease my forehead. *Why would he ask me to do that?* I don't ponder over it much though, I just agree. And so we both shift a little closer, turn a bit so that we're facing each other, while still holding hands.

This isn't a challenge. This is secretly a boon Aiden has presented me on a silver platter. Now I can look into his mesmerizing eyes for as long as I want and I don't even need an excuse to do that.

And so it begins.

It's a little weird at first. And I understand now why Aiden wanted me to hold his hand. I keep getting this urge to look away from him. I feel so . . . shy. I just want to look away, hide behind a curtain or something so that I don't have to control the blush that's threatening to color my cheeks. His touch makes all this even weirder. It eventually gets better though. I'm a lot more at ease after a few seconds.

Has anyone ever looked at you, like *really* looked at you? Now remember, there's a difference between looking and seeing. When someone looks they notice, they observe. They don't just access the whole picture briefly. They *actually* look at you as if they can see through your soul. They look at you because they *want* to and not because they *have* to.

That's how Aiden and I *look* at each other. Even though it's only his eyes I can stare at I still analyze it. I notice how long his lashes are and the brown of his eyes. I notice how they sparkle just a little. He looks at me too. I know he's just not seeing me, not just staring for the sake of it. It's like he's making the most of this moment too.

These few minutes could have easily been hours—they were perfect. I couldn't see anyone but him, couldn't *hear* what was going on around me. It was just us, locked up in our tiny little bubble, separated from the rest.

Tring!

The bell rings and everybody gets up to leave. Aiden and I are the only ones who don't move. Our hands are locked into each other's and we're staring straight into each other's eyes, totally engrossed in this game…or each other.

Everyone spills out of the classroom and it gets a little quiet. It's lunch break. I hear footsteps coming in our direction. But I don't look up—I can't. I cannot lose this game. I *can't* let him win.

"Oh!" I hear a short gasp. It's a girl. The tone of her voice speaks *volumes*. It's that gasp people make when they stumble upon something they shouldn't have. It's that gasp people make when they're embarrassed because they barged in on something intimate and not meant to be seen. *Does it look like Aiden and I are doing something intimate? Does it?*

I can't help it. Her surprised gasp makes me look away from Aiden so that I can see who it is. I drop his hand too.

"Oh, I'm *so* sorry, did I interrupt something? I just wanted to . . . wanted to—" It's Marion and she looks embarrassed—exactly how I'd been picturing her.

"N-no—" I begin speaking but Aiden interrupts me.

"As a matter of fact *yes*, you did interrupt something," Aiden says coolly. The way he says it makes it sound so wrong.

"What he means is, you interrupted this *game* we were playing where we're supposed to look into each other's eyes and not blink and—" I try to reduce the damage.

"Just tell us what you wanted." Aiden cuts me off. My mouth drops open and I turn to gape at Aiden.

"I just wanted to . . . borrow Scarlett's notes, if that's okay," she mumbles.

Aiden grabs my notebook and hands it over to her without even asking me.

"Here, have it. Now *leave*," he says, sounding annoyed.

Marion squeaks a 'thank you' in my direction and then rushes away.

I whip my head towards him. "What the *hell* Aiden?!"

"What?" he says like he has *no* idea.

I roll my eyes, annoyed, getting up and packing up my stuff. His hands grab my arm and pull me down, so that I plop down on the seat beside him.

"Hey, you can't go. If I'm not wrong, you just lost the staring battle. So *I'm* the winner."

I glare at him before giving him my 'are-you-shitting-me' look.

"A deal is a deal Scarlett. And since *I'm* the winner I get whatever I want."

"*What* do you want?" I ask, giving up.

"You."

I freeze. My heart soars in my chest and for a second my mind goes completely blank. Before I can fully comprehend what he just said, Aiden starts to laugh.

He *actually* starts laughing. And that's when it hits me. That jerk was joking.

Of course he was.

My cheeks heat up and I look away, biting my lip urgently. *God, this is SO embarrassing.* Beside me, Aiden is laughing like a hooligan. He actually has tears in his eyes from all that laughing and he's slapping his hand on the desk like he just cracked the funniest joke *ever*.

I smack his shoulder with my hand—hard.

"Ow! What was *that* for?!" he exclaims, rubbing the spot I just hit.

"You know *what* it was for." I glare at him, not bothering to hide my annoyance. I start heading towards the door when I feel his hand grab my arm once again.

"Hey, don't go!" he says like he's actually disappointed to see me go. I turn around to glare at him.

"Let go of my hand, Aiden."

"Don't go, *please?*" he actually *pouts* when he says this and bats his eyelashes at me like a clingy girlfriend would in those cliché teen movies.

I can't help giggling. He just looks *so* ridiculous. I slap my hand over my mouth and double up laughing. "Oh my god Aiden what *was* that?!"

"That was the one, and the only Aiden Walker pout. It's extremely rare and has been sighted only once or twice in human history."

"You're *such* a dork," I say shaking my head, still giggling like an idiot. I've completely forgotten about that mean little trick he pulled a couple of minutes ago. I sit down on the seat adjacent to his and turn to him. "So what do you want O winner of the mighty staring battle?" I say in a patronizing voice.

"I'll let you know when something strikes me. Right now, I've got all I want." He smiles at me. I feel those butterflies infiltrate my belly. I turn away, trying to had the fact that I'm blushing right now.

"C'mon, lunch is halfway over. We better get going or we'll miss out all the edible stuff."

And so we both head to the cafeteria side by side. I feel this rare sensation—like I'm floating away in a bubble—a bubble of happiness. I can't stop smiling and I just feel so . . . blissful.

All because of him.

As we continue walking, I'm not able to take my eyes off of him. How did he get this gorgeous? I swear to God he wasn't *this* good looking last year.

He hasn't changed. He hasn't changed at all. The only thing that has changed here are your feelings for him.

He's just so. . . how do I even describe it? Now that I think about it, I can *totally* understand why so many girls at school drool after him. His eyes are this *really* deep shade of brown that reminds me of those dark chocolates my dad brought from this trip the tips ever so slightly and stands straight up on his head. And there's his smile . . . It's so . . . perfect.

And currently, he's giving me that perfect smile.

God, I like him.

I like my best friend.

Oh, and he has a girlfriend.

I feel scared admitting these feelings to myself. I *don't* want to have these feelings. It just feels wrong. And for him of all people! We are just friends. I am probably like a sister to him. He's crazy about his girlfriend. There is absolutely *no* hope. Then why?

I need to control my feelings before they get out of hand. And he can never know—never. It'll make everything so much more awkward than it already is.

Aiden suddenly stops in his path, and I with him. It's Hailey. She's here. Just a second ago he was smiling at me and now he's passing her that same smile. I stifle a groan.

God, what does he see in her?

I know the inevitable is about to happen—Aiden introducing me to Hailey. He was supposed to do that ages ago, but never got around to doing it. I must admit, a lot of it was my doing. I'd somehow distract him, making him forget, or vanish at the last moment. But I guess I can't avoid this anymore.

"Scar, I don't think you've met Hailey before, have you?"

God, why are you torturing me?

"Uh, no you haven't." I smile awkwardly at Hailey who is absolutely beaming right now.

"So Scarlett, this is Hailey . . . my girlfriend."

Ouch. That hurts.

"—and Hailey, this is my friend Scarlett."

Friend.

This hurts even more.

"Hi!" she chirps, then wraps me in a warm hug. I'm left speechless.

The worst part is she's probably a nice person. If she was a mean bitch, I would have a genuine reason to despise her. But she's actually a good person and the only reason I can't seem to like her is because she's Aiden's girlfriend. Pathetic, I know.

"Aiden's told me a lot about you. Like, he literally never shuts up." She giggles as and looks at Aiden. I notice Aiden's already looking at her with that adoring look in his eyes. He really likes her.

"I'm glad I finally got to meet you too Hailey!" I hope she doesn't notices how strained my voice sounds right now.

She smiles at me.

She's just so bright and bubbly, so happy and outgoing. She's like the complete opposite of me.

How can I ever compete with someone like her?

Chapter Six

Scarlett

"You ready for your first ever detention Miss Stevenson?"

"Unfortunately yes, Mr. Walkers," I chime back, trying hard not to glare at him.

Together we make our way to the library. Of course, we wouldn't be going where we are going if it hadn't been for him. Aiden landed us in detention. We'd been sitting in class. I was taking notes. Or at least, trying to. Aiden had been relentlessly whispering lame jokes to me. Sometime during the hourlong lecture, I'd lost my composure and burst out laughing. It would have been okay had Aiden not started laughing too. Seeing him laugh made me laugh even harder. Now here we are—sent as a punishment because neither of us could shut up.

I meet Aiden on the way to class after school. I've just returned from my locker and now I'm heading for detention.

In the library, the librarian points us over to a huge pile of books and instructs us to assemble them in their proper shelves. She settles down in her chair, sipping coffee, telling us to get to work.

Well, this is boring.

My flats click-clack against the library's wooden flooring as I get to work. The hour passes by slowly, but I enjoy myself nevertheless. Initially it's really boring—grabbing books and arranging them on the shelves. But eventually, I lose myself in the library. There are so many books here, *so many*. I come across some really interesting titles as I work. Some of the shelves I visit, I would have never thought of visiting them. But now that I have, I keep coming across books that peak my interest. I note down their names, making a mental note to check them out later.

And so the hour breezes by. I was down to my last fifteen minutes, yet I still had close to twenty books to arrange. I grab a couple of books and head over to the history section. I check the serial number and realize that they need to go on the top-most shelf.

Just my luck!

I stretch my legs, trying to balance on my tiptoes as I struggle to place the book where it belongs.

I don't succeed.

I groan, giving up. Suddenly someone snatches the book from me. I turn to look at the intruder and see a smug looking Aiden.

"What the hell?!" I glower.

He smiles cheekily at me. "Try to not take books that go on the top. You're so short you won't be able to reach it." He places the book where it belongs, then dusts his hands in an exaggerated manner. "Whatever would you do without me?"

"Whatever," I murmur.

Trying to get back at him, I grab the heavy book he's holding. I look at its serial number so that I can identify where it goes. I swear it's almost a thousand pages. Unfortunately, it goes on one of the top shelves, and Aiden knows it. He's trying very hard not to smirk. He cocks his eyebrow at me mockingly. It's too late to back off. I stick my tongue out at him, feeling equally cheeky. I'm going to do this.

To prove my point, I extend my hand as high as I can, getting back up on my toes, trying to put the book where it belongs. But as I reach up, the book starts to slip from my grasp.

I panic, trying to hold onto the book. But what it really led to is me losing my balance. My feet starts to slip, and the next thing I know, I'm falling. My hands flail around for support, but in vain. I squeeze my eyes shut, awaiting the inevitable pain.

But the pain never comes.

I pop open my eyes, realizing I'm not falling anymore. Instead, I see a hand wound tightly around my waist: Aiden's hand.

"Scar, you okay?" He looks worried. I nod uncertainly at him, too flustered to give a coherent reply. "Are you sure?" he asks again.

I nod again. I try to calm down my heart. It's beating so erratically. Maybe it's the sudden fall, or maybe it's my close proximity to Aiden: the way his arms feel just right around my waist, but I feel nervous

None of us speak.

We're doing that thing again: staring deeply into each other's eyes like we can see each other's soul.

None of us look away.

His gaze shifts, stopping on my lips, then immediately jumps back to my eyes. It's just like that night…that night of the party. Something invisible is at work here. There's this weird energy between us and it's pulling us closer. We're like the opposite poles of a magnet—the attraction is undeniable.

Oh my god.

He starts to lean in. Warning bells go off in my mind. I should stop him right now. But I don't. When only an inch's space separates our lips, he pauses. I feel his warm breath on my face. Goosebumps erupt down my arms. Holy shit, who knew I could get this nervous?

I want him to cover that teeny-tiny distance between us desperately. But at the same time, I know I can do that too. But I don't. It's like I've frozen and my senses are all jumbled up. I can't even form coherent thoughts.

Tring!

Tring!

The school bell causes us to snap out of it. His hands instantly drops from my waist. I jump away from him like his body is a ball of fire. My heart beats hard against my chest: *ba-dump, ba-dump.* I'm struggling to breathe properly and it's not because of this musty library smell.

"I . . . uh . . . I need to go," I murmur. I turn around and rush away. The library book lies forgotten on the floor. I can feel Aiden's eyes on me as I turn away but he doesn't stop me.

I run as fast as my feet can carry me, dying to get out of the confines of the library. My heart is beating so frantically. I'm sure it's going to burst right out of my chest. I've never felt this way—never. I've never felt so nervous, so frantic, so excited, and annoyed at the same time. What happened a few minutes ago had been overwhelming.

I exit the library real fast and head over to the school grounds. My small run soon morphs into short strides, ultimately turning into a slow walk. I'm desperately trying to calm my heart. But it's futile. There are knots in my stomach, tightening by the minute. This feeling, it feels good and bad at the same time. I don't exactly like it, but I don't want it to stop either, which is crazy, you know?

I sit down on a bench and snap my eyes shut, reliving what happened a few minutes ago.

I can still feel his warm breath on my skin and his arms around my back. It feels so real. But it *was* real. It really *did* happen. Aiden almost kissed me. It wasn't a dream.

I groan. *How can I suppress these feelings after what just happened? How can I?* I'll never be able to forget the look in his eyes as he leaned towards me. I'll never be able to forget how he held me. Most of all, I'll never be able to get over the fact that it had felt so amazing.

God, I really like him.

I wish I'd kissed him that night of the party instead of running away. I wouldn't be sitting here, wondering how his lips would feel on mine, if I had. I'd already know.

Suddenly my cell phone starts ringing, disrupting my daydream. My eyes pop open. I quickly take out my phone from my bag. My heart almost gives out when I see the caller ID—it's Aiden.

My hands tremble as I stare at my phone. Is this for real? He's calling me after *that*? I want to answer the call, but I resist. I don't want to pick up the phone immediately; it'll make me look desperate.

After five short rings, I can't resist anymore and hit the answer button. My heart is practically in my mouth.

"H-hello?" I stutter.

"Hey."

"Uh . . . what happened?" I ask.

"Where did you go?" he asks.

My heart flutters. *Was he indicating that he hadn't wanted me to go?*

"We have dance practice today."

Oh. So *that's* why he called. Not because he was annoyed I left or because he wanted to talk to me or whatever. He called because we had dance practice.

"Oh, I'm sorry I forgot," I mumble.

"It's okay. We're practicing at my place today, right?"

"Yeah, just like we'd planned."

"Okay, well, I'll see you there." He hangs up.

He could have asked me if I wanted a lift. But he didn't . . .

I leave the school and make my way back home so I can freshen up before leaving for Aiden's house. I keep replaying our conversation on the phone and the library incident in my head. I can't help smiling whenever I remember how close we'd come to kissing each other. But why should I even be thinking about that? It's not like it means anything. At least not to him.

Back at home, I take a quick bath, change into a comfortable tee and a pair of shorts, and then head over to Aiden's house. After a fifteen-minute bus ride, and a short walk I reach his place. I head to the door and am about to ring the bell when I notice the door is slightly ajar. I roll my eyes—typical Aiden, always in a hurry.

I enter the house and find it completely quiet. He has to be home; his car is outside. Maybe he's upstairs, in his room.

I smile to myself. How about I quietly barge into his room and scare him? His expression would be priceless.

As I reach the landing I see the door to his room is slightly open. I walk over, making sure not to make any noise, ready to jump right into the room. But I stop right in time.

My eyes widen as I take in the scene before me. Disbelief washes over me, and my stomach tightens. Hailey and Aiden are on the bed, kissing each other fervently, making out.

Something inside me crumbles up. I feel someone has punched me hard. I stop breathing for a couple of seconds and my chest starts hurting as a result. I didn't expect it to hurt as much as it did then. I bite my lip hard. For some strange reason I want to burst into tears.

I won't cry. I won't cry. I won't cry I chant inside my head as I silently turn around and leave exactly as I'd come—quietly and unnoticed. I don't know where I'm going but anywhere is good as long as it's away from him.

I remember seeing William and Angelina kiss each other in the hallway once. I'd never felt like this then. I used to just feel grossed out and would look away. But in this case, I feel so…I don't even know what I feel. Just that it's not a very good feeling.

I'm just glad they didn't see me. How embarrassing would *that* have been.

Chapter Seven

Scarlett

The doorbell rings. I look up from the novel I'm reading. *Who could it be?* It's a nice Saturday afternoon and I'm not really expecting anyone. I don't get up and wait for Mom to open the door. The doorbell rings again.

Oh wait, nobody's home.

Reluctantly, I get off my bed and head downstairs. The doorbell rings again. "I'm coming, geez!" I yell. The person on the other side of the door has probably never heard of this thing called 'patience.' I finally reach the landing and rush to the door so that this person, whoever he or she is, doesn't get the chance to ring the doorbell again. I unbolt the door and pull it wide open.

And immediately regret it.

"Oh." I pause. It's a long awkward pause. "Hey . . . Aiden," I say, sounding hesitant.

He looks grim. He doesn't smile at me like he usually does. I feel a pinch of pain.

"What's wrong?" I ask.

"What's up with you?" he asks, looking solemn.

"What do you mean?" I inquire, confused.

"You never showed up yesterday."

No you idiot, I did.

"What's going on? Are you like avoiding me or something? Why would you even . . . oh." Realization dawns upon him. "Wait, it's not because of what happened at the library, is it?" His eyes look straight into mine and somehow I'm not able to look away. "It was . . . okay, I admit it was sort of awkward. But I swear it won't happen again. You don't have to avoid me because of it, alright?"

"I'm not avoiding you." I assure him.

My heart thuds hard against my chest as I remember what had happened yesterday. I'd been able to take it off my mind for a bit but seeing Aiden here again has just brought everything back.

He smiles with relief. "Thank god for that. I thought you were. You didn't show up for practice yesterday and didn't even call me to tell you won't."

"Come on in. We can practice now if you want."

He agrees and as usual follows me to my room.

Up in my room, I attach my iPod to my sound system. I go to the album containing all the Enrique Iglesias songs and play them. Many of his old songs have that fast salsa beat in them. As the music starts, I gesture for him to take my hand.

We hold each other's hand and stand in the basic stance. Then start with the most basic salsa move—swaying our hips and trying to coordinate our foot work. We practice a couple of lifts after that. We fail miserably in doing most of them. I seriously don't know where we're going with this.

I run towards him and jump; he catches me right on time. I wrap my hands around his neck and we stay like that for two seconds before he swiftly drops me, grabs my hand, and starts twirling me round and round and round.

"Okay, get ready!" This time we're practicing the move where I'm supposed to run towards him. He then has to grab my hand, twirl me once, after which I'll lift my leg high up in the air, and bend backwards, while he supports me.

I run towards him. His hands clasp around my waist for a fraction of a second, after which they slowly start to slip away. I panic and before long, I find myself falling. One second, I'm on my feet, and the next I'm not. I fall down flat on my ass—hard.

"Ow. Ow. Ow. Ow." Tears blur my vision for just a second before I feel a hand wiping them off.

"I'm so sorry Scarlett! I'm *so* sorry. I didn't mean to—I swear I just—I'm sorry!" Aiden keeps begging for forgiveness, and I realize that if I don't tell him to shut up, he won't.

"For God's sake Aiden, shut up! It's okay, alright? I'm fine! Just a little...hurt." I try to get up. My butt's killing me. Aiden grabs my arms and pulls me up. He leads me to the bed.

"Damn . . . that hurts," I moan as I plop down on the mattress.

"I can make it better, you know? Do you want a nice, sensual butt massage?" he teases, wiggling his eyebrows. I bite back a giggle and roll my eyes.

"You don't ever get tired of joking around, do you?"

"Who said I'm joking?"

I roll my eyes at him.

I ask him to get something for me to eat. He gets me some snacks and soda from the kitchen. We lounge on my bed after that, munching sandwiches and talking about random things, until it gets very quiet.

The songs have stopped playing. I excuse myself, so that I can restart the playlist. As I start getting up, Aiden grabs my hand to stop me.

"What?" I ask.

"Scarlett . . . I just remembered something." Aiden begins, his eyes lighting up. "Remember that staring battle we had some time back? Well, I'd won and I *still* haven't asked for my prize."

Oh no, not that.

"Oh c'mon Aiden—" I protest.

"Nope. I won fair and square. Now you must follow up with your part of the deal. You have to do what I ask of you."

I start feeling nervous. *What is he going to ask me to do?*

"I want you to dance—with me." He demands.

I immediately start to make excuses. "You know my butt still kind of hurts. Besides, haven't we practiced enough for today?"

He rolls his eyes. "I didn't mean practicing our dance routine when I said let's dance. I meant I want you to *dance* with me—*slow* dance—you know, where two people hold each other and sway to slow, sappy music, and look into each other's eyes? That."

My eyes widen. I look at him, trying to assess whether he's joking or not. His expression say it all—he's not kidding. He's a hundred percent serious.

"B-but why would you want to do that?" I stammer.

"I haven't slow danced before, and I want to experience what it feels like." He shrugs.

"You've *got* to be kidding me! What did you do in all the school dances?"

"*Other* stuff," he says suggestively.

Typical Aiden.

"C'mon, please! *Please*?" He coaxes, widening his deep brown eyes innocently. He heads to my iPod and after scrolling through my playlist a bit, he then selects a song.

I don't argue further. This could have been *so much* worse. Slow dancing is a relatively simple task to accomplish.

I realize just what I've agreed to do when I find myself standing in front of him with only a few inches separating us. As the music starts, his hands slowly wrap around my body and slip down my back, landing a little below my waist. I suppress a gasp.

The sexy music fills the room; its soft beats bounce off the walls. I try to ignore how fast my heart is beating, or how close we are to each other. He pulls me towards him, fastening both his arms around me firmly so that I'm pressed up against his chest. I hesitantly wrap my arms around his neck. I can feel his breath on my face.

We sway our bodies to the soft rhythm of the music. My breathing comes out uneven and fast. I don't look at him. I just can't. Whenever I try to meet his eyes, my heart starts to race. I can't make myself look into his eyes, scared that he'll figure out exactly how he's making me feel.

"I was right," he murmurs.

"About what?"

"You don't like our proximity. You can't bear my touch."

I lift my gaze to meet his eyes. "W-what are you even saying? Of course not! I mean . . . I mean—" I look away, defeated.

"And there, you're doing that again," he whispers sexily.

"Doing what?" I ask. I can't comprehend a word he's saying. I can barely breathe much less make myself focus on what he's saying.

"Not looking at me, averting your gaze. *Look* at me Scarlett." He commands softly.

I look up at him, just so I can prove him wrong. I regret it. I regret it *so* bad. When I look at him, and I mean *really* look at him—straight into his eyes—I forget to breathe. It causes this strange pain to erupt inside my chest. I want to just run away.

Being this close to him makes me realize I'm holding everything I can never have. It makes me realize for the first time that this thing we have...that these feelings *I* have . . . it's going nowhere. All I'll ever get are these small, precious moments with him—nothing more. It makes me realize he will never be mine.

It hurts.

We're still slow dancing. It's not even dancing. It's more like stepping from the left leg to the right leg. My heart is beating *so* fast. I'm scared I'll end up doing something I'll regret; something wrong like kissing him and risking our friendship. I need to get away from him before I do something and make a fool out of myself. In the library we'd come really close to crossing the lines. We'd literally been saved by the bell. But here? Here there's no escape.

"You blush a lot, you know?" He observes.

I bite my lip nervously. "Yeah . . . " I look up into his eyes and am caught off-guard by how intensely he's looking at me. But the strange thing is, it's not my eyes he's looking at it. It's my lips.

Does he want to kiss me?

The music fades away, leaving us in pure silence. I realize we're still holding each other. None of us tries to step away. It's...strange. There's no music to dance to but here we are frozen in time, looking straight into each other's eyes.

The very next second Aiden starts leaning towards me. It's like the library incident all over again. Except this time, I don't run away. This time I stay.

I press my eyes shut and start leaning towards him too. A second later our lips brush against each other's ever so slightly. I feel electricity run through every core of my body. I tremble.

Aiden suddenly pulls away. My eyes suddenly pop open at the same time. We both realize just *what* is happening. I freeze. He immediately steps back.

"I think . . . " I'm not able to form a coherent sentence, but somehow he understands exactly what I'm trying to say.

"Yeah, you're right. Bye Scarlett." He quietly turns around, then leaves.

"Bye Aiden," I whisper.

Chapter Eight

Scarlett

"Damn!" I curse under my breath. I am beyond pissed. The weather outside is terrible. It's raining heavily; and oh, I just missed the bus I was supposed to catch *fifteen* minutes ago.

For a minute or two, I contemplate not going to school altogether. But then I remember our teacher is going to cover a very important topic in physics today—something related to magnetic fields.

"Mom, how do I go to school today?!" I complain.

I look outside the window in dismay. Sinister looking clouds loom in the sky, and thunder crackles every few minutes.

"Your dad will drop you, of course," she replies.

I immediately look at Dad. His face is hidden behind the newspaper, only the top of his mousy brown hair is visible. He's oblivious to the ongoing conversation.

"Dad!" I exclaim, trying to catch his attention. He looks up from his newspaper, startled.

"What?" he asks.

"Can you drop me off at school?"

He replies in the negative. "Sorry dear, but you know my office is on the other side of the city. I'll be late if I do. Why don't you just ask your brother?"

If my brother drives, why do I still use the school bus? Because he's really unreliable. He skips school *a lot*. Plus he usually jams with his buddies after school. I couldn't rely on him for rides, so I had to settle for the bus.

Well, I'll have to go with him today.

I stomp up to his room and barge in. Surprise! Surprise! He's asleep.

This boy.

"Darren, wake up!" I screech.

He groans, burying his head further under the blanket.

"Go away Scarlett."

"Darren get up. I need you to give me a ride to school. Don't *you* have school?!"

"Okay whatever," he murmurs, completely ignoring my question.

"Darren! You need to get your ass up and ready within twenty minutes or I'm going to be late."

"Calm down woman!" he exclaims, sounding fully awake now. "I promise you that you'll be at school on time."

"Okay..." I look at him suspiciously, before exiting his room.

Fifteen minutes later, the doorbell rings. My mom orders me to get it. Wondering who it could be so early in the morning, I pull it open, seeing the last person I expected to see.

"What are *you* doing here?!" It's Aiden.

He shrugs. "Darren told me you needed a ride for school today, so here I am!" he says, opening his arms wide.

Ugh Darren you lazy bastard! I could have called Aiden on my own. *Why didn't I think of it?*

"No hug for me?" Aiden asks. "Okay." He put his hands back down.

No wait, I want to hug you! Wait!

"Come on let's get going. We'll be late if we don't."

Aiden follows me. As we reach his car, I sigh in delights. His car is a sleek black Mercedes Benz, and I have a thing for black cars. It's gorgeous, really. It has these soft plushy, totally comfortable seats and an awesome sound system installed in it.

I get in the passenger seat and off we go. We sit in the car in silence. Aiden, being his usual self, is humming a tune of some song. The radio's playing, but at a very low volume. A couple of minutes later, one of my favorite songs comes on. I immediately reach over to increase the volume. Aiden leans forward to do the same, causing our fingers to brush against each other. I immediately retract my hands and put it on my lap, pretending nothing happened. This doesn't go unnoticed by Aiden.

I know the way I act is ridiculous. But ever since I've discovered the feelings I have for Aiden, I try my best to stay away from him, physically at least—for my own sake.

"I don't have skin disease you know?" he says, looking right at me—his dark eyes looking squarely into mine, holding my gaze.

"I know you don't, I just . . ." I resist the urge to look away. Attractive boys make me nervous, and just my luck, I realized a few days back that I find my best friend *really* attractive.

"No seriously, I don't bite. Well . . . unless you ask me to," he says suggestively, cocking his eyebrows. I can't help blushing.

"Perv!" I punch him lightly.

Then I do something which even surprises me. I reach over and put my hand right onto his. He looks up at me, surprised. Then he smiles and puts his hands over mine; it completely covers mine. I feel goosebumps appear all over my arm. I love the way it feels, all warm and rough to the touch.

We sit quietly. The drive seems a little long, but I don't mind. He occasionally glances at me, and when he catches my eye, he smiles at me—my heart does somersaults in my chest. I smile right back at him, feeling uncertain.

I *want* to feel happy. I want to feel content, but I can't. I know this is transient. These small moments are all I'm going to get. He'll never be mine the way I want him to, not really.

He suddenly stops the car and I look up expectantly. Did we reach school already? Isn't it a bit too quiet for school? Then I realize we're not there yet. We're parked in front of a house. I glance at him questioningly.

"Hailey. I'm her ride for school," he explains.

Oh, of course. She's his girlfriend and they always go to school together. How nice.

He texts Hailey, asking her to come outside. A minute or so later, Hailey emerges out of her house, her hair cascading down her shoulder in perfect ringlets. As she nears the passenger seat, she frowns, her eyes narrowing ever so slightly as they fall on me.

She makes no move to open the car door. Instead, she clears her throat, gesturing me to step out. She wants to sit in the front. I feel anger pulse through my veins. It makes me want to combust into smoke and ashes. I'm really tempted to punch her in the face.

But the anger's gone as soon as it comes, leaving behind a feeling of melancholy. I have no right to be angry. She is his girlfriend. She goes to school in his car every day. She always sits next to him and he holds her hand as he drives. This is *their* routine. She's not the intruder—*I* am.

So I push open the door and go sit at the back, letting her sit next to him. I can feel Aiden's eyes on me. For a second or two,

I almost believe he wants to say something to Hailey but then he doesn't. He silently watches me as his girlfriend takes her rightful place. It hurts.

She starts to smile as soon as she sits next to him. "Hey baby, how're you? I missed you *so* much," she coos. Then she leans forward and smashes her lips onto his. He protests for a second or two before kissing her back. The way she kisses him is aggressive. There's nothing affectionate about it. It's almost as if . . . as if she's marking her territory.

I look away, my eyes burning with unshed tears. If I could leave right now, I would. But it's still raining outside and I still need a ride.

Aiden starts the car again, and off we go again. I notice their fingers are intertwined. She's whispering into his ear, and he's smiling and responding back. They both are lost in their own bubble. It's like they've completely forgotten that I'm here. I force myself to look away, and stare outside the window instead.

I . . . I want this. I want to have this sort of relationship with someone too. I want someone to look at me the way Aiden is looking at her. I want someone to hold my hands and kiss me and make me feel beautiful. I want this.

But I don't have it.

I shove in my earphones for the rest of the ride, blasting angry pop music. I block Hailey and Aiden's mushiness, making the car ride bearable to some extent. Ten minutes later, Aiden parks his car at school. I bolt out as soon as the car stops. There's only so much I can take. Not that Aiden notices of course; he's too occupied with his precious girlfriend.

* * *

Hailey

Aiden kisses me goodbye just outside of my class, his lips moving affectionately over mine, giving me butterflies in my belly. When he breaks the kiss I smile at him, and he returns the gesture, unleashing a swarm of butterflies. I bid him goodbye and enter the classroom.

My so-called friend passes me a knowing smile as I take my designated seat.

"I still can't believe you're dating *the* Aiden Walkers," Amyra gushes.

I roll my eyes. "You speak of him as if he's a celebrity," I mutter, extracting my history notebook from my bag.

"He might as well be. He's *so* hot."

"Uhm are we forgetting he's *my* boyfriend?" I point out.

Amyra rolls her eyes, ignoring my remark. "You know, I need to tell you something important. It's about him."

"Tell me what?" I ask, curious.

"Do you know a certain Scarlett Stevenson?"

I immediately freeze. "W-what about *her*?" I hope I don't look as tense as I feel.

"Nothing much. It might be false but I heard these rumors about her and him . . ."

"Him? As in Aiden? What rumors?"

"Just that they have this thing going on or something. This girl in their class saw them together after their class ended. They were staring into each other's eyes. They looked pretty cozy . . ."

"That's bullshit!"

"It could be false, but if I were you, I'd be a little more careful, especially of Scarlett. She looks so sly." I can see Amyra is enjoying my discomfort. She's always been like this. I don't even know if I can even consider her my friend. But she's all I have.

"What can I do about it?" I ask her.

"If I were you, I'd go to Scarlett and . . . talk. You know, just make it clear who's the girlfriend here."

"You want me to ask Scarlett to keep her distance from him?" I can't believe what Amyra is suggesting me to do.

"Pretty much, yes. But again, it's all up to you. You can sit here and do nothing—let her flock around him and let her wound him around her finger. *Or* you can set some boundaries."

The teacher chooses this moment to enter the class so we stop talking.

"Think about it," Amyra mouths.

And I *do* think about it.

* * *

I decide I won't say anything to Scarlett. As much as her closeness to Aiden makes me uncomfortable, she hasn't done anything out of line (yet) I have no reason to walk up to her and lash out. And this is exactly what I tell Amyra when she asks what I've decided to do.

She makes a face. She'd clearly been anticipating drama.

"I didn't want to do this, I *really* didn't. But you leave me no choice. This one's gonna hurt," she says mysteriously, like she knows about something I don't.

"What are you talking about?"

"Come with me." That's all she says. And like the fool I am, I follow her. I know this will make us late for the next class but I'm really curious. She takes me through a series of corridors before I realize we're in front of our school's dance studio.

I pass Amyra a quizzical look. "Why are we here?"

"You'll see."

And I do. I see Aiden, and I see Scarlett. They are dancing with each other. I pass Amyra a bored look. "So? Aiden told me

he's been assigned this dance project with her. It's no big deal."
We're both hidden from view, peeking in through the slightly ajar
door.

"Are you sure it's not a big deal? Look *closely*."

I look at her quizzically, then turn back to look at Aiden
and Scarlett. They both are laughing now. It would have been
normal, really—two friends laughing about something. But this
was different. There was something . . . more. Her hands were still
wrapped around his neck and his around her waist. They were
looking into each other's eyes as they laughed. Then slowly the
laughter subsided, morphing into perfect silence.

I expected them to move away from each other then,
since the music had stopped. However, they didn't. They just . . .
stood there, looking at each other, *staring* into each other's eyes.

With my heart in my throat, I looked at them. They were
close to each other—*too* close.

What is Aiden doing?! Why isn't he pushing her away? What will
he do?

They step away a minute later. But that minute is a minute
too long. By the time it happens, I've already decided something.

Scarlett and I . . . we need to talk.

* * *

Scarlett

I glance at my watch and see that the next class begins in
fifteen minutes. Good, I need time to calm myself. People give me
curious glances as I rush to the girl's washroom, like my ass is on
fire. But my ass isn't—my heart is. I just can't stop thinking about
the car ride this morning.

I sigh with relief when I see the washroom is empty. No annoying freshman girls gossiping about "that hot senior guy." I put down my bag and take out my hair brush and start brushing my hair repeatedly. It pacifies my turbulent mind. I feel much better. I sigh, trying to smile confidently at my reflection.

I'm a smart, beautiful, independent girl. I don't care if my best friend doesn't have feelings for me. It doesn't matter. I don't care if he likes that Hailey girl. It's—

I hear the door of the washroom being pushed open, creaking just a little as it slides over the tiled bathroom floor.

Speaking of the devil . . .

Hailey confidently strides in. I'm once again reminded of the car ride, of how tense the atmosphere had been. I hope against hope that she will head to one of the cubicles. No such luck.

Instead of heading there, she walks to the mirror and sets down her bag right next to mine. She spends a minute or two looking at herself, running her fingers through her auburn tresses. She dabs her lips with a peach colored lip gloss next. She zips up her purse, picks it up, and turns around to leave.

Thank heavens!

She stops in her path and turns around to face me.

Oh god no.

"Oh, hello Scarlett! I didn't see you there," she murmurs.

"Um hi . . ." I try to smile at her.

"So sad, seems no one ever sees you."

Huh?

"Especially Aiden . . ."

I freeze as she says this. *Is she implying what I think she is implying?*

"It must be really hard to clamor for your best friend's attention *and* affection but fail *miserably* every time."

My heart stops beating in my chest for a moment. I ball my hands into fists.

Hailey turns to fully face me, an annoying smirk plastered on her face. It quickly morphs into a cold frown. "Now you listen to me Scarlett and listen *carefully* because I won't repeat myself. Aiden is *mine*. He is *my* boyfriend."

"I know that—"

"Do you? Do you *really*? Don't act all innocent. I saw how you were holding his hand in the car this morning. And don't think I haven't noticed how you stare at him from afar. But by all means, you can stare at him the whole fucking day, as long as you remember that it's the only thing you can do—stare." She takes a step closer to me, intimidating me with her hateful glare. "But don't you dare come any closer or you'll be sorry—I promise you." She glares icily at me. "As long as we have this established, we're good."

Then she turns around and sashays out the door, leaving me dumbstruck.

Chapter Nine

"—and then she walked away." I finish telling Susan about what happened today with Hailey.

She gasps on the other side of the line.

"*Oh my god!* I can't believe that bitch—"

"But Hailey's right. Aiden is *her* boyfriend. I'm just his . . . friend," I murmur.

"*So?!* It doesn't give her the right to act like this. It's not like you have been throwing yourself at him. You're his *best friend*. She needs to suck it up and stop acting like an insecure piece of shit."

I stay silent, not knowing what to say.

"Wait, you're not really considering what she said, right? You're not going to push Aiden away, you hear me?"

"I don't know…"

"Shut up! Let *Aiden* decide who he wants to be with. You don't have to distance yourself from him, okay? Just be the friend you've always been to him. Anyway, what did *you* say? I hope you fought back!?" Susan questioned.

"It was so sudden: one second we were touching up our makeup, and then the very next second she exploded like a bomb; dropping her I'm-oh-so-innocent `façade and shouting at me. I just didn't know what to say—"

"You didn't know what to say? Are you kidding me?! You knew *exactly* what to say. You just had to tell her to get over herself and fuck off. You didn't. Know why? *I* know why. When the hell are you going to start standing up for yourself?!" Susan bellows. I stifle groan. I hate it when Susan lectures me.

"I just . . . I was caught off guard, okay? That's why I didn't say anything. I'll stand up for myself next time, I promise." We both know I'm lying. But Susan doesn't push the topic further. Maybe it makes me a coward, but I've never liked confrontations. I know she's right. I need to stop letting people stomp all over me.

"Anyway, I called you because I wanted to tell you about this carnival. Everyone's going."

I think about it. *Going to a carnival wouldn't be too bad...*
With Aiden.

"Can I bring Aiden? I have not hung out alone with him since summer and I really miss it."

"Oh sure, sure. Some people from my school are going to be there anyway so I'll hang out with them."

"You don't have to—"

"I know I don't, but you need that alone time with him. You should have it."

She promises to text me the address and time. We talk a little on the phone and then she hangs up. I immediately shoot Aiden a text.

Hey.

After two *very* long minutes he responds.

Hey

I don't reply back immediately, since I don't want to seem desperate.

Me: Sup?

Aiden Walkers: Just talking to Hailey ;)

I feel annoyance bubble up inside me. *Why the fuck does he always have to bring her up in our conversation?!*

Me: Oh, cool! :D

(Translation: I don't give a fuck.)

Aiden Walkers: :)

Our conversation stops here. I wonder how to continue it. Fortunately, he double texts.

Aiden Walkers: So . . . what are you up to?

Me: Was just reading about this Carnival in town. I think I'll go check it out tomorrow. You wanna tag along?

Aiden Walkers: I might, not sure though. I'll confirm and tell?

Me: Sure :)

* * *

"Where is he? Where is he?" Susan asks me for the hundredth time.

"I don't know! He said he'll come, but I can't see him anywhere . . ." I sigh.

"Text him!"

"No way! It'll seem like I'm really eager and—"

"Shut up and text him!" Susan demands.

"No way in hell!"

She grabs my phone from hand and sends him a text at the speed of light. I gasp, snatching back the phone. I glare at her accusingly. She simply smirks. I read the text she just sent him.

You here yet?

I groan and am about to scold Susan for texting him, when my phone vibrates. I stare down at it to see that Aiden has replied. I hurriedly read his text.

I'm near the hotdog stands.

Immediately my eyes fall on the hotdog stand, a few meters away from where we're standing.

"Hey, did he reply?" Susan inquires, but I'm too aghast to respond.

"I can't believe he did this." I fume, my voice laced with venom.

"Did what?"

"What is his problem?!" I exclaim, not able to contain my anger.

"What happened?!" Susan inquires but I ignore her.

"What now, are they stuck at the hip or something?!"

"Will you tell me what the fuck has happened?!" Susan shouts, finally losing her temper.

"See for yourself, just look at the ho-dog stand. He's there," I reply dryly.

Susan cups her hand over her eyes and looks at the hot dog stands. She lets out a low whistle a couple of seconds later. "Damn, that's him in the dark blue jeans, isn't it? He looks hot."

"Oh, that's him alright! But look *carefully.*"

Susan frowns at me. "What the hell are you going on about?!" I gesture her to simply look. She turns back. This time she understands what I mean.

Her eyes widen as she witnesses Hailey snake her arms around Aiden's Waist and pulls him closer. "Don't tell me that's his girlfriend," Susan scoffs.

"That's *exactly* who she is. Can you actually believe he brought *her* along?! I really just wanted it to be us. He's been cancelling plans ever since he met her. And now he's brought her here too! Now I'll be stuck feeling like a third wheel. I *can't* meet him now."

"Well, in that case, we'll just have to get rid of her." Susan shrugs.

"How?" I cock my eyebrows in question. But I don't let her respond. I know what he has in my mind before she even says it. "No way Su, we're *not* doing anything to her."

"Who said we'll *do* anything? It'll just be an 'accident'," she says, feigning innocence.

"*No*. We're not doing anything," I declare, shaking my head adamantly.

Susan sighs, slumping her shoulders. "You're such a party pooper. But I'm telling you, my idea could have worked."

"Well, I should be heading there now." I lament.

"Girl, you really think I'll let you go off on your own?"

"So you'll come with me?" I ask her.

"No, but someone else will." I look at her, perplexed. She tells me to wait and starts tapping away on her phone. Two minutes later, she looks up and smiles at me. "Done!

"Done what?"

"Since we'll be doing this, I better tell you about Adam. He's this guy in my history class."

"Oh, the one you rejected last year?"

"Uh-huh. And even though he's pretty much over me, we're still good friends, and so he's agreed to help us out," she explains

"Help us with what? I don't understand..." Confusion lines crease my forehead. I don't know what Susan's up to, but it's probably something terrible.

"Adam's going to be your date for today."

"D-date!?" I cry out.

"Fake date, to be precise. He's cute, funny, and sweet—the perfect guy to make Aiden jealous."

"J-jealous?!" I stammer. Susan nods. I pull my hair, frustrated. She's out of her mind! She's insane if she thinks Aiden will get jealous.

"Not just jealous. Think about it, wouldn't it be pathetic if you just walked up to them all by yourself? You'll have to follow them around the whole day. Hailey will get another excuse to laugh at you. It's better this way, trust me."

I nod. She actually has a point.

"Awesome!" I squeal, giving Susan a tight hug. She's a genius! She just saved me from undergoing a hell lot of humiliation. We both silently wait for this Adam guy to arrive. I feel a little hesitant, since I have to pretend I'm on a date with someone I've never met before. But Susan trusts him, so I guess I can too.

A few minutes later this lanky looking guy with dirty blonde hair appears at the scene. That has to be Adam. On closer inspection, I notice he has brilliant blue eyes and an easygoing smile. He's definitely cute.

Susan introduces us to each other, and then explains the plan to him. He chuckles, then turns to me, giving me a full-fledged smile.

"Even though I know you can trust him." Susan turns to Adam "Still, *stay* in your limits. If you try anything on her—" She threatens him.

He mock salutes her. "Aye, aye, captain!" inducing a small chuckle from me.

"What about you? Where are you going?" I ask her.

"I'll chill with the people from school."

"Oh, alright." I nod. I hug her goodbye; then Adam and I head off to meet Aiden. We hold hands like couples do. It feels strange holding a stranger's hand out in public.

"So . . . this Aiden guy, you're trying to make him jealous?"

"Uhm, not exactly. I just don't want to be the third wheel," I explain.

He chuckles. "Don't worry, we'll make him jealous."

"Actually, we could have fun too. This doesn't have to be boring."

"Who said it'll be boring?"

Wow, I like this guy already!

My heart starts beating faster as we approach Aiden and Hailey. Adam gently squeezes my hand, offering a reassuring smile. Aiden is the first to see me. He waves from afar. I wave back. A smile immediately plasters on my face, and I'm pretty sure my eyes are sparkling with delight. I can't help it; it's a reflex.

"Stop smiling like you've just won the lottery or something. Play it cool," Adam whispers to me, and I immediately stop smiling.

"Hey Scar!" Aiden exclaims, stepping forward to wrap his arm around me. I am momentarily surprised. Aiden never greets me with a hug.

I savor the hug as much as I can, enjoying his strong and sturdy arms around me, even if it's only for a few second. I glance over at Hailey and see her scowling. I smile gleefully at her.

Take that, bitch!

"Oh hey Hailey, I didn't see you there," I greet her rather icily.

Hailey passes me a tight-lipped smile. "Scarlett, I'm *so* glad you told Aiden about this carnival. We hadn't had the chance to go out for a while. But today we get to go out on a cute date, thanks to *you.*" She turns to Aiden, "Baby, we'll ride the Ferris wheel, right?"

He gently presses his lips against her head. "Yeah babe, we're going to do *all* the things you want." She giggles in response.

Stop giggling bitch, or I might just strangle you.

I pass Hailey another sugary smile before turning to Aiden,

"I'm so glad you brought her along. I'd been a little worried worried that you'd show up all by yourself. It would have been a little weird for Adam, since he doesn't know you."

"Oh! Uhm, who's Adam?" Aiden asks, confusion lines creasing his forehead.

"Oh right, I didn't introduce you guys. Aiden, this is Adam, my date and Adam, this is Aiden . . . my friend."

"Date?" Aiden sounds a little puzzled.

"Yeah! We met through some mutual friends. In fact, he's the one who told me about the carnival in the first place." I shrug.

Aiden fist bumps Adam, and they greet each other like guys usually do. Then Aiden returns back to Hailey, and Adam takes my hand again.

"So what do you want to do first, sweetheart?" Adam asks me, putting our plan into action.

Will this even work?

"Uhm, I wanted to try out a couple of those carnival rides, how about you?"

Adam hugs me closer and smiles. "Whatever you want, babe," he murmurs, unleashing the B word. I glance at Aiden sneakily, trying to see if he looks even slightly bothered.

He doesn't. Instead he's busy talking to Hailey, whispering softly in her ears. She's laughing at whatever he's saying. I feel annoyance bubble up in my chest. I try to ignore it and focus on Adam instead.

We all start walking and soon reach this ride called 'The Teacups.' It consists of a bunch of giant teacup shaped seats arranged on a round base. The base moves round and round, and also up and down, causing the teacups to move about. I gesture towards it, indicating I want to ride it. Aiden groans.

"Don't tell me you want to ride that," he says making a face. "That's a ride for babies."

"I want to ride that!" Hailey exclaims at the same time.

Adam and I double up laughing. "Looks like your girlfriend is a baby," I remark, smirking.

"Yeah, but she's *my* baby," Aiden says, pulling her closer to him, giving her a small peck on her lips. Hailey smirks at me.

I look away, feeling hurt. Adam notices my downtrodden expression and tries to cheer me up. "C'mon, let's go ride it." He grabs my hands and off we go. Aiden and Hailey follow close behind. We sit down side by side on the ride and soon enough it starts.

"Don't worry, we *will* make him jealous—I promise," Adam whispers to me. I smile back in return.

"Thanks Adam for helping me out. It really means a lot."

He smiles back. "It's nothing, honestly. You don't need to thank me."

The ride starts. We begin to move round and round. I clutch the edge of the giant teacup we're sitting in. A strong wind whips against my face. As the rotational speed increases, I let out a scream, pressing my eyes shut. I feel so dizzy.

This was a bad idea.

Adam urges me to open my eyes and enjoy the ride. But I can't. I feel terrified and queasy. If this is a "ride for babies," then I don't want to go on anymore rides. The ride ends a couple of minutes later and we get down hurriedly. I feel slightly dizzy and make a mental note to not get onto anymore rides for now.

We all wait for a couple of minutes, calming our nerves before walking further.

"Oh my god, we need to try this out!" My eyes shine with excitement as I stand in front of the haunted house. It's a single story building, quite small actually and looks a little creepy. I can hear screams coming from inside.

"Please, can we try this out?" I plead. This time Aiden and Adam both look equally excited. Well, Hailey doesn't.

"Uh, I think I'll skip. I don't feel so good after that ride," Hailey says, looking slightly queasy.

"Aw c'mon Hailes, it'll be fun!" Aiden encourages her.

"Yeah Hailey, it'll be fun. You should totally come. Unless you're scared, of course. I mean I totally understand if you're scared." I assure her. Adam stifles a laugh.

"I'll meet you outside, once you guys are done." Hailey glares at me, and then walks away.

I shrug. "So are you guys coming or what?" I ask, and then head inside, not bothering to wait for them.

We pay for the tickets, and then head up the porch of the rickety old house. A high-pitched scream pierces my ears as soon as I step inside the house. That was *definitely* a sound effect. It's very dark in here, but a sick greenish glow illuminates our path slightly. I touch the walls, as I make my way, realizing they aren't made of solid brick, they are hollow. I can feel someone banging on them from the other side. It's really creepy. We take small uncertain steps. Wails and screams envelope us as we walk further.

A couple of steps later, I get my first fright. A slightly cold and clammy hand wraps around my ankle, causing me to scream loudly. The hand vanishes a second later, and I'm left to stare around in the dark, trying to figure out where it came from. Adam and Aiden are staring at me as if I've gone crazy.

"What happened?" Adam asks, sounding concerned.

"Uhm, it was nothing. Someone just grabbed my ankle, that's all," I mutter.

Aiden doubles up laughing. "Whoever it was did an awesome job! Your reaction was priceless!"

I narrow my eyes at him. "Yours would be too if someone grabbed your leg out of nowhere in the goddamn dark!"

We follow the ghostly green colored glow that illuminates our path. Suddenly the walls vanish, and my hand comes in contact with something slimy. I let out a yelp.

"Scarlett watch out!" I hear Adam, and before I can contemplate what is happening, he pushes me away. My back comes in contact with the wall, while Adam provides me cover in the front. Something big and white swoops down again, like a pendulum.

Aiden brings forth his hand and grabs its. "Chill guys, it's just a dummy, covered in a white cloth, nothing to be scared of."

We walk cautiously, carefully assessing our surroundings. More such objects swoop down at us, hitting us a couple of times. More ankle grabbing follows. Skeletons jump out at us, and once something very similar to a bat, swoops downs at us, shrouding us in darkness for a few seconds.

By the time I spot the exit, I'm frustrated. This haunted house wasn't scary, it was annoying. I make a run for the door, not letting myself wait any longer. As I started running, the floor beneath me starts vibrating like crazy. The leveled floor suddenly morphs into a slope, causing me to lose my balance and hurtle forward. Someone wraps his arms around my waist, steadying me before I fall on my face.

"Are you okay, Scar?" Aiden's familiar voice soothes me. I nod, not able to muster a reply. That was a close call. I almost got a mini heart attack. Aiden's scent surrounds me, as he stands close to me, with his arms still wrapped around my waist.

"Y-yeah." I muster up a reply. Aiden gently lets go of me, and I walk away. As I emerge out of the haunted house, I notice Hailey sitting on a rock, under a tree nearby, texting away on her phone, a slight frown plastered on her face.

My cheeks are still warm from earlier when Aiden had so swiftly taken me in his arms to break my fall. We'd been so close. I'm suddenly hit with a desperate longing. My eyes linger on Aiden, and I realize what this longing is. It's him.

As he presses his lips softly onto Hailey's for a moment, I feel something deep inside me shatter—my heart. I quickly look away, hoping that if I don't see them together, the pain would go away. It doesn't. It's still present somewhere deep inside, but I do a good job of hiding it.

I catch Adam looking at me, a concerned expression on his face. He passes me a weak smile. "It's going to be okay, you just wait. We're going to make him jealous before the sun sets, and that's a promise!" I'm overwhelmed by his sweetness. He's not getting anything from doing this, but he's still helping me out. Feeling a little sentimental, I wrap my arms around him and give him a hug. "You don't need to do this. But you still are. Thank you."

After briefly hugging Adam, I step away from him, and pass him a soft smile. As I turn around, I notice Aiden's eyes on us. He immediately averts his gaze.

Hailey wants to try out the gaming stalls next. So we all head there. She is practically glued to Aiden which doesn't in anyway help to improve my sour mood. The only thought comforting me right now is that Adam, whose here right next to me, is going to help me make Aiden jealous.

To make someone jealous, they must feel something for you. And he doesn't feel anything for me.

We arrive at a stall where we need to throw paint-filled balloons at an old man. He's sitting on a plastic seat that's attached high up on the wall. Whoever succeeds at hitting him a certain number of times will get the toy he or she desires.

"So which toy do you want?" the stall in-charge asks us. The boys instinctively turn towards us.

"Uhm, that one!" Hailey and I simultaneously point at the same plushy baby pink bear.

"Uh . . . I'd suggest one of you to choose a different one. How about this? This one's cute," The guy presents us with another teddy bear that looks exactly the same, except its baby blue in color.

"Scarlett, you'd be okay with the other bear, right?" Hailey prompts.

"Uh, no. I want this one. Why don't *you* take the other one?" Honestly, it's not even a big. But I'm just *so* sick of compromising. First I had to adjust all my plans, just because Hailey decided to tag along. And now I'm supposed to choose a different toy too? She can't always get her way.

The one in charge, noticing that neither of us are budging, presents us with another alternative. "Let's tweak the rules a little then. Earlier, you all were supposed to make twenty-five hits within five minutes. Let's change the rules and turn this into something more…competitive. Whoever manages to make more hits during the set ten minutes wins the bear. How about that?"

Hailey and I nod. No, I *actually* like this. This could be fun. Wiping that smug look off Hailey's face would be fun.

Aiden and Adam pay for the balloons and get a bucket each, both filled with about fifty balloons. Adam gets a bucket full of blue colored paint filled balloons and Aiden gets red. The instructor blows the whistle and Aiden and Adam start chucking balloons from the bucket at the man, while the instructor keeps count.

Aiden being the good athlete he is, is doing a better job, although Adam isn't far behind. Hailey starts cheering for Aiden. His speed immediately increases.

Oh yeah? So if I cheer for Adam, I get the teddy bear? Bring it on!

So right there and then, I start cheering for Adam too. "C'mon Adam, you can do it! You're going to win this!"

But as the game proceeds, the number of balloons seem to never lessen. Adam begins to look tired. The smile on Hailey's face increases by the second. I know I must do something, and so I step forward, telling Adam to let me handle things from here on.

I start throwing the balloons at the old man forcefully. I flinch when it hits him hard on his belly. His body is splattered with red and blue paint. Poor old man, how much is he getting paid for doing this?

Aiden eventually gets tired too, so Hailey takes his place.

The whole agenda of the game instantly changes.

The aim now isn't to win the bear. It's to win, period. It's to show Aiden his girlfriend is a loser. It's almost like we're competing *for* him. It gets real aggressive real quick. We're throwing balloons and yelling profanities at each other. Forget the teddy bear; we're almost out to get each other.

That's when it happens: the first balloon comes flying towards *me* and not the old man. I gasp when it lands across my belly, splattering me with red paint.

I glare at Hailey. "You bitch!" I roar, swinging my arms and tossing a balloon straight at her.

Splat!

It hits her square on her face, the paint ruining her makeup and hair. I let out a loud guffaw and double up laughing.

Her mouth drops open. "How dare you?!" She throws another balloon at me.

I manage to duck, simultaneously hurling as many balloons as I can in her direction. The in-charge is gaping at us. Aiden and Adam are urging us to stop, but not coming anywhere close. They don't want a balloon to accidently hit them.

It starts to get uglier and uglier by the minute. The balloons in our bucket long gone, we both start looking around for more balloons. Our eyes fall on the giant balloon-filled tub behind the counter at the same time. We make a beeline for it. We're about to start launching balloons again when Aiden suddenly shouts on the top his voice.

"That is ENOUGH!" he thunders, startling us. He steps forward and stands between both of us. We immediately drop the balloons we'd grabbed to throw at each other. I instantly feel embarrassed for having acted like an absolute child. All signs of anger drains off his face once we stop. Hailey and I wait for him to continue.

"It's just a teddy bear, why are you girls getting so worked up?" he sighs.

Oh honey, if only you knew.

"Well, tell your so-called friend to control herself!" Hailey seethes.

"Me?! Are you serious?! Aiden tell your stupid girlfriend to stop blaming me for her own childishness!"

"*I'm* not childish!"

"Oh yeah? *You* were the one who started this!"

"I did not!"

"What a two-faced liar!" I snap.

We both start to bicker, and another war of abuses begins. It's pretty obvious at this point that Aiden is losing his cool.

Suddenly we hear someone giggling, causing us both to stop. Our eyes fall on a young girl. She's adorable, except for the fact that she's clutching the teddy bear, the one *we* both had been competing for. She walks away with it, while we're left gaping.

"Well, that's that. No point in fighting now. The bear's gone," Adam ventures.

Oh, if only he knew that this isn't a petty teddy bear dispute. It's much more than that. The balloon fight was just an excuse for us to express our anger towards each other. Of course, Aiden and Adam are too dense to realize this. Especially Aiden, who is clueless about the fact that I, his best friend, hate his girlfriend. The feeling is definitely mutual.

Hailey smirks at me for just an instant. It's so short-lived that it goes unnoticed by everyone else. The smirk vanishes instantly, replaced by a small frown and sad eyes welling with unshed tears.

Oh my god, she's faking it. She's fake-crying. That conniving bitch!

"Oh Aiden, I only wanted to have fun, and spend some time with you. That's all. I didn't know this would happen . . . I shouldn't have come. It would have been better if you'd just hung out with her." Then she bursts into tears. For a second even I'm confused. *Is she really crying, or is this simply an act?*

No, of course she's not crying. She just wants Aiden's sympathy.

"I guess I should leave. I'm so sorry for ruining today. I'll get going now," she murmurs and starts walking away.

"Wait no, don't go Hailey. Please! This wasn't your fault." He turns to me. "Scar, I think you should apologize to Hailey."

Wait, what!?

"*Look* at her Scar, she's *crying.* I'm not blaming you for all this. But you were really hateful to Hailey. Please just say sorry to her."

My mouth drops open.

What. The. Fuck.

Is he serious? Has he forgotten it was his girlfriend who started this balloon war and the name calling? And he wants me to apologize? No way in hell.

I glare at Aiden. I've never felt this angry before.

I have some self-respect too. I'm not apologizing for something I didn't do.

My anger reaches its peak when I notice Hailey's expression. She's smiling triumphantly at me.

Not even if Aiden asks me to.

"No."

"What?" Aiden sounds surprised.

"I said no. I am *not* apologizing. She should just suck up the fact that she's acting like a drama queen and accept that *she's* responsible for all this," I snap back.

"Scar—"

"It's okay Aiden. I wasn't really expecting anything from her anyway. I don't know what's wrong with her or why she's behaving like this. I'm sick of all this. Let's just go." Hailey grabs Aiden's hand, pulling him away.

Aiden looks at me again, silently asking me to do what I will never, ever do. He notices the adamant expression on my face and realizes I'm not going to budge. He sighs and walks away with her, hand in hand. I start walking away too, feeling a mix of anger and hurt.

Usually Aiden and I never get angry at each other. Sure, we have our moments when we can't help but argue. But this is completely different. We've never had a real fight. Not like this anyway. We're officially mad at each other.

I hear footsteps behind me, and suddenly feel hopeful. Did Aiden suddenly realize he was acting like an idiot and decided to come back?

"Scarlett, wait up!" It's Adam. *Of course,* Aiden isn't here. He's with *her.*

"Are you okay?" Adam asks me. I want to lie to him. I want to tell him I'm alright, that what happened did not affect me in the least. Instead, I confess that I feel miserable.

"I'd been so excited for today. I'd thought Aiden and I would hang out together or something. I'd thought this was going to be one of the most memorable days of my life. Instead, it's turning out to be one of the worst."

Adam pats my shoulder soothingly and tries to reassure me that things would turn out to be okay. "You're not giving up on our plan yet, are you? We still haven't made him jealous."

"How are we going do it anyway?"

"We just will," he replies.

We head towards the food stalls. I get weird looks from people, since my dress is covered with splotches of red and blue. But I don't care. The only thing worrying me right now is the fact that Aiden is not talking to me. *Should I go and apologize to him for my rash behavior?*

But that would mean apologizing to Hailey, which I definitely don't plan to do. So that leaves me with no option except to wait it out; wait for Aiden to realize he was being stupid.

"By the way, what about that stall in-charge? He must be pretty pissed about our behavior," I ask Adam.

"Oh, not exactly. He was actually scared of you girls." Adam starts laughing. "Plus, it's not like you guys caused any damage. It's all cool."

"Wait, you had to pay to him for all those balloons, right? I completely forgot we're not on an actual date. You don't have to pay for me or anything. Just tell me how much I need to pay you."

"No, I'm not taking money from you! But if you really insist, you can treat me with an ice cream." He shrugs.

"Sure!" We head towards the ice cream stall where we both end up ordering double chocolate chip flavored cones. The sweet delicacy helps to get my mind off Aiden for a minute or two. But the ice cream finishes a little too soon, and the thoughts of Aiden return to haunt me again.

"Adam, I don't think we'll be able to make Aiden jealous. He has left anyway. Let's just drop this idea. It's not going to work. I'm just glad you stuck around with me, otherwise I would have felt like the third wheel, and this day would have been disastrous."

Adam opens his mouth to argue, but then shuts it again. He knows I'm right. Aiden is *not* going to get jealous.

"Well okay, if you say so." He agrees. We spend some more time in the carnival. Going from stall to stall, and ride to ride. But it's pretty obvious that my heart's not in it.

"I guess we should leave." Adam suggests.

"Uh, yeah," I murmur. "I'm really sorry, Adam, for ruining your day. You could have enjoyed so much more if it wasn't for me. But thanks a lot. I mean it." I smile at him. Then suddenly hit with a wave of spontaneity, I rise on my tiptoes and softly kiss him on his cheeks. "Thank you," I say again.

A slight blush colors Adam's soft cheeks, and he smiles at me.

"You don't have to thank me. It *was* fun. But there's this favor I need to ask of you. Can you help me out?"

"Of course! What is it?"

"Well , I don't fake date girls for fun, no. I only did it for Susan. Because she's your friend, and she needed my help. I . . . I really like her Scarlett. She's *amazing*! If it's not too much, could you . . . could you convince her to go out with me? Just once! Just *one* date, that's all I need."

My mouth drops open in surprise. Well I hadn't been expecting *that*. Gosh Adam is *such* a sweet guy! I don't know *why*

Susan rejected him. I find myself nodding. "Of course Adam, I'll definitely talk to her."

His face lights up. "Thank you *so* much! You don't know how much you're helping me."

"What are friends for?" I pause. "I mean I can consider you my friend, can't I?"

Adam laughs. "Definitely! If you need to make that silly guy jealous again, reach out to me. I don't know why he's wasting his time with that girl when he has *you.*"

I blush, then shake my head in refusal. "No Adam, no more of this 'getting him jealous' thing. It was stupid anyway. But thanks for offering!"

I step towards him, and give him a warm, friendly hug.

"Thanks for hanging out with me today! I owe you one."

"Talk to Susan for me, and *I'll* be in your debt."

I promise him I will. I definitely will. Susan's an idiot if she'll let a guy like him get away.

* * *

Aiden

I stare at Scarlett from afar. She's with that Adam guy. Hailey is still complaining about her. I pretend that I'm listening, when really, her constant complaining about Scarlett is getting on my nerves. I admit Scarlett had been rude, but Hailey isn't all that innocent herself.

Scarlett is talking to Adam as they nibble on their ice creams. Then suddenly, she creeps closer to him and gives him a little peck on his cheeks.

What is she doing? She barely knows him.

Adam says something to her, making her laugh. I can't help glowering at him from a distance.

That ass is probably feeding her a string of romantic cliché stuff anyone can easily get from the internet, and she's probably eating up those words. Can't she see he's fooling her?

But who says he's fooling her? Maybe he actually means it?

Yeah right! I'm a guy; I know how our minds work. I don't trust him.

Hailey's constant jabber of "Aiden" suddenly catches my attention.

"Aiden can we please ride the Ferris wheel now?"

I nod. "Sure Hailes, let's go." I reluctantly follow her to the Ferris wheel, which is just a few meters away. I don't want to go ride the Ferris wheel. I want to go talk to Scarlett and tell her I'm sorry for acting like an ass. I *hate* fighting with her. We usually argue over small, minor things. But this is different. This is real.

This is terrible.

After paying, we both wait in line for our turn. Our turn comes within a couple of minutes, and we both take a seat. Hailey immediately clasps my hands, her eyes shining excitedly. I'm overcome with a wave of affection for her.

We rise higher and higher, as the wheel turns. My eyes suddenly widen when I realize I can see Scarlett again. She's still sitting on that bench with Adam. They've finished eating their ice cream. My eyes stay glued on her. It seems like they are still talking to each other.

Thank god they're not doing something else.

Wait, I don't care if they do!

Or do I?

Scarlett suddenly scoots closer to him and wraps her arms around him. What is she doing? Are they kissing?!

"Baby!" Hailey croons, grabbing my face in her tiny little hand. "Kiss me!" She demands, leaning towards me.

"What, why?!"

"Because we're on a Ferris wheel! I always wanted to be kissed on top of the Ferris wheel," Hailey explains.

I don't reply, distracted by Scarlett. I'm still trying to see if she's kissing him or not. The moving wheel is making it hard for me.

"Aiden!" Hailey exclaims, a hint of annoyance lacing her voice.

"Hailey I can't, I feel dizzy." I make an excuse, hoping she will stop pestering me. She groans.

No, Scarlett isn't kissing him. They are hugging. Okay, I can deal with hugging. This is okay.

I turn to look at Hailey again. She looks disgruntled. "I'm *so* sorry." I apologize to her. To make up to her, I pull her closer and softly press my lips on hers. She instantly kisses me back. The mood lightens up again. Hailey isn't angry anymore.

We stop kissing when the Ferris wheel stops. Personally, I don't understand the logic of kissing on top of the Ferris wheel. How are you supposed to enjoy the view if your eyes are closed, and you're busy kissing someone? I verbalize this thought and convey it to Hailey.

She rolls her eyes. "You're *so* unromantic Aiden. Not everything needs to make logical sense, okay? People kiss on top of the wheel, because it's romantic, that's it. It doesn't need to have any other reason."

I want to argue further, but I don't. I'll probably just piss Hailey off if I do. If Scarlett was here, we'd continue this argument. She'd put forward a few points, logically forming an argument, and I'd lose. She's just *really* good at debating and stuff.

Wait, why am I thinking about her? She's probably not thinking about me. She's busy with him.

Once we get off the Ferris Wheel, I realize that I need to apologize to her. I can't stay like this, without talking to her. It's driving me insane! So I drag Hailey to the ice cream stalls, hoping Scarlett's still there. Hailey gets excited, thinking I want to buy an ice cream for her. I'm disappointed when we get there a few minutes later.

Scarlett's already gone.

Chapter Ten

Scarlett

I adjust the strap of my school bag before heading towards my locker. Today started off badly. Apparently, my alarm clock forgot to ring, and the only reason I even woke up was because my mom barged into my room an hour later, shouting that I was late for school. I had a quick shower, put on a decent outfit, and rushed downstairs to grab some toast. I almost missed the school bus.

On the way to class, I realized my books were missing. I hadn't put them in my bag once I'd finished with homework last night.

Feeling morose because everything is going so unexpectedly, I walk towards class. I plop down on the only available seat in class. The teacher strolls in a minute later. I sigh, relieved. I made it just on time!

I look around, my gaze falling on the person sitting on my right. I immediately stiffen. Of course. *Of course* it's him.

It's officially proven—this is one of the bad days. The kind of days where nothing goes your way. The days where you look like crap, and feel like crap too, where everything goes wrong. This is one of those days, and I'm not at all excited.

My eyes flit over Aiden for a second before I look away, reminding myself that we're not talking. I could say I'm sorry for yesterday, except I'm *not* sorry. I don't utter a single syllable to acknowledge his presence. It's agonizing. Sitting right next to him like this, our bodies almost touching, and not even looking at him—it's torturous. He doesn't do anything to improve the situation either, and so we continue to ignore each other.

The first period seems to drag on for hours it seems. I let out a long tired yawn once the class gets over. This day is already off to a bad start, how much worse will it get?

The next couple of periods pass by in a blur. And by the time lunch break rolls in, I'm yawning like crazy. This day has been absolutely eventless.

I walk towards my locker alone. Usually Sharon accompanies me but the teacher made her wait after class today because she hadn't submitted the homework we were supposed to.

I suddenly stop. My eyes widen, and my heart races in my chest. What the hell is he doing *here*?! Aiden Walkers is leaning against my locker, texting away on his phone. I frown. This is *not* good.

What am I supposed to do? We're not talking. Doesn't he know that's my locker he's standing against? How do I tell him to move?

I decide to not stop by the lockers at all. I can grab my books *after* lunch is over, when Aiden isn't anywhere in sight.

It happens as I'm passing by. It takes him less than a second to realize I'm not stopping. He quickly steps in front of me, blocking my path. I freeze. What is he up to? I look up at him, confusion fresh on my face, and am shocked to see his familiar smile.

He's smiling at me! What even . . .

"Uh, hey," I murmur, feeling awkward.

After ignoring each other the whole morning, we're finally conversing. It feels so strange.

"Let me get those," he says and grabs my books. "They must be heavy."

I gape at him. He doesn't wait for me to respond and takes my books.

"Uh, thanks." I open my locker and take the books from Aiden, putting them inside.

"Aren't you hungry? C'mon let's go eat," he quips, taking my hand in his.

What the hell is going on?!

I don't ask him why he's talking to me all of a sudden, like we're back on friendly terms, like nothing ever happened. I don't bring up yesterday. I secretly hope he went through some sort of memory loss and completely forgot our fight. Of course, I know the truth is far from it. He remembers everything. Maybe he's secretly angry. I don't know why he's pretending to be so amiable. I silently follow him into the cafeteria, my mind flooding with a thousand questions. We both take a seat in the corner.

"I'll bring our lunch trays," he says, leaving me alone. I sit there speechless.

Is this a joke?!

Aiden returns ten minutes later with two lunch trays in his hands. He smiles at me as he takes his seat. My heart beat quickens in response. He starts eating his food, talking to me between bites. I don't respond to a single sentence he utters. It doesn't faze him, he keeps on talking anyway. Not able to bear it any longer, I decide to demand for answers.

"Aiden—"

"And then he stood up and cursed right in front of the teacher. Can you believe it?! Right in front of Mr. Brookes and everyone was so astonished that—"

"Aiden—"

"—he had the audacity to do that after all that drama, but he did it anyway and now he's—"

"Aiden—"

"—going to spend the whole year in detention. I pity him, I mean—"

"AIDEN!" I scream, losing my patience.

It startles him. People around us look up. My cheeks immediately turn red. I ignore them and focus my attention on Aiden instead.

"What do you want?" I ask solemnly, sounding dead serious.

"W-what do you mean Scar?"

"Quit it Aiden. What are you playing at? Why are you talking to me?"

He sighs, giving up. "I'm sorry." He apologizes. I don't respond, so he elaborates. "I'm sorry I acted like an ass yesterday. I shouldn't have asked you to apologize to Hailey. I had absolutely no right to do that."

"Damn right you didn't!"

"It was stupid really. It's not like Hailey had been completely innocent. I just . . . I felt *so* terrible later on. I hate fighting with you Scar. I hate it. Can you please forgive me?"

My anger at him dissolves a little. I'm just glad Aiden decided to apologize and end this fight. I roll my eyes. "Yeah okay, I forgive you. Just don't act like a dick again, okay?"

He nods. "Promise."

"You know, I just want you guys to get along. What with you being my best friend, and her being my girlfriend. You both are so important to me, and I hate to see you two fighting with each other. Can't you try to get along with her just for my sake?"

I sigh. I want to refuse. I want to tell him that there's *no* way in hell that'll happen. Not after the way she has been treating me. He's so, *so* naïve. Can't he see her for the manipulative two-faced bitch she is? Here he is trying to dissipate the problem, while all she ever tries to do is stir up drama.

Boys! They can be so stupid sometimes, always going for the bitches—the stupid, dumb, brainless bitches.

"I'll try to get along with her, for your sake." I finally give in, smiling at him.

He grins, looking genuinely happy. She does *not* deserve him.

"Great! So can I assume you will meet me at my place after school, for a movie marathon with Hailey and me?"

"Wait…movie marathon? What? Where did this come from!?"

"Look, I just want you and Hailey to get along, okay? So I thought we all could watch a couple of movies. You, me, her and well, anyone else you'd like to bring. How about that…that Adam guy? It'll be fun!"

I stare at him, dumbstruck. Okay, so I'd said I'd get along with her, but that did *not* mean I'll hang out with her and torture myself. What I really meant was that I'll be civil to her and try not to strangle her whenever she pushes my buttons. Which as it is, would be hard. But this? I'm *so* not doing this. No way!

"No Aiden. No!"

"But you said—"

"I know I did. But that doesn't mean I want to spend time with her, pretending we're buddies or something. I know she means a lot to you but I despise her, okay? Stop looking at me like that. You heard it. Yes, I *despise* her! I can't pretend to like her for your sake anymore. I hate her."

He lets out a sad, defeated sigh. "Here I am trying *so* hard to make things right and you—whatever, I know I can't change your mind. So I'll just drop it. I just wanted you guys to bond with each other and become friends. But I guess that's too much to ask." He gets up. "I need to go Scar. See you later." He stomps away.

Ugh, what a drama queen.

I notice Aiden has left his lunch tray here. I grab the juice and apple he hasn't eaten to give it to him later. Right now, I don't know what to do or think. Can I really tolerate that bitch for a few hours, just for Aiden's sake? I can't get his hurt expression out of my mind. I hate to see him down, especially when the reason is me.

Of course. Of course, I'm going to go after him and say yes. He just has this way of making me do things I would never do.

* * *

Once lunch ends, I head back to the lockers. I spot Aiden immediately. He is busy looking for something in his locker. I suck up my breath and let it all out in a whoosh, trying to pacify myself. I walk towards him, gently tapping on his shoulder to get his attention. He looks over his shoulder, seeing me, he turns back again, ignoring me.

Crap, he isn't making this easy for me, not by a long shot.

"Aiden . . . please just listen to me? Please?"

His shoulder slumps in response. He turns back around. "You wanted to say something?"

"Uh, yeah, about that movie marathon you proposed? I think I'd like to join you guys," I say, smiling hopefully at him.

After yesterday's drama, Aiden had taken the first step into reducing all this awkwardness. If it hadn't been for him, we wouldn't even be talking. The least I can do is try to get along with his girlfriend. A smile instantly erupts on his face. He isn't angry at me. I feel relieved.

Aiden offers to drive me to his place once school ends. But I refuse. I cannot endure another car ride with Hailey and Aiden. Instead, I decide to approach Sharon after school.

"Sharon, are you free right now?" I ask her as we exit the school building a few hours later. I know Aiden said I could invite Adam if I wanted, but I'd rather not. I don't want to drag him into this mess. But I don't want to go alone either, for obvious reasons. But Sharon…I'd like to take Sharon.

"Yeah, why? Do you want to hang out or something?"

"Yeah! What do you think of watching movies?"

"Sounds awesome!"

"Uhm . . . at . . . Aiden's house?"

She scrutinizes me carefully. "Aiden's place? What?"

"Would you like to accompany me to Aiden's? We're planning to watch movies."

She scowls and turns away. "No way in hell!" she scoffs.

"Oh please Sharon, you *must* come! I kind of promised Aiden that I'll join him for a movie marathon at his house, and I don't want to go alone!" I beg.

"I don't like him, you know that. Besides, why do you want me to come anyway? *You're* his friend. *You* go."

"But his girlfriend will be there!" I exclaim. I sound so desperate. Cut that, I *am* desperate. Sharon *must* come. She's my only hope of surviving the afternoon.

"So?" Sharon inquires, cocking her eyebrows accordingly.

"I'll feel like the third wheel if I go alone."

"You *are* the third wheel Scarlett. Let the couple enjoy themselves. Why must *you* go?"

"Please Sharon, I'll explain everything later. Just *please* come with me."

"Okay, fine. But first, you need to answer my questions." She demands. "Something is up with you, something you're not telling me."

I stare at her, perplexed. "What do you mean?"

"What's the deal with you and Aiden? C'mon, spill it. You always act so weird when I mention his name."

I realize that no matter how many excuses I make now, she will not budge. Not this time. Defeated, I grab her hand and lead her towards a bench nearby. I suddenly feel nervous. It's not that I don't trust Sharon. I trust her *completely*. It's just that I *know* she won't approve. She detests Aiden. She will never approve of my crush on him—never.

"I *like* Aiden like 'more than a friend'." It comes out more directly than I'd intended it to. I'd been thinking about beating around the bush a bit, and then gently telling it to her, instead it all came out in a rush. But it's only after I let it out, do I realize how much I'd wanted to all along. It's like a big weight has been lifted off my chest.

Sharon's response isn't as quick as I had thought it would be. She takes her time analyzing what I just said and thinking it through. When the truth finally registers though, her mouth drops open in shock.

Thank god, at least she reacted. I thought she was petrified.

"You like . . . Aiden?"

I simply nod, not knowing what else to say.

"But doesn't he have a girlfriend?" Sharon says.

"So? I said *I* like him. I never said he likes me back. In fact, he doesn't even know about my feelings for him."

"He doesn't?" Sharon sounds surprised. "He sure as hell shows a lot of interest in a girl he has no feelings for," she murmurs. "Since when has all this been going on?"

She seems genuinely curious and so, I tell her. I don't go into a lot of detail. But I tell her everything from the start, the start being the day when I'd been helping him with Hailey's birthday surprise. I think of mentioning the start-of-summer party too, the one where we almost kissed, but then I don't. What's the point? He met her that night. That almost kiss isn't significant anymore.

After a good twenty minutes, I'm done. And *then* comes the lecture I'd been dreading.

"A crush, huh? Well there's no harm in that. But Aiden? Seriously? He's a fuckboy. I don't like him at all. Besides he has a girlfriend now. I know you guys are friends, but you stay away from him Scar. He's not worth all the mess you think he is. I really think you should move on. It can't be that hard. You've just been crushing on him for a few weeks. How serious can it be?"

I want to tell Sharon that my feelings for him are quite serious. No, I'm not in love with him or anything. But my feelings are quite strong. And I *know* Aiden. I'm his best friend. I know things about him no one else does.

He is not who everyone judges him to be. That's just the part of his personality he chooses to display. There's another layer hidden behind it all; the layer only those who really *know* him know about. Deep down, he's a sweet, romantic, and sensitive guy who loves and cares for people with all his heart. He can be torturously annoying when he aims to be, but he can also be the most amazing person without even trying.

God, I like him.

A goofy smile appears on my face on its own accord. Sharon notices that silly expression on my face and gently smacks me. "Get a hold of yourself!" She grabs my shoulders and shakes me dramatically. "I think I *need* accompany you to his house. I don't trust him, and I really don't trust *you* around him."

"Thanks Mom!" I retort, giggling.

She rolls her eyes and sticks out her tongue at me. "So what are we waiting for? Let's go!" I feel relieved knowing that Sharon's coming with me. She'll make this terrible afternoon a little bearable.

* * *

After a ten-minute ride, we reach Aiden's home. This is the first time Sharon has come here. She doesn't bother hiding her curiosity. She keeps looking here and there. I feel a nervous tremor run down my body as I ring the doorbell. I'm mentally preparing myself to see him.

Except I don't get to see him when the door opens, not right away anyway. His girlfriend opens the door. Her smile falters when she sees me. She glares at me, not trying to hide her anger. I guess Aiden didn't tell her I'll be coming to join them.

"What the hell are *you* doing here?" she hisses.

Oh this is going to be fun—not.

"I'm here to watch movies with Aiden. He invited me."

"You guys are *still* talking?"

"Of course we are! Your stupid little melodrama at the carnival didn't succeed in breaking our friendship," I spit out.

She narrows her eyes at me. She's about to say something when she's interrupted by Aiden. "Hey Scar, you came right on time!"

"Hey Aiden!" I greet him, and before I can change my mind, I take a step forward, and gently wrap my arms around him, giving him a hug.

It lasts for less than two seconds. It's very short, not at all romantic—more of a sweet and friendly gesture. But it's enough to make Hailey's blood boil. I see her showing me the finger behind Aiden's back, her eyes shooting daggers at me, venomous words burning on the tip of her tongue, just waiting to be unleashed. I smirk at her, not bothering to hide my triumph.

"Hello Aiden," Sharon greets him casually.

He talks to her politely for a change and responds back nicely. Then we follow him inside the house. His house isn't huge, but it's big and nicely organized. He has a separate laundry room, an audio-visual room containing the music system, TV, and the computer along with his Xbox, and of course the kitchen and bedrooms.

Comfortable rugs have been laid down around the couch in the audio-visual room. Various chips, popcorns, and soft drinks surround the rug. A stack of CDs are laid down on a table nearby. I feel excitement bubble up inside me when I look at the scene before me. How exciting, to spend the whole afternoon watching movies with him!

"So which genre do you guys want to watch?" Aiden asks.

"Romance!" Sharon, Hailey, and I shout simultaneously.

"Cut me some slack girls. I'm the only guy here, you know? I don't want to watch chick flicks."

"But I don't want to watch an action movie!" I whine.

"And there's no way I'm watching a horror movie!" Hailey retorts.

In the end, it's Sharon who gave us the idea. "Let's have a Harry Potter marathon!" she exclaims enthusiastically, and so that's what we settle on.

The next couple of hours fly by. Aiden and I keep bickering every few minutes, exchanging interesting Harry Potter trivia. This is one of his big bad secrets. He's a Potterhead. Not that he'll ever admit to it if you ask him this in front of everyone. He has read all the books and seen all the movies. I also have a feeling that he has a secret stash of Harry Potter merchandise somewhere in his bedroom.

By the time we've finished watching three movies, Sharon and Hailey look annoyed, and tell us they don't want to watch anymore.

"But you can't stop now! The Goblet of Fire is the best out of all the Harry Potter movies and—" Aiden protests.

"We would watch it if you two would at least *try* to shut up," Sharon interrupts. By 'you two' she means Aiden and me. "We know you both have seen the movies a million times and know the dialogues by heart. But you don't need to repeat them when we are watching the damn movie!" Sharon exclaims, pissed.

Hailey looks really sour too. But she doesn't say anything. She keeps looking at me in a strange way like she's looking at me for the first time. She almost looks sad.

"Okay, we'll try to keep our mouth shut. Can we please go back to watching the movies now?" I plead.

Sharon shakes her head in refusal. "Nope, I'm done. It's getting late anyway."

Aiden turns to Hailey, hoping she will choose to stay. But she refuses too (thank god!) "I've got to go. My mom and dad have to go out somewhere and I must stay at home and look after my brother." She makes a face, and then plants a soft kiss onto Aiden's lips. "Drop me home?"

"Actually, I'm heading off home too. I can drop you on the way." Sharon suggests. They both get up to leave. I'm not sure if I should stay or leave too, but I figure I can always leave after them. Hailey opens her mouth to say something but is cut off by Aiden.

"Actually, that's a good idea. Besides I need to finish up some of my pending school work. Scarlett, would you help me out with it, please?

That clearly means I don't get to leave, right?

Hailey nods, a little hesitantly. Her eyes flit over on me. She gives me a weird look like she's warning me to stay away from Aiden.

Just before leaving, Sharon turns to me and shoots me a soft smile. That's when I realize what she's trying to do. She wanted to get me some alone time with Aiden, that's why she offered Hailey a ride. Even though she detests him, and doesn't approve of him, she somehow knows how much he means to me. That's why she's doing this. My heart melts at the gesture, and I smile back at her, mouthing a 'thank you.'

Sharon and Hailey drive off in Sharon's car, leaving Aiden and me alone.

We head back inside the house. He runs up to his room to get the books. Apparently, he's having trouble with a few geometry problems. We settle down on the couch and for the next hour and a half, I clarify all his doubts and help him solve the questions.

"Do you want to take a break from all this?" he says after a while. I nod. I do feel tired from discussing all these questions. "Why don't you want to help me water the plants?"

"Seriously? First, you make me do your homework, and now you want help with chores?"

"Oh c'mon, it'll be fun! We'll just walk around the garden splashing water all over. That's *fun*."

"Oh what the hell!" I shrug. "Let's go."

We exit the house and head towards the garden shed. He unbolts the door and grabs a long hose, then heads outside and attaches it to the garden tap and starts the water. He's also brought along a watering can, which he hands over to me after filling it to the brim. "You water the flower beds, and I'll water the trees." I shrug, and then walk to the other side of the garden. What an unusual thing to do.

We spend the next twenty minutes watering the garden, occasionally making small talk. I eventually find myself standing next to Aiden, watering some rose shrubs. Aiden is randomly sprinkling water onto the nearby grass.

"God it's so hot out here. Plus the mosquitoes keep biting me!" I whine.

"Oh, so it's hot?"

"Yeah, I wish I could submerge myself in ice-cold water. I really want to shower right now." I complain.

I realize my mistake a little too late. "Your wish is my command *milady*!" Aiden exclaims, with a mischievous smile playing on his lips.

He turns the hose towards me and tightens his hold over the pipe, increasing the pressure of the water. The water gushes out and drenches me from head to toe in a matter of seconds.

My mouth drops open in shock. "Y-you! How dare you? You jerk!" I shriek.

"You were the one who wanted a bath." He shrugs, laughing at my helplessness.

I stare at the water can in dismay. It contains very less water. All the same, I don't hesitate to empty it upon Aiden's head. *He* gasps. He hadn't been expecting that.

I make a run for the garden tap and start refilling my can. I am in the middle of splashing the newly filled water on him, when he takes the can from my clutches. I try to snatch it back but in vain. He succeeds in pouring the water *I* filled on *me*.

I stomp my feet in anger. "Ugh! I hate you!"

But Aiden simply smiles at me. "I love you too darling!"

Freeze—that's what I do, I freeze. I freeze as he utters those three simple words I've been dying to hear from his mouth.

I love you.

I glance at him again and see his casual expression, his goofy smile, and I finally get some sense knocked into me.

He doesn't love me they were just . . . just some words, of course. It just slipped out.

Focusing back on the task at hand, which is to drench Aiden, I look around, and my eyes fall on the garden hose. Aiden had dropped it near the trees when he'd decided to chase me. I run towards the trees and grab hold of the hose. Aiden is hot on his heels and comes running behind me.

I apply pressure to the pipe and drench Aiden with the water.

"God stop Scar! No, stop!" He protests. But I simply laugh and continue to do it. He lunges for the hose and grabs hold of it for a second, directing the flow of water towards me. But I'm pretty quick and succeed in pulling the hose form his grip. We both struggle there under the trees for the upper hand, both desperately trying to emerge victorious.

Finally, I get hold of the hose and succeed in pulling it from his clutches. My eyes widen in surprise when I notice that I actually succeeded. "Oh my gosh! Yay! I won! I won!" I start jumping excitedly.

That's when it happens.

I slip. My body loses its footing over the wet mud and I feel myself falling down, gravity doing its job. I grab hold of Aiden's shirt for support and pull him down with me too.

Plop!

Down on the ground we both fall; him on top of me.

Aiden

I'm on top of her. We're close, so close. Scarlett's eyes are wide with shock. She actually looks scared.

Why is she acting this way?

Wait, she's probably never been so physically close to a guy before. Her love life is non-existent, after all.

The position I'm in is slightly uncomfortable since I'm supporting all my body weight onto my ankles and elbows so that I don't crush her. So I roll off her, and gently fall down on the muddy ground beside her. Scarlett gets up and gives me her hand. I take it, and she pulls me up.

"Uh, sorry for that." She smiles sheepishly, her cheeks are red. She's blushing again. She blushes so much. But I'm not complaining. It's actually kind of cute.

She grabs the hose, again.

Oh god no, not again. I'm sick of us soaking each other with water.

Surprisingly, instead of aiming the water at me, she aims it at herself. I find myself confused as I stare at her pouring all the water on herself. Then I realize that she's actually washing off all the mud on her body. I just stand there awkwardly as she runs her fingers through her wet hair.

Then she removes the jacket she's wearing. My jaw drops open. Her thin white shirt has become transparent due to all the water and is clinging tightly to her body. Her denim shorts cling tightly to her hips, making her look . . . sexy.

Holy mother of—

Her head snaps in my direction. Wait, did I just say that out loud?

Crap.

She cocks her eyebrows at me. A second later her eyes widen. She instantly turns around in the other direction, covering her chest with her arms. She glares at me.

"Aiden you jerk, you could've could've . . . said something! You were just standing and staring—"

"Uh, I'm sorry?" I say, raking my eyes down her body, taking in every inch of her wet skin.

If possible, I make her blush even more. Her cheeks are on fire. Wait, is she angry with me? She starts to walk away.

"Scarlett wait, I'm sorry—" I grab her hand and pull her towards me, to stop her from walking away. Her body crashes against mine; our chests collide. Our noses are almost touching now. *That's* how close she is to me. I can feel her chest rising, feel her soft breath on my skin. It makes me shiver. My hands wrap around her waist on their own accord, pulling her even closer to me. I gently cradle her face in my hand, remembering the night of that summer party. The night we almost...

"Aiden—" Her big brown eyes gaze innocently into mine. I caress the soft skin of her cheeks.

Was Scarlett always this beautiful?

"Aiden—" She begins to speak again. I interrupt her. Again.

Only this time, I do it with my lips.

Chapter Eleven

Scarlett

Have you ever been in a situation where everything seems too good to be true? A situation where you are a hundred percent positive that it happened but you still can't believe it because such amazing things never happen to you? Well I am in one such situation right now.

Aiden's been staring at me for what seems like an eternity. I am confused. *Why is he not letting go of me?* We both just stand there for a couple of seconds, staring at each other intensely. Then in the blink of an eye, he crosses the tiny distance separating us and claims my lips.

He's kissing me.

Aiden Walkers, my best friend, is kissing me.

On the lips.

I freeze as soon as his lips touch mine. He cups my face in his hands. The kiss is soft, a light touch that slowly builds into something a little more intense. I want to reciprocate, but I'm too shocked to react. I simply stand there as he kisses me. I've never kissed anyone before—never.

Butterflies swarm my belly. My heart is beating so fast. I'm only aware of one thing, and one thing alone: Aiden. The only thing I can feel are his lips. Everything else vanishes. His hands run down my back and land on my hips, leaving a trail of blazing fire, igniting my skin. My thoughts don't make sense anymore. Nothing makes sense. I *can't* think. He has taken over my body, soul, and mind. I feel euphoric.

He stops kissing me a few seconds later. I start panicking internally. I don't want him to stop. But I know he will if I don't respond to his touch. So, for the first time ever, I kiss him back.

Like I said, I've never kissed anyone. So I don't know if I'm even doing it right. Aiden has kissed so many girls, and I'm completely inexperienced. But I don't let that faze me. I kiss him back with all I have, pouring all my feelings through that single kiss.

I'd never understood why people enjoyed kissing. I'd also thought that swapping saliva with someone was disgusting. But then, I'd also never known it felt like *this*. This . . . what *is* this? I can't explain. But it's everything I never knew I wanted. I never want to stop.

But stop we do. A few minutes later we both break the kiss, stepping away from each other.

"What . . . was . . . that?" I gawk at him, not able to grasp what just happened.

"I . . . don't . . . know?" He looks flustered. There's a nervous edge to his voice.

He doesn't know? He kissed me and he doesn't fucking know?!

I try my best to calm myself. I still feel a little breathless from the kiss we just shared. And my heart? It's beating faster than it has ever before. And in the midst of all this confusion and chaos, I realize with a start that I, Scarlett Stevenson, just had my first kiss. I bring my fingers to my lips and touch them, not able to believe it. I look up at Aiden, and see confusion written all over his face. My heart jolts inside my chest.

What if . . . what if he regrets doing this?

My heart beats painfully; my stomach suddenly hurts. I feel as if someone is twisting the bones inside my body and blocking my wind-pipe. Unshed tears burn in my eyes. He's regretting it. I can see it on his face. He doesn't even know why he did it. He's—

Calm down Scarlett. Don't get so worked up. Ask him why he did it, get some clarity.

I take in a long breath. That little voice inside my head is right, I need to calm down. I look at Aiden again. He looks normal now. He has probably gathered his thoughts and pacified his chaotic mind.

Right, I must ask him now.

"Aiden?" I venture, my heart thundering inside my chest.

"Yeah?"

"W-why did you kiss me?" I stutter, suddenly losing confidence.

His gaze meets mine for a fraction of a second, before fluttering away. He sighs; he sounds sad and tired. My heart clenches inside my chest.

"I don't know why I did it Scarlett. Please forgive me. I shouldn't have done it. It was a mistake."

A mistake.

Isn't that what I was scared to hear? Imagine your crush telling you that the intense kiss you shared with him was a mistake. Now wouldn't that break your heart? I don't know about you, but it sure as hell broke mine.

"A-a mistake?" My voice cracks.

"Yes. I'm *so* sorry. I shouldn't have done that. Can you please forget about it? Please?" He sounds really desperate. My heart throbs inside my chest.

I don't want to forget it. It's my *first* kiss for God's sake! How can I forget it? Tears well in my eyes.

"Please don't tell Hailey about this. It'll break her heart." He pleads.

Even after all this, the only thing he's worried about is her. This breaks my heart even more.

No, just no. Suddenly the grief I feel subsides, making way for red hot anger. He does *not* get to say that kiss was a mistake, not after wreaking havoc in my life like that. No fucking way.

I quickly wipe my tears and turn to look at him.

"No."

"What?"

"No, I *won't* forget that kiss. And no, it was *not* a mistake. That was my *first* kiss, you prick! You should have thought things through before stealing it like that. And now that it's done, you have *no* right to tell me it was a mistake!" I seethe, giving him the most hateful glare I can muster.

He slowly advanced towards me. I know what's coming next. He's going to apologize again. He's going to look straight into my eyes and coax me out of my anger. He'll break my resolve, and I'll end up forgiving him. He will succeed.

Well, I can't let that happen. Not this time.

"Goodbye Aiden," I hiss, then walk away.

* * *

I'm sitting in my room right now. My initial bout of anger has vanished; all that remains in its place is sorrow and regret. I'm so sad Aiden called the kiss we shared a mistake. This experience was supposed to be special. I shouldn't want to cry every time I remember my first kiss. I should be dancing around the room, smiling to myself. Instead, I'm lying on my bed, replaying each and every word he said, and trying not to cry. It's really unfair.

I can't believe I shouted at Aiden and pushed him away. This is so unlike me. I never raise my voice, I never confront people and stand up for myself, as pathetic as that sounds. I wonder if he's mad at me right now. Maybe I shouldn't have...

No, he deserved it. He shouldn't have done what he did.

But he *had* apologized, and I still walked out on him. I doubt he will talk to me again. I should be angry. I should be angry at him after what he did. And I *am* angry. But I also miss him.

If I could undo this afternoon, I would—even if it meant not knowing how his lips taste, not knowing what it feels to come alive. Even if it meant to not know how it felt to be held in his arms, to not know how his touch ignited my skin. I would turn back time and give it all up if it meant having Aiden back in my life.

A sudden knock on my door interrupts my stream of thoughts. A second later, it opens and in enters my mom.

"Scarlett? Someone's here to see you."

"Send them in, I don't feel like going all the way downstairs." My mom simply nods, and leaves. I look pretty terrible at the moment—my hair all unkempt, wearing an old t-shirt and boxer shorts. But then, it's probably Susan or Sharon.

A few minutes later, the door to my room slowly opens. I look up from the book I'd been trying to read earlier, and almost fall off the bed. It's Aiden. *He's* here.

"Scar? Can I talk to you?" He slowly sits on the edge of my bed, not shifting his eyes from me.

"Depends. Do you plan on telling me the kiss we shared was a mistake? Or even worse, are you going to act as if it never happened?" I demand, sounding rather cold. I'm not going to make this easy for him. Not by a long shot.

"No." He shakes his head in refusal. "I'm not here for either of those."

"Then what do you want?"

"I want to apologize." I open my mouth to speak, but he doesn't let me. "No, I'm not apologizing to you because I stole your first kiss. I'm apologizing, because I called it a mistake. That kiss? It wasn't a mistake. You know why? Because I don't regret it." He grabs onto my shoulders. His eyes bore into mine, burning with sincerity.

"Then why did you ask me to forget it? Why did you say it was a mistake? *Why?*" I demand. Aiden is confusing me *so* much. He's pushing me off the edge, only to grab my hand at the last moment. *That's* what this feels like.

"Because *I* wanted to forget it. I wanted to shrug it off as a mistake, and pretend it never happened. I know I'm being very selfish. But after I kissed you, I realized I'd kissed a girl behind my girlfriend's back. The guilt was literally killing me. I was trying to convince myself that that kiss didn't mean anything."

"So…what does this mean for . . . for us?" I ask him, dreading the answer as soon as the question leaves my mouth.

His forehead creases with confusion. "What do you mean? *I* have a girlfriend. You are my best friend. Does it have to be any different now?"

Yes, yes it has to be different. I want it to be different. Is that too much to ask?

"Scarlett I know you're probably feeling very awkward about all this. I'm *so* sorry for acting like a hormonal idiot. I wasn't thinking . . . I don't even remember how it happened; it just did. But I promise that it won't happen again. Maybe this was bound to happen. You and me . . . we had a lot of sexual tension between us.

But it's all out of the way now. We kissed, and we got over it. I doubt it'll ever happen again."

I want to slam my head against the wall—slam my head because he's an idiot, slam my head because I *hate* the situation I am currently in.

How do I tell this fool that it's not just chemicals and hormones for me, but so much more? *How* do I tell him that I'm dying to feel his lips on mine, right this second? *How* do I tell him that things *won't* go back to the way they were, not after the way he kissed me, not after I just realized how utterly smitten I am.

Not after I realized the intensity of my feelings for him.

For me, things will never be the same.

Chapter Twelve

Scarlett

"So, will you go out with me this Friday? We can go watch movies or something. We could chill at the beach too. Heck, we'll go anywhere you want. What do you say?" Aiden suggests.

My heart skips a beat. If only, he was *actually* asking me out on a date, I mean. He isn't though. He's just asking me to hang out with him this Friday as a friend. In fact, the only reason he's probably asking is because his girlfriend is going to be out of town for two weeks. I bet he doesn't want to spend the weekend by himself.

"Uhm, I don't know..." I hesitate, feeling unsure.

"Oh c'mon! You probably have nothing better to do on Friday nights anyway. You just sit at home. The least you can do is hang out with me!" he says, raising his arms in exasperation.

My mouth drops open. "You're basically saying that I completely lack a social life!"

"Well, what I'm saying is true though, isn't it? You *do* spend your Friday nights all by yourself, am I correct?" he inquires, cocking his left eyebrow dramatically.

It wasn't always like this, was it Aiden? There was a time when all my Friday nights were spent with you.

"Well yeah, so what?!" I snap.

"So, go out with me!"

Oh why does he have to phrase it like that! It makes it sound like he's asking me out on a date! Which he isn't, so can't he frame his sentences differently? Something like, "let's spend some time together this Friday." But then, that would sound a little romantic—

"Earth to Scarlett! Hello?" Aiden waves his hand in front of my eyes, trying to get my attention.

"God yes, I'm listening. What's your problem?"

"*You* are. So tell me, will you come?"

"I'll think about it."

"Seriously? 'Think about it'? You're torturing me, you know?"

I flash him a smirk. "Take it as it is, leave it if you won't." I shrug.

"You're mean, you know that right?"

"Mean's my middle name, baby." I wink at him mischievously.

"Oh c'mon Scar, give in already. Are you going to make me beg for it?"

"Should I?" I tease.

"No, *please.* Just come with me?"

I pretend to think for a moment, when in fact I've already decided. I just wanted to make him work for it. "Yeah sure whatever," I say, trying to sound nonchalant.

He passes me a dazzling smile. "I'll pick you up at seven, alright?"

I shrug. "Fine by me."

* * *

I glance at the clock every other minute. It's almost seven; he said he would be here by now. My stomach churns due to all the nervousness. I feel light-headed.

I step in front of the mirror, making sure everything is in place. I look pretty good—beautiful if I dare say so myself. My dark brown hair is hanging down my shoulders in soft beach waves. I'm wearing a cobalt blue frock that I'd bought at the mall last month. It hugs my figure in all the right places. I've kept my makeup to a bare minimum, just some eyeliner and lip gloss.

I'm in the middle of brushing my hair again when the doorbell rings.

He's here!

I feel butterflies swarm my belly. My breath comes out rapid and short. I haven't even seen him yet and I'm already feeling faint. What will happen when we come face to face?

The doorbell rings again. Great! I forgot nobody's home. Which is good, to be honest. They'll assume that I'm going on a date, and then tease me about it. For some reason, my whole family thinks Aiden and I have a thing going on.

Ding!

The bell rings a fourth time before I finally open it. My eyes immediately fall on Aiden. He looks . . . delicious. He looks so . . . I don't even know how to describe it. Dark denim jeans hugs his lean waist. A casual white t-shirt hugs his torso to perfection. His hair just the perfect amount of messy, is falling on his face, accentuating the dark brown of his eyes.

Breathe Scarlett, breathe.

His eyes widen slightly as he takes in the sight of me. His mouth drops open just a little. "Can we go now? If you're done checking me out, that is." I smirk.

His expression doesn't falter. "It's not my fault I can't take my eyes off you."

"Then whose fault is it?" I ask, cocking my eyebrows.

He leans in, caressing my cheek with the tip of his finger. "Who do you think?" He winks.

I blush. Aiden smirks, knowing he's had the desired effect. Satisfied, he steps back. "C'mon let's get going, or we'll miss the start of the movie."

I nod and follow him outside after locking up the house behind me. He stops in front of a black motorcycle.

Wait, a motorcycle?

"Where's your car?" I ask him, my eyes wide like saucers.

"At home? I wanted to ride this baby today. Why, is there a problem?"

"N-no! I just—my hair would get ruined," I mutter. Which is true. Riding on that monstrous vehicle would totally put all the time I invested styling my hair to waste. Besides I haven't sat on a motorcycle before. I must admit, I'm slightly nervous.

I turn toward the motorcycle again. "Besides, how do I sit on it?" I don't want to accidently flash him my underwear as I try to sit on it.

Aiden rolls his eyes at me. "May I?" He doesn't wait for an answer. Before I can contemplate what is happening, his arms are around my waist. He lifts me off the ground easily, as if I was as light as a feather and puts me onto its seat. I gasp. "What the—"

Next, his hands reach for my hair. He gently twists them into a small knot. His fingers softly brush against my neck as he does and I feel goosebumps appear down my arms.

What is happening to me?

The impact of his touch lasts for a few seconds. Finally, he puts the helmet on my head and removes his hand. "Hold on tight, alright?" he says as he climbs atop the motorcycle himself. He puts on his helmet, starts the engine, and off we go. Initially I hesitate, not knowing how to hold onto him. Not wanting to fall off and break some bones, I'm forced to wrap my arms around his torso.

He doesn't respond to my actions; he doesn't even shift in his seat. I'm not scared about falling off the motorcycle anymore. In fact, I am actually enjoying myself. The evening breeze is rushing against my body. The speed at which we're going brings about an adrenaline rush. It's addictive.

Twenty blissful minutes later he stops the motorcycle near the local multiplex and gets off. "A movie, like we decided?" he asks.

I nod. Now it's not like we're on a date or something, so I take out some money from my purse to hand over at the ticket counter. Of course, Aiden with his man pride and everything, stops me from paying.

"I *can* pay, you know?" I argue.

"This was my idea, so *I'll* pay."

"But—"

"No buts," he retorts and pays for my ticket too.

"Fine. But I'll buy ice creams when we hit the beach, alright?" I say.

"Okay!" He smiles at me. I feel my heart do a somersault inside my chest.

The movie we're watching is a horror movie, and guess what? I *love* horror movies. I stare at the hideous movie poster, grinning. This is going to be *so* much fun. Aiden chuckles when he notices my expression.

"There was no way I was watching romance, and I know you don't like action movies. So I settled for horror." He shrugs.

"Good choice Mr. Walkers." I beam up at him. The movie starts at seven. We buy an extra-large popcorn tub, and an extra-large coke with two straws. We figure it would be better this way. As throngs of people envelope us, Aiden catches hold of my hand so I don't lose him in the crowd. It feels so . . . good. The feel of his hand in mine does.

We enter the movie hall and find our seats. The movie begins ten minutes after we're seated. I stare excitedly at the screen. I can sense Aiden's gaze on me. I smile, loving every second of it.

* * *

"No! Oh my god, are you insane? Don't go in there!" I exclaim. A couple of people sitting nearby turn to glare at me, annoyance clear on their faces. I ignore them and continue to shout at a slightly lower volume, "Don't go in there. You will *die*!"

Aiden laughs beside me. "Scar, it's just a movie. Relax."

"I hate the fact that most of the people in horror movies are dumb. Like if they even had an ounce of brain, they could actually survive." I complain.

He wraps his arms around my shoulder. "Don't worry, next time we'll go for a film that has smarter characters."

Next time? There's going to be a next time?

I smile to myself.

I dig my hands inside the popcorn box and realize Aiden's hands are in there too. Our fingers brush against each other. Suddenly, he intertwines his pinkie finger with mine, our hands still inside the popcorn tub. I'm momentarily surprised. I glance at him and see his eyes are glued onto the screen. A hint of a smirk is visible on his face.

Oh he loves riling me up, doesn't he? Well two can play the game.

A few seconds later, Aiden drops my hand and grabs the straw of the extra-large cola we brought, sipping the cola in.

Taking the chance, I lean towards him, and sip from the other straw. Aiden stiffens as I lean in close. Our lips are so awfully close. I slurp the coke slowly and then remove the straw from my lips. I lick my lips before moving away.

I notice his eyes are glued onto my lips instead of the screen now.

Mission accomplished.

It's my turn to smirk.

Aiden doesn't give any sort of response. Instead, he turns back to look at the screen. We don't talk during the rest of the movie; it's all very quiet. It's not like I don't *want* to talk, he just seems distant, lost in his own thoughts. I wonder if it's because of the little teasing I did a while back. Did I go a little overboard?

By half past nine, we've finished watching the movie and are heading to the beach. Aiden is being very quiet tonight.

"So uhm, wasn't the movie great?" I try to strike a conversation.

He glances at me and then looks away. "Yeah, it was," he murmurs unenthusiastically.

I frown.

What is wrong with him?

I wrap my arms around him affectionately. "Hey, it's okay if you're missing Hailey. It must be so hard to be—"

"No, I'm not missing her Scarlett. It's not always about her, okay?"

"Uh okay, if you say so." I shrug. "Well in that case, let's head to the beach. I still have that ice cream treat to give. Or would you rather pass?"

Please don't leave yet, please don't go.

"Ice cream sounds good." He offers me a small smile. I smile right back at him, relieved he isn't leaving yet.

* * *

"One chocolate chip and one black currant." I order.

I hand over the black currant ice cream to Aiden after paying. Honestly, I'm not even sure how anyone can like black currant better than chocolate ice cream. Chocolate's the best. It's like an unwritten rule in the book of desserts.

"You know . . ." he remarks.

"Know what?" I ask, confused.

"That black currant's my favorite. Even Hailey doesn't remember that," he says, sounding rather surprised.

I shrug. "I have a sharp memory. I'm good at remembering things," I say like it's no big deal. Except it is. I don't remember what my brother's favorite ice cream is, but I know his! I know so many things about him—his favorite songs, how he likes his coffee, the number on the back of his jersey, the brand of the cologne and soap he uses.

I sound like an obsessive stalker.

We finish our ice creams in a matter of minutes, sitting cross-legged near the shore. The waves come all the way to our legs, but don't touch us any further. We sit there quietly under the star-lit sky, not uttering anything, just sitting. And this silence? It may mean nothing to him, but to me it means everything. It's just so beautiful. I don't even care about ruining my dress. I'm just happy sitting here next to him.

"Oh, I almost forgot," he says and stands up.

"Where are you going?" I ask.

"Just a second, alright?"

I nod and wait for him as he vanishes off god knows where. He returns a couple of minutes later, with a paper bag. Plopping down on the sand, he takes out two beer cans from it.

"Beer? Are you serious? We just had ice cream."

"And now we're going to have beer." He stretches his legs out in front of him comfortably.

"Where did you get this from anyway?" I ask.

"I'd got it earlier and brought it along for our beach picnic. Anyway, take this." He hands me the can of beer.

"I don't drink," I mumble, feeling embarrassed. I suddenly feel like a child. I'm sure Hailey loves beer. I bet they both sit like this on the beach, sipping beer off their identical looking cans. I bet Aiden wishes she was here next to him, instead of me.

"I know, that's why I bought you a can of cola. You can mix it with the beer."

I can't help smiling. I drink half of the cola, then I pour in some beer in what remained of it. Next time I take a sip, the cola's flavor is tinged with bitterness, and when I swallow it, it burns my throat slightly. I give the leftover beer to Aiden.

I don't know how long we sit there, talking about random things. The tide had gotten considerably higher, so we had to shift back, to avoid getting wet. My cheeks are hurting from all the laughing I've been doing for these past couple of hours. I glance at Aiden, his eyes are twinkling, and there's a smile on his face.

"I've missed this," he says suddenly.

"Missed what?"

"Talking to you for hours about random things, just being with you in general."

I smile. "We don't spend much time together these days, do we?"

He nods in agreement and takes a sip. He's been drinking non-stop since we got here. "No, we don't. But I wish we did."

We both lie down side by side, with the sound of the ocean buzzing in our ears. The star-studded sky greets us. Our hands unconsciously reach for each other's, our fingers intertwining

"Scarlett?" Aiden prompts.

"Hmm?"

"If you could freeze a moment in time, forever, and ever and live it a thousand times over, which would you choose?"

"I-I don't know. I've never really thought about it. What about you?"

I was expecting him to choose some moment he spent with Hailey or his family. So I was really surprised when he answered my question with: "if I could freeze a moment in time, and live it a thousand times over, I would choose this: you and me, lying on the beach on a such a beautiful night, looking at the stars, and just talking. There's this feeling in my chest I can't quite name. I feel so completely at peace, so utterly happy. I could stay like this forever."

I feel my heart do a somersault in my chest. How can he say something like this, and not expect me to fall in love with him? I want to feel elated. Instead, I feel sadder than I've ever felt before. He's so close, yet so far. He's with me, but not really mine. And he'll never be.

As soon as this realization strikes me, I remove my hand from his. I get up and shift away from him. I'm not strong. I'm not strong enough to hold his hand and hear these things he's saying, and then forget all this and accept the fact that he has a girlfriend.

Aiden's brown eyes snap onto me. "Did I say something wrong?" he asks, noticing my expression.

"N-no, you didn't." I can't meet his eyes. I can't bear to sit so close to him and act like everything's normal, act like I'm not losing my mind right now.

Aiden sits up and faces me. "Scarlett, are you okay?"

"Of course." I tremble. "Why wouldn't I be?"

"Are you really going to lie to me now?"

"I'm not lying Aiden, *drop it*," I say with my teeth clenched.

He decides to listen to me and doesn't discuss this further. Instead he says something that makes me lose my mind even more. "You look really beautiful tonight, by the way. You always do."

His words catch me off guard. I hadn't been expecting him to compliment me so randomly.

He has a girlfriend. This doesn't mean anything.

"Anyway, how're things going with you and Hailey?" I ask. The intricate details of their relationship are the last thing I want to hear right now. But at the same time, I need him to remind me *why* I should control these things I'm feeling.

He looks annoyed almost immediately. "Why do you keep bringing her up?! I'm here with you, am I not? Can't we talk about something else?"

"Geez, okay! No need to get mad at me. I don't know what's up with you. You've been acting moody the whole evening. What's wrong? Did you guys get into a fight or something?"

"God, it's *not* about her! It's not *always* about her, okay?!"

My eyes snap onto him. "Then what is it about?! *Tell me.*"

"Nothing, forget it," Aiden replies stiffly.

I shift closer to him, looking him dead in the eye. "*Tell me* Aiden Walkers, what is it about?"

"It's about you!" I gape at him. I'd clearly not expected him to say that. "Yes, you! The reason I am here with you right now, is because I wanted to spend time with you. I just wanted to be with you."

"But you *are* here with me, aren't you? Why are you so angry then?"

"I'm not angry. I'm just—I'm frustrated. There are these things that I'm feeling and they keep messing with my head—"

"What things? Why don't you tell me?"

"I *do* tell you; I try to, at least. But you almost always brush me off. You *never* take me seriously. Then you flirt with me like it's no big deal—"

Wait, what?!

"—back in the movie hall, you have *no* idea how badly I wanted to kiss you. But you were just being a tease. It's not easy Scarlett. *Controlling* myself around you, controlling these feelings, it isn't easy. And it's with so much difficulty that I succeed. But then you end up doing something like that—flirting with me, heck, just *smiling* at me, and I lose it. I *fucking* lose it!"

"Aiden, I don't understand—"

"There, you're doing it again! You *perfectly* understand what I'm saying. You just *don't* want to believe it."

"What?! Aiden I *don't* understand. I really don't. You have a *girlfriend*. None of this makes sense."

"I *like* you Scarlett. I think I have feelings for you," Aiden says, cupping my face in his hands. How did this night turn from casual to intense in a matter of minutes?

"W-what kind of feelings?"

"The confusing kind? I don't know…why don't you just believe me?" Aiden sounds desperate. His deep brown eyes pierce me with their gaze.

I look away, not able to meet his eyes any longer. "Aiden you're with *Hailey*. And me? I'm just your friend."

"No! With you . . . with you it's different. With you *I* feel different. When we kiss, there's this heat, this passion. I know you feel it too. It's not the same with her."

I back away from Aiden, letting his hands drop. "Aiden no, you're confused. You're—wait, how many of those have you drank by now?" I ask, suddenly realizing something.

Aiden Walkers is drunk.

"A couple." He shrugs.

Of course! He's not sober. He's drunk. He doesn't know what he's saying.

"C'mon Aiden, let's take you home. You're drunk."

"I'm *not* drunk! I can handle my liquor. You need to understand—"

"No, c'mon let's go—"

"No, listen. I *know* what I'm saying. I *like* you." I freeze. Hearing him say these words…it's almost like I'm in a dream. I'd never thought I'd get to hear this from his mouth.

Aiden takes advantage of me being temporarily motionless and leans in. He brings his hand to my chin and gently lifts my face towards his. A second later, his soft, soft lips claim mine. Shock descends upon me almost immediately.

Almost unconsciously, I start kissing him back. Slowly at first, then harder. I can taste the hint of alcohol on his lips, smell his heady cologne. A dull, hazy voice in my head tells me to step away from him, to stop kissing him. But I ignore it. He moves in closer, causing our chests to collide. His hands encircle my waist, pulling me closer.

I run my hands up and down his back, finally reaching out for his wavy brown hair, entwining my fingers, gently tugging at them. Our lips fit perfectly, as if they were made for each other.

His tongue flicks against my lower lip, his hands press on my thighs. Against my better judgment, I open my mouth wider, letting him in. I let out a strangled moan when his tongue comes in contact with mine. The gentle tickling sensation makes my toes curl just a little.

He wraps his arms around my waist, lifting me off the ground, and pulling me onto his lap. His hands ignite my body with their touch. I wrap my legs around his waist, as we continue to kiss.

He is the first to break it.

"What are you doing to me Scarlett?" He moans.

We are face to face, our noses almost touching. My chest rises and sinks rapidly, just like his. That kiss has left us breathless.

"Stop making me want you." He leans in, brushing his lips against my neck, making me tremble. I remain quiet, not knowing what to say. The gravity of the situation is slowly dawning upon me, the grave realization of just what we've done . . .

"I like you Scarlett. Be my girlfriend."

I gasp.

Calm down Scarlett, he's drunk. He doesn't know what he's saying.

"Aiden, you already have a girlfriend. Her name is Hailey, remember?"

"It's *you* I want. You. Only you and you alone."

My heart aches. Does he really mean all this? There's no way I could be certain. At least not right now.

I get up. "Let's go home Aiden. Let me call someone to come pick us up. You're in no condition to drive."

"But—"

"*No.* C'mon, stand up now. We're leaving. We'll continue this conversation when you know what you're talking about."

His shoulder slumps in response, but he doesn't argue further. I decide to call Darren, asking him to drive us home. He arrives a few minutes later in his car, along with one of his band mates. His band mate drives Aiden's motorcycle to his place, while Darren gives Aiden and me a lift. It's good that Aiden has passed out; because he'd have been very, *very* reluctant to let anyone else touch his motorcycle.

During the ride home, Aiden keeps mumbling incoherent things. He also refuses to let go of my hand. Darren looks at us with this weird grin on his face. Once Aiden mumbles something that sounds suspiciously like my name. Darren smirks when this happens.

Twenty minutes later, Darren drops Aiden off at his home. I can't help thinking about everything Aiden had said and done this evening.

Silly Aiden. He's not even going to remember what happened when he wakes up.

Chapter Thirteen

Aiden

"I looked so gorgeous in that dress. I'm telling you, you wouldn't have been able to take your eyes off me. The pictures don't do me justice. It really sucks that you're not here. I miss you *so* much," Hailey whines.

A soft smile appears on my face when she says she misses me. "I miss you too," I say. But as soon as the words leave my mouth, Scarlett's face appears in mind. Guilt descends upon me almost immediately.

All I can think of is how Hailey will feel once she finds out I've kissed Scarlett—not once, but twice. She doesn't deserve this, her boyfriend kissing another girl behind her back. I want to tell her what has happened. But I don't know how to tell her something like this without really hurting her feelings.

"Aiden . . . hello? Aiden are you there?" Hailey's slightly panicked voice breaks my chain of thoughts.

"Yeah, I am. Sorry I just . . ."

"Are you okay babe?" she sounds worried. She really cares for me; she really does. And what am I doing? Kissing Scarlett behind her back. Unlike Scarlett, Hailey actually *has* feelings for me. Scarlett? She doesn't feel that way about me. That's why she shuts me out every time.

"Yeah babe, I'm okay." I assure her. "Can't wait for you to get back."

"I'm cutting my stay short since I miss you so much. I'll be back in a couple days, and then we'll go out, okay?"

"Yes, definitely! I'll be right here, waiting for you."

"Bye babe, I'll call you again tonight."

I remember most of the things that happened last Friday. I've been able to recall almost everything in bits and pieces over the weekend. I remember watching that horror movie with Scarlett, then heading over to the beach. Then we talked. I don't exactly recall our conversation. But we talked mostly. Then I kissed her.

If there's something I clearly remember, it's how her lips felt against mine. All I can remember with perfect clarity is how it felt kissing her, with our bodies pressed against each other's. It had been . . . I don't even have words to describe what it felt like. Surely, she felt something for me if *that's* the way she kissed me, so passionately, so wildly.

Probably not.

* * *

Scarlett

The football tournament starts in a couple of weeks, and Aiden is practicing *so* hard. His days start with it. He comes up to school early in the morning and practices for two to three hours every day, and then sometimes practices during school hours too. And then he practices some more after school is over, and then goes home. I can see how much it tires him. But there is a lot of pressure, being the captain and all. It is his first time as the captain, and he is really nervous. Not that he shows it. He maintains a cool façade, but I know what's going deep inside that head of his.

And on top of that he has to manage his grades too. The weekly tests are coming up and he has to study for them. Whatever time he can take out, he spends it with his girlfriend Hailey. I get to spend some time with him during the classes we share, but that is about it.

Neither of us have brought up the kiss we shared on the beach that day. He probably doesn't even remember it. I still don't know if he meant the things he said that day. And I guess I never will. I know I should have asked him about it, but I didn't and now it feels like it's too late.

It is our gym class right now, and we are outside. The boys' football team is practicing. I sit down to, well, ogle Aiden. It takes me a while to find him. My eyes search the crowded ground and finally, I see him. He is wearing his trademark red jersey, and let me tell you, he looks hot with a capital H.

He's weaving his way through the players, heading for the goal. A few minutes later, he scores a goal. He laughs and jumps up in the air, triumphantly. I feel my heart melt on the spot. This sport means so much to him. He's so dedicated to it. I really, really, hope he leads the team to victory. He deserves to win.

I spend the remaining hour ogling him. He is oblivious to the numerous people doing the same. Aiden had always been popular among girls.

After the class ends, I see him making his way to the bleachers. The first thing I notice is that he's not wearing his jersey anymore; he's half naked. A thin layer of sweat covers his abs due to all the sweat from playing outdoors. I feel my heart jump inside my chest.

Now I know it's not a very big deal. He's just showing some extra skin. All the same, I can't help ogling his bare torso. Hours, and hours of football has toned his chest and mid-riff. Why is he not wearing a t-shirt? When did he remove it? Why is he coming *here?*

Breathe Scarlett, breathe.

He waves at me, making his way towards me and before I know it, he's standing right in front of me.

Hotness overload. Hotness overload.

"H-hi!" I stutter.

Don't stare at his body. Don't stare at his body. Don't stare at his—

"Hey!" He smiles at me, sitting down next to me. "Did you watch me play?"

"Yeah." I nod.

"How was I?"

Perfect.

"You were pretty good."

He cocks his eyebrow. "Just good?"

I roll my eyes. "You were fucking splendid! Happy now?"

He laughs. "Yes. But really, how was I?" he asks me in a serious tone.

I turn to look at him, our eyes meet and I ignore how my heart skips a beat. He looks worried. "You were amazing." I assure him. "You totally kicked ass out there. I'm sure you guys will win." His eyes twinkle as he smiles at me this time. There is something different about this smile. It seems more carefree, more genuine— more *real.* He wants to say something. I know he does. He's looking at me so intensely. He opens his mouth to speak . . .

Suddenly a white-black football comes soaring through the sky, right at us. Instinctively, I wrap my arms around my head, to protect myself. But the ball never hits me. I peek from the back of my hands, and notice Aiden standing in front of me, the football clutched in his hand. He's yelling at someone down below—Damien, I think.

"What the hell did you do that for?!" Aiden fumes.

"You both were looking really cozy up there; couldn't resist!" Damien chuckles.

Aiden glares at him and throws the football back at him. It hits him in the chest, and he lets out a groan. Damien gives him the finger, and then walks off.

Aiden turns back to me. I know almost immediately that he won't be saying what he'd been planning to earlier. The moment we'd shared earlier is over now. The intensity had vanished.

"Anyway, what do you think of my abs?" he says, posing like a model and making seductive expressions. I burst out laughing.

"What the hell do you mean!?" I can't help laughing.

He motions towards his body. "Aren't they amazing? Don't you like them?"

Like? I love them.

I roll my eyes. "They're . . . okay. I've seen better, you know?"

He narrows his eyes at me. "You know what you just did? You hurt my man pride." He reproaches, looking grim. "You need to be punished."

I burst out laughing.

"Oh, so now you're laughing, yeah? Let me make you laugh harder."

"Huh? What do you mean?" The meaning of his words dawn on me a second later. "Oh no! Aiden, no. You wouldn't—"

He steps in closer, and I let out a scream. "NO!" I shriek and start to run with Aiden hot on my trail. I rush down the bleachers, trying my best not to slip. Then I make my way through the throngs of people, smacking against them as I run. Aiden closing in on me. It won't be long before he—

"Aaaahhh!" I scream. People shoot us dirty looks, but Aiden ignores them. He wraps his arms around my stomach and starts tickling me. I squirm. Tears burn in my eyes as I laugh hysterically. "Oh no, please stop!"

"Say you're sorry."

I try to pry off his hands but in vain. He continues tickling me. I can feel his warm, sweaty body pressed against my back and feel his toned muscles. If only he wasn't tickling me, I could stay like this forever.

"Okay, okay fine. I'm sorry!" I breathe out. I know Aiden's not really offended. He just wants to make me miserable.

"That a good girl," he says, letting me go.

I calmed my heart, before turning around to look at him. A mischievous smile grazes my lips. "I'm sorry you've got terrible abs!" I shout, running away.

But I'm not able to run far. After all, he'd been standing right next to me. His hands wrap around my waist for the second time today. His fingers tickle my sides, and I let out another series of shrieks. This time he doesn't let me squirm out of his grasp. He tickles me some more before lifting me off my feet, and tossing me over his shoulder, so that my head is hanging down his back. His arms maintain a tight hold around my waist as he starts to walk. I continue punching his back, shouting at him to leave me but it only makes him laugh harder.

"You hurt my man pride darling," he quips.

People look at us weirdly and point at us too. I feel embarrassed but Aiden doesn't let me go. Feeling frustrated, I pinch his butt hard.

"Ow! What was that for?!" Aiden exclaims.

"That was for making me hang down your sweaty body Mr. Walkers."

"Don't act like you're not enjoying every minute of this."

He receives another pinch in the butt for that.

"Pinch me all you want cupcake, I'm not letting you down. The whole school's going to see me carrying your cute butt down the hallway."

I try pinching him some more, and even punching him a bit. But to no avail. After a while I get tired so I stop all protests and simply lift my head up a bit. How he's able to carry me I have no clue, but it's kind of fun. I smile.

I'm hanging down Aiden's back.

Chapter Fourteen

Scarlett

I check my class schedule. Just my luck, I have chemistry. *God, why are you torturing me?* Chemistry is the worst subject ever. Even math is better than this. I mean, who the hell care if the oxides of metals are acidic or alkaline? I don't. And what's more, the monthlong renovation of our chemistry lab just got finished. We'll have practical classes from today.

Such fun.

Well, at least I won't have to deal with a whole day of school. They cancelled all the afternoon classes so the students could watch the football match that'll be taking place this afternoon. Aiden's going to be playing then.

Sighing, I start walking towards the laboratory. On the way I come across my friends. They have this class too. We enter the lab one by one. I immediately take one of the seats in the last row. I'd rather die than sit in the front during chemistry. Sharon is about to take the seat beside mine when Aiden appears out of nowhere and plops down on it.

"What the—!" Sharon gasps.

He chuckles. "You can go sit somewhere else, I came here first."

"Not fair! Get off this seat before I kick your ass. You know I won't hesitate to do it." She warns him.

He shakes his head in refusal. Sharon passes me a pointed look, silently asking me to tell him to leave. I resist the urge to groan. *Why can't she leave?* I mean I sit with her in most of the classes anyway. She *knows* I have a crush on him. Can't she let me sit with him for once?

Andrea and Kayla who are sitting nearby look pointedly at me, waiting for me to do something. God, I'll *have* to ask him to leave, otherwise they'll get suspicious.

I turn to Aiden. "Can you please leave, Aiden? Sharon wants to sit here."

"She can sit somewhere else."

"Stop being difficult Aiden."

"I'm not leaving."

"Ai—"

"Good morning class!" Mrs. Nelson, our chemistry teacher, enters the lab. "I'm *so* thrilled. We can finally start with the practicals!"

At least someone is excited.

Sharon, knowing it's too late to do anything now, walks off to sit somewhere else, looking annoyed. I silently feel happy about it: another blissful hour right next to Aiden. It's so weird that even school gets less boring when you get to hang out with your crush.

The teacher starts to explain about the different lab equipment we will be using this year. She instructs us to wear our lab coats and eye protectors. It came as no surprise when Aiden and I end up as partners.

He smiles triumphantly. "So I guess an A+ is guaranteed in chemistry!"

"What do you mean?"

"I'm partnered with *you*. I'll definitely get an A!"

"Listen mister, you're not getting an A unless *you* work. So you better pay attention in class."

"Well that, I must admit, will be hard. How can I focus on anything when I have someone so hot sitting next to me?"

I try not to blush. "Stop with the flirting pretty boy and pay attention."

"Who said I was flirting with you? I was talking about her." He gestures to the person sitting on his other side.

I burst out laughing. "Oh really? So you find Jake hot? I didn't know you played for *that* team." I burst out laughing.

His eyes widen, surprised. "What do you mean?" I gesture for him to look behind him. Aiden's joke backfired on him.

He looks flustered. "Not funny!"

"Yes, it is!" I laugh yet again.

He rolls his eyes and focuses his attention back to Mrs. Nelson. I giggle. He looks so cute when he's embarrassed.

A few minutes later we are sent to the work stations to do some simple acid-base reactions and record our observations in our files.

Of course, Aiden with his impeccable timing, bombards me with the worst question ever.

"Scarlett, why haven't you brought up that kiss?" Aiden inquires, catching me off guard.

I stiffen as the words leave his mouth. *Oh god, things were going so great, and he had to suddenly bring up this.*

"I-I don't know. I'm surprised you even remember it, seeing as you were so drunk that night," I mutter, hoping he'll drop it.

"*Of course,* I remember it. But *you* weren't drunk. Why didn't *you* bring it up?"

"Honestly, I didn't think it mattered." I shrug.

"Of course, it matters!" he retorts exasperatedly.

"Does it? You were *drunk.* You obviously didn't know what you were doing. I didn't want you to call this one a mistake too." Low blow, I know. But it's true. I didn't want him to say kissing me was a mistake and feel that pain in my chest that I was oh so familiar with.

He sighs. "It *wasn't* a mistake. I—"

"Scarlett and Aiden! It seems you both are done with the experiment." Mrs. Nelson rebukes us, shattering the silence. Aiden and I look up.

"Um no we haven't finished yet," Aiden responds.

"Then *why* are you both talking when the rest of the class is busy doing their experiment?!" Mrs. Nelson glares at us. She can be scary when she wants to.

That shut us up. We both don't talk for the rest of the period. By the time the bell rings, Aiden has to leave to discuss last minute strategies with the team.

"All the best! I know you're going to do great." I assure him.

"Thanks Scarlett." He smiles at me.

I shake my head. "Don't you *ever* thank me."

His eyes look straight into mine, not budging. He's doing that staring thing again. His chocolate brown eyes make my heart beat so painfully. I like him *so* much, and the worst part is that he doesn't even know. He has no clue how important he is to me, how very, very important.

"How did you become so important to me?" he says, breaking my train of thought. I stare at him in awe, not knowing how to respond. He just verbalized what was on my mind.

"Aiden—"

"I like you Scarlett, I mean it. I can't take this anymore. I need to know how *you* feel."

"How *I* feel? Aiden, you don't need to know that."

I hurriedly gather my books after putting away the lab equipment, and then leave class with the rest of the students. I silently will for Aiden to leave. I'm not ready to have this conversation with him yet.

"Scar wait, please!"

I keep walking, refusing to stop. I need space, space to breathe and think. But whenever he's around it gets so hard to do just that. I can't think right, can't breathe right. And it's so hard to act like he doesn't affect me, to pretend I'm okay, to act like I don't feel *anything*. It's *so* fucking difficult.

"Scarlett, for God's sake, wait damn it!" he yells. I freeze.

"What?" I ask, turning around.

Before he can speak further, he is interrupted by Damien, one of his teammates.

"Man, what are you doing here?! Coach's going berserk. We need you ASAP! The match's about to start."

Aiden sighs and informs Damien that he'll come in a couple of minutes. Then he turns back to talk to me. I nervously wait for him to speak. I've never seen him look so serious before

He stares intensely into my eyes, moving closer. "I like you Scarlett. I have feelings for you. Just give me the word. Just tell me you feel the same, and I'll leave Hailey. I promise."

My eyes widen in surprise. What is he saying? He can't be serious. This seems like a sick, twisted joke. He can't really mean it, can he?

"Wha—Aiden, you can't be serious."0

He steps forward, taking my hand in his. I stare nervously into his beautiful brown eyes. Is he serious? Could it really be this easy? So that's all it'll take? A simple yes, and the thing I've craved for so long, would be mine? Just like that?

I don't say anything. I am scared. I don't know what to believe. I don't know if he really means what he's saying. My heart aches for his words to be true. The tone of his voice was urgent. I'd never heard him sound so desperate. He'd chased me down the corridor. His hands are clasping mine so tightly. His eyes staring so intensely. Surely, he couldn't be lying?

"Meet me after the match and give me your answer. I'll wait for you."

He slowly drops my hand, and then walks away. I stand there frozen, not knowing what to do. This can't be real, he doesn't mean it. He's probably joking. This is unbelievable. I look at him as he turns around and walks away. The steps he takes match the beat of my heart—fast and hard.

Could this really be it? Is this the moment I've been waiting for?

I'm not gorgeous or confident. There's nothing extraordinary about me. I am, I must accept, shy and insecure. I'm not good at socializing with people. I'm definitely not popular. I look awkward in those skirts and dresses the girls at our school pull off so effortlessly. I'm stubborn, and never back down from a fight. I'm dreamy, and I trust a little too easily. I'm definitely not the kind of girl he has dated in the past.

So why would he want to now?

I groan. The more I think about it, the more confusing it gets. Why now? Why so suddenly? Aiden has had plenty of chances to get with me in the past. But he's always gone for those other girls—the beautiful, confident ones who do as they please, who are not afraid to be themselves, the social butterflies with exuberant personalities. The type of girl Hailey is and I'm not.

So why now?

"Here you are!" Sharon's familiar interrupts my thoughts. "What are you doing here? C'mon the match is going to start soon. We need to hurry or else all the good seats will get taken." As much as I'd like to be left alone and ponder over everything that has happened, there's no way I'm missing the chance to watch Aiden's first match as captain.

I let Sharon lead me through the crowded field. We head up the bleachers and sit down next to Andrea and Kayla who have fortunately saved us seats. The match is about to begin in five minutes. The cheerleaders are currently doing their pre-match cheering and the crowd is waiting for the match to start.

The whistle is blown and the players from both the teams enter the field. My eyes immediately stop on Aiden who is the front-most player in the line. The two team captains shake hands, and the players immediately take position after that. Aiden looks up towards the stands and his eyes meet mine. He offers me a smile and waves. My heart skips a beat. My legs tremble just a little.

Beside me, I hear my friends gasp. "Did Aiden just *wave* to you?" Kayla asks, astonished.

I feel my cheeks heat up. I don't reply. I simply avert my gaze and shrug. The girls giggle beside me.

"Is there something going on between you two we don't know about?" Kayla prods.

Should I tell them?

"*Of course* nothing is going on between them. How many times do I have to tell you guys? They are just friends. Aiden has a girlfriend, right Scarlett?" Sharon interjects. I nod, shooting her a gratuitous smile.

My thoughts inevitably come back to Aiden. I feel myself transport back to the hallway where Aiden and I last conversed. I can't help remembering the way his brown eyes had captured mine, how he'd held my hands. My heart automatically starts beating faster. Just over ninety minutes later, when the match ends, Aiden will expect me to give him my decision, a decision that could change everything. Am I ready for that change?

To be honest, I might *never* be ready for that change. I'm not good with changes. I'm so used to my current state; the thought of things changing thrills me and scares me at the same time. I can't sit here in fear and miss this opportunity. I might never get this chance again.

I've decided. I know what to do now. If the match ends on a good note, I'll head over to Aiden right there and then and tell him. Yes, that's what I'll do.

I focus my attention back onto the field. The referee blows the whistle, and the match begins

* * *

Everybody stands up, holding their breath. Aiden's heading straight for the goal. A member of the opposite team charges towards him, but he swerves expertly. Racing across the last few yards, he throws the ball. It smacks down on the ground, just beyond the line.

Touchdown!

We won. *Aiden* won.

Excited cheers and hoots erupt from the crowd. Aiden turns around, taking in the huge crowd chanting his name. 'Walker! Walker!' is all that you can hear. I can't help grinning. I feel so proud of him right now. He'd been so nervous for this match. But the endless practice sessions had paid off. They won.

I realize with a start that *this* is it. It's time to do what I'd decided. The time has come. It's now or never. I can't back out now.

I take in a deep breath and get up. Sharon looks up at me, confused. I tell her there's something I need to do and leave before she can offer to come along. I need to do this alone. I want to drink in the smile on Aiden's face when I say 'yes.'

I head down the bleachers, pushing through the excited crowd. The cheerleaders are dancing to a victory song. I can hear their chants. I finally get off the bleachers, and see Aiden standing a few feet away, with his back to me.

With every step I take, I feel surer of my decision. This is what I want. This is what my *heart* wants. It wants Aiden. It wants him with everything it has.

I run over to him. He's just a short distance away now. My heart threatens to burst out of my chest, it's beating so fast; this has little to do with my running, and everything to do with this gorgeous boy in front of me.

I stop a few meters away from him, mentally preparing myself for the conversation that is to take place. *What will I say? How will I say it?*

Yes, yes Aiden, I want to be with you. I like you Aiden, leave her for me. No, that doesn't sound alright. It sounds too . . . desperate.

Hey Aiden, I've decided it's a yes. I'd love to be with you. No, not this either. It's too enthusiastic.

I groan. This is so frustrating. *What am I going to do?*

I imagine how it'll go once I tell him about my feelings. I can totally imagine the dazzling smile he'll offer me, and how his brown eyes will sparkle when he'll hear about my decision. I can almost hear his laugh and feel his arms around me as he hugs me.

Oh screw it! There's no point in contemplating it over and over again. I just need to go with the flow.

With butterflies fluttering in my belly, I take slow, hesitant steps towards him. He's so close now. I reach out my hands to touch his back.

But then I don't.

I see Hailey run into his arms and envelop him into a tight hug. She buries her face in the crook of his neck, wrapping her legs around his waist, as he supports her. "Congratulations baby!" she exclaims, before smashing her lips onto his.

I stand right behind him, frozen, taking in the way she's kissing him. She entwines her fingers through his hair, kissing him harder. I know he's kissing her right back.

What are they doing? Why are they kissing? Why is he kissing her?

The answer comes to me immediately. And when it comes it hits me hard—a hundred times harder than it has ever before like someone has punched me in my stomach hard. The realization makes my insides twist painfully. I had never thought emotional pain could hurt a person with *this* magnitude and intensity. It actually feels like someone is ripping my heart out of my chest.

He's kissing her because he *wants* to. He's kissing her because he's *with* her. And why wouldn't he? She's his *girlfriend.* *That's* when I realize the ridiculousness of this situation. What am I doing here? Why am I standing here? What am I waiting for? For them to stop kissing? And what after that?

I realize how *wrong* this is. They are together. They *love* each other. And who am I? An outsider. I have no business being here. They *belong* together.

I take a step back. Then another. Then another. Before I know it, I've turned around and am running, away from them, away from Aiden, away from the boy who was never mine to begin with.

Chapter Fifteen

Scarlett

"So students, how far have you come with your project may I ask?" Miss Levine inquires. Everybody instantly looks confused. Which project is she talking about? "Why do you all look so lost? I hope you haven't forgotten about that project I assigned you all some time back?"

That's when it clicked. The project, the dance project—salsa.

With Aiden.

Oh my god.

"It's due in a month. I want all of you to submit it. And those of you who have to *perform* something will do so in the school; we'll all be going to the auditorium for that."

Oh crap! I am *so* done. This is the end. Just—just kill me now. *How am I supposed to rehearse with Aiden if we're not talking?!* This is insane. This is . . . I am *so* dead.

Yup, you heard it right. Aiden and I? We're not talking.

It was my decision actually. After what happened at the game, I decided that staying away from Aiden was the best choice.

Because who am I kidding? It's too late to curb my feelings for him. I can't be friends with him and secretly torture myself like that anymore. This is the best way: distancing myself from him until my feelings slowly fade away.

It's not easy, far from it actually. But I'm trying.

The first day had been the worst. I'd been sitting by myself. The class was about to begin. I'd purposely decided to sit directly in front of the teacher's desk, knowing it would be the last place Aiden would decide to sit at. But I was proven wrong. Aiden had strolled in three minutes later and plopped down right next to me.

He'd looked at me and I'd already guessed what he was going to do next. I could already see his lips forming a smile. I'd turned away before he could do that. I didn't want to feel it— those butterflies in my stomach when he smiled. I didn't want to like him. I just wanted to forget about all this, about *him*. And so, I'd looked away. I'd glanced at him again a few seconds later. My heart had almost broken in two when I'd seen the hurt and slightly confused expression etched across his face.

That was just the start. For the rest of the period, I'd pretended to be occupied with reading Shakespeare and listening to the teacher explain about his works. I'd told Aiden to not talk whenever he tried to, saying I wanted to focus. I did not even laugh when he had whispered lame jokes to me like he always did. I wanted to. Hell, I was *dying* to: to laugh and talk to him and be like I always was with him. But I couldn't. I needed to control myself. It was the only way to get over what I felt. I needed to build a wall around me to keep him from getting in. When the bell rang forty minutes later, I left the class in a rush like even being next to him for another minute would've killed me.

Aiden didn't need to be a genius to figure out I was giving him the silent treatment. After all, I'd ignored all his texts and calls after the match and had started avoiding him at school too. Eventually, he stopped trying and left me alone. I should have felt relieved. After all, this is what I'd wanted, right? Except, I didn't. It felt wrong, being so far away from him. Seeing him but not talking to him. It was torturous. I wanted to be near him, touch him, *talk* to him—be the reason he smiled. It's been two weeks since we stopped talking, and it hasn't gotten easier.

My eyes flicker towards Aiden, only to see him looking right back at me. My heart skips a beat when our eyes meet and I quickly look away. Things are *so* weird between us right now, and I'm supposed to *dance* with him?! *How* do I do that?

I wait for Aiden to come over to discuss the project. To at least *tell* me that he doesn't want to do it anymore. He doesn't. He sits right where he is. Minutes pass by and the situation doesn't improve. With only five minutes before class ends, I decide to talk to him. I've been ignoring him for the past two weeks, and now I'm going to do just the opposite of that.

Lord help me.

"Uhm, Aiden? Can I talk to you for a second?" I ask after walking up to him. My heart does cartwheels and somersaults in my chest. I think I'm going to die.

He turns. Our eyes meet and a surprise flashes across his face. It vanishes instantly though, like it'd never existed in the first place, leaving his face blank.

"Yeah sure, what is it?" he replies nonchalantly.

I feel a little hurt because he didn't reply enthusiastically or smiled at me. But then again, I kind of deserved it. Oh well, at least he didn't walk away. That would have been *really* embarrassing.

"Uhm, it's about the project, you know, the dance? We haven't rehearsed for a for a while. We've not even choreographed the whole sequence, and it's due next month."

"Okay, so? What about it?"

"I was wondering if you were free this afternoon, you know, so we could practice?" I ask hesitantly.

"Sure, but we can't practice at my house today. Mom has some clients coming over."

"Oh, that won't be a problem. I think we could stay back and rehearse in the dance studio here?"

He nods. "Alright, I'll meet you there after school's over. Bye."

Our eyes meet again, and I swear I can see a hint of a smile form on Aiden's lips. But before it could turn into a complete smile, I turn away. I cannot do this. I just can't. I just know that seeing him smile at me would wipe out all the progress I'd made in two weeks.

* * *

The last bell of the day rings and I feel my heart beat speed up. It's time now. With my heart in my throat, I make my way towards the dance studio.

My phone suddenly starts ringing. It's Sharon, probably asking me if I want a ride back home. I quickly inform her that she need not wait for me.

Once I meet Aiden in the dance studio, we don't waste time making small talk; we start practicing immediately. We rehearse the dance routine; at least, as much as we'd succeeded in choreographing.

Aiden's arms are secured tightly around my waist. Our legs are moving in perfect coordination, not a step out of place. He finally throws me up in the air, turns me around, catches me and then we stop. We've managed to dance perfectly up to this point. Only a little bit more remains to be choreographed and then we'll be done.

We decide to take a short break. We've been in this studio for an hour, and we're dead tired. The awkwardness has vanished, but that doesn't mean the previous comfort has returned. It's still weird. We're sitting quietly when suddenly Aiden asks just the question I'd been dreading.

"Why Scarlett? Why have you been ignoring me?" He demands to know.

I sit there motionless, not knowing how to respond. What do I say? How do I tell him that ignoring him is the last thing I want to do? How do I tell him that I want to *be* with him but I can't? How do I tell him that this is the only way?

"After the match, I waited for you for an hour. I called and texted you *countless* times. I thought some emergency came up. I got *so* worried, you have no idea! But then I thought you'll probably call me later, or at least reply to my texts. A couple of hours went by, then a day, then two. Then you started ignoring me at school too. What *is* your problem!? Do you enjoy playing this cat and mouse game with me, where I chase you and you keep running?!" Aiden looks absolutely distraught. I've never seen him like this. I feel waves of guilt wash over me. I shouldn't have cut all ties with him, not like this, not so abruptly.

"Scarlett I'm tired. I'm tired of chasing you around. I-I just want to know. I want answers and I need them *now*. No more running away from me. You *have* to face me. Tell me. *Say* it." He scoots closer to me, resting his hands on my shoulders, forcing me to meet his eyes. I can't face the fierce intensity of his gaze. I can't. I feel my heart speed up, and my insides twist uncomfortably.

I get up and walk away. "I-I don't know what you want me to say," I murmur.

He gets up, and walks up to me, looking furious. "You know *exactly* what to say. You just don't want to say it!"

"What do you want me to say, huh? What do you want?!"

Aiden steps closer to me, beholding me with his intense brown eyes. "I just want to hear you say that you feel the same as *I* do. That your heart is beating as fast as mine is right now. That you—"

"I-I don't feel anything for you Aiden, I don't," I state, silently pleading him to drop it.

"You're lying!"

"You're delusional Aiden, you just don't want to—"

"Really Scarlett? Really? You're going to *lie* to me, your best friend?"

"I'm not lying Aiden."

"Oh you're not, are you? Then tell me. Tell me your heart doesn't threaten to burst out of your chest every time we're this close." He challenges, taking a few steps towards me. My heart starts racing almost immediately. I take a few uncertain steps back, only to feel my back hit the wall. With nowhere to escape, the only thing I can do is meet his eyes.

"Tell me you feel nothing when I do this," he whispers, reaching out to touch my face. He tucks a stray lock of my hair behind my ear. His finger trails down my cheek, caressing it. He then gently takes my face in his hands, pauses for just a fraction of a second, silently asking me for permission. I know I should push him away. But I can't. I'm so fucking weak when it comes to him; it scares me.

He leans forward, brushing his lips against mine. I tremble, not able to help myself. "Look into my eyes and tell me you don't feel anything when we kiss." He pants. Then he crushes his lips against mine. I feel my breath leave my body, feel my heart stop. His hands run down the length of my arm, before wrapping around my waist, pushing my body against his. I let out a moan. He takes my bottom lip in between his, sucking it. Then he slowly breaks the kiss, leaving me breathless.

"Stop resisting me, Scarlett. Stop lying to yourself. Say it. I want to *hear* you say it."

I open my mouth, almost giving in. There's no point in lying about it. He can see right through me.

"I—"

Before the words can leave my mouth, the door to the dance room bursts open. Our heads snap in its direction. My eyes widen, my mouth drops open.

Hailey's standing at the entrance looking very, *very* pissed.

Oh shit.

"Is *this* how you guys practice? By sucking each other's face?!"

Oh fuck.

She turns to me, her face a mask of fury. Her cold eyes glare at me.

"You! I warned you to stay away from him, didn't I?! You sly bitch! I'm going to—" She starts marching up to me. *Oh no . . .*

"Hey Hailey wait, stop!" Aiden exclaims, stepping in front of me. "Don't blame her, it's not her fault."

She narrows her eyes at him. "Then whose fault is it, huh!? Stop defending her—"

"It's mine. *I* kissed her."

Silence. Loud, deafening silence.

"W-what?" Hailey's voice is barely above a whisper. She looks stunned.

"Yes, I did it. It's *my* doing. Shout at *me*, not her."

I gape at him, not knowing how to react. How did things get so fucked up in a matter of minutes?

"I-I think I should go," I mumble.

"Yes, you should!" Hailey seethes, her eyes shooting daggers at me.

With one last glance at Aiden, I walk away.

* * *

Hailey

"How long has this been going on?" I demand, feeling anger pulse through my veins. Aiden sighs apologetically.

"For a while," he murmurs.

That's the thing about Aiden, he is a very good liar, but once he knows his secret's out in the open, he'll be hundred percent honest. So I am sure that whatever he tells me now, will be hundred percent true.

"Why?" That's all I ask.

I just need to know *why* he had to go to her. What does she have that I don't? What does he have with her that *we* don't? I need to *know*.

His face falls. He looks guilty. "It's complicated—"

"Uncomplicate it then."

"I think I have feelings for her." He admits.

My world comes to an abrupt halt. This is what I'd been dreading. I'd seen how she used to look at him, I had sensed it long back, maybe even before *she* knew about it. I'd just known that she had feelings for him. And now, it turns out, he likes her too.

"And what about me?" I ask, feeling more and more unsure by the minute.

"I like you. You know that."

Do I? I don't know.

I know I should have walked away then and there. I should have respected myself enough to do that. But I didn't. I *couldn't*. When I looked at Aiden, all I could see was the time we'd spent together. He was the first boy I'd felt so deeply for. How could I let this relationship slip away so easily?

So instead, I forgave him.

"You really hurt me Aiden. But I'm willing to overlook this . . . this mistake. What we have . . . it's good. *We're* good together. Don't throw this away for someone you're not even sure about. Make a decision and tell me. Me or her."

He is at a loss for words. *Why is he thinking so much? Why is he even thinking? Isn't the choice simple? Is he really even considering being with her?*

"I-I need to think Hailey."

My second clue. I should have left him then and there. He needed to *think* who he wanted to be with. But I was and have always been a fool for him.

So I let him think. I give him time.

Chapter Sixteen

Aiden

I emerge out of the shower and put on a new set of clothes I grab from my locker. My head hurts and there's a dull ache in my muscles. I run my fingers through my wet hair. In the seventeen years of my existence, I've never had to deal with girl problems. And now, I'm in the middle of this drama that involves not one, but *two* girls.

"Hey man, can I get a ride today? My car's at the mechanic's so…" Damien comes up behind me, interrupting my train of thoughts.

"Yeah sure." I nod. "Let's go."

"You don't sound very good. Something up?" Damien asks, concerned.

I consider telling him about my dilemma. Usually if I'm in some sort of trouble, I go to Scarlett. She's pretty good at giving advice and stuff. But not this time. I sigh. Well, beggars can't be choosers. And I really need an outsider's perspective. "Yeah, there's this problem . . . C'mon I'll tell you about it on the way."

We walk side by side to the parking lot. On the way a bunch of girls from the cheerleading squad pass us with coy smiles, giggling. Normally, I would have stopped to engage in a conversation or two, leaving with their numbers. But one, I already have their numbers, and two, for the first time, I'm not interested in the slightest. Girls are a nightmare, and I'm already involved with two.

Once we're in the car, Damien turns to me.

"So . . ." He prompts.

"Yeah so, you know Scarlett, right?" I ask him.

"Of course, I do. What about her?"

"Well, I like her," I say slowly, taking my time, trying to understand the significance of those words.

"Ha! I knew it!" Damien exclaims, suddenly jumping up.

"Wait, what!?" I gape at him.

He shrugs. "I had a hunch that you guys were into each other."

"Wow, you're more observant than you look. But you're kind of wrong. She's not into me. I mean, I don't know. We've kissed thrice, and I told her how I felt but she didn't say it back."

"Hmm . . . Scarlett doesn't seem like the kind of girl who casually kisses just anyone. What's the problem anyway? So you like Scarlett, big deal! She'll give in sooner or later."

"Dude, I already have a girlfriend, remember?"

"Wait . . . you're still with Hailey?" I nod. "Well, I don't understand. Why are you with her if you like Scarlett?"

"Because . . . I don't know. I kind of like Hailey too, I can't deny that. I need to make a decision now. Sometime back, I'd been so sure that Scarlett's the one. I was ready to leave Hailey for her. But then Scarlett completely cut me off—wouldn't respond to my texts, wouldn't even look at me. And now, I just don't know. Maybe I don't mean as much to her as I'd thought. Hailey on the other hand, she genuinely feels for me. We actually have something. Should I throw it away for someone who probably doesn't care about me?"

Damien nods thoughtfully. "What you're saying makes sense. Besides, I think you're better off with Hailey anyway. I mean, don't get me wrong, Scarlett's a great girl and all. But you guys . . . you just don't fit."

I frown. "What do you mean?"

"Girls like Scarlet, and I'm only guessing here, but girls like Scarlett, they are the emotional kind. They get too attached too easily. And *you're* not cut out for that shit."

"No, that's not—"

"Don't even try to deny it. You change your mind too much. You've dumped girls within a week. You get bored too easily. Do you really think it's worth risking it with Scarlett? You'll break her heart the first chance you get."

"No, I won't! I—"

"You will Aiden, you will. And how do you think *she* will handle it, huh? It'll completely break her." I try to argue again but Damien doesn't let me. "Hailey on the other hand, she's a tough one. She'll not only kick your ass if you mess with her, she'll be able to bounce back if you hurt her."

I hate the fact that what he's saying is a hundred percent true. He is right. I *will* hurt Scarlett. And it'll completely destroy this bond we have. I'd rather just be friends with her than risk losing her friendship.

"You're right but, you don't understand—I *like* her."

"Move on."

"How!?"

"I don't know man, stay away from her maybe. You need a little distance. You both are together all the damn time. What you need is space. Go back to Hailey and leave Scarlett alone. You'll move on in no time."

I wish I felt better after knowing what I should do. Instead, I feel worse. I don't want to distance myself from Scarlett. I'm not sure I can do that.

Which is precisely why you should do it Aiden. Back the fuck off before it gets too late.

I sigh. If walking away from Scarlett is the right thing to do, why does it feel so wrong?

* * *

Scarlett

Have you ever wanted time to speed up, things to go faster? Like that time when you were stuck in the middle of a boring lecture and you wanted the bell to ring already. That's how I feel right now. I can't wait for the clock to strike eight, so I can finally meet Aiden at the park. He called me a few hours ago, requesting me to meet him there so we could talk face to face. Since then, I've been constantly dreaming up different scenarios inside my head about what might happen once we meet. I don't know why he wants to meet, but he sounded serious. We'd been having an intense conversation before Hailey had interrupted us.

Maybe we'll finish it today. I haven't felt this strongly for anyone ever. I've had my list of crushes, but this, it's so much more than that. These feelings are stronger, deeper. And I don't want to give up on them, give up on the first person ever who made me feel like this.

I don't know; I'm just scared. I don't know if I should embrace these feelings with open arms or deny them. I just don't know. I guess today would finally seal the deal—I will finally know what I should do, be with him or simply try to move on.

"Are you sure about this Scar?" Susan asks me.

She's plopped on my bed and is licking Nutella off a spoon.

I groan and shut my eyes close. "I don't know Su, I don't know anything. This is just too much, it's making my head and heart ache, but in a good way."

She scoots over, so she's sitting next to me. "I just want you to be careful, that's all. I don't want you to get hurt."

"I don't know about that. Every time I decide to tell Aiden how I feel, something fucks it up, and makes me realize why I shouldn't. But I'm done waiting. I'm going to tell him tonight."

"I just don't want you to get hurt. Is Aiden really worth all of this?"

"I know the answer to this—he isn't. Aiden isn't anyone special or extraordinary. But he makes me happy. He gives me butterflies and when I'm with him I feel complete, and happy. My happiness is worth it, isn't it? It's worth the risk. *This* is worth the risk. And even if I do get hurt in the process, that little chance of me possibly getting what I want, the chance of me being with him is worth the risk and all the pain that comes with it."

Susan sighs and passes me a sad smile. "Oh Scarlett, I think you're falling in love with him."

I want to deny it, to tell her that she's mistaken, that it's just a crush. But I don't. For the first time I feel that there could be some truth in her words. And for some reason, that doesn't scare me at all.

I feel fearless.

* * *

The park where I'm supposed to meet Aiden is close to my home. It takes me approximately ten minutes to walk there. While I'm walking, my heart beat keeps increasing, until it gets impossible to breathe. I have to stop every once in a while and pacify myself.

When I finally reach the park, I realize I've arrived earlier than decided, so I go and sit down on one of the swings. It's still 7:45 PM, and it'll be another fifteen minutes or so before Aiden arrives.

And what then? What happens after that?

I push away all the negative thoughts, trying to remain optimistic. I lightly swing on the swing and enjoy the fresh cool breeze that makes my hair fly. I can see the pale white moon in the distance, shrouded by grey clouds.

Please, not tonight. Don't rain tonight.

It's not that I don't like the rain. I *love* it. I love the delicious smell of the wet earth that comes with it and the beautiful water-droplets that settle on plants making them look greener. I love how the wind gets cooler. I love the rain, I do. But the rain can also be very depressing like one's mood—dark, gloomy, and cold. I don't want this night to be anything like that.

Aiden

Scarlett's looking at her phone's screen, probably checking the time; it's still five minutes to eight. I've been standing here, behind some trees for the past ten minutes, staring at Scarlett, trying to build up the courage to do what I'm about to do.

I stare at her, at her wavy dark locks that are flying carelessly in the wind. I get this intense urge to run my fingers through them, to caress the soft skin of her cheeks, to look into her beautiful eyes, and kiss those impossible-to-resist lips one last time.

I could make this easy. Instead of walking away and simultaneously breaking my heart in the process, I could choose to stay. I could risk it all and see how it goes. Maybe, just maybe, it'll work out. Maybe I won't break her heart. Maybe she'll be the one, the girl that finally makes me stay. Maybe this won't affect our friendship. Maybe.

But that 'maybe' is a big 'maybe.' A 'maybe' I can't risk. So I slowly step out from the shadows, willing myself to do what must be done.

Scarlett notices me almost immediately. Getting up from the swing she walks over to me. Her eyes are wide with anticipation. She's trying to look composed but I can see the hint of uneasiness on her face. She steps closer to me and a waft of her heady perfume invades my senses. The urge to bury my face in the curtain of her hair overpowers me.

"Scarlett—" I begin but she interjects.

Scarlett

"Yes." I announce.

He looks at me, confused. "What?"

"Yes, I'll be with you. Leave her."

His face falls.

"What's wrong?" I ask, feeling apprehensive.

"You, me, us—everything." He sighs.

"What?" I ask. A hint of anxiousness creeps into my voice but I try to compose myself.

"You're an amazing girl Scarlett, really. I mean it. You're beautiful, smart, passionate . . ."

"But? I know there's a 'but' coming. What is it?"

"But this can't go on. *This* has to stop. I don't know what we have, what we *had*, but it's *got to* stop. This—this . . . flirtationship. It needs to end *right now*." My heart forgets to beat as those words roll off his tongue.

"We shouldn't be together. We're just so wrong for each other. I'll never be able to give you what you want. I'm not that kind of guy. You're looking for forever, but all I'll give you is an inevitable goodbye. That's how it is with me. I can't change. Not for you, not for anyone." The stark reality of it hits me then. He *can't* change. He *won't* change. If he really, truly, had feelings for me, he would at least *try*. But he's not even willing to do that.

And that's when all the air abandons my lungs. Tears blur my vision, and all the warmth deserts my body, leaving me cold.

He steps closer to me, putting his hands on my shoulder. "You deserve someone so much better than me Scarlett, someone who will give you *exactly* what you want. Someone who's capable of giving you love, and—"

I stop listening to him. I *don't* want better. I want him, only him. *Why doesn't he understand?*

Tears threaten to spill down my cheeks as I step away from him, not able to bear his touch. I stare down at my feet, unable to meet his eyes. I feel so humiliated and used. Was it all a lie, or did he just change his mind? Did it mean anything to him? Those stolen kisses, those tender touches, those secret smiles; did they at all? Was he just having 'fun' or did he ever, even for a single second, feel something for me?

"It's okay. Like you said, we're not good for each other. I'm not hurt. I had no substantial feelings in the first place. This . . . whatever it was . . . was nothing," I respond.

Lying—it's so easy to do. Maybe that's why Aiden does it all this time. No substantial feelings? Who am I kidding? It wasn't even a crush. It was so much more than that, so much more. But he doesn't need to know that. He doesn't need to know anything. He doesn't need to know that he has single-handedly crushed my heart into a million pieces.

He gently pushes my chin, so I'm forced to look into his eyes. It hurts. I blink the tears away. I won't cry here, not in front of him. He doesn't need to know how much I love him.

Love him.

Wow, I love him.

This sudden awareness about the true extent of my feelings makes this even worse. Why did I have to realize how I truly feel in the midst of this heartbreak? Why did I have to realize it at all? I was better off ignorant. I was better off unaware of the fact that Aiden was like the air I needed to breathe.

"Scarlett, I'm sorry."

How many times will you say that Aiden? How many times?

I shake my head. "It's okay, don't be sorry about it."

"You'll find someone better." He assures me, pressing his lips tenderly onto my forehead. Somehow *this* gesture hits me harder than any of the kisses we've shared. This seems more real, more genuine.

"*Of course,* I will! I'm amazing, am I not?" I try to smile, but it pains me to do so. This is so easy: lying, pretending like his words and action are not affecting me.

He suddenly freezes, as if he's just remembered something.

"What now?" I ask.

I'm *this* close to having a cardiac arrest. I just *know* that this, whatever it is, is going to be so much worse than what happened earlier.

I'm not sure I'll be able to handle it.

Aiden

"I can't—I can't be friends with you."

Oh fuck.

Okay, so that's *not* how I'd wanted it to come out. It sounds all wrong now that it's out of my mouth.

I wanted to tell her that I needed a little space, some time away from her to get a grip on myself. God knows it's hard being so close to her, forcing myself to remember that she's my best friend and that I need to stop. Like Damien said, I can't move on if I'm always around her.

I am about to clarify myself when Scarlett speaks up.

"Hailey told you to stay away from me, didn't she? She doesn't want us to be friends anymore. She told you to choose— me or her."

I gape at her. *Oh no.*

"Scar—"

"And clearly you've made your choice—her," she says coldly. She instantly steps away from me. "God, I can't believe you! I hate you *so* much!"

"Listen—"

"There *is* nothing to listen to, okay? I can't believe I cared for you and wanted you when all this time I meant nothing to you. Was this all just a game? You had your fill, and now you're leaving the first chance you get. I get that you don't want to be with me, but our friendship? How can you throw *that* away? How can you throw it *all* away?!"

Angry tears spill down her cheeks, but she hurriedly wipes them away. I extend my hands to touch her, to calm her down, but she slaps it away. "Don't touch me! I hate you! Just leave me alone!"

My heart aches in my chest. "Scarlett please, listen to me—"

"I don't want to listen to anything! Just go, leave me alone, like you intended to do all along! *Just let me be!*"

I want to argue. I want to stay. But when I see the stubbornness in her fiery eyes, I know I have lost the battle. She's made up her mind. She won't listen to me. At least, not right now.

"What did you call us, called what we *had?* A flirtationship? Yeah? Well this *flirtationship* is over officially. So now you can fuck off!"

My shoulders slump in response. I turn and look at her one last time before walking away.

Scarlett

I head back to the swing and stay there for what feels like hours, not moving. The same words keep repeating in my head, stabbing me like a knife.

You're not good enough, not for him, not for anyone. You deserve to be alone. That's why he chose her over you.

I know it isn't true, at least not all of it. But when your brain constantly tells you the same thing again and again you sort of start to believe it. Maybe I *am* not good enough. Maybe that's why he chose her over me.

It starts to rain, but I remain frozen on the swing, not moving, barely breathing, but definitely not crying. After the first few tears that spilled, I didn't cry at all. I refuse to cry. I won't cry not anymore.

I sigh. I wish I'd known he wasn't worth all that crap I went through. I'd just thought he was different, you know? Don't we all? We think this exact same thing before we start falling for him. We think he's different, and that it'll be different this time, that he won't hurt us. Or we think that we'll succeed in changing him. We're usually wrong, and then we start blaming ourselves for being stupid. I guess that's what I'm doing now: blaming myself.

The rain gets heavier, making me shiver due to all the cold and wetness. But I still refuse to leave. I really need to be alone.

Of course, that doesn't happen.

A few minutes later, I'm surprised to see Susan in front of me. She has an umbrella with her. She grabs my hand and pulls me up. "What the fuck Scar!? Why are you sitting here in the rain, do you want to fall ill?! C'mon now!" I follow her silently as she takes me to her car. The umbrella succeeds little in saving me from the rain. We reach her car within minutes. She quickly yanks open the door to the passenger seat and shoves me inside before heading over to the driver's seat. She immediately turns on the heat, start the engine and we're off.

"God, how can you be so stupid? We all were worried sick, wondering where you were."

"I'm sorry," I mumble, staring out of the window, losing myself in my thoughts.

She puts her hand on my shoulder, soothingly. "Hey, it'll be okay. We're going talk about what happened, because I *know* something did. But first, you need to take a nice warm shower and have a cup of hot chocolate." I nod, not saying anything. The rest of the ride passes in silence. I don't let her turn on the radio; I'm not in the mood for music.

At home, after Mom scolds me a bit for being so irresponsible, I head to my room and take a long warm shower and emerge outside, being greeted by a delicious cup of hot chocolate. While sipping the tasty liquid, I discuss the events of the night. My voice comes out bare and emotionless; I don't shed a single tear. I've promised myself today that I won't cry because of him anymore.

Susan listens to me, wide-eyed. Then she starts muttering a string of very colorful curses, aiming them at Aiden. She gets up, threatening to beat the absolute shit out of him.

"Susan, sit down. You're not going to do anything. The deed has been done. There's nothing left to do. There's nothing that I'd *want* to do. It's done. *I'm* done."

And I was.

Done.

Chapter Seventeen

Scarlett

I'm busy doing differential calculus, with earphones shoved in my ears. Susan says something to me, forcing me to take out an earphone and turn to her.

"What?"

"I said, how long are you planning on staying like *this*?"

I roll my eyes and turn back around. "What's wrong with this? Studying is good."

"You've completely shifted into this shell, you know? You don't talk to anyone, you don't laugh anymore. You don't read books, which made you happy by the way. You've stopped listening to music. All you do is study all the time."

I want to tell her that this is me—this is me when I'm sad. I need to distract myself by doing something productive, something that doesn't need my emotional investment—like vigorously exercising to or solving boring math problems. If I don't distract myself I'll end up overthinking about every tiny aspect of the situation.

I don't explain all this to Susan though. Instead, I simply close my books, switch off my iPod and get up, stretching my arms wide. Heartbreaks do have their pros, like me completing all of my pending school work.

But then it has its cons—obviously. It's really hard, and it hurts like hell. But I know there's nothing I can do to change this situation. He's with her now. He's happy, and me...well, I could be better.

Ding.

Well, that has to be Sharon. I excuse myself and head downstairs to open the door. Sure enough, it's her. She comes inside, hugs me, and follows me upstairs to my room. Susan and Sharon greet each other. They recently met a couple of days back after all the drama that ensued with Aiden. They both were really worried about me and had come to my house to see me, and that's when they met each other.

No, I hadn't been an emotional wreck when they'd arrived. I'd just been really distant and emotionless—empty. So they'd forcefully made me watch silly RomCom movies and stayed for an impromptu sleepover. The movies triggered my tear ducts and I ended up crying like a baby after watching it.

After entering my room, Sharon drops a pile of papers onto my desk. "The notes from our chemistry teacher."

"Thanks a million!"

I actually skipped school for two to three days, and Sharon has been bringing in all the work that I missed. Today was thankfully a Friday and so, I don't have to go to school for another two days. Yay!

Sharon plops down on the bed next to Susan. I turn back to the table and start going through the notes she's just got. *Great, I have something new to distract me now.*

"So anyway, I was wondering if you wanted to go to this party…" Sharon begins to speak.

Mine and Susan's head snap towards her at the same time. The only difference is, I groan while Susan gasps excitedly. "Oh my god, when is it?!" she exclaims.

"Today actually, and Eric's hosting it! You know Eric, right?" she asks me. "He's kind of an idiot but he throws the best parties ever. We should totally go. Plus it's been a while since we've gone to one. It'll be a nice change from all this dullness."

I do not respond. Going to a party is the last thing I want right now. I just want to be alone.

"Scar, I really think we should go. Especially you, Scarlett! It'll be a nice change for you after all that, uhm all that happened." I glare at her for almost mentioning what happened with Aiden. It's been two weeks since then, and it still hurts like a bitch.

"Thanks, but no thanks. I'm seriously not in the mood," I mutter.

"Aw c'mon!" They both groan.

Maybe going out wouldn't be too bad. Getting drunk could be a good distraction…

* * *

"Hot—that's the word," I say, flipping my hair dramatically as I make a sultry pose in front of the mirror.

"Word change, you mean *sexy*," Susan pipes in.

The past three hours have been completely blissful. We spent it in the most girly way possible—trying on various outfits and doing each other's makeup. Susan and Sharon had gone off to their houses to grab as many clothes, accessories, and shoes they could and had returned in half an hour's time. Then we'd tried out different combinations to come up with the best outfits.

I am currently wearing a purple blouse with elbow length sleeves, a pair of black hot pants (courtesy of Sharon) and a pair of purple colored pumps. I usually avoid excessive makeup, but I've decided to experiment today. I'm going with the classic smoky eye, with my dark brown eyes lined with a kohl pencil and an eyeliner. I've even shaped and darkened my eyebrows to make them look on fleek. I've even gone as far as straightening my usually wavy hair. I look quite different, as a result.

Sharon here is wearing a strapless electric blue minidress. She's topped it with a pair of silver stilettos. Her hair is slightly curled at the tips. Her eyes are done up with silver eye shadow and bright cherry lips, she looks ready to party.

Susan looks gorgeous too, in a silver sequined minidress and black strap heels. Her hair is at its usual wavy self. She's applied a little blush and eyeliner and is mostly going with the nude makeup free look. All in all, we three look drop-dead gorgeous.

"Time for a group photo bitches!" Sharon cheers, taking out her phone. We spend like an hour taking each other's photographs and clicking selfies. I mean, we don't look this good every day, do we?

My mom gushes over our outfits when we start heading outside. She also spends like ten whole minutes reminding us to be safe and come back on time.

Tonight's going to be a good night.

Susan is the designated driver. We turn up the music and drive away into the night. I stare out the window as the music plays; silently pretending I'm in a music video. I wish they both were playing sad, melancholic music. But Sharon, who always makes it a point to play the cheesiest, and the most mainstream songs, is the self-appointed DJ.

"I want us to let loose tonight and forget about all the problems and drama in our life," Susan says as she drives.

I nod. "I think you're right. Screw everything, let's just live this night like it's our last," I reply.

They both gawk at me.

"What?"

"You did not just say that! That was basically you saying YOLO."

I shrug. "Well that's me, and I meant what I said."

"You know what? Let's make a party bucket list," Sharon suggests.

"A what?!" Susan and I exclaim together.

"*A party bucket list*—a list of things we'll do at this party before we leave; especially Scarlett, because she's been so down in the dumps these past few days. You're not allowed to leave before doing all of them."

I nod, feeling a little skeptical. Fifteen minutes later the list is complete. It's scrawled haphazardly over a crumpled tissue paper.

The Party Bucket List:

    1. Get drunk

    2. Sexy Dance with a guy

    3. Play beer pong

    4. Play Truth & Dare

    5. Play Never Have I Ever

    6. Kiss Someone

    7. Exchange phone numbers with someone

"Okay, that list is *completely* ridiculous!" I exclaim once Sharon's done with it. "I mean I don't drink so getting drunk is out of option; so is beer pong and never have i ever. Truth and Dare is okay, and what's this sexy dancing crap?"

"You know, sexy dancing—grinding and dancing like sensually, like you're making love on the dance floor," Sharon says it casually, as if it's no big deal.

"And how are you planning to get drunk? You're the designated driver." I turn to Susan.

"This bucket list is for *you*. We might indulge if we want to, but it's not compulsory for us."

"Me?! What? When did we decide on that?"

"It's only given that *you'll* have to do it seeing *you're* the one who needs to enjoy the most. The only reason we're even at this party is because we wanted to lighten your mood."

"Oh my god, why are you guys ganging up on me? What have I ever done to you?" I groan. "I'm starting to think coming to this party was a *very* bad idea."

I can hear the loud music already. We're almost there. The street is crowded with cars parked on both the sides and teenagers are trudging towards the big white house at the end of the street. Suddenly, I feel this intense urge to turn around and bolt. I feel my stomach churn with anticipation.

What's going to happen tonight?

Little did I know that I'll be doing every single thing on that party bucket list tonight.

Chapter Eighteen

Scarlett

I can literally *smell* the booze. The loud beat is making my heart pound really hard against my chest. Eric's house—if it can even be called a house, it's so big—is almost completely filled with teenagers. They keep moving from one place to another, talking obnoxiously on the top of their voice. The garden area is decorated with fairy lights. People are sprawled across the lawn drinking and dancing. I don't know why, but this party seems like one of those crazy parties that tend to get out of hand.

"Here, a little something to lighten you up," Sharon says, passing me what looks like a liquor flask.

"Where did you get *that*?!" I exclaim.

"I smuggled it from home, duh! Now drink it up."

I shake my head, refusing. Sharon tries to coax me, but I'm pretty adamant.

Giving up, they both turn around and we head inside. I sigh as I follow my friends. The music is almost ten times louder here; my ears hurt. The music is almost making the room vibrate;

the beats are jumping off the walls crashing into each other. God, I'll probably go deaf before the night ends.

"Okay girls, there's not much talking we'll be able to do. But tonight, I want us to dance till our feet hurt, forget all our problems, and live while we're young!" Susan shouts over the music.

I see a group of teenagers playing truth and dare in one corner. They're sitting comfortably on the couch and an empty beer bottle in front of them. It's turning round and round and round. The game looks really interesting. Sharon's Bucket List immediately enters my mind. Wasn't playing truth and dare a task too?

Hmm…maybe later.

"C'mon let's dance!" Susan exclaims, dragging me and Sharon towards the throng of dancing teenagers. Before we know it, we're shaking our body to the beat of a pop song. I can feel the sudden rush of energy; I feel excited. My hair whips as I move. I can feel everyone's eyes on us. This is so exhilarating.

An hour later, tired from all that dancing, we decide to take a short break and head towards the kitchen. This place is really crowded too; it's almost suffocating. Couples have occupied almost all of it. They can be spotted at every other corner, kissing and feeling each other up: some against the walls, some on the kitchen mantle tops. There's a giant fridge in the rightmost corner and that's where I go. I squeeze my way through the crowd and open up it up. Su and Sharon immediately grab a can of beer each. I look for something non-alcoholic. The drinks refresh our minds, and then it's back to dancing.

Someone changes the music, swapping the loud hip-hop number for a sappy ballad. A few people groan, while couples immediately scramble onto the dance floor, hogging the chance to slow dance. Seeing all these couples wrapped intimately around each other, swaying slowly to love songs takes me back to the time I'd done the same.

Slow dancing…

…I remember slow dancing with Aiden.

I can almost feel his arms wrapped around my waist, and my hands around his neck. I can almost feel the warmth of his body seeping into mine; feel his light breath tickling my skin. And it hurts, it hurts so bad. It hurts so bad to realize that I'll never get to feel that way again—feel that sense of completeness.

I push away the painful memories. They are not worth thinking over; because they are just that—memories. And we don't get to experience the same things twice.

My eyes travel across the dance floor. The mushiness here is making me sick. I just want to get out of here.

"Hey Scarlett? Uhm, let's go out for a bit," Susan says suddenly.

I cock my eyebrows at her. "Why? You just said you were going to ask the DJ to change the song."

"I changed my mind. Fresh air, we need some fresh air. Let's get out of here."

"But I want to dance. Can't we—"

And that's when I see him, them—to be exact: Aiden and Hailey . . . slow dancing. I'd not expected it to hurt the way it did then. I hadn't even guessed it was humanly possible to feel the way I felt then. The pain hits me hard. I can feel this heaviness slowly spreading through my chest. It's getting harder to breathe. Just seeing them together had triggered all the feelings, all the thoughts I'd been trying so hard to avoid.

I want to look away, but I can't. Susan tries to pull me away. But I can't seem to move. I can't stop looking at them, looking at her, with her hands wrapped firmly around his neck. His strong arms are holding her waist protectively. Eyes—they are looking into each other's eyes, so deeply, so intensely.

I could have been there instead, you know? I could have been there, with his arms wrapped all around me, feeling the flutter of his heart every time he leaned in. *I* should be there, running my fingers through his wavy tresses. But I'm not. He doesn't look at me the way he looks at her. And he never will. He's made that much very clear.

My deep trance is broken when I realize that Hailey and Aiden are slowly leaning towards each other.

God, I need a drink—right now.

I don't wait to see what happens next. I swiftly turn around and head back to the kitchen. I push past the people in my way and open the damn fridge, taking out a bottle. I don't even glance at the label. I don't even think. I simply pour some (a lot) of it in a glass, mix it with some juice, and then swiftly drink all of it. Then I grab the bottle and head back.

Susan and Sharon are still here, looking around for me apprehensively. So that's why Susan wanted some 'fresh air.' She'd hoped I wouldn't see them. Now I wish I hadn't either. But it's too late for that now, isn't it?

Not able to stop myself, I glance at where I'd seen Hailey and Aiden. They're kissing frantically. There's nothing really romantic about that kiss though. There's a lot of touching involved, yes. But there's something missing.

With my stomach churning, I gulp down some of the alcoholic liquid. It immediately triggers my gag reflex, and I feel like spitting it out. But I ignore the feeling and continue drinking. A warm sensation envelopes my belly.

A hand comes up and snatches the bottle from me. "What the hell!?" I curse, annoyed. I need it. I need it to lessen my pain and distract me; to blur everything.

"You don't want to drink. You *hate* drinking. Why *are* you drinking?" Susan asks, sounding worried.

"Isn't it obvious? I want to forget a certain douchebag."

I try to take the bottle back from her, but Susan's taller than me. She lifts it farther beyond my reach. I let out a growl,

"Su, give it to me!"

"Give it to her, let her drink," Sharon says.

"But—" Su tries to protest but Sharon cuts her off.

"Seriously, let her drink. She needs it. She has a right to let off some steam and just . . . relax and not think about all this. Wasn't that the point of coming here tonight?"

Susan looks reluctant, but she hands the bottle back to me. I eagerly grab it and gulp down some more of its content before slapping down the bottle on the table. I can feel myself losing the clarity, the preciseness of the situation little by little, with every sip. I wipe the drink trickling down my lips and breathe.

So that's why people drink when they're upset. It helps them lessen the pain, forget it even.

I feel lighter, more energized. The alcohol has done its work. I don't feel like dwelling on my thoughts. There's this unused energy in my body and all I want to do is expend it.

"I need to get out of here," I say to Susan and Sharon. I don't wait for their response and head to the room adjacent to this. On the way, we come across Kayla and Andrea. They're all decked up for the party in skintight short dresses of metallic tones. I introduce them to Susan and vice versa. We hang out for a bit, then head back to the dance floor as soon as the sappy music is replaced by some good ol' EDM.

Ten minutes into dancing, Andrea leans in, beckoning all of us to come closer so we can hear her.

"What is it?"

"Extremely hot guy at 3 o'clock, and he's not even a stranger," she squeals. "Oh, oh don't you all turn to look at him at the same time!"

"Well, who is it?" I ask, curious.

"William Hayden," Sharon states, finally noticing who Andrea is talking about.

My eyes widen as the name registers in my brain. William. William Hayden. The guy my friends think—

"You mean the guy Scarlett has a massive crush on?" Kayla responds. I immediately feel my heart beat double up. God, how could I forget *that*? My friends still think I like William, they have no clue about my feelings for Aiden. I never even liked William like that. I just found him attractive, *still* find him attractive. But then, who doesn't?

William does look really hot tonight, if I must admit. His dirty blond hair is messed up in just the right way. He's wearing a pale blue shirt that compliments his blue-green eyes. Compared to the rest of the boys, he looks so classy.

"You should go dance with him." Andrea suggests when she notices me looking at him from afar. He's surrounded by a couple of people, all of them showering him with attention. He's moving on the dance floor like he owns it. Every inch of his body moves in synch with the beat of the music and holy hell, I can't dance with someone so . . . so terrifyingly gorgeous.

"Yeah right, as if!" I roll my eyes at the ridiculous suggestion.

"Why not? Just do it. The night is young, and so are you both," Kayla says cheekily.

"Actually I agree with her. Just *go*." Susan urges me.

My head snaps in her a direction and I pass her an incredulous look. She knows I like Aiden, then *why* is she asking me to go dance with another guy?

Should I do this? That's what parties are for, right? To socialize, to meet new people?

"You know what? I think you guys are right. I'm going to go up to him, and we're going to dance." They cheer me on. I gulp down some more of the alcohol and then head towards William.

I admit that I *want* to talk to William, see how it goes. But then, I'm also kind of hoping that Aiden will notice me from across the room, see me talking to William, see me laughing, and regret what he did. I want him to know that what he did didn't affect me in the slightest, and that I'm completely over it. Which is of course, a big fat lie. But he doesn't need to know that.

Now usually, in such situations, I'm a nervous wreck. I can't randomly walk up to strangers for the life of me. But I'm slightly tipsy at the moment and have found this new sense of confidence I didn't even know I possessed. The thought that I might make a complete fool of myself doesn't enter my mind and I confidently walk up to him.

William Hayden is standing right in front of me. Not dancing so much anymore, he's busy talking to two girls, a cup of beer clutched in his right hand. His trademark smirk makes its appearance and the two girls almost swoon on the spot. He proceeds onto saying something, which causes both the girls to let out high pitched giggles.

This guy is good, and I mean really good. He knows how to wrap a girl around his finger perfectly.

Not prolonging the inevitable, I walk up to the trio and speak up. "Hey!" I greet. All three pair of eyes fall on me, their eyebrows cocking slightly, wondering who the hell I am and what do I want. "Mind giving this bored girl some company?" I say casually, hoping I don't sound as nervous as I feel.

William's face breaks into a smile. "Sure! The more the merrier, right?"

The volume of the music here is much lower, making it easier to converse. It's initially awkward, but not too much. William does a good job of letting me join the conversation so I don't feel left out. He fills the awkward silences with his contagious laugh and witty comments. The two girls leave after a while, leaving me alone with him.

William hands me a cup of beer and I drink it up without any hesitation. By now I'm so used to its bitter taste, but the warmth that follows and wraps me up is so worth it. "How do you feel about dancing, huh?" William asks me.

I nod almost immediately. This is what I came here for in the first place: dancing. He extends his hand towards me. I bite my lip shyly before taking it. I haven't talked to my friends for half an hour. I haven't even thought about Aiden. Sure, he's always in the back of my mind but with alcohol and William combined, the thoughts of Aiden haven't bothered me much.

We head to the main dance area where the music's louder. And when he steps closer and wraps his arms around my waist, I don't stop him. I put my arms around his neck and let myself inhale his scent.

"What would your girlfriend say if she sees us dancing?" I whisper in his ears.

He chuckles, causing his eyes to twinkle. "I don't have a girlfriend," he murmurs.

"Then who's that girl I see you so often with? Dark hair and—"

"Oh, she's my best friend Angelina. Our relationship is purely platonic. I suppose you don't have a boyfriend that will mind *us* dancing together?"

"Oh, no I don't!"

That's all the encouragement he needs. William pulls me closer, our chests gently collide. We start swaying our body to the fast beats of the music. As the tempo builds up, so does our speed. My hair flies around my face, and I can feel William's arms wrapped tightly around my body. He flips me around so that my back is against his chest, and I can feel his hand graze my hips. His hot breath fans the nape of my neck, making me giggle. God, am I drunk already?

As the music changes from fast and energetic to a slow, R&B number, I start rolling my hips to match the beats of the song. William follows suit, doing the same. Our waists roll in the same direction, my back touching his front, and before I realize it, we're grinding. It's not the disgusting, raunchy kind you usually see at parties. Our bodies are touching, but only barely. We've got a comfortable amount of space between us for this to not be overly intimate.

Does this count as 'sexy dancing'? Yeah, I guess it does. One of the tasks on the party bucket list is officially done.

Aiden

God, what the hell is she *doing*?!

I see Scarlett just a few feet away dancing with a guy who looks vaguely familiar. I'd actually let myself appreciate how sexy she looks tonight if she wasn't cozying up to that guy like that. Who is he *anyway*!?

I feel anger pulse through my veins when I see that guy's hands dangerously close to Scarlett's butt. I swear if it goes there *one more time* I'll—

"Aiden! Aiden, hey!" I jolt, surprised. I realize its Hailey calling me out. She's standing right next to me. We'd been dancing together until I noticed Scarlett with him, whoever he is.

Hailey notices what I'm looking at. "Hey, isn't that Scarlett—holy shit! What is she doing with *him*?!"

"Wait, you *know* him?"

"You do too! Look carefully! That's William Hayden."

Wait . . . William Hayden. William Hayden. William—

Suddenly it clicks. I know who he is. It's William Hayden. He's a notorious fuckboy, and right now Scarlett's dancing with him.

I feel my protective instincts kick in. But I stop myself. I can't just go there and stop them from dancing with each other, especially after what happened between Scarlett and me. We both, we're not on speaking terms. I have absolutely no right to—

I see him smirk before he wraps his arms around her waist, pulling her closer.

Fuck this! I don't care what Scarlett thinks. I'm going there right now and—

"Aiden, *where* are you going!?"

"Hailey I just need to—"

"Just *stop*, okay?! I'm *not* blind. I've noticed you've been looking at her for a while. I thought you both were done!?"

"We are, it's just—"

"Just what?! *I'm* your girlfriend, and I'm standing *right here*—beside you. Can you just stop—just stop focusing on *her*?"

"Yes, I'll stop, I *promise*. I just need to—just wait here, okay? Give me a minute, I'll be right back." Before Hailey can start arguing again, I walk away. I make my way through the throngs of sweaty teenagers until I'm directly in front of Scarlett and that guy.

Scarlett is the first to notice me. She freezes momentarily before looking away. Whatever, I'm not here to talk to her anyway. The one I'm here for is *him*. I grab his arm, pulling it away from her hips. William looks up, looking visibly annoyed. "What the fuck!? Who are *you*?" He snaps, pulling his arm away from my grasp. Scarlett's looking at me now. Her eyes are wide with shock.

"It doesn't matter who I am. I just need you to get your hands off Scarlett right *now*. And if I see it going back there again,

I'm going to break it, and that's a promise," I reply coldly. My eyes lock onto his and I glare at him hatefully.

William glares back at me, before turning to Scarlett. "I thought you said you didn't have a boyfriend?!" he asks, sounding a little irritated.

"I don't!" she exclaims almost instantly.

"Then who is *he*!? And what's his damn problem?"

"Oh no, he's just my best—" Scarlett stops. "I mean, he's—he's no one. Forget him; let's just get out of here," she says taking his hand into hers.

I feel a not-so-familiar pain jab my chest. She was just about to call me her best friend. But then she didn't. *Fuck, but it really hurts.*

"Yes Aiden, let's get out of here too." Hailey steps up, appearing suddenly. We're all a little surprised to see her. Scarlett looks really pissed right now, and William? Poor guy has no idea what's going on. Hailey glares icily at Scarlett before wrapping her arm around me and pulling me away.

Only when we're a little distance away does she let go of me.

"I can't believe you! Was it really necessary to go there and create a scene!? It's not like he was harassing her! They were just dancing."

"You don't understand—" I try to explain.

"Are you jealous Aiden!?" She snaps, making me forget what I was about to say earlier. "Are you jealous that she's dancing with some guy, someone who's not *you*? Because that's what it looked like. No wonder he thought you were her boyfriend or something. You acted like a possessive piece of shit."

"W-what!? No that's . . . that's not true. I . . . look, I just went there because the way he was touching her—I don't know, I don't trust him okay. And just because I've stopped talking to her doesn't mean I've stopped caring about her. She's *still* my best friend, okay?! And I was looking out for her. That's all. I wasn't . . . I wasn't jealous."

Hailey rolls her eyes at me. "Seriously? Look, frankly, Scarlett seems to have no problem with how he's touching her whatsoever. So *you* need to mind your own business and let her do whatever the heck she wants. The only thing you should be focusing on right now is having a good time with me. And if I see you pulling another shit like this, I'm leaving. I came to this party with *you*, so that I could hang out with *you*. I'm not in the mood for crap like this."

I grudgingly nod, knowing what Hailey is saying is hundred percent correct. "I'm . . . I'm sorry. I don't know what came over me. But I promise not to do that again. C'mon, let's go get a drink. I feel really thirsty."

And irritated.

I think of what Hailey accused me of the first time— jealousy. Was I really jealous? Is *that* why I went there in the first place?

Well, not really. I mean I really didn't like the way he was touching her, but that's only because I was feeling protective over her, right? Not because I was jealous?

Yeah, I suppose so.

"Alright, let's go." She nods, turning around and walking towards the kitchen. I follow suit.

Chapter Nineteen

Scarlett

"I'm *so* sorry about that. I had no idea he'd barge in like that and behave so rudely." I apologize to William. I don't even know why *I'm* apologizing to him when *Aiden's* the one who acted like a prick in the first place. But I can see that what happened earlier has irritated William and I really don't want him to stop talking to me, at least not yet.

William sighs. "Who was he though? Your ex-boyfriend?"

I chuckle. "No, my ex-*best friend* actually. We had a fall out recently. I don't know what came over him—"

"Relax. It's okay. He was just looking out for you, I suppose. I would have done the same for Angelina."

I look up at him, my brown eyes meeting his blue ones. He smiles at me, reassuring me that everything is fine. "So anyway, since we're already out here, let's take this opportunity to talk. As fun as it was dancing with you, I'd like to get to know you more."

I feel the familiar anxiety return. Here we have an extremely attractive boy who wants to talk to *me*. I have absolutely no idea why but I'm not complaining.

"So, I think I've seen you before, but I'm not really sure. Although, I don't know how I'd forget coming across someone as pretty as you," he remarks. I resist the urge to roll my eyes, feeling slightly turned off. He's so gorgeous, and so charming. *Why does he have to be cheesy?*

"Maybe you should keep your eyes more open then." I suggest, sending a cheeky smile his way. I don't mention that one time I crashed into him in the school hallway and he helped me gather all my books that had fallen. I'm not surprised that he doesn't remember me at all. I'm not exactly the kind of girl who leaves an impression.

I analyze him—his face, his expressions, the way his hair is styled, the way his eyebrows move animatedly when he talks. He is really good looking, no kidding there. *How in the world did I get so lucky?* Someone as good looking and popular as *him* is showing interest in someone like *me*.

You see, I've never really been very social. I'm just me— simple and quiet Scarlett. Well, not really quiet but you know what I mean, right? I've always been an introvert. Things have started changing a bit now. But I'm still *me*, even now.

I'm not a dork, or a loser. People don't avoid me like the plague and I'm not exactly at the end of the social ladder. But I'm not the kind of person people notice either. I'm the girl people cross in the hallway without pausing to spare a single glance. I'm the girl people don't usually bother to know about, because they don't notice her. I'm the girl who looks so boring and ordinary from the outside that people don't bother to know what's on the inside. That is *me*. If this was a movie, I'd be an extra.

And to think that someone like me has captured his attention is just unbelievable. People don't notice me, especially people like *him*—the popular kind. William is definitely one of the most popular guys in the school. He is this sexy, talented guy who can dance and sing and always plays the lead in school plays. Our worlds are *totally* different. But now, here we are, talking to each other, getting to *know* each other. A few months back, when I'd seriously been crushing on him, I would have never guessed such a day would come. But here it is now.

We spend the next twenty minutes getting to know each better. He tells me things about him that I already know—that he likes to sing, dance, and play the guitar, and that he's the head of the drama club. Then he tells me a couple of things I didn't know: that he likes to write (songs mostly) and that he's going to audition for Juilliard School of arts a couple of months later.

And then it's my turn to speak, and I feel the familiar nervousness settle in. I hesitate at first. What if he thinks I'm weird? What if he realizes he's wasting his time with a girl like me? But then I convince myself that I'm overreacting. William is still waiting for my response. He's opening his mouth, about to repeat the question, thinking I didn't hear him the first time. So I start speaking. I tell him that I write, and that I'm obsessed with this boyband, and my favorite color is black and I'm a huge Potterhead, and a self-proclaimed fangirl. I keep waiting for him to leave, or worse, laugh at me. But he does nothing of that sort. Instead, he does something I'm not used to. He *listens*. He sits back and listens to me as I speak and it's a brand-new experience. I've never spoken ten minutes straight without being interrupted once or twice. I've always been more of a listener, never the one to lead a conversation. But here's William, listening to me with his eyes wide open and a soft smile playing on his lips, as if he's genuinely interested.

I could get used to this.

"So can I read something you wrote someday?" he asks, still smiling at me.

"Sure, if you want to." I shrug making a mental note to write something that isn't about my former best friend. All the poems I've written recently are in some way about him.

Aiden.

I suddenly feel, so, *so* tired. God, what the hell am I doing here? All dressed up, surrounded by kids high on booze. I tried to fool myself into thinking I could forget about him for at least *one* night. I was so wrong.

God, my head hurts.

"Uhm, I think I . . . I've got to go," I say, suddenly getting up to leave.

William frowns. "Why? Aren't you enjoying yourself here?"

I nod. "I am. I'm just . . . tired. I think I'll go hang out with my friends for a bit."

He shrugs. "Okay, sure. Catch you around?"

I nod. "Definitely." I wave goodbye and start walking away, away from the crowd and away from the headache inducing music. I contemplate looking for my friends, but one look at the humongous crowd trapped inside the house, and I know I'll be doing no such thing. Instead, I head to the rear of the garden. I hope it'll be slightly less congested.

Well, it's not secluded but it's relatively less crowded. There's a big pool filled with crystal clear water. The sky blue tiles give it a dramatic look. Teenagers are lounging around it with bottles in their hands, dressed in scanty swimwear. A muscular guy cannon balls into the pool, causing a huge splash.

I walk away from the commotion and take a seat in a secluded corner, near a cluster of trees so I'm hidden from view. I am in no mood to be disturbed. God, my feet hurt so much. I drag a plastic chair from nearby and sit on it. I remove the pumps I'm wearing, and softly massage the sole of my foot. It feels quieter here even with the music going on faintly in the background. I lay down my back against the support of the chair and gaze up at the night sky. It's full of twinkling stars, absolutely void of any clouds. I don't know for how long I sit there, simply gazing at the star-lit sky, feeling as if I'm in my own world. I think I can spend the rest of the night here by myself, doing absolutely nothing, just being here.

Suddenly, I hear someone coming. I can hear them walking over the pathway, causing the gravel to crunch under their feet. God, I hope they don't plan on staying. I want this place to myself.

"Aiden! Stop, what if someone sees us?"

"I don't care. I just really want you."

"But we're in a garden!"

"Like I said, I don't care."

I freeze. That's *definitely* Aiden and Hailey, and they're really close by. God, the last thing I want is for them to see me all here by myself and think that I'm stalking them or something. That would be absolutely mortifying.

"Aiden *stop*." I hear her giggle.

"It's your fault. Why do you always look so irresistible?"

"God Aiden, I want you too, like right now. But we have to be patient, yeah?"

Eww.

My thoughts are interrupted by the sudden ringing of a cell phone. For one terrible second, I think it's mine, and that any second now, Aiden and Hailey will spot me sitting in the shadows...

"Hello?" Hailey's voice comes on. *It was Hailey's phone. Thank heavens!* "What?! Oh my gosh, is she okay? No, of course she isn't. Okay yeah, okay, okay yes. Sure. Okay bye, I'm coming." She hangs up and turns to Aiden. "I'm *so* sorry but I have to leave."

Aiden groans. "*Why?!*"

"My friend's boyfriend of two years just broke up with her. We're all going over to her place to cheer her up."

He groans again. "Do you really have to?" *Silence.* "Alright, alright, I'm kidding! Go cheer her up."

I think she bids him goodbye then. I have a suspicion that the goodbye actually comprised of this really long (barf) goodbye kiss. But after a few minutes, I'm surrounded by silence again. I think they left.

Ah . . . sweet seclusion.

I hear the crackling of the gravel again.

Someone's still here!

And when I twist my head around to see who it might be, I see the person I'd been trying to avoid the entire night.

Aiden.

His eyes widen as soon as they meet mine and I feel my insides twist horribly. Just one eye contact—one, and it's enough to trigger all the feelings I'd tried to stash away. They resurface. Their impact is massive. Like a giant wave they drown me, leaving my stomach in painful knots.

I'm the first one to look away. God this is *so* awkward. I hope he's planning to leave. The last thing I want right now is to talk to him. But what happens next, surprises and disappoints me at the same time. He sits down on a chair a few feet away.

What the hell!?

I can't conceal my shock. What does he want? I take out my phone from my pocket and start tapping randomly, pretending I'm texting someone.

God, just leave already!

"So I see you've already exchanged numbers," he remarks.

Hold on, is he talking to me? "Excuse me?!" My head snaps in his direction and I glare at him.

"Where did Wilbert go? I thought you were hanging out with each other? Did he ditch you for some other girl?"

I glare at him, not trying to hide how much I despise him currently. "Care to mention how it is *any* of your business? And his name's *William*, not Wilbert!" I seethe.

"William, Wilbert, no big deal. Nobody cares anyway," he says nonchalantly. Suddenly serious, he continues, "What are you even doing with him Scar, you don't even know him."

"I'm socializing. Ever heard of that term? That's what parties are for?"

He narrows his eyes at me. "This is a serious matter Scar. I don't trust that guy *at all.* I think you should stay away from him."

"Well, then it's a good thing that I don't care what you *think*, because I'm not planning on staying away from him anytime soon." *The nerve of him!* First he breaks my heart, then ends our friendship and ignores me for days, and then he has the guts to come up to me and tell me to stay *away* from someone. I can't even—

"He's a not a good guy Scar! Maybe you find him charming, but don't fall for that. He . . . he dates dozens of girls every year. He's a notorious heartbreaker."

"Does it even matter? I'm just trying to have a good time here. It's not like I want to date him or something."

"Oh, so you don't? Then why were you dancing so intimately with him earlier, huh?"

"For fun! I was just trying to have a good time! And I was too, before you came along and ruined it."

"For fun?!" He spat out. "Who *are* you? Because the Scarlett I knew would have never done something like that; throwing herself at guys!"

My mouth drops open. "I wasn't *throwing* myself at anyone!"

"Look Scarlett, I'm just trying to look out for you. I just want—"

"Aiden, I *don't* care what you want, don't you get it?! I just want you to leave me alone. *Please.* I'm absolutely sick of you. I'd rather cut my tongue off than waste another minute talking you. So please, don't bother me again," I say as coldly as I can muster, and turn to leave. I can feel his gaze burning a hole through my head but I continue to walk away.

* * *

I stumble and almost land on my butt. The room is spinning slightly. *God, beer pong was NOT a good idea.*

I'd been so frustrated with Aiden, I'd ended up playing beer pong to distract myself. Now half an hour later, after drinking from half a dozen cups, my head is spinning. I guess I can tick off another thing on the party bucket list. And if I'm not careful, I'll have to cut off one more—getting full on drunk.

"Oh my god, where *were* you?!" I hear Susan's familiar voice directed towards me. I turn around and see her in front of me, small worry lines marking her forehead. She looks tired, and her forehead has a thin layer of sweat.

"Oh you know, around…" I mumble. "Where were *you*?"

"Dancing in the main area. I thought you'd still be there. You know, with William. But I didn't see you."

"Oh, we left after a while, to go somewhere quieter."

"Did something interesting happen?" She cocks her eyebrow, smirking at me.

I roll my eyes. "Nothing happened."

"Yet," she adds, that silly smirk still adorning her face. Anyway, we'll be leaving soon, like maybe in two hours. You staying with me or what?"

"Uhm . . . I thought I'll go play some truth and dare."

"Are you sure?" Susan asks me, suddenly sounding worried.

I nod. "Yeah, plus I've already completed two things on the list: sexy dancing and beer pong. I'll be able to cut off one more after this."

Susan nods. "Okay, I'll catch you later. Take care, okay? And give me a call once you're done with the game."

I promise her I would, and then I head to where I'd spotted the group of kids playing truth and dare earlier when I'd arrived. I pray that they're still there.

It's not hard to spot them. The number of people has increased. They are all sprawled around a glass table, some lounging on the couches and chairs, other standing. There are many who aren't playing but watching from a distance. I'm just wondering how to include myself in the circle when I notice William's curly mop of blonde hair. He's sitting on the couch, pressed against a redhead, and a guy with jet black hair. I make my way around the circle, and I'm just about to greet William, when he raises his head, and his eyes meet mine. He offers me a warm smile. He asks the redhead to make some room on the couch. I squeeze in between them, passing him a gratuitous smile.

"Ah, so we meet again," he quips, his voice a little above a whisper as he leans towards me.

I feel my cheeks heat up at our proximity. "So, you playing spin the bottle?"

"My chance hasn't come up yet, but yeah. Are you going to join?"

I nod. "I think I will."

I shift my attention from him and look around, taking in everybody's faces, until my eyes stop on a pair of familiar chocolate brown eyes. Well, *this* is unexpected.

What is Aiden doing here?!

I notice him glaring at me, so I pass him an equally hateful look, only to realize he's not glaring at *me*, he's giving the evil eye to William.

Is he following me?!

I can't believe it! I *told* him to stay away from me, didn't I? *Why is he so damn stubborn?!* I bet the reason he's frowning is because I'm with William again. I shift even closer to William just to piss Aiden off. I'll hang off William's arm the whole night if that's what it'll take to enrage him.

"Okay guys, so I'm starting another round, alright?" A brunette with glittery eye makeup announces as she gets ready to spin the bottle. "Just remember, you have to do what you're dared to do, alright? Otherwise the consequences will be severe."

We all nod and then she spins the bottle. The bottle spins four time, before slowing down, its mouth pointing towards a guy with spiky blonde hair. "Truth or Dare?" she asks him challengingly.

"Uhm . . . truth?"

"Have you ever kissed a guy?" She smirks, like she already knows the answer. His face turns crimson. He stutters a bit before his shoulders slump and he slowly nods his head.

"Yes, I have," he replied.

Everyone around us gasps. So he's clearly *not* gay, that's why people are so surprised.

"Hey, don't judge me! It was just an accident. I'm no homo."

The girls with that dramatic eye makeup chuckles before she murmurs "that's what *he* said," causing everyone around them to laugh.

After this the guy who answered the question spins the bottle. My heart's pounding against my chest. *What if it lands on me? What will I choose?*

I almost get a heart attack when the bottle stops in front of me, only to realize it's not pointing towards me, it's pointing towards the redhead next to me. She jumps up excitedly, calling out "dare" before anyone can even ask.

The guy smirks, like he'd been anticipating it all along. "Give me a lap dance, baby girl." My eyes widen, and I silently thank the gods that the bottle didn't land on me. But unlike me, the redhead has absolutely no qualms about giving a random stranger a lap dance. She stands up, exposing her long, long legs, and a dress that barely covers her butt. Within minutes, she straddles him, and is sitting comfortably on his lap. Then she starts rolling her hips in circles, causing the guy to let out a low moan. They're at it for like two minutes, before someone in the crowd tells them to "get a room." They decide to follow his advice, leaving hand in hand. I feel even more nervous now. *What if I get a sleazy dare like that?!* I could choose truth, but what if they ask me something really personal and humiliating?

What have I gotten myself into!?

Aiden

"So truth or dare?" This blonde girl, I think she's a senior asks me. I don't think much. I choose dare.

"Play the rest of the game without your shirt on." She smirks. I roll my eyes. That was relatively easy. Sure, two years ago I would have been completely mortified if I had been given a dare like that. But times have changed now.

I start unbuttoning my shirt. One by one the buttons come off, exposing more and more of my toned chest. My eyes suddenly fall on Scarlett, and I can't help smirking when I realize she's ogling me. She looks away, embarrassed. *I bet she's blushing right now.* Her eyes return to meet mine a second later. I look into them defiantly, challengingly. *Am I making you nervous?* In the dim light I see her swallow nervously.

She's so distracted that she doesn't notice that another round has come and gone. I've spun the bottle, it has landed on someone, I've asked them a question (they chose truth) and now that person is spinning the bottle again. She's staring at her fingers.

"Truth or dare?" a voice breaks her out of her trance. She looks up, only to realize that the bottle's mouth is facing her, and the question is directed towards her. "Uhm—uh—dare," she stammers. Her eyes widen as she realized what she just said. She'd clearly hadn't wanted to choose dare. But it's too late now; the deed has been done, and now she must face the consequences.

"Kiss the person sitting across you on the mouth for three full minutes," the girl who has spun the bottle dares her.

Suddenly alarmed, my eyes dart around the circle, wondering who Scarlett is supposed to kiss, only to realize...

I'm sitting across her. She has to kiss *me.*

She realizes it at the same time as me, and I know she's not happy about it. "Ha-ha *no way*, I'm not kissing *him.*"

"You have to. It's a dare." That girl argues.

I'd be lying if I said I didn't want Scarlett to kiss me. On the mouth. For *three whole minutes.* I know I could intervene. I could say I have a girlfriend who wouldn't approve. I *know* I should intervene. But I kind of want to know what she'll do.

"No." She refuses, shaking her head. "I'll take the punishment. *Anything* but him." The way she says it . . . hurts. She's really good at this, at making the other person feel like absolute shit. Because that's how I feel right now. She's been so hateful and rude towards me the entire evening. But then, it *is* my fault. I hurt her. I deserve this. I deserve everything she throws my way.

"Are you sure? The punishment could be worse."

She nods. "I'm positive."

"Well, in that case, do you see that table? I want you to climb on it, and dance to a song of my choice in front of *everyone*."

Nervousness is apparent on her face. She should have kissed me when she had the chance. Now she'll be making a complete fool of herself in front of *everyone*.

"Can I get a drink?" she asks.

They pass her a bottle of beer, and I stare at her, confused. Scarlett doesn't drink. My mouth drops open when I see her chug down almost half the bottle in one big gulp.

Oh boy, when did that happen?

Scarlett walks towards the designated table, removes her pumps and then climbs onto it. She stumbles a little but balances herself right in time. I notice William looking at her, a sleazy smile playing on his lips. He's *totally* ogling her butt. I just know it! That son of a—

The girl walks over to the DJ and tells him to change the song. It takes me a while to realize that the song she has chosen for Scarlett is Britney Spears' *Toxic*. She couldn't have chosen worse. Scarlett turns around so that her back faces us and starts swaying her hips to music.

As soon as Britney begins to croon the lyrics, Scarlett turns around to face us. Her hair flips dramatically in the air. She looks confident and just about ready to slay it. She sings along to the song, moving her hips sexily and doing complicated dance moves with her hands and legs.

Everyone in the room is looking at her by now, but she's immune to their attention. Her eyes are glued onto William; he's the only she's focusing on. She flutters her eyes and smiles seductively at him from time to time. She doesn't look crazy at all. In fact, she looks . . . sexy. I let out a groan.

Holy shit.

When the chorus comes she raises her hands up in the air and moves them round and round in circles, in coordination with her hips. Everyone has their phones out and are capturing a video of her dance performance. She's going to be all over Facebook very soon.

By the time the song ends, everyone is already applauding. Every single pair of eyes is on her. Sometime during her dance performance, William left his seat on the couch, and now he's standing a few feet away from the table she's standing on, looking at her in awe, like he's seeing her for the first time. He seems to be in some sort of a trance.

I walk up to him and clear my throat to catch his attention. He blinks, suddenly much more aware of his surroundings. He looks visibly embarrassed. *Serves him right.*

I turn away to look at Scarlett now. She's getting off the table, putting on her high heels. I look around and see that almost every guy in the room is ogling her right now.

When did *this* happen? When did she get so bold, so confident? Or had she always been this way, and I, as her best friend, failed to notice?

"She really is something, isn't she?" William speaks up.

I look at him, realizing a second later he's talking to me.

Then I nod, slowly.

She really is.

Chapter Twenty

Scarlett

It takes every bit of my strength to get off the table and back to the couch without falling on my butt. I know I shouldn't have drunk so much! Sure being drunk has its own pros, like not caring that you're making a fool of yourself in front of basically half the school. But there are the cons too: this spinning of the room and this ever-increasing urge to throw up.

The game continues once I return. Since I'd refused to do the dare that I was initially given, I don't get to spin the bottle for the next round. I spend another twenty minutes playing spin the bottle after my dare. Time flies by in the blink of an eye. I spend most of the time talking to William. Something has changed. He keeps smiling at me for no reason.

Once I've had enough of this game, I decide to go and do something else. I'm just about to tell William I'm going when the bottle stops in front of us, its mouth facing William this time.

"Okay William, what do you choose? Truth or dare?"

"Uhm . . . I don't know. Dare? But please don't ask me to dance," he adds, jokingly. Everybody knows he's an amazing dancer.

"Alright then, go and kiss the person you find the most attractive in this room." I notice a lot of people, including both boys and girls looking at William, silently hoping he'd kiss them.

"I can't kiss myself!" he exclaims, looking aghast. Everyone bursts out laughing.

"Ha-ha very funny mister cocky! Let me be specific: kiss the person you find the most attractive in this room other than yourself."

He turns to look at me, offering me another one of his smiles. I smile back. He's been awfully smiling the past few minutes. As soon as I smile back at him, he starts leaning towards me.

Now wait a minute…

My eyes widen. I realize William's going to kiss me just a second before his lips press softly onto mine.

What the—

It's all happening so suddenly, so fast, I don't know what to make of it. My heart jolts painfully in my chest while I sit frozen as his lips caress mine. I sit there, motionless like an idiot while his lips continue to move against mine. I sit there, not doing anything, just waiting for it to stop.

And when it does, I quickly excuse myself and leave. My eyes involuntarily fall on Aiden as I'm walking away. He looks as stunned as I do. My head hurts so much. I massage my temples.

What the hell was that?!

It was so sudden, so out of the blue. Oh god, my chest hurts. I'm not good with surprises, especially surprise kisses. I don't know how to feel right now. On one side, I'm kind of happy that William thought I was the most attractive person in the room.

But at the same time, I don't know if I appreciate being kissed by a stranger like that.

I'm suddenly hit by a realization—I completed two more tasks off the Party Bucket List: I got drunk, and I kissed a random stranger. There are just two more tasks left, so why not go on with it, right?

I call Sharon and we meet outside the kitchen. Noticing my intoxicated state, she gets some lemon wedges from the fridge and makes me suck on them.

"William kissed me," I tell her, grinning like a weirdo.

She spits out the beer in her mouth. "What?! When did that happen!?" she exclaims, looking at me incredulously.

"Two words: Truth or Dare."

Sharon squeals. She actually squeals. "Oh my god! Tell me everything!"

"I'll tell you everything on the way home. Patience, girl."

We decide to play 'Never Have I Ever' next, so I can strike another task off the list. The voice inside my head warns me to not drink any more, but right now, I really don't care. They hand us a cup of beer each. "Here you go then, you'll be needing this."

Just before the game begins Aiden's familiar form (now with his shirt on) takes one of the seats. I gawk at him. *Seriously? He's actually following me? What does he even want?!*

Sharon notices him too, and she doesn't back down from expressing her distaste. She glares at him until he looks away, then she turns to me. "Do you want to leave? Because we can totally do that."

I shake my head in refusal. I'm not going to stop having fun just because of him.

"Okay, I'll start," this girl Ashley, from one of my classes speaks up. "Never have I ever hooked up with someone in a crowded room." I don't drink from my cup. I'm one of the three people who don't drink. The rest of them chug down the beer in a single gulp, Sharon included. I can't help looking at Aiden as he drinks, remembering how just a few hours ago I'd seen him and Hailey lock lips in the middle of the dance floor.

The next person who speaks is Damien, Aiden's friend from the football team. "Never have I ever . . . danced with someone to a sappy love song." My hands shake as I take my very first sip. I clearly remember that one time when I danced with Aiden. It seems like it happened ages ago. Everything is different now. Everything.

I don't see who the next person to say the statement is, but I hear the statement clearly. "Never have I ever shoplifted." I don't touch my drink and neither does anyone else around me, except two girls who happen to be friends. They smirk before downing their drinks.

The next voice comes from the person sitting right next to me. "Never have I ever had a crush on a teacher." The only person to take a sip is Damien, so he's forced to tell everyone about 'this really hot biology teacher' he had in eighth grade.

Before I know it, he's finished telling his story and it's my turn. I wrack my brain for something but can't come up with anything cool. So I finally settle for something a little more...personal. I stare straight into Aiden's dark eyes as I say this: "never have I ever broken someone's heart." This was for him. He knows it was. Aiden the self-proclaimed heartbreaker, who goes around changing the girl on his arm every week, the popular football player who broke his best friend's heart. He lifts his cup and takes a sip. I look at him accusingly. He has no idea how much it hurt. No idea.

From my other side, Sharon's voice comes up next. "Never have I ever fallen for my best friend." I almost choke on my spit. I snap my head to glare at her. "Seriously!?" I mouth. Leave it to Sharon to pull a stunt like that. She smirks at me, before gesturing towards my cup, silently telling me to drink up.

I turn to look at Aiden, the bane of my existence. Our eyes lock, fire meeting fire. No words are spoken yet we end up saying so much more than we'd ever had. Then slowly, we both raise our cups and drink its content. I'm not drinking because of the game anymore. I'm drinking to wash away the taste of his mouth that still lingers in mine. I'm not drinking for fun, I'm drinking to forget.

We both are the only ones drinking this time. Each and every person in this circle is looking at the both of us. I hope their alcohol-infused minds are too chaotic to realize that Aiden and I were best friends, that we both fell for each other.

Why is he drinking though? It's not like he ever felt anything for me.

He's lying, Scarlett. Don't believe him. You never meant anything to him. It had been so easy for him, so easy for him to walk away. He never had feelings for you. It was all about the chase. And once he had you wrapped around his fingers, he left. He left when you needed him the most. He lied.

"Never have I ever had a one-night stand." The voice breaks my train of thought. About half of the people in the circle drink, Aiden included.

"Never have I ever kissed someone in the rain." A few people drink from their cups. I don't, and neither does Aiden. I am a little surprised to see that.

And finally, it's Aiden's turn to speak. The beer in my cup is almost finished by now. He stares straight into my eyes as he says what he says next: "Never have I ever lied about my feelings."

What does he mean? That he wasn't lying, wasn't pretending to have feelings for me all those times when he made me feel special, made me feel like I was the only one?

I don't drink the leftover beer. I don't know about him, but I lied. I still lie. I lie to myself every second of everyday that I don't need him, that I can live without him. I try to convince myself that this emptiness in my heart will go, that one day I'll move on, that I'll get over.

I lie to myself every day, and it still doesn't get easier.

Chapter Twenty-One

Scarlett

After finishing with 'Never Have I Ever', I decide I've had enough of this party. Sharon agrees with me and doesn't try to coax me into staying longer. We call Susan, asking her to meet us at our car. I feel so queasy right now. I swear I'm never going to drink again.

Ten minutes later, we find ourselves in the parking lot, next to Susan's Ford. She isn't here yet. Sharon and I wait for out in the cold. I can feel the cold air against my bare legs, and I just want to get in the car and turn on the heat.

I'm busy typing a text to Susan when I feel someone's presence looming over me. I look up from the screen of the phone and am greeted by William's familiar face. His blue eyes twinkle in the dark as he smiles at me.

"H-hi, I hadn't been . . . expecting you," I murmur, trying to sound unsurprised. Looking at his face inevitably reminds me of the kiss we'd shared during the game of truth and dare. Well, not *shared*—more like *he* kissed me as I stood there motionless, not able to comprehend what's happening.

"Hi," he greets me, smiling softly. "Um…are you leaving?" I nod in response. "So soon?" he asks, surprised.

I shrug. "I have a curfew." *Also, I'm sick of this party. I just want to go home and curl in my bed.*

"Seriously? A curfew? That's so—"

"Lame, I know. But tell that to my mom, why don't you?!"

He looks at me, his expression a mix of pity and sadness.

"Well, at least we go to the same school. Will I see you around?"

"If you'll keep your eyes open, you will," I reply cheekily. *Great, alcohol makes me even more sassy.* "Anyway, what are you doing here? Is there something you . . .?" I trail off.

He nods. "Actually yes, first, I wanted to apologize for kissing you like that. I hope you're not mad or anything. It was just a dare." I look at him pointedly. "I'm not denying that I didn't want to kiss you though." Against my better judgment, I laugh. He visibly relaxes, knowing I'm not angry. "Second, I wanted to ask you for your number."

My eyes widen. I'm not sure I want to exchange numbers with him. I mean sure, he's a nice guy and once upon a time, I used to have a crush on him. But that's a thing of the past. I don't like him like that anymore. Do I really want to get involved with him? Even if it's as a friend? Before I can make up my mind, Sharon grabs my phone, and hands it over to William. "Here, type in your number." She orders.

I stare at her, wide-eyed. *What even . . .*

He doesn't need to be told twice. He does just that, and then gives himself a missed call using my phone, so he has my number. I stare at my phone in dismay. I feel like I've lost control of everything, like everything has slipped out of my clutches *Oh Sharon's so going to get it!* I glare at her. Why do my friends think it is okay to meddle in everything I do? Why do they think they need to push me into everything?

Sharon smirks. She knows I won't get mad at her, at least not in front of William. I turn to William, who smiles at me when he notices I'm looking at him. Then suddenly his face becomes a mask of seriousness, and he steps forward, gently taking my hand in his. He brings my hand to his mouth, pressing his lips softly onto my knuckles.

"I just want you to know that I'm glad I met you tonight. I had a lot of fun and I hope to see you around." His blue eyes trap me in their gaze. He winks at me, smiling flirtatiously, then walks away.

* * *

"Is there something on my face?" I ask Sharon, perplexed. She shakes her head no. I look away from her, only to catch a group of girls staring at me. When they realize I've caught them in the act, they quickly turn away.

What is going on?!

I spot another pair hurriedly looking away as I turn in their direction. I turn to Sharon once again. "No seriously, is there something on my face? Or is it my hair? Is there something…wrong with me?" I smooth the creases on the navy colored frock I'm wearing.

What is everyone's problem!?

"Dude, you look completely fine. Why do you keep asking this?"

I sigh. "I don't know. Everyone keeps . . . staring," I mumble.

Sharon shrugs. "I don't see it, whatever they're seeing. You look normal enough. Maybe it's not you."

But ten minutes later, when Sharon had left for her early morning economics class the stares still hasn't stopped, and I have no idea why. It's not even blatant staring. Its hushed whispers and discreet glances. It's unnerving.

So I do the only thing that comes to my mind: I head to the washroom. Away from all the staring eyes, I examine myself in the mirror. There's nothing stuck in my hair, there is nothing on my face, and my clothes aren't bunched up or folded in someplace they shouldn't be. I look perfectly . . . normal. *Then why—*

The door to the washroom bursts open. My head snaps in the direction of the door, and lo and behold, I come face to face with none other than my ex best friend's girlfriend Hailey. For a second or two we both just gape at each other. Then I force myself to look away, trying not to feel awkward.

What do I do now? Ignore her completely or talk to her indifferently? Taking to her would be like walking on treacherous grounds. It's no news that we both despise each other. To force a conversation between us would be pointless. I'd rather not engage in one. Sooner than later, we'll end up arguing. So I silently pray that she'll choose to ignore me and won't acknowledge my presence.

But of course, that doesn't happen.

Two minutes into touching up her makeup, she goes, "So I saw you with William at that party. Glad to know you've stopped chasing Aiden." My eyes snap onto her. "But no surprise there. I mean now that you're obviously done with Aiden, you *had* to go and grab someone else, yeah?"

I turn to her completely, my eyes narrowing down at her.

"What is your problem!?" I glare at her. The look I gave her is full of hate and disgust, but she doesn't even flinch. Instead, she glares right back at me, her hazel eyes burning aggressively.

And that's when I snap. *What is her problem!? I didn't ask for this, did I?* Did I want to fall in love with my best friend who so happened to be her boyfriend? No! I didn't run after him or force him to kiss or touch me. It just . . . happened. I never wanted things to get so complicated. But they did. And now I'm in love with a guy who doesn't even talk to me, who doesn't even care. Who never cared. It's pathetic.

"What do you *want* Hailey?! Haven't you done enough?" I burst. "Why don't you just leave me alone? Why do you have to find excuses to torment me?! You've got Aiden, and you're happy with him. Isn't that sufficient?"

Hailey's face goes blank for a few seconds. She's like a deer caught in the headlights. And suddenly it all makes sense.

"You're *not* happy You're . . . you're still insecure, aren't you?" I realize. "Everything is *not* good with you and Aiden." I chuckle. "Honestly, I'd feel bad for you if you weren't such a bitch." I wait for her to throw insults at me. Instead, I realize, she's actually *listening* to me. So, I go on. "Honestly Hailey? Maybe you should look a little closer to home. Maybe it's not me, maybe it's *him*. You *know* how he was before he got with you. He was never the kind of guy who could commit to one girl. What makes you think he's changed now? Maybe we both are just deluding ourselves." With that, I turn around and leave. She doesn't call after me. She has no reason to; she knows what I said is absolutely true.

I check the time on my watch and see I'm already twenty minutes for class. I decide to skip it altogether. I hope the teacher won't notice my absence.

After loitering around a bit, I head towards the school auditorium. I'm sure no one would be there this early in the morning. So I can spend the rest of the period here in peace. I push open the large wooden doors and slowly step inside. The auditorium is completely dark except for a couple of spotlights lighting up the stage. When it's clear that its devoid of people, I take out my iPod and plop down on the nearest seat. I'm about to shove the earphones in my ears when I see something that makes me stop.

There's someone on stage, I realize, surprised. It's too dark to clearly see who that person is. Judging by their broad shoulders and lean stature, it has to be a guy. He is propped up on a stool and has a guitar clutched in his hands, his head is bent downwards. He's strumming the guitar strings with the tips of his finger.

I find myself silently moving towards the stage on my own accord. He's so absorbed in playing the guitar, he doesn't realize that there's someone else in the auditorium.

I soon realize, on reaching closer to the stage, that he's not just playing the guitar, he's singing too, albeit in a soft, faint voice.

"And you don't, you don't know
How long I've been waiting for"

I silently ease into a seat and listen to him as he continues to play his guitar and sings the rest of the song.

"But you should, you should know
You're the one I've been looking for"

He continues to sing while I listen with rapt attention. When the song's finally over, he looks up and our eyes meet. I stifle a gasp. I stare at him in awe. Who would have thought it would be *him*! But *of* course it's him. I should've known—

"Scarlett, is that you?"

I slowly stand up, suddenly feeling embarrassed. "What are you doing here, William?"

He stands up with the guitar still in his hands. "Isn't it obvious?"

I walk towards him. "So you sing sappy ballads in your spare time, huh?"

"Ha-ha something like that," he murmurs, his eyes glinting under the spotlight.

"I didn't know you sang so beautifully."

He shrugs again as he gets off the stage, walking towards me now. "Singing is one of the many talents I possess."

"I'd like to see your *other* talents," I respond coyly, surprising myself. *Did I really say that?!* Was that . . . was that my feeble attempt at *flirting*?

"I'd *love* to show you sometime." His mischievous eyes promise me an experience I'll never forget.

"I'll look forward to it."

I'm surprised I haven't turned a deep shade of red yet.

He chuckles and steps closer to me. We're standing chest to chest now, his face a few inches from mine. And suddenly my lungs forget to breathe, and my heart rate picks up. All that confidence from earlier vanishes in the blink of an eye and I step away from him, ruining the moment. I realize I'm the same old me—the same old socially awkward Scarlett who is a nervous wreck around attractive boys. And William is a *very* attractive boy.

William offers to walk me to my next class when the bell rings. Our conversation takes a casual turn and he tells me about his love for music and how writes music in his free time. We both walk together through the crowded hallways, side by side. I notice a few people turn to look at us, girls mainly. I'd like to think it's because of William, but I have a feeling it has more to do with the fact that he's walking around with me today. I suddenly realize that my hanging around with William in front of everyone would only substantiate the rumours.

But you know what? I don't care. Not anymore.

Five minutes into class, our teacher Miss. Summers announces: "a reminder to all of you that the semester projects are to be submitted by the end of next week, and if any of you haven't finished it yet, I suggest you try to wrap it up as soon as possible."

I immediately freeze.

The semester project—salsa—with Aiden.

Crap.

"Shit!" I curse under my breath. Oh god, how could I forget?! Aiden and I are supposed to dance together! And it's too late to even switch projects *or* partners. I am so screwed. I will have to *dance* with him! Well, *if* he'll dance with me. I'm sure he doesn't even want to see my face, and the feeling's quite mutual if I have to be honest. I bury my face in my hands and groan. This couldn't get any worse!

"I'm giving this period off to all of you so that you can discuss your projects with your partners. If you have any queries you can come to me," she declares before sitting down.

Everyone scrambles off to their partner until I'm the only one left sitting by myself. Someone taps on my desk. I look up. Aiden is the last person I'd expected to see, but there he is, towering over me. His deep brown eyes stare coldly into mine.

"We forgot about the project," he says, his voice cold and emotionless.

"I know," I reply curtly.

"We need to practice."

I sigh. "Do we really have to? I don't even want to do this anymore."

"You think *I* want to do this? I'd rather pick up trash or raise disgusting bugs than *dance* with you!" he exclaims.

Ouch.

What he said then shouldn't have hurt as much as it did. But if he's capable of giving up on our friendship for his girlfriend than he probably doesn't want anything to do with me anyway.

Dance is probably one of the long list of things he's disinterested in doing with me.

I sigh and get up, forcing myself to look into his eyes. I almost flinch. He's staring at me so coldly, almost as if *I* was the one who ended our friendship and not him. Not able to bear the constant hate emanating off him, I glare right back at him.

We have exactly fourteen days to choreograph and perfect a four-and-a half minute long dance routine. *How* are we going to do that? In order to accomplish this feat we need to cooperate and try not stab each other while we're in the same room. Despite the numerous dance tutorials available on YouTube, we need guidance, *actual* guidance.

But who can teach us how to dance in such a short time?

The answer comes to me almost immediately. Why, it's so ridiculously simple! Maybe we won't fail after all.

I turn to Aiden. "Meet me at my place at four today. We'll practice."

He shrugs, then turns around and leaves. I turn to my phone.

I need to send an important text.

* * *

Aiden

I ring the doorbell twice before Scarlett comes and opens the door. Her hair is wet; she probably came out of the shower a few minutes ago. She smells like lemon and cinnamon. *Girls and their sophisticated bath products.* She's wearing a baby pink camisole and boy shorts. *Don't stare Aiden, don't stare.*

She shifts aside so I can come in, then closes the door behind me. Judging from how quiet her house is, nobody is home except for her. I turn around to ask her what exactly she has in mind for our dance practice, when I notice she has plopped down on the nearest couch and is busy texting away on her phone.

Okay then.

I stare at her, perplexed.

"Okay so . . . can we start?" I ask, realizing she's not planning to stop anytime soon.

She doesn't even look up. "Nope, not yet. You'll know when we have to start."

Okay, what the heck is that supposed to mean?!

I don't argue with her though. Instead, I sit down on the couch opposite to hers and pull out my phone from my pocket. I glance at Scarlett; she's completely absorbed with whatever she's doing. She has a pair of earphones on and she's bobbing her head to whatever music she's listening, murmuring the words under her breath. She looks kind of cute.

I decide to take my phone out too. I've got a new text; it's from Hailey.

Hailey: Are you free rn?

I quickly type up a reply.

Aiden: Not right now but will be in a couple of hours. Why?

Hailey: Just wanted 2 see u. I miss u.

Aiden: Miss u too babe x

Hailey: So...see you in a few? We can continue where we left off at the party ;)

Whoa . . . so she's really serious about it, huh.

Aiden: You sure about this babe?

Hailey: 100%

Aiden: Cool, cyu soon then. Love you

Hailey: Love youuuu xoxo

Are we ready for this? Are we at that level of our relationship, ready to join mind, body, and soul? Or is this too soon?

Are you hearing yourself Aiden?! When was the last time you put so much thought into doing someone? What's wrong with you?

My train of thought is interrupted by the doorbell ringing. I glance quizzically at Scarlett. What the hell is going on? It's been fifteen minutes since I've arrived, and she's made absolutely no move to start practicing. And now someone's there at her door.

Scarlett gets up, removing the ear phones and heading over to open the door. Half a minute later, I can hear her talking to someone. I'm obviously annoyed. She called me over to practice and all we've done till now is text away on our phones.

She steps away from the door and a tall guy enters. He briefly hugs her, and there's nothing, absolutely nothing, friendly about that hug. His hands linger on her lower back for way too long, and the way he's pressed up against her body is making me want to go over there and pull them apart.

Who is he?

Scarlett turns around to face me, giving me a view of a very familiar face.

"Hey Aiden, you guy haven't met officially but this is William, and he's going to teach us how to salsa."

Chapter Twenty-Two

Scarlett

It has been half an hour since William has arrived. We've been practicing ever since. He completely changed the choreography. He did like the song I chose though, so we're keeping that. He is quite a talented dancer. He looks so focused and determined, I'm impressed. I've been enjoying our practice session so far. Not that I can say the same for Aiden. Unlike me, Aiden looks sour and disinterested. I have to occasionally remind him that I'm not the only one who's supposed to dance, that this project requires teamwork.

"No, no, no, no—not like that! See, you're doing it all wrong. You're not supposed to move your waist like *that*." William instructs me. He walks over to me, forcing Aiden to shift to give him space. He proceeds to plant his hands on either side of my waist, pushing them first left, then right, and then left again in a fluid manner. My cheeks immediately burn with embarrassment. "Move it like this, understood?" I nod.

He returns to where he had been standing initially. Aiden returns to his place too. I can see a scowl plastered on his face.

He's been like this ever since William's arrival. I reluctantly put my hand on his shoulder and let him wrap his around my waist. I seriously don't want to do this *anymore*. Sure, I like him but I don't like him like *this*. I don't like how he's constantly scowling, getting pissed at the smallest of things, and not being cooperative at all.

"And now, start from the beginning, alright?" William instructs. I turn to look at Aiden. I immediately feel my breath hitch. My heart beat quickens. The feel of Aiden's warm breath on my face makes it hard for me to breath. How can I hide my feelings when he gets *this* close to me and makes me feel like *this*? And those eyes; those deep, dark brown eyes will be the death of me.

I force myself to look away.

We both start dancing as soon as the music begins to play. One step back, one step forward; freeze, twist; one step back, one step forward. His back feels stiff under my touch. His fingers are digging into my skin, just a little above my hips. We're not looking at each other.

"Stop, just stop both of you." William interrupts us. We both turn to look at him. I feel a prickle of annoyance. *What now?!* "There's no . . . chemistry, no heat." Aiden and I stare at him incredulously. "Both of your bodies are too far apart, there's a lot of distance. This is salsa, alright? It's like making love on the dance floor. Your bodies need to mold into one. Your steps should leave a trail of fire on the stage. When you hold each other, it should seem like you were *made* to hold each other. *Where's* the energy, the sexiness?" William demands.

Oh I don't know. I think it died, just like our friendship.

"Here, let me show you both exactly what I mean." He asks Aiden to step aside, and then proceeds to takes his place. His hand replaces Aiden's around my waist, and I hold onto him firmly, one of my hands resting on his shoulder and the other holding his hand. William puts his hand on the small of my back and pulls me close. He looks completely poised while I'm close to having a heart attack.

I've never been one of those girls who could be completely natural and carefree in front of hot guys. I've always had trouble talking to attractive boys or feeling comfortable around them. Worst case scenario: I've become a stuttering mess, shutting up completely. And now here's this gorgeous guy standing just a heartbeat away from me. I think I'm going to faint.

The music begins and I start to scramble internally for the dance steps William had taught us a few minutes ago. I don't have to think too much. My hands and feet automatically react to the beats of the song and I start dancing, as if the steps are etched deep into the recesses of my mind. Not a step goes out of place. I'm a little lousy, but all in all we dance in coordination, not missing a single beat and by the time we're done I'm panting for breath, my chest is heaving and a thin layer of sweat covers my forehead.

"And that's how we do it!" William cheers. He looks amazing; not a hair out of place. He doesn't even look tired. No one would be able to guess that he'd just danced energetically to a salsa routine.

I wish I could say the same for me.

Silence settles around us and I realize that the song came to an end about fifteen seconds ago, but William's still holding my hands and I his. His piercing green eyes are two tiny pools of hypnosis. A soft smile is playing on his (really kissable) lips. His eyes shift. They're not looking into mine anymore. I think he wants to kiss me. Does he want to kiss me? Oh no—

William's hands reach up to my face; his fingers gently caress my cheeks before removing a stray curl that's falling over my eyes. Now I might look calm; I might even look at ease. But that is *so* not the case. I just want to run away from the room.

Is he going to kiss me again?

"Okay, we get it now! So can you . . . give us some space and let *us* practice? Because *we* both are supposed to dance in front of everyone together." Aiden's stern voice shatters the silence. I don't need to look at him to know he's annoyed.

I hear foot-steps. A second later, I see Aiden in front of me. I was right. He does look pissed. The question is why. His intense brown eyes are narrowed on to William. "Move," he mutters rather rudely, almost shoving William aside. William looks at him quizzically, probably as confused as I am. "I said *move*." Aiden's hands clasp William's arms, ready to push him if need be. My heart beat quickens. I feel warning bells ringing inside my head. I can sense it, Aiden's anger. It's raving, boiling, burning.

What the hell is his problem?!

"Okay, okay. See? No harm done." William raises his hands up in surrender as he steps back. I gulp, feeling scared. I've rarely seen Aiden like this and honestly, seeing him like this scares me. He's aggressive but never to this magnitude. There have been very few times I've seen him this angry though. Like that one time he punched a member of the swim team because he insulted Aiden's mother. When Aiden gets angry, he loses it completely. He gets violent; he says and does things he doesn't mean to. Things almost always get out of hand, which is why I'm scared something bad might happen.

However, that doesn't happen this time. I sigh with relief when I see William back off, giving Aiden space instead of getting offended by his behavior. He turns to talk to me before walking away.

"I don't think your friend here likes me very much."

"He's not my friend," I say before I can stop myself.

Aiden ignores me. He glares at William instead.

"You're right, *Wilbert*. I don't like you; I don't like you *at all*. If I had any say in this, you wouldn't even be here right now. We *don't* need your help. We were doing perfectly fine before you came along. So why don't you just *leave!?*"

"Aiden!" I gasp. Something is seriously wrong with this boy. I just don't understand.

Aiden

I'm still glaring at William. I don't know why but I dislike him. Oh I dislike him *a lot*. Not just dislike, I think I *hate* him. This has to be a record. I've never developed such an instant hate for anyone. Taking my eyes off him, I turn to look at Scar. Her expression is a mix of shock and fear right now. I know she doesn't approve of my behavior, of how I'm treating him.

I know I have no right to be like this, to interfere. What she does is *her* business. I'm not even her friend anymore. I don't have the right to do *anything* for her. But a part of my heart will always be protective for her, will always look out for her. For me, she'll always be my innocent little best friend, the one I protected like a brother, loved like a best friend and wanted to touch like a lover. And no matter how hard I try, I *cannot* ignore that part of my heart, however small it may be. Not that it is small, no. I think it gets bigger and bigger every day.

"I think . . . I think you should leave," she says, interrupting my train of thought, only to realize a second later that she is talking to me, *me*! I can't fucking believe this!

Okay, I get it. She wants me out of her house. She's worried I'll end up bashing William's head against the wall.

Hmm . . . not a bad idea though; not a bad idea at all. Maybe I should do just that.

"Why should *I* leave?! *I'm* your dance partner. *We're* supposed to practice together."

"I think we've had enough of practice today. We'll continue this later. Now, you should leave. Goodbye." She practically shoves me out of the door and shuts it close behind me.

Great, fucking great! My ex best friend just kicked me out of her house, and now she's inside, all alone, with that psycho.

* * *

Ding!

I look up from my notebook; I'd just been in the middle of completing my math homework. Or rather, I'd been *trying* to complete my math homework. My mind just can't focus.

Who can it be? I know Mom won't be home until later tonight. She is in a meeting with a new client. And my younger brother is off for his karate classes, so he won't be back until later too. I pack up my books and put them away before heading off to open the door.

It's Hailey. I stare at her, confused. *What is she doing here?*

"Aren't you going to let me in?" She cocks her eyebrow.

"Oh um, yeah, come in." I step aside and give her room to walk in. Confusion lines still mark my forehead as I stare quizzically at her, wondering why she's here. I mean no, it's not abnormal for her to turn up at my house. She's my girlfriend after all. But she always calls before she does.

"Is everything okay?" I ask.

A brilliant smile plasters her face. There's something hidden beneath that, something sly and secretive. She walks towards me.

"Is anyone home?"

I shake my head in response. "No, it's just us."

"Good, then we won't have to waste time going up to your room." With that, she gently pushes me onto the couch and straddles my lap. Not giving me a chance to speak, she plants her lips fully onto mine. Her tongue enters my mouth a moment later. It moves with a fervor I haven't seen before.

God damn.

She guides my hands to her hips, urging me to grab them. Her fingers mess up my hair and her lips leave a trail of moisture down my neck. She backs off a few minutes later, looking into my eyes, searching for something in mine. That secretive smile is still playing on her lips.

What is going on?!

She lifts her arms and pulls off her tank top, revealing a lacy black bra underneath. She starts guiding my hands higher, towards her—

Now hold up right there!

I grab her hands, stopping them. "What are you doing?" I ask her, perplexed.

"Kissing you," she murmurs, diving down to press her mouth against mine. I shift my face away.

"Hailey—"

"What?" she asks, sounding annoyed. "We decided to finish off what we'd started, and now we are. So why don't you just let me…" Her fingers expertly unbutton the first few buttons of the t-shirt I'm wearing. Gesturing me to lift my arms up, she strips me off the t-shirt I'd been wearing. The air around us tickles my bare torso and I suddenly remember the series of texts we'd exchanged in the afternoon, when I'd been at Scarlett's place.

Her fingers reach for the buttons on my jeans but I grab her hands. "Wait Hailey—"

She looks up at me, visibly annoyed. *"Now what?!"* she asks, exasperated.

"Are you sure about this? Maybe we should . . . we should wait, take it slower, think it over maybe."

"What *is* there to think over? I love you and you love me, shouldn't that be reason enough?"

"Yes but—" *I don't think I love you.*

She sighs, getting off me, and sitting on the couch adjacent to mine. "What is *wrong* with you?! You'd been excited enough a few days ago. You were barely able to take your hands off me. What changed?!"

I realized I'm not in love with you.

"Nothing, I guess I'm just not in the mood. Look Hailes, I'm feeling really tired right now. We'll do this some other time."

She glares at me. "Serve that bullshit to someone who'll actually buy it. I'm not an idiot Aiden. Something's bothering you and I need you tell me what it is."

I shake my head in refusal. "It's nothing—" How am I supposed to tell her I'm *not* in love with her? That for me, we're not there yet. That it just feels wrong. I can't do this.

"Fine. Don't tell me." She snaps, putting on her top again. Then she starts heading towards the door.

"Wait, you're leaving?"

"Yes. This is the end of our so-called conversation. We won't be talking again until you decide to tell me why you've been so distracted and moody. Goodbye." With that, she pushes open the door she came through and leaves, slamming it behind her.

And that's when, that's *exactly* when it hits me. There, sitting shirtless with my jeans unbuttoned, with the front door open wide apart, I realize why I'd been so distracted.

Scarlett.

Oh god, how could I have left her there all by herself with William!? God knows what he's done. Maybe I should go check—

No Aiden, stop. You don't want to go there and give her another reason to think you're a blithering idiot with no sense of shame.

But—but she's there—alone! With *him*. I *know* I shouldn't have left! I'm so stupid.

Not thinking twice, I grab my t-shirt, button my jeans, and leave the house, locking it behind me. Jumping atop my motorcycle, I put the key in the ignition and bring it to life. The engine sputters bouts of smoke, and I drive away.

* * *

Scarlett

Ding!

"Scarlett! Get the door, will you?"

"Yes, Mom!"

I let out an annoyed huff. Must I always get up to open the door? I'm a busy girl. I've got things to do!

I head down the stairs, looking visibly annoyed and pull open the door. *I swear to god if it's Mrs. Norman again—*

I freeze.

Aiden.

What is he doing here?!

"What are *you* doing here?!" I ask. I turn around and take a quick scan of the couch, and the coffee table near it. Nope, he hasn't left anything here. I turn back around and gave him a questioning glare.

"I—"

"Aiden? Is that you? Oh, I thought it was you! Hello, it's been a while since I saw you, hasn't it?" My mother, ever the social butterfly, interrupts me. "Why don't you come in?"

"Actually, he was just leav—"

"Oh I'd love to, Mrs. Stevenson," he responds, giving me a pointed look before crossing the threshold and entering the house.

Damn it.

"So how you've been? And Mr. and Mrs. Walkers?"

"I've been great, and so have they. It's really nice to meet you again. Mrs. It really *has* been a while. I think the last time we met when Scarlett brought you to school for the annual parents-teacher meet."

"Yes, yes, I remember. You should come here more often!"

I just gape at the two of them. Why does my mom have to be so nice and chatty with everyone?!

"Okay, give me just five minutes; I'll fix you a nice snack."

"Really Mrs. Stevenson, that's not necessary," Aiden protests. I feel like banging my head against the wall. No seriously, *why* is my mom so . . . so damn warm and welcoming and talkative?!

"Oh alright then. But you better come around sometime for dinner. I'll be mad if you don't," she tells him.

"Oh, I definitely will. You can count on it."

She nods at him pleasantly before walking away, finally leaving us alone.

Wasting no time, I turn to Aiden. "

Well?! Are you going to tell me why you're *here*?" I try hard not to raise my voice.

"I just wanted to see…"

"See what?!"

"If he was done giving you your private dance lessons! I was worried!" He growls.

Now hold up *right* there. He was…worried? What even—

"What makes you think he stayed? He left right after *you* did." I stare at him incredulously. "And what do you mean you were worried? Aiden, William is a *good* guy, okay? You *really* need to change your attitude when it comes to him. You were so rude to him this afternoon. Honestly, what is your deal?!"

"I don't trust him Scar, he's not—"

"Stop! You don't even know him."

"And you *do*?!"

I let out an exasperated sigh. "*Aiden!* Stop! Honestly, he's just trying to help us with the dance and everything. Can you at least *try* to be civil to him? He doesn't *need* to do this. He's only helping us because I requested him to. And we *need* him. Please remember that before you start running your mouth the next time William's with us."

"I'm not making any promises. If he starts—"

"Sorry for the delay kids, I started making coffee." My mom returns from the kitchen, laying a tray of cupcakes and two cups of steaming hot coffee on the coffee table.

I'm worried Mom is planning to stay and make conversation with Aiden. But she spends only a minute or two asking how his studies are going before retreating back to her room, leaving me alone with him.

He stares at me awkwardly for a second or two, before taking a sip of the coffee. After a long stretch of silence, disrupted occasionally by the slurping, Aiden speaks up. He looks calmer than he had been. A faint smile grazes his lips and he speaks up, "So, how have you been?" he asks me casually.

I almost answer him back, answer him back with the way too overused 'oh I've been good.'

Almost.

Except, I realize I'm *not* good, that it's a lie. Me? I'm miserable and melancholic. It's so hard to fall asleep at night. His face plagues me every time. Waking up seems like an impossible feat. Going to school every day and pretending I'm alright, even more. So me? Oh, I'm not good, not at all. And the reason? Oh the reason is sitting right in front of me, running his fingers gently through his messed up hair as he casually asks me how I am.

So no, I don't tell him how I am or how I feel. Because these days I don't feel anything at all. It's like I'm trapped in a glass case, locked away from the rest of the world. It's all grey and bland, the colors have abandoned me. Everything's empty and numb. It's a side effect of giving away too much of your soul, for loving someone too hard and too intensely, for handing someone your fragile heart on a silver platter, only to have it smashed to pieces.

"Why are you doing this Aiden? No, I'm genuinely curious. Why are you asking me how *I* am? We're not friends anymore. We're nothing! You made sure of that. So what makes you think I want to sit here and talk to you about how I've been?!"

He's hurt; I can see it in his eyes. But he's not shocked, no. Like he'd seen it coming, like he'd totally expected me to blow up on him. I feel a tiny tinge of remorse, but that quickly vanishes. I'm *so* done. I'm so done letting him get away with doing whatever he wants. Who does he think he is? What did he think would happen? That'd I'd start talking to him, sidelining everything that has happened over the past few weeks? No, definitely not.

"Fourteen days from now, that is, in *exactly* two weeks, we'll perform the dance, after which, I assure you, you'll never have to talk to me again. We'll be free from each other for good. I'll be able to go back to my life and you to yours. No more uncomfortable and awkward situations. I won't be a problem to you or your girlfriend; everyone will be happy."

His eyes widen ever so slightly, the hurt in them intensifies. But I don't care anymore, remember?

"Just two weeks Aiden, just two weeks."

Chapter Twenty-Three

Scarlett

"Are you nervous?"

I resist the urge to roll my eyes for the nth time. No seriously, *why* does everyone I talk to asks me this? *Of course,* I'm nervous! My stomach is a mess. I have to constantly remind my lungs to breathe. My palms are slightly clammy; my heart thinks it's a good idea to beat *really* fast and I swear to God if *one* more person asks me if I'm nervous I'm going to choke them using their own entrails.

"Nah, I'm fine," I murmur.

"You look really, *really* pretty by the way."

I smile at her. "All thanks to you. Thanks for letting me borrow your dress."

She shakes her head dismissively. "It's no big deal, honestly. Now you just go out there and burn the stage, you hear me? *Burn it.*"

I can't help laughing out loud. "Ha-ha, thanks for the encouragement Sharon." She hugs me goodbye and leaves.

Good, now I can panic in peace.

My stomach hurts. I am a nervous wreck right now. I just want to run away. I swear I will never do something like this *ever* again. With my heart in my throat, I take a step forward and peek from behind the curtains. The auditorium isn't completely filled. It's not even a real crowd, just a bunch of bored teenagers. I shouldn't be so worried, only the juniors will be coming.

What's the worst that could happen anyway? Our performance could suck; we'd get bad grades, so what?

And you might end up making a complete fool of yourself in front of sixty people, so there's that.

I just love my brain and how supportive and encouraging it is. Just love it.

I tug at the edge of the emerald green dress I'm wearing, trying to make it longer. The dress is slightly tight on me, since Sharon is so skinny. It keeps sticking to my body and riding up. I run my fingers down the shimmery silvery green sequins adorning the bodice of the dress. I never, *never* wear something so bright and shiny; it's just not my thing, you know? But here I am, all decked up. I'm going to stick out like a sore thumb, I just know it. But I guess, that's the whole point of it.

My hair is secured in a tight, elegant bun resting firmly atop my head. I glance at the pair of dark green four-inch heels I'm wearing. I hope I'm able to balance myself in them. How humiliating would it be if I end up falling off the stage while dancing just because of them?

The door leading to the backstage area creaks open. I turn around.

Aiden's here.

He looks so classy in a crisp white shirt, and a pair of skin-fit black pants. His hair's all gelled and slicked back for a change. In short, he looks really, really, sexy.

And I should stop checking him out right about now.

I turn back around.

Our performance is towards the end. A few more people have to perform on the stage, be it singing, reading poetry or acting out a play. Within minutes the back stage is occupied by some more teenagers, who slowly trickle onto the stage as their turn comes.

My nervousness increases.

Half an hour, for half an hour I sit glued to the chair, awaiting my turn. For half an hour I feel all choked up and shaky. Then finally, the stage assistant rushes over to us telling me it's time.

I try not to puke.

Well, there's no point in sitting here and scaring the heck out of myself. Might as well get up and ready to humiliate myself.

What if I forget a step? What if I slip and have a wardrobe malfunction? What if—

"Stop overthinking Scarlett. It's going to be alright," Aiden's voice pulls me out of my thoughts.

"H-how did you know I was overthinking?"

"You were doing that thing with your face where you slightly scrunch up your eyebrows and stare off into space, looking slightly constipated," he murmurs.

I gasp. "I was not!"

He chuckles. "Whatever you say Scar, whatever you say."

I want to stop talking to him now. Today's the day. After this, we'll be done with each other for good. So yes, I want to stop talking to him and just get on with it, but I can't. I'm such a mess right now and I don't even understand why. So, I don't stop.

"But . . . what if we—" I start speaking.

"We won't. *Stop* doubting yourself. You're going to do great. *We're* going to do great. We've practiced a lot after all, haven't we?"

He's got a point there. We've worked our ass off the past two weeks: danced, danced, danced until our feet were sore and our muscles cramped. Aiden surprisingly was civil towards William, though not necessarily polite. We had regular practice sessions and mastered all the steps.

So why am I so nervous?

The curtains start to rise and I feel my heart bungee jump in my chest. My hands start to shake; my legs tremble. *Oh god I need to get a grip.* Out of nowhere I feel Aiden's fingers intertwine with mine. The shaking stops. I look at him, trying to ignore the butterflies in my stomach. He squeezes my hands reassuringly. Warmth spreads through my insides and I feel myself relax.

"We're going to slay it together. I promise."

I find myself smiling.

"Aiden?"

"Yeah?"

"Please don't let me fall on my butt this time."

"Even if I promise to give you a sensual butt massage later?"

"*Even* if you promise to give me a sensual butt massage later."

He chuckles "Yes ma'am!" A full-fledged smile adorns his face now. The warmth in my belly doubles up.

Our eyes meet and for a few seconds everything vanishes. The crowd, the curtains, the empty stage—they all vanish. All I can see is his blindingly beautiful smile and his soft browns eyes that are currently looking at mine. For a few short seconds, I'm transported back in time and it almost feels like we're back to where we began, back to when I was all about him, and he was all about me and it was us, just us.

Before I know it, we're both walking onto the stage, hand in hand. The initial nervousness has subsided and all I can think about is that this is it, the very last performance, after which we won't have to dance again. After which, there will be no more after-school practice sessions. I won't have to wrap my arms around him as we move and pretend my heart is functioning normally. This is it.

The beats of the music begin, echoing through the sparsely populated auditorium. Under the influence of the music and Aiden's touch, my body comes alive. He slowly wraps his arm around my waist; his other hand clasps mine. He pulls me closer, our bodies collide, and we freeze in this position. Two seconds later, he twirls my body round and round, before I take a leap and he catches me. We freeze again. He puts me back on the ground, and we start doing the basic step: one step forward, one steps back.

The dance moves come naturally to me, like they've been encoded into my system. My muscles relax; my posture improves. My body movies fluidly, as I let the music possess me. Aiden and I dance in complete coordination, not a step out of place and not a single missed beat. The dance is very sensual and our bodies are always in close contact.

And then, the very last part of the dance sequence arrives. We weren't able to completely master this step during the practices. But it was the most beautiful part of the choreography so we didn't change it.

I look straight into Aiden's eyes; he nods at me, encouraging me to go ahead with it. It's now or never.

And so, I charge towards him, running as fast as my four-inch heels will allow me to. At the very last moment, I take a leap. I press my eyes shut, waiting for my body to hit the ground. But it never does. Aiden, like he's supposed to, grabs my body on time. I instantly wrap my legs around his waist. His hands go under my back and support my spine. Then he starts to spin.

Round and round he goes. I refuse to let the dizziness get to me, I refuse to loosen my grip. After two full circles, he lifts my body up in the air and I stretch out my arms, striking a pose. He circles twice again. Then he tosses me up in the air. I don't scream. I don't let the fear invade my heart. I just close my eyes and relax.

I trust him; he'll be able to pull this. I trust him. He won't let me fall.

And I don't fall, he doesn't let me fall. He catches me in his arms. I gasp; surprised we succeeded in doing this. I open my eyes and find myself staring straight into his. And suddenly it's like I'm in a movie and someone has hit the slow motion button. The beat of the music, the murmur and applause from the crowd are almost inaudible now. What I can hear is my tumultuous heart. It's beating so hard, so fast, so intensely. What I can hear is the sound of Aiden breathing. In, out, in, out, the air leaves his body in a whoosh, causing his chest to rise up and down. The world around me is a kaleidoscopic blur. But Aiden's eyes, the brown in them is so vivid and dark. My body can sense nothing but him. It's like his beautiful entirety has consumed me.

Our lips are just a few inches apart. It'll be so easy for me to cross this little distance and claim his lips for my own—so easy. But I can't. It's like I'm in a trance. Everything's within my reach but I can't grab it. In that moment I am nothing; nothing but scattered fragments of my whole, floating away in the wind. I am not a solid, rigid being, but a fluid soul; melting in the arms of the one I love. In that moment I'm too much, and too less. Too empty, too hollow but completely full at the same time. In that moment, I am nothing and everything.

And I have a feeling that I'll never get to feel this again, something so intense, so powerful. It's enrapturing, maddening, overwhelming, all-consuming. It's perfect. And I'll never get to experience this again.

Dark, and depressing thoughts cloud my mind. My heart thuds painfully to a stop. The flames running through my veins, scorching my chest vanish. The air of electricity trapping us in its cage seizes to exist. And just like that, our moment's gone, never to come back again.

Aiden

I feel my heart drumming painfully against my chest. What *is* this I'm feeling? My lungs have forgotten what air is. My heart has been running a marathon. My skin is tingling from head to toe. I've never felt this way before. Maybe it's because of the dancing.

Or maybe it's Scarlett.

My heart jumps in my chest when I realize her body is still wrapped around mine, chest to chest, skin to skin, our fingers intertwined. Her magnetic eyes are fixated upon me, long lashes grazing her cheeks. Her hair is an untamed mess; escaped locks encircle her beautiful face. Her legs are wrapped sensually around me, her warm breath falling on my face. Her chest rising and dropping rapidly in a rhythmic fashion; it's like music.

What are you doing to me Scarlett?

Now that dance, that was quite steamy. I know the people around me agree. I can see it in their awestruck eyes. Throughout the performance everybody had been screaming and clapping, blowing whistles and recording the performance. The performance had been so fiery. But now it's over. The *project* is over. No more after-school practice sessions, no more excuses to spend time with her. When I decided to distance myself from her, I'd thought it would be easy, that I'll be able to do it. And once I regained control over these unexpected feelings, things could go back to normal.

But no, I had to screw things up. So now, all that I'd been feeling? It's increased a thousand-fold. I always had an inkling that my feelings for Scarlett were more than just platonic. I tried to repress them though, whatever they were. I always saw them as an unnecessary baggage, an unexpected attraction that would soon pass. I was, obviously, wrong. Now things have gotten so out of hand that Scarlett won't even look at me. This conversation we had. This . . . moment we shared, it's probably never going to happen again.

Suddenly Scarlett grabs my hands. I look up at her, surprised; only to see that she's facing the crowd ahead. She tugs at my hand, beckoning me to take a bow. And so, I bend my head low, alongside her. Our performance has come to an end.

We turn around and head backstage. It's all so bittersweet. On one hand I feel this giddiness, this little bout of happiness, bubbling in the pit of my stomach, making me want to jump and shout. Maybe it's because of how successful the performance was, or maybe it's because today was the first time in weeks Scarlett and I spent not shouting or fighting but just living in the moment together.

But then there's this other feeling; the dark, melancholic one. It keeps whispering in my head, telling me there's nothing to be happy about. In fact, today, this day that I'm so happy about, is nothing but the end of something beautiful, something important.

No, no I'm not going to let that happen. This isn't how it ends.

I'm going to apologize to her. I'm going to apologize for everything I've put her through. In the end, it doesn't even matter if she feels that way about me or not. All I need is her. If just being her friend is what it takes, so be it!

I'm going to make everything okay. I have to.

Determined, I follow Scarlett backstage, only to find a certain annoying male specimen waiting for us there: William. I immediately feel the familiar flare of anger run through my veins. I swear to god this guy makes my blood pressure rise!

He's smiling, flashing his dazzling white teeth. Even his god damn teeth are perfect. I mean, is there *anything* about him that doesn't scream perfection?! No wonder Scarlett likes him.

Yes, she likes him. I mean, it's *way too* obvious. And why wouldn't she? He's so . . . clean and well managed and poised. Compared to him, I'm such a mess.

Scarlett runs up to him. He instantly wraps his arms around her, lifting her little body up in the air and twirling it around. I hear her laughing. She sounds *so* happy.

"I saw your performance. It was phenomenal!" he exclaims.

She jumps up and down excitedly, squealing girlishly. "You did!? No but seriously, were we really that good?"

William nods. "Yes, you were. I've taught you well, dear student." He winks flirtatiously at her, patting her head.

Oh hell no! I'm not letting him ruin this moment for us. This moment . . . it belongs to us, to me and Scarlett. *We're* supposed to get excited and hug each other and congratulate each other for rocking the stage out there. William is nothing but an intruder, an unwanted presence who is distracting her.

I'm about to walk over to them, but something stops me. For the first time it hits me that maybe, just maybe, *I'm* the one who is unwanted. I look at them, standing so close, laughing and talking animatedly, and it's not too hard to guess who is unwanted here. It's me. *I'm* the one who should leave, not William.

And it's not fair. It's not fair that he gets to make her so happy while all I get to do is see her smiling from afar. He gets to hold her in his arms and hug her, while I stand here wishing I could be in his place.

Oh it's completely fair Aiden. You hundred percent deserve this.

All that has happened, *everything* that has happened, it's just been a big fat mistake. It wasn't my intention to hurt her. It never was. How could I ever think of hurting *her*?! But somehow, I ended up doing just that.

And suddenly I feel like I'm losing her. It's all so strange and sudden, I don't even see it coming. I'd probably lost her that night itself, when I told her we couldn't continue being friends. But for some reason, I feel that sensation of loss right *now*. In this moment, I can feel her slowly slipping away.

I see him caress her cheeks and tuck a strand of stray hair behind her ear. I hate the way he touches her, so softly, savoring every second of it. Because he knows, he knows how precious she is.

I see him lean in. Their lips connect. She doesn't pull away. There's something so vivid and about this particular movement. I know I'll remember it for a long, long time. This moment right here, it changes everything.

He understands what he has. He understands what I didn't. And I hate it, but there's nothing I can do about it.

Scarlett

I step away from William, surprised. Now that's the *second* time he's caught me off guard kissing me like that. My cheeks burn red with embarrassment.

"What was *that* for?" I ask.

"I don't know . . . I'm just really happy I guess?"

"Happy?"

"Happy to see you, to be standing here and talking to you."

I feel nervous butterflies swarm my belly. This is so new for me. Someone actually *wants* to kiss me. I make someone happy just by talking to them. And I guess it's *okay* for William to feel this way, to want to kiss me. There's nothing wrong with it. Maybe he likes me, who knows.

So I don't scold him for kissing me out of the blue. However, I don't make a move to kiss him back again. I don't want to give him the wrong idea. He's nice and all, but I don't feel that way about him.

"You were *really* good out there. I know I've said it before, but really, your performance was amazing!" William's just trying to fill the silence, and I appreciate it.

"I never thought I'd be able to do it, you know? And that too so well. But I guess I was wrong. It wouldn't have been possible without Aiden though." I turn around to face Aiden, only to see he's not there.

Where did he go? Just a minute ago he was standing right there and now he's gone? I feel slightly hurt to think he left without saying goodbye. I'd really thought things could be normal now. Yes, I'd thought of nothing but distancing myself from him once the project came to an end. But something changed.

Something changed when he held me in his arms and danced with me like it was the end of the world. I felt . . . special, wanted, *needed*. Something changed. And for just a few seconds, it felt like I meant something to him; that maybe he felt the same way. That he wanted me as much as I him. And somehow, the thought just worked its way up to my mind that things will go back to normal now. No more fighting; no more awkwardness. I'd been *so* sure that we could work things out and be friends again. I guess I'd been wrong.

I feel my mood deteriorate.

I guess I was wrong. He obviously didn't feel the way I thought he did.

"Uhm . . . where did Aiden go? Did you see?" I ask William.

"I didn't see him leave, since I was talking to you. I don't know. But you know what I *do* know?"

"What?"

"That this occasion calls for a celebration."

"Celebration?"

"You know, you were an amazing student, and this performance pretty much proved it. So…I want to take you out for lunch, or dinner? Whatever suits you. My treat!"

"Why should *you* treat me? I should treat you with a dinner since *my* dance went well."

"But you're my favorite student, so *I'll* treat you."

I chuckle. "And I suppose you've had a lot of students to yourself?"

His eyes twinkle. "A few," he murmurs secretively. "So tomorrow evening works for you? You free?"

"Absolutely."

"It's a date then."

This guy . . . he's so freaking smooth. I never saw it coming.

"William, you *do* know I don't feel that way about you…"

"Yet. You don't feel that way about me yet. Give me a chance Scarlett, let me change your mind," he says, his demeanor oozing confidence. "Just one harmless date, that's all I want."

I sigh. "Well . . . alright then. It's just one harmless date after all."

Chapter Twenty-Four

Scarlett

It wasn't just one harmless date.

It was more than one. And they were definitely not harmless. One followed the other, and then another. I'd promised myself that this would be a onetime thing, but William succeeded in coaxing me to go out with him every single time. I can't say I minded very much. I liked spending time with him, talking with him. We didn't have a whole lot in common but William was a great listener, and for the first time I came to realize how much I actually had to say.

Our dates were fun. The first time, he took me out bowling followed by a quick dinner, nothing fancy. We bonded over bowling pins and burgers. He'd lost at bowling from me, and I'd teased him about it endlessly. The date was friendly and light and I enjoyed myself. He didn't try to kiss me when the night ended. I guess he was trying to take things slow. Weird thing is, I didn't really mind.

Once it was over, I thought—there, that's that. We went on a date and now it's over. I can head back to my normal, stable, uneventful life. I'll probably not go on another date for a while. And again, I was okay with that. Why? Because going on dates is a stressful affair. *Boys* are a stressful affair. Especially attractive ones. So I was happy knowing that the much needed peace and calm would return to my life now.

But William called me three days later telling me about this really cool Pizzeria, that I *must* visit with him. And he was being so persistent and I wanted to say no, but the words got stuck in my throat. So I just agreed instead.

After another three days, amid the heavenly smell of baked garlic bread, and warm melting cheese, William and I spent yet another evening together, getting to know each other. Again, it was fun. Every now and then, we'd be shrouded by a blanket of awkward silence, but it never lasted very long. He made sure of that.

When it was time to leave, he asked me if we could take a picture together, you know, for the memories. I obliged. So we took a selfie, smiling widely at the camera. His arm was wrapped around my shoulder the entire time.

After finishing up our pizza, we went for a walk on the beach. It felt completely wrong. This beach . . . this was *our* thing, Aiden and mine. He was the one I came here with at night. It felt completely wrong to be here with some other boy. But here I was, with William, holding his hand and pretending I wasn't just waiting to get the hell outta here.

It's nothing personal. It's just this place. It reminded me of the night Aiden and I lay here on the sand; of how he kissed me when he got drunk. I'll never forget how it felt when he cupped my face in his hands and kissed me like I meant something to him.

By nine, I was back at home, curled up in my bed, ready to fall asleep. Little did I know of the nightmare tomorrow would bring.

* * *

The stares begin as soon as I enter the school premises. "What is it now!?" I mutter under my breath, feeling extremely annoyed. I am getting really sick of this. *Why can't someone just come forward and tell me?*

And then someone did, no two people did: Kayla and Andrea.

"When were you going to tell us?!" they exclaim as soon as they see me.

"Tell you what?" I ask, genuinely perplexed.

"That you and William are dating!"

I gape at the two of them. "How—how do you know we—did you see us together?"

"What? No!"

"Doesn't matter anyway. *Everyone* knows you both are dating," Andrea explains.

"But how?"

"Aren't you on Instagram?"

"No, I'm not very photogenic, remember? What's that got to do with it anyway?"

"Everything," Sharon pipes in, suddenly arriving out of the blue. "Here, check it out." She hands me her cell phone.

I look at the screen and feel the air leave my body. It's that picture of us—William and my selfie from last night. William uploaded it on Instagram. There's also a caption beneath it which says:

'We look so cute together #datenight'

I don't know how to react. On one hand, I feel really flattered that he's showing off the fact that we're dating. But, that's the problem, we're *not* dating. It was just two dates and if I have my way, there won't be any more. But now William has blown things out of proportion and everyone thinks we're together or something.

Before I can fully react, the school bell lets out a shrill, piercing noise that tears through the entirety of the school. First period has just begun.

I hand Sharon her phone back. "Ugh, never mind. I'll deal with this later. I need to get to class."

"See you at lunch! We'll be waiting for the juicy details." Kayla teases before bidding me goodbye.

I almost run to class. My problems didn't stop when class started. It only got worse.

As if everyone's reaction wasn't enough, Aiden decides to start acting like a jerk.

I see him sitting across the room, in the front, with his back against the wall, sitting sideways. I feel his gaze follow me, as I make my way through the classroom. When I look up to meet his eyes, he quickly turns away, his visage a cold uncaring mask.

I decide to ignore his weird behavior for now and take a seat at the back of the classroom. The teacher drawls on and on about the structure of atom—about protons, electrons, and quantum numbers. I feel my eyes getting heavy, sleep slowly creeping upon me.

If I could just keep my eyes open for another fifteen minutes...this class is almost over.

* * *

I slowly open my eyes.

Empty. The classroom is empty.

Alarmed, I fish out my phone and look at the time. It's been ten minutes since second period started.

I slept. Shit!

I quickly get up, scrambling to collect my book, backpack and notebook.

My eyes fall on a lone figure, sitting at the corner of the class, with his head down on the desk. Aiden is fast asleep.

I can't believe it! We both fell asleep and nobody thought of waking us up.

I slowly walk up to him. He looks so peaceful, so serene, with his wavy dark hair falling on his face, and his lashes resting gracefully on his cheeks. He looks like an angel; a really hot angel.

I almost hate myself for waking him up, but I have to. I can't let him sleep and miss all his classes. He'll land up in a lot of trouble. So I shake him gently, hoping he'll open his eyes. I speak out his name a couple of times.

After a minute or two, he stirs. His eyes open slowly, his gaze falling squarely on mine. I feel my breath hitch. The dark swirls that are his eyes look right at me, and for a few confusing seconds, I feel as soft as mush. Brown, so brown. I feel all the emotions I'd buried somewhere deep, come up, like a big, violent ocean wave that refuses to be tamed.

"Scarlett?" he murmurs groggily, sounding confused.

"Get up, you fell asleep in class," I reply, trying to ignore how fast my heart is beating right now.

He sits up, stretching his toned arms above his head, causing the t-shirt he's wearing to ride up and reveal a few inches of his skin. I pretend I didn't just gawk at him like a perv.

"So . . . I fell asleep?"

"Yeah, pretty much."

"Why are *you* here and not in class?"

"Same reason, I fell asleep too."

He looks amused. For a second, I want to mirror his expression, smile that goofy smile so apparent on his face. Then I remember how he left right after our dance performance ended; without even saying goodbye, like things between us were truly over; how he's been ignoring me this whole week, not even looking at me once, much less exchanging words. Even today, he'd been so cold when I entered the class. Why does he always act so strange?

It's like he's mad at me half of the time and decides to act cold just to hurt me. But that tough, rude exterior melts away when we come face to face.

Why is he like this? Does he enjoy this strange game we keep playing? I'm so tired of this.

So I shun the urge to smile, turn around and start walking away.

Aiden

"Hey Scar, wait!"

She stops, rather reluctantly it seems. For a minute it felt like she was going to ignore me and walk right away. But she didn't. She stopped.

The realization of what we've become, the harsh reality, hits me full force when our eyes meet. I hate the way we've become. But so much has happened in so little time, and now even thinking about going back to the way we were seems impossible.

A question has been gnawing me since last night. In fact, not since last night, but last week. I don't think I can take it anymore. I *need* to know.

"Can we talk?" I ask her.

I see her blank expression dissolve into one full of anger and irritation. *Well, I should've seen that coming.*

"Oh, so *now* you want to talk? Where were you the past week?! In fact, *where* were you once our performance ended!? You just—just left. Why?!"

"I had to go," I murmur; the confidence I had earlier vanishing in an instant.

"You *had* to, or you *wanted* to!?"

I needed to.

Because the way I felt when I saw you with William, was downright unbearable. Because I'm stupid, and selfish and an idiot. Because I—

In the end, I don't end up saying any of that. I know I should have, but I don't. My mouth has its own mind, it seems. "I was just trying to give you and William some privacy, seeing as you both were busy kissing each other." I fail to hide the bitterness in my voice when I say these words.

"And you were giving us privacy, huh? For how long? A week!?" She demands.

Of course, I hadn't meant to go MIA *completely*. I could've finished what I'd initially set out to do—I could have apologized some time during the next week.

But I didn't.

I just couldn't face her. I felt angry.

I just . . . felt betrayed, you know? I felt abandoned and forgotten. I know I was over reacting, but that's how I felt.

But most of all, I felt replaced.

"You know what? At this point, I don't even care. Just get on with it. What do you want?" she says.

"I need to know—I need to know if you are with William. Are you together?" I finally ask.

"*Well,* as you can see . . . I'm quite alone right now. So I'm obviously not *with* William."

I give her a pointed look. "Seriously? This is the time you decide to get cheeky? You *know* what I mean."

Now it's *her* turn to give me a pointed look, as if saying 'really?! That's what you think?' She opens her mouth to say something, but then changes her mind at the last moment.

Shaking her head, as if I'm testing her patience, she goes: "honestly Aiden, I don't see how this is any of your business. I'm not talking about this with you, so just leave me alone."

Before I can so much as get another word out of my mouth, she leaves. Now I don't want to be all dramatic and chase after her and yell at her to stop, because I know Scarlett can be quite stubborn when she wants to.

So I drop it for the time being. Knowing one way or another, she'll eventually give in.

But it's hard to not think about it. Not if every second person is talking about it. I hear two girls passionately discussing beside my locker, whether William is dating "that junior" or not, discussing as if their very life depended on it.

"She's rather plain, don't you think? William can't be dating *her.*"

"Yes but look at the picture he uploaded! It clearly states they went on a date together."

They both lean over the phone one of them is holding, in order to get a better look.

"Honestly, even if they *are* dating. They're probably not in a serious relationship. You know how William is. He's probably just using her to satisfy his needs."

My curiosity piqued, I softly tap on the shoulder of the girl standing nearest to me. Both of them look up from the phone and at me.

"Um, can I take a look at that?"

"At what?"

"*That,*" I say, gesturing towards the phone. She rolls her eyes.

"Yeah, sure."

Scarlett's face greets me from the screen of the phone. But it's not just *her* face. William is right next to her, his cheeks almost touching hers as they both smile at the camera.

I feel annoyance bubble up inside me almost instantaneously. *God I hate him. I don't even know why. He's just really annoying.*

My gaze falls on the caption below the photo. I wrinkle my nose as I read it, worry lines creasing my forehead.

'*We look so cute together #datenight*'

"No, you don't look cute together," I mutter, irritated.

"I know right?! She's *so* ugly. She doesn't deserve someone as gorgeous as him, don't you think?" The girl hears me, and says in response, taking back her phone.

Her tendency to repeatedly insult Scar gets on my nerves. I decide to shut her up. "Actually no, she's beautiful. Like, *really* beautiful. I have no idea how *he* scored a girl like that. If she was single, and there was even a *little* chance that she'd date me, I'd get with her before you could blink your pretty little eyes."

Both of them gape at me for a second or two before throwing me a weird look and walking away.

Then in the locker room in gym, I catch a bunch of guys discussing whether "that short chick" William is dating now is hot or not. Two of them think she is.

"William just doesn't date anyone. She's probably good in bed."

"I think she's kinda hot. I wonder why I never noticed her before though. Is she a new student?"

I immediately walk away, before I end up losing my cool and punching one of them. I know all too well how vulgar and crass the conversations in the boys' locker room are. I do not want to witness this particular conversation whose main subject happens to be my best friend.

All the same, despite trying to not let my curiosity get the best of me, the question keeps gnawing me. Even though the evidence, the facts are staring me right in the face, I refuse to believe it. I continue to cling onto the hope that maybe, just maybe, all of this is a lie.

I spend the lunch alone, in the football field, sitting by myself on the bleachers, going through the photos of Hailey and me that are stored in my phone.

It's been about three weeks since Hailey and I had a proper conversation. Ever since that day, when she'd walked away because I was, and I quote "distracted and moody", we haven't sat down together properly and talked, never mind kissing and all those other things couples do.

We did talk twice via text, only to end up arguing.

We'd initially decided to take a small "break" from each other, let things cool down, give each other some space. But I'd recently been thinking of making this break more permanent.

It just didn't feel right—being with her. There was something missing. And it didn't feel like something teensy that would appear over time. It was something significant.

Just thinking about her didn't give me butterflies anymore. Heck, even *looking* at her didn't. *Poof!* It was as if all my feelings had vanished overnight.

Now don't get me wrong, I still care about her, and yes, she's *still* important to me, but not in the way the person you love should be.

It's how I've always felt after getting with those other girls. A few days would be up, and everything I'd like about them would vanish, the feelings, if they were any to begin with, would get less intense after which they'd become non-existent. This was something quite similar.

I'd thought Hailey was the one. I'd been *so* sure. But I think I was wrong. Whatever we had, it *still* lasted longer than I'd expected, but ultimately, it just ended up like the rest.

I think the time has come.

Hailey and I, we need to end it.

* * *

Scarlett

Lunch is a nightmare. My friends hog me for details, even Sharon! And no matter how hard I try to deny the existence of anything serious between me and William, they just don't believe it.

I see William sitting at his usual table—thank god for that. I want to talk to him. I need to clear things out, set things straight; tell him we're not dating exclusively. It was just a one (two) time thing. But he's busy with his friends, and there's no way I'm going to try to grasp his attention or walk over to him in front of so many people. It would only add fuel to the fire.

So there's nothing I can do but sit at my table and endure the exhausting conversation my friends keep engaging me in.

"At least tell us *something*!" Andrea pleads. "Is William a good kisser?"

"You both *have* kissed, right?" Kayla questions.

Now because I'm possibly the worst liar ever, I'm not able to pretend William and I haven't kissed. Instead, I end up blushing. All of them squeal excitedly. "Details! Details!" They demand. I can feel a headache coming.

So yes, lunch passes excruciatingly slow, just like the rest of the day. And by the time the school bell rings at two thirty PM, I'm more than done with the day. I can't wait to go home, take a long shower, and go to sleep. But there are still things to be done, things that cannot be avoided.

Shortly after lunch, I'd sent a text to William, asking him to meet me after school is over. I'd asked him to meet me near the stairs leading to the roof. I was sure that place would be secluded and away from prying eyes.

He's not there. I feel a pang of irritation. I hate it when people don't come on time when they have an appointment with someone. I hate unpunctuality.

He strolls in about seven minutes later, his bag-pack dangling casually down his left shoulder. "Hey there! Sorry, got caught up with my friends, took a while to get them off my back."

I accept his apology. There's not much I can do about it anyway.

"So how are you?" he asks me, sounding like he genuinely cares.

"I'm . . . I'm good. Look William, I wanted to talk about—about us."

A gorgeous smile springs upon his face. "About us, you say? I like the sound of that." He leans against the wall, folding his arms across his chest, giving me his full attention. "What do you have to say Scarlett? Do you want to hang out during school hours? I don't have a problem with that. I was just trying to take things slow, which is why I didn't bother you today."

"No, it's—it's not that. Look, we—William we aren't—we're not a 'thing', okay?"

"Yeah I know. We're just two people getting to know each other."

"No, you don't understand. We're not . . . we're not dating exclusively. We're not . . . there aren't going to be anymore dates."

The smile falls off his face. "Whoa, why not? Wait, if you didn't enjoy last time, I get it. Pizza and a walk on the beach? That's so boring. I should've taken you somewhere else—"

"No, no William it wasn't the place, the date or *you*. It's me. I just can't do this right now."

"But why?"

"I just . . . can't. You're a great person, I'm just—I can't—"

He drops his bag on the ground and takes a step towards me, then another, then one more. He tenderly cups my face in his hands. I can't help but look into his eyes. I don't have any words to explain what I'm going through, why I can't be with him. How do I tell him there's not anything of me left to give? That I'm essentially empty, because everything that I'd ever been was given to Aiden; *is* given to Aiden.

"What's stopping you Scarlett? Why are you so reluctant to give me your heart?"

Because it's broken, and the only person who can put it back together doesn't want it.

"I know everything's new, and awkward, and strange right now. We barely know each other. Maybe it even feels forced. But I promise you that will change. You just need to give us a chance. You just need to *try*."

I can't. I think it's futile. I've already fallen too far.

"I won't hurt you Scarlett, I hope you know that. You need to let go of your inhibitions and *try*. I know you can do it. Give me a chance, and I swear you won't regret it. I'll make you happy."

He sounds so genuine, his eyes the epitome of honesty.

I remember the first time I talked to him—when I approached him at that party. I also remember *why* I did it—to stop thinking about Aiden, to distract myself.

Maybe this is what I really need—a guy like him. Someone who genuinely cares about me and wants to make me happy. Someone who won't hurt me. Because God knows I've had enough of this heart break.

I need a break, a break from all this pain and drama.

And who knows, maybe he's the one. Maybe I was wrong all along. Maybe Aiden was never meant for me. *And how will I ever know if I don't give him a chance? How will I let go if I don't let go?*

He's right. I need to let go of my inhibitions. I need to take this opportunity life is giving me. How long can I continue like this? Moping after a guy who was never mine to begin with? Who never will be? This is good for everyone. I'll finally move one. Saying yes would make William happy. Hailey would finally stop feeling so insecure and realize I pose no threat to her and Aiden's relationship. And Aiden and I . . . maybe we could start over: be friends. Like, actual friends and none of that flirtationship thing.

Maybe the dance really *did* mark the end and the beginning—the end of me and Aiden, and the start of something new with William.

I take in a huge breath, then wrap my arms around William's neck and pull him closer.

He's surprised to say the least. I've never been the one to initiate anything. But this is me now, the new, post-Aiden me who is *trying*.

I stand up on my tiptoes, grab his collar, and pull him even closer. By now he knows exactly what I want. Our chests collide. In a second his lips are upon me, and for the first time, I don't hold back.

I kiss him back, committing the taste of his lips to my memory, erasing someone else's at the same time. I try to take as much in as possible, to make most of this sensual experience. I try to take everything in—from the texture of his lips, to the soft sizzle of his tongue, to the way his fingers feel running through my hair, how hard and shapely his collar bones are—everything.

I don't hold back.

I let go.

Chapter Twenty-Five

Scarlett

A hand slowly wraps around my waist, causing me to jump in surprise. I turn around to see a familiar pair of blue eyes.

William.

He leans in and presses his lips softly onto my cheek. He throws a sweet smile my way. It's like a cup of hot chocolate on a cold winter morning. Yes, *that's* how nice it is. So nice in fact, that for a few blissful moments I forget the reason I feel so sad.

I thought I could do it. I thought I'll just have to push myself a little and it'll get easier but it hasn't. Every time I'm with William, all I can think about is that I'm not with Aiden. Pining after someone unattainable is one thing; you still hold onto that tiny strand of hope. It makes you miserable, yes. But it doesn't drown you in it.

But this, this is different. When you accept defeat, when you finally back off, it's *completely* different. The hope is gone. And no matter how courageous you'd felt when you made this choice, you feel like you've let go of something extremely important. And you know it's wrong to want to go back, that you'll only end up feeling miserable. But somehow, being like this seems so much worse.

William's still smiling for some reason. He's hiding something. I can almost sense it. Now what is he up to?

"Why are you smiling like that?" I ask, cocking my eyebrows.

"Why? Can't I smile when I see my most favorite person ever?"

"Oh, so I'm your most favorite person now?"

He simply smiles in response, pulling me closer so that my body presses gently against his, his arms still firm around me waist. He guides me through the crowded school hallway.

My heart drums painfully in my chest.

Ba-dump. Ba-dump. Ba-dump.

I feel so self-conscious. I can *feel* their gazes on us, on me. I've never been under so much public scrutiny. We enter the cafeteria together, with his arms still around my waist. I feel awkward and want to step away from him, so we don't look so conspicuous.

Now usually, around this time, we part ways. I go off to sit with my friends at our table, and he walks away to the table where he sits with his senior friends—that big table at the very center. Even though I did agree to give him a chance, give *us* a chance, we've been taking things rather slow. We just talk in between classes, and sometimes after school. We text in the evening.

But things go a little differently this time. He keeps walking towards his table, taking me with him. Confused, I turn to him.

"Why are we going there? I don't sit there."

"I thought we could sit together today, you know, just for a change? I even invited your friends to sit with us, so that you don't feel awkward."

I nod, feeling a little surprised. That was quite thoughtful of him, to invite my friends. I feel really thankful that he thought of that, because there is *no* way I would have survived the lunch with a dozen seniors without feeling out of place.

I feel relieved to see my friends huddled up together at the right side of the table. I go and take a seat next to them. William plops down onto the seat beside mine. Shooting one last smile at me, he turns to his friends.

"I can't believe he invited us to sit with him!" Andrea whispers.

"Yeah. I think he really likes you Scarlett," Kayla pipes in.

I feel my cheeks heat up, and quickly duck down, so that they can't see my face. I blush so easily. This is probably why my parents name me Scarlett. My cheeks are red like half of the time because I'm always getting flustered.

"Scarlett?" William suddenly prompts, resting his hand gently on mine. I jump a little in my seat, surprised. I turn to him.

"Yes?" I ask.

"I wanted to introduce you to my friends. Is that okay?"

I nod, mentally preparing myself to greet a dozen different people, and memorize their names and faces.

The first person he introduces me to is Angelina, his best friend. Yup, she's the one who we all thought was dating William. Well, turns out they really weren't. She's this gorgeous Latina with the most stunning pair of green eyes I've ever seen. She's sitting across of him, on the other side of a table. I've heard a lot about her. She's a straight-A student, top of her class and head of the debate and culture societies. She's one of those people who exude confidence and authority. I think she got an early acceptance into an Ivy League, Columbia or Brown, or so I've heard. She gives me a tight-lipped smile before turning to her cell phone.

Okay then...

"And here's Joshua." William points to a skinny guy, with curly black hair, sitting next to Angelina. He gives me a small wave and a forced smile, before turning back to his lunch tray.

What's the matter? Don't they like me?

They probably think I'm not good enough for William or something. Or maybe they don't think it'll last. William's always bringing girls to the table. What makes me any different?

"And that's Karen and Tasha." He points toward two girls sitting next to Joshua. They both have blonde hair. Tasha's nose and lips are pierced. They both smile nicely at me, making me feel slightly better. They even add a 'hello' to go with it. At least they both are much friendlier than Angelina or Joshua. He introduces me to a couple of more people, finally pointing to the guy sitting on his left (Derek).

Once he's done introducing his friends, I introduce mine, and within a few minutes, everyone starts talking to each other. I smile to myself. This wasn't so hard. My friends are talking to his, and his are talking to mine and we're all talking to each other. I've never been part of a huge group, but I could get used to this.

"So . . . I wanted to do something, and I need everybody's attention," William says. As soon as those words leave his mouth, I start feeling queasy.

I knew he was up to something!

He turns to me. "Now what I'm about to do, I could have done it in a much more romantic way. And I *will* if you will tell me to after this. But I figured that doing it this way was so much better and meaningful, since I'm doing this in front of everyone."

All of his friends are giving each other knowing looks. I'm the only one who is clueless. Before I can ask him what he's planning to do, he stands up from his chair. Joshua and Derek follow suit. Putting two of their fingers in their mouth, they both let out a high-pitched whistle that succeeds in catching everyone's attention. A few people look up, confused. But most of them just seem curious.

"So," William begins, once he knows he has everyone's attention. "A lot of you must have seen me hanging around this beautiful lady, Scarlett. And a few of you probably are aware of the fact that we're dating. But I never officially asked her to be my girlfriend."

My breath hitches in my throat.

Oh no. Oh no.

"So I thought, hey, why don't I do it today, here, so that *everyone* will know how much I like you."

If I could dig up the earth and bury myself alive, I would. Seriously, why does William have to make a spectacle of everything!? I mean geez, if he'd asked me to be his girlfriend when we were standing by the lockers that would have been cool too.

But no, he has to do everything on a large scale. Life is a stage for him, and he's always under the spotlight.

This isn't the first time he's pulled a stunt like this. Last year, he'd changed the lines of the school play during the rehearsals, making it this intense romantic monologue, and had sat down on one knee to ask the girl to be his girlfriend. Of course, she'd said yes.

He'd broken up with her a month later.

When a relationship is private, whatever happens in it, affects only the two of you. But when you make a spectacle of it, it becomes everybody's business. And what happens when it doesn't work out? Nobody lets you forget about it. So yes, I'm a little worried about being asked like this, in front of everyone.

Then to make matters worse, William starts to sing. *To sing!*

He sits down on the edge of the table, props his guitar on his lap and starts to play. It's that song I'd heard him singing in the auditorium that day. It's sweet but...

Why couldn't he just sing it to me in private!?

It's extremely cheesy, excruciatingly embarrassing, downright mortifying, but also kinda romantic.

For a few unnatural minutes, I'm not the 'behind-the-scenes girl' but the leading lady of a teenage movie. I'm directly under the spotlight, no longer in the shadows. All eyes are on us as he serenades me.

Is this even real life?!

I'm almost breathless by the time William finishes singing the song. My heart is pounding hard against my chest and my cheeks are hurting from all the blushing.

Can I just die already?

And then, he walks over to me. The guitar in his hand is replaced by a large bouquet of roses that his friend just handed over to him. I hear gasps and *awws* from every corner of the room.

Oh my god this is so embarrassing. I would have enjoyed it more if there weren't so many pairs of eyes staring at us.

It gets very silent. All I can hear is the beat of my heart and the words that come out from William's mouth. "Scarlett, will you give me the pleasure of calling you my girlfriend?"

I'll have to give you that pleasure. You leave me no choice, asking this in front of everyone!

But I'd already decided, hadn't I?

I'd already decided to move on and give William a chance. So why is this so hard? Why is this so difficult?

"So? Will you be mine?" He prompts. Another rush of 'aww's and *oohs* and *aahs* fill the room.

I feel my palms getting sweaty and my stomach twisting into knots. A deadly silence has taken over the room, and all I can do is just stand there, wondering what to do. I can't delay anymore. It'll get awkward.

If I say 'yes' then that's it, there's no turning back. But if I say 'no' I'll not only break his heart but embarrass him in front of *every single person in school.*

You could say I was feeling the pressure.

"William I—"

I pause, as if hoping for a miracle. A miracle that involves Aiden rushing here, standing in front of everyone and proclaiming he has feelings for me and that *he's* the one I should be with.

But this isn't a movie or a romance novel. It's real life. Which is why nothing of that sort happens.

I can't waste another moment. I slowly nod, feeling super awkward.

"Yes William, I'll be your girlfriend," I declare. I feel the air rush into my lungs, feel the knots in my stomach loosen. It's like someone has hit the play button on the stereo again. The silence vanishes and is replaced by noise, so much noise. Everyone is cheering.

William pulls me into a tight hug, lifting me off the ground, twirling me round and round. You would think that I'd just agreed to marry him or something.

* * *

Aiden

I quietly get up and walk out of the cafeteria. I walk slowly, trying to appear as relaxed as possible. I try very hard to look blank and unaffected by what I witnessed a few minutes ago.

Nobody notices me leaving.

Outside, I punch the lockers lining the hallway. Then I punch at the same place again. And again. And again.

It leaves a dent.

I kick the wall next to it three times.

All that punching and kicking and I *still* feel angry.

I slump down on the floor, suddenly drained of all energy. I feel really, really terrible. I don't think I've ever felt this way before. I want to break things. I want to hit them, and crush them, and rip them apart.

I can't get her out of my head. All I keep seeing is the two of them—William and Scarlett, him holding her in his arms...If someone would have gutted me with a knife, it would have hurt less.

I feel squeamish and my head hurts. I regret coming to lunch today. Maybe I should've spent it at the bleachers like I'd been doing for the past week. It would have definitely helped me avoid seeing William and Scarlett together.

But no, I had to go to the cafeteria today. *And just my fucking luck...*

So that's that. Everything is crystal clear now. She likes him. She has actual feelings for him. She never liked me like that. To her, I was just a friend. And to think I'd been chasing after her like a desperate idiot, hoping against hope that we could something more.

Okay yes, so I was partly at fault too. I kept holding onto Hailey. And maybe that had something to do with it. But it doesn't matter anymore. Scarlett's with someone else now and she has feelings for him. She—

I hear someone coming, feet slapping against the tiled hallway. I look up, wondering who it could be.

It's Hailey.

Worst timing ever. We've not talked for like a month and today's the day she decides it's okay for us to start talking again.

I look at her and feel an intense wave of anger. An anger directed at myself.

Damien was right, I'm not meant for serious commitment. The first time I decide to give relationships a chance, I end up hurting my girlfriend.

I thought we'd last. I'd thought it was real.

I'd thought wrong.

"Aiden?"

I shake my head. "Not now Hailey, I need to be alone. I-I can't do this right now."

"You *have* to do this right now Aiden. I'm tired. I'm so, *so* tired. I saw you walking away, you know? I saw the way you left as soon as Scarlett said yes to William. Don't pretend this has nothing to do with her."

I turn to look at her.

It's time. I have to do this. I need to end this for good.

"You're right." I nod. "It has everything to do with her."

Somewhere deep in my chest, my heart cracks a little. I have to do this. I've avoided it for too long: dragging it on and pretending that things will flip back to the way they were. That I'll get over my best friend and give Hailey the love she deserves. But I was wrong. I can't.

Sometimes feelings fade. Sometimes it futile to hold onto something that wasn't supposed to work out from the beginning. And I think Hailey knows that too.

"Is that why . . . why you didn't . . . didn't do it with me that night?" she asks.

I nod in response. "I didn't think it was right," I say. "I didn't think it was right for us to do something so special when I didn't feel that way about you."

"You love her, don't you?" she asks me. She doesn't sound angry, just curious.

I nod slowly. "Yes, yes I do."

It was her, it was her all along.

She lets out a deep, heartbroken sigh. "I knew it."

My eyes widen. "Wait, what do you mean you 'knew it'?"

"It was so obvious Aiden. Anybody could see it. *Anybody.* I was in denial, of course. I didn't want to believe it. If only I'd had the courage to face reality, I wouldn't have to go through what I did."

I shake my head fervently. "Please Hailey, don't blame yourself. It's not your fault. It's me. *I'm* sorry for making you go through this. *I* was the shitty boyfriend. You . . . you were perfect."

She stares at me, pain evident in her eyes.

"I think deep down, I always knew it, knew I had feelings for Scarlett. I just didn't want to face it. I thought I could avoid feeling that way. I thought I'd get over it. Trust me, when I asked you to be my girlfriend, I meant it. I genuinely wanted to be with you. You were amazing and you cared about me and I cared about you. I was ready for the whole commitment thing. I wanted to make it work.

I was an idiot though. I obviously failed and it's totally not fair that *you* have to be the one to suffer because of me. I didn't do right by you, I know. And I don't expect you to forgive me, because what I've done is terrible. It's because of me that everything got so out of hand. And you have no idea how fucking sorry I am about that. I hurt you, and it's because of me now that you'll think a hundred times before you trust a guy ever again.

But I promise you, it wasn't a lie. I *did* have feelings for you. I *did* care. I still do. You'll always be an important part of my life. The memories we have together, will always be there in my heart. I just . . . I just don't feel the way I'm supposed to anymore. And I wish there was some way I could change that but I can't."

She's crying now, and it hurts, god it hurts. The guilt is eating me alive. Hailey did not deserve all the crap I made her go through. And I wish I could go back in time and take it all back. I wish I'd left her the moment I knew I felt something remotely non-platonic for Scarlett.

But then, I guess I wouldn't have gotten with Hailey at all. *After all, I met her that night at the party . . .*

My thoughts take me back to that start-of-summer party. Scarlett and I had been dancing together. Right there, under the lights with her hair flying all over as she laughed, all I'd wanted to do was take her in my arms and kiss her. I'd tried to that too. I had leaned in, my heart drumming like crazy, ready to claim her lips. But she'd given me the curve. She practically ran away from me and I'd been so embarrassed, I clung onto the first girl I could. I wish I hadn't. I wish I'd waited for her to come back.

I've been running from my feelings from the start. I avoided Scarlett all summer, going on numerous dates with Hailey, hoping what I felt would fade. I know I hurt Scarlett in the process. I was being so selfish but I was in denial. Then I got close to Hailey and suddenly things seemed to be falling into place . . .

Except on Hailey's birthday, when we'd surprised her; I'd spent the whole day with Scarlett, planning everything. It had been one of the best days ever. And on the roof, just before I'd texted Hailey, there had been this moment—this weird moment where this voice in my head had said:

Are you sure about this Aiden? Do you really want to do this?

And I'd looked at Scarlett: seen her smiling that beautiful smile of hers, as her wavy hair whipped carelessly in the wind; seen her looking out towards the distance, lost in thought and I'd thought, *god damn! But she's so beautiful.* And I'd realized no, that I wasn't sure if I wanted to do this. I wasn't sure if I should ask Hailey to be with me.

But then Scarlett was urging me to call Hailey and everything happened so fast and before I knew it, Hailey and I were weeks into dating each other. I'd forgotten about that little moment with Scarlett on the roof.

I should've realized Scarlett meant more to me than I'd thought.

And then we got that project together and I went to her place for the dance practice and things got so awkward. I could've realized it then too.

Then that library incident—when we'd come *so* close to kissing each other. God, it feels like a lifetime away. She looked so beautiful that day; she always does. She'd looked flustered, *so* flustered. And her eyes were wide and innocent when she'd looked at me and I'd never wanted to kiss someone so badly before. I wanted to kiss her like those romantic heroes kiss the heroines in those sappy RomCom movies. I'd wanted to run my fingers through her hair and make music against her lips.

Or when we slow danced and I'd held her in my arms. It had been the most magical thing ever. That day, I'd understood why couples enjoyed something so slow and simple. It is because in those few moments, you get to hold this really special person in your arms. You get to look into their eyes and feel their heart beating against yours, feel their soft flesh grazing your skin as you lost yourself in their embrace.

I should've realized. I had *plenty* of moments to, but I kept ignoring the signs, kept ignoring my *own* feelings, and now here we are today in this mess.

Hailey shakes her head. "I was stupid. I thought I'd be the one to finally change your mind. I was wrong. It was never meant to be me. I guess I knew that it wasn't working. But I just kept pushing and pushing and pushing, fighting for something that didn't exist. I should've walked away before. It's partly my fault."

"It's not—"

"You know what, at this point it doesn't even matter. It's all done and over with."

"I'm so sorry Hailes. I didn't mean to screw everything up like this. Relationships require work and I didn't put enough effort. And on top of that, I was unfaithful. Which again, was not what you deserved. I'm sorry."

Hailey suddenly looks uncomfortable. "What? What is it?" I ask, confused.

"Actually . . ." she trails off, sounding hesitant. "Actually, I wasn't completely faithful either."

I gape at her. Okay so, I didn't see *that* coming.

"What?" I'm not angry. That would be hypocritical of me. I'm just really shocked.

"I was just *really* lonely. I swear it didn't start as that. You were always so distracted and lost in your own world. Half of the time it felt like you weren't even there. Physically, you were present. But mentally, you'd checked out of our relationship a long time ago. I was just too blind to realize it," she explains. "So this one night, I got really lonely. Then I met this guy online and we got talking, and we immediately hit it off. He was great. He *is* great. We met up a few times and I wasn't really planning on anything. But one thing led to another and it just happened," she says, sounding guilty. "That's what I wanted to talk to you about Aiden, I can't be with you anymore. I don't *feel* that way about you anymore. I think we've been together without really *being* together, you know? Yes, we had feelings for each other. But now they're just…"

". . . gone," I finish, nodding. "I understand. I mean, yes, I am a little disappointed and shocked but I get it. I'm not going to hold a grudge over this or hate you because I know this is partly my fault. If I'd been there for you—"

She shakes her head. "It doesn't matter. What's done is done."

"So this is the end."

She nods. "This is the end."

I smile sheepishly. "I guess we just weren't meant to be, huh?"

"I guess not."

"Are things going to be okay between us?" I ask her.

"If by okay you mean me not holding a grudge over you, and not referring to you as my dickhead of an ex-boyfriend, then yes, things are going to be okay between us." She smiles.

I smile right back at her. "Take care Hailey, and once again, I apologize for all the crap I gave you."

She shakes her head. "Don't fret over it. We're even now . . . sort of. You take care too, okay?"

I nod.

Somewhere, the bell rings, marking the end of lunch break. Students start spilling through the doors, making way to the lockers and the classes they have to be at. I start walking away.

"And hey, Aiden!" Hailey shouts out. I turn around, curious. "Do something about the Scarlett situation. I hate seeing you moping around like a loser. That's not you."

"Ha-ha, I'll try," I reply, chuckling. She's right. That's not me.

But it's easier said than done.

Chapter Twenty-Six

Aiden

I decided to skip class.

After my conversation with Hailey, I felt really, really tired. Today has been a long day, *is* a long day.

I wouldn't have been able to focus during class anyway. I just can't stop thinking about Scar. All I can see is this image of Scarlett locked in William's embrace. It's downright torturous.

One of my biggest nightmares has become a reality—Scarlett is with someone else now. Scarlett has a boyfriend. Nerdy, socially awkward Scarlett who never had a love life has a *boyfriend* now. A boyfriend with whom she'll do couple things.

She'll kiss, and he'll kiss her back. With tongue. Lots of tongue. William seems like the type of guy who likes tongue. He'll touch her like . . . everywhere. *Everywhere.* And she's going to touch him right back.

At night, when she feels lonely, *he* is the one she will call, and they'll talk on the phone for hours. He will be the first person she thinks of when she wakes up. When her favorite boy band will release some new music, *he'll* be the one she'll force to listen to their songs. She'll steal food off *his* plate and smack *him* when she's irritated. He'll get to witness her laugh firsthand, and then he'll act like a dork, just to make her laugh again. Because god, that laugh of hers, is the most beautiful sound ever. And I really *do* hope he acts like a dork to make her laugh. She deserves to laugh. A lot. And when she's nervous, she'll go to *him* and she'll text *him* when she finishes reading a book, and cry to *him* about all the characters who broke her heart, and the evil antagonist, and the one she fell in love with.

All the things she did with me, she'll do with him now.

And I never explicitly appreciated these tiny things Scarlett did but now she's gone, truly gone and I *know* I'll miss every single thing about her. All of them.

Well of course, she's not dead or whatever. But things will change. Things *have* changed. We're not even friends anymore, and even if by some miracle we do become friends again, there will always be this crack in our relationship. It'll never be the same again.

I wish I could go back in time and do things over. Say things when I should've said them, express my feelings directly and immediately. I wish I'd never let her go.

I sneak out the little metal flask from my locker, hide it beneath my t-shirt, and then go to the roof. I never returned those keys Scarlett and I stole off the janitor. I guess he must have a duplicate pair with him, because he never changed the lock. So now I go to the roof whenever I feel like skipping classes.

I take out the flask and sip the bitter liquid stored inside. It's a really concentrated form. I usually mix it with water or soda to get a light buzz when I'm up for it. But I don't want a light buzz today. I need something stronger.

I just hope I don't get hammered.

* * *

Scarlett

My phone vibrates for the *fifth* time. I let out an exasperated sigh. Who the hell is texting me in the middle of class?! Everybody knows I never reply to texts during school hours.

However, since I'm extremely irritated, I fish out my phone from my backpack, and tap on the message icon. I glance at the teacher to make sure she isn't looking in my direction. I turn back to look at the phone.

Five text messages.

From Aiden.

Five.

My heart jumps in my chest. My insides twist, and I suddenly feel breathless. I hate the fact that just seeing his name on the screen of my phone has such effect on me.

Without wasting any more time, I start reading his message.

The most recent one states:

Plz don't ignore me Scar, it hurts.

Okay…weird.

I decide to start from the earliest text.

Congratulations Scarlett, u finally have a boyfriend.

Then the second one:

I hope you're happy with your decision.

The third is the longest:

Do you really think he'll keep u happy? He doesn't deserve u Scar. You can do so much better. And by so much better I don't mean me. I just mean better in general.

Then the fourth:

Fuck I just really miss you

Reading these messages saddens me. I don't know what to make of it. He's not happy about the William thing. But that was a given. He disliked William from the very start. As for ignoring him, I just can't flit back into his life and pretend everything's alright. Because no, it isn't.

I need space. I need to be away from him. Maybe I've spent so much time with him that I fooled myself into thinking what I felt for him was the real deal. But who knows? I need to experience new things with different people and see the person I am when I am not with him.

I need time.

I try to focus on what's going on in class, trying to curb my curiosity about Aiden and stop wondering where he is right now and if he's really drunk, or was I mistaken and those texts were a result of some serious introspection.

I bid Sharon goodbye once class ends. Then make my way through the crowded hallway, walking to the next class I've got.

Suddenly, a hand pops out and grabs my left arm. And before I can so much as react, it pulls me into the nearest classroom, shutting the door behind. The classroom is empty, I realize. I feel my heart pounding in my chest—hard, and blood rushing through my veins. I find myself pressed against the wall, with two arms on either side of me, blocking my escape. Someone's breath tickles my face. It reeks of alcohol.

What the hell is going on!?

My panic is short-lived. I find a pair of familiar brown eyes looking down at me, and I feel myself relax. No need to worry. It's Aiden.

"Aiden? What are you doing?!"

"You and I . . . we need to talk."

"So talk."

All I can do is stand still and meet his intense gaze. I want to look away, because it's making me uncomfortable. But somehow, I'm not able to. He doesn't speak. Instead, he stands there, quiet and motionless. The only movement is that of our chests slowly rising and falling against each other's as we inhale and exhale air.

I find myself a little out of breath due to my proximity to Aiden.

When he doesn't speak, I go on. "Aiden, we're in school. Why are you drunk!? You could get in so much trouble."

"I'm just a little tipsy."

"No, you're drunk. Do you know how much trouble you'll be in if someone finds out? They'll suspend you."

"Not for underage drinking. The most I'll get is a few weeks of suspension."

"And that's nothing!? Aiden—" He doesn't let me finish, planting his hands on my mouth, smothering my voice.

"Shhh Scar, you worry too much. Breathe a little. Nothing is going to happen." My insides turn into mush. His husky, drunk voice is probably the sexiest sound I've ever heard.

"Do you love him?" he asks, shattering the silence. My eyes widen. Is *this* what he wanted to talk so urgently about? I feel irritated. I could be in class right now, but he wants to "talk."

I just want to tell him to get lost. That I'm not going to answer these stupid questions of his. But Aiden looks so determined. I know he'll not leave me alone unless he gets these answers. Plus, what does it matter? He might not even remember all this once he sobers up.

"Of course not," I answer.

"And me? Do you love me?"

My breath hitches, my heart jumps so hard in my chest that it leaves behind a dull ache.

There is so much I want to say, but not like this. Not when he's drunk and will forget everything I say now. Not when whatever I say won't change things. He'll still be with her, and I'll be with William. Because after everything that has happened, I know one thing for sure—Aiden and I, we're not good for each other.

He accepts my silence as a "no," which is fine by me. Fat good it'll do me by confessing my feelings!

"Do you think he loves you?" Aiden goes on. I open my mouth to speak, but he cuts me off. "—because no, he doesn't. Not like—"

He shuts up suddenly, his voice stopping abruptly, as if someone cut off his vocal chords.

"Like what Aiden?"

He shakes his head. "Nothing, nothing, it doesn't matter."

I sigh, suddenly feeling tired. I push him away, stepping away from the wall, so that I'm not pinned against it anymore. "Do you have anything important to say? Because if you just want to complain about William, then sorry, I don't have the time for that."

He slumps his head, looking rather ashamed. "I'm sorry. Instead of being supportive like I should, I'm giving you a hard time. I'm really sorry for my behavior." He looks up. "I don't know what's wrong with me. I should be happy for you. In fact, I am. I *am* happy if *you* are happy. If this is what you truly want, then

yes, I *am* happy for you. I hope he treats you better than I did."
Aiden offers me a weak smile.

I suddenly feel awful for the way I've been treating him.
Maybe I have been a little too harsh. Yes, he's been a jerk. Yes,
he's been super annoying. And yes, he bailed out on our
friendship. But I can't hold that against him forever. It's really
exhausting to hate someone, to hold a grudge against them. I'd
rather just let it go.

"Here's to you and William," he slurs, and takes a long
swig from a metallic flask I hadn't noticed before. "Cheers! You
want some?"

The pungent smell of alcohol hits me full force.
Disgusted, I grab the flask, and take it away, before Aiden can
drink some more.

"Hey! Give that back, you can't take it." He protests. His
voice sounds so mellow. His eyes are drooping with lethargy, like
he could pass out any second.

"No, *you* can't drink what's inside it. We still have three
hours of school left and if any teacher catches you in this state,
you're done for!"

"Ugh, why are you such a party pooper Scar? Live a little!"

I roll my eyes. "C'mon, I'm getting you out of here," I say,
grabbing Aiden's arms and leading him out of the classroom. I
don't feel like going to class anymore, not when I'm almost twenty
minutes late. Besides, I don't want to leave Aiden all by himself.
He's drunk off his ass and I don't want him to get in trouble.

I realize I will have to sneak him out of the school
premises, which is not going to be easy—at all.

I push the door of the classroom, and peek through the
gap. The hallway is devoid of people. This is our chance.

Our shoes slap against the tiled floor as we run towards
the lockers to grab our things. I pray the principle isn't on one of

her strolls around the school. I have no idea how I'll ever be able to explain *this*.

Once we've taken our bag and books, I guide Aiden towards the school grounds. Thankfully, he doesn't question where we are going. But that doesn't mean he is, by any means, keeping his mouth shut. Oh no, he's happily chattering away if we're out for a nice walk. I would have happily indulged in the conversation if the situation wasn't so serious.

"Scarlett, where are we going?" Aiden asks me.

I sigh and turn to look at him. "We're getting out of here."

"What do you mean?"

"We're leaving the school premises; I think we'll have to climb over a wall or something."

"But we can't do that! It's against the rules. We could get caught and—"

I gape at him as if he has suddenly grown three heads. "Since when did you start caring about the rules?"

My question stumps him. And for a second, he stares out into the distance, his face slightly crumpled as he tries to make sense of his sudden respect for rules. Then he turns to me, realization suddenly dawning upon his face. "You're right. Since when did I start caring about rules? C'mon let's get out of here."

I lead him towards the walls lining the hind part of the school grounds, the one where the field and bleachers are. The walls here aren't as tall as in the rest of the campus, and there's a thick cover of trees here, that will hide us if anyone comes while we're crossing it. There are a few bricks piled up in the corner. We can use them to give us some leverage.

I beckon Aiden to go first. He doesn't need the bricks, he's tall enough. He grabs the edge of the wall, hoists himself up, and voila, within minutes he's perched atop it. I follow suit, arranging 4 bricks, one atop each, and step on them. However, I'm still forced to take Aiden's help to get on the wall. I sigh with relief once I end up on top too. I look on the other side. There's no foothold or anything. The ground is bare. We have no choice but to jump.

This time too, Aiden is the first to go. He pushes himself off the wall and lands smoothly. For being drunk, his sense of balance and control over his body is quite good. I on the other hand, feel uncertain and afraid. I'm not sure I can make the jump. I'm short and I'm terrible at all things athletic.

"C'mon Scarlett, what are you waiting for? Jump!" Aiden encourages me. I smile weakly at him, telling him I'm scared. "Don't worry, I'll catch you!" I stare at him, my heart drumming against my chest, wondering if I should just give up. *I'm* not the one who is drunk, he is. And he is already out of school, I can always go back. But what if he gets lost or passes out somewhere? I can't leave him like this.

"Okay, I'm jumping. Catch me?" I ask. He nods reassuringly in response. Here goes nothing. I'll have to trust his drunken self to catch me and not let me fall. I scoot my hips towards the edge of the wall and then push off. I start my descent.

My first instinct is to scream. But before I can even start, I've already reached my destination. Like I said, the wall wasn't very high. Aiden arms are supporting me, as he holds me bridal style. He's looking down at me, his eyes fixed on mine and a brilliant smile is plastered on his face. My heart is racing away in my chest. Whether it is because of the jump, or because of Aiden, I'm not sure.

Once Aiden puts me down, I dust my and jeans and ask him, "How did you come to school today?" I silently pray that he came via his car.

No such luck, he tells me he drove his motorcycle to school.

Now we're in trouble.

I'm not letting him drive when he's drunk, obviously. That would be a death wish. I guess we'll have to walk to the bus stop. The bus stop that is twenty minutes away. We'll have to walk there in the heat.

I groan.

Or . . . I could just drive his motorcycle . . .

I mean, how hard can it be?

"Keys. Give me your motorcycle keys," I say, extending my palms towards Aiden.

"What? Why?"

"So that I can take both of us away from here."

He shakes his head rapidly. "No way in hell! You're not driving it. Do you even know how to?"

"No, but I know how to ride a bicycle. It can't be much different."

He simply gives me an 'are you shitting me?!' look. When he realizes I'm one hundred percent serious, he begins to protest again. "No, no way at all. I'm not letting you drive. What if we die? *I'll* drive."

I snort. "And that's supposed to be so much better because? The probability of us dying increases if we let *you* drive. *You're* the one who's drunk!"

He sighs, his shoulder slumping in response. "Okay fine but let me teach you first." He walks over to me and spends the next ten minutes giving me precise instructions and details about this vehicle. After assuring him I've got it, I climb onto the motorcycle and take hold of the handlebars. Aiden stashes our bags in the compartment under the seat and a second later the seat behind me dips and Aiden takes his seat. His arms immediately snake around my body and I gasp.

"Aiden, what are you doing?!" I exclaim.

"What? I'm letting you drive my baby. I should get some benefits too."

His warm torso is touching my back. I can sense whenever he inhales or exhales, feel the gentle thump of his heart beating against his chest.

I kick the motorcycle to life. It takes me a few tries but once it starts, I rev the engine and off we go. I stifle a giggle as I think about how we both look right now. Me, a petite girl, driving a deadly vehicle and Aiden sitting behind me, his arms secured tightly around my body. We must look ridiculous.

"Let's go on a long ride and never come back!" Aiden shouts on top of his voice. I laugh in response.

Driving this vehicle is no piece of cake. It's heavy and if I lose even a bit of focus, we'll lose balance and fall. And I'm trying *so* hard to not lose my focus right now. Which is saying something because hey, how can you not lose your focus when your crush is pressed up against your body and you can feel his warmth seeping through your skin, causing goose bumps to erupt down your arm? Yeah, like I said, I *cannot* focus.

Suddenly, I feel something heavy plop down on my right shoulder.

It's Aiden's head.

Oh my god, please don't tell me he passed out!

"Aiden? Aiden!? What the hell are you doing!? Are you okay?!"

"Huh? What? My head kind of hurts, I'm just putting it on your shoulder."

"Oh thank god you haven't passed out," I sigh with relief.

I feel him nuzzling my shoulder, consequently making me shiver. He's pressed up so tight against me, his arms locked around my middle.

I glance at Aiden. "What are you doing Aiden? Would you err . . . mind giving me some space?"

"Nope, I'm good."

"I didn't ask you if you're comfortable! I told you to move!"

"But I don't want to! Now shut up and drive."

"But I can't! You're distracting me!" I complain. "Damn it Aiden, why are you torturing me like this?!"

I glance at the road and I see something that makes my heart stop.

A big bus heading straight at us.

We are going to die.

A few seconds, just few seconds I lose my focus and *this* happens.

"Oh no!" I shout out, terrified.

This catches Aiden's attention. He withdraws his head from my shoulder and looks up. "What happened? What happened?"

"We're going to die. We're going to die. We're going to die. We're going to—" I start chanting. The bus is coming closer. I've forgotten everything, my mind is blank. My limbs are paralyzed. I don't know what to do anymore; except maybe scream.

"Aaaaahhhhh!!!"

His hands immediately replace mine at the handlebars, and at the last moment he swerves the motorcycle, away from the bus's path. The bus passes us, blaring its horn. The driver gives us the finger.

Aiden's driving now, even though he is seated behind me. My hands are hanging limp by my side. I can hear the blood pounding through my veins. I think I'd stopped breathing.

"Phew! That was close," Aiden sighs with relief.

"Close? That was close?! You almost got us killed!"

"I? I got us killed?! Excuse me, but if it wasn't for *me* we'd both be dead by now! So you should thank me instead of shouting at me and maybe throw in a few kisses for saving your life."

This guy.

"It *was* your mistake! If you weren't so hell bent on distracting me, I would have been paying attention to the road. In fact, if you weren't so keen on getting drunk in the middle of the day, not to mention in the school premises, we'd be happily alive and worry-free, sitting in a class. So yeah, I'm going to blame *you* and no, you're not getting any thank you kisses!"

He lets out a puff of air. "I missed this. I missed you." He rests his head on my shoulder again.

"I missed you too Aiden. I missed you too."

Chapter Twenty-Seven

Scarlett

I've been standing behind the couch for the past five minutes, staring at my brother. He's watching TV. His hair is all mussed up and there are bags under his pale blue eyes. There's a milk carton in his hands.

Now.

I crouch, gently leaning forward so that my mouth's right next to his ear. Then:

"Boo!" I shout.

Darren jumps on the spot, spilling the milk everywhere. "Jesus fucking Christ, what is wrong with you?!" He curses. All I do is laugh uncontrollably, clutching my stomach hard.

The couch is all messed up now. But this was *so* worth it. It's a good thing Mom isn't here. She'd have a seizure if she saw all the spilt milk.

Mom and Dad have gone out of town. It's an annual Stevenson tradition: a weeklong get-together at Grandma and Grandpa Stevenson's place that is *awfully* boring. The signal there sucks and all you get are rows after rows of empty farmlands, and ratty relatives who leave no chance to criticize you.

Our parents love it.

Darren and I just don't fit in there—not with the adults, not with the kids. We only get bored out of our minds. My parents are crazy if they think I'm going there again.

So of course I'd lied.

"Are you sure you don't want to come?" my mom had asked me while loading her luggage in the car.

"I'm sure. I have a lot of school work and an upcoming math test, so I really can't go." False. In reality, I didn't want to travel hundreds of miles only to meet my boring relatives. I just wanted to have the house to myself; chilling with my laptop and listening to loud music, and maybe binge watching some of my favorite TV shows. That's all I wanted: complete solitude.

Darren slumps back down on the couch, munching dry *cornflakes. And* he's drinking milk right out of a carton again. Ew.

"Did you want anything? *Will* you want anything? I know Mom and Dad aren't here so technically, I'm the boss and I need to babysit you—"

"What!? No! I'm not a child—"

"Good, because I'm kinda busy this week. I have a lot of plans and I don't really want to have to look after you."

"Oh, aren't you the most caring brother ever," I mutter under my breath.

"I have band practice almost every day. Next month, a music producer is coming to hear us play. Not from some major label or anything, but it's a start. So yeah, I'll be busy with band practice. And a couple of my friends from school are coming later to hang out. And oh, I'm throwing a party on Saturday."

"And Mom thinks you're responsible. Boy is she wrong!"

He ignores my comment. "I'll be here watching TV if you need anything. I *hope* you don't need anything though."

I roll my eyes at him; then start heading upstairs to my room, when suddenly, the doorbell rings.

"Are you expecting someone?" I ask Darren.

"I told you, some friends from school are coming over." He turns back to look at the TV. "Can you get the door please? I can't miss this part of the match."

I sigh and head towards the door since he's too lazy to move his ass. I open it and just about die.

What the hell is *he* doing here?!

I can't help gaping at Aiden who's standing right in front of me. He looks equally shocked to see me.

"Uhm . . . come in," I murmur awkwardly.

We're *still* ignoring each other. That brief bit of companionship lasted only while he was drunk. After that, it was back to us not talking to each other. Things have somehow gotten even worse than before. He's not only been giving me the silent treatment; it's almost like he doesn't see me. Earlier, he'd at least look at me, maybe even glare at me. He'd sometimes go as far as being rude. Now? Nothing. It's like I don't exist. He looks right past me. Sometimes I see him glaring at William, but that's about it. To him, I'm invisible.

So what is he doing here? What does he want now?! I'm just about to ask him this when Darren speaks up:

"Oh you're here. Where are the others?"

"Jake had to go run some errands for his dad, so he bailed out and Ashton said he'll try to swing by later. He's not sure though."

He's here to meet Darren? What the hell!?

I mean yeah, they know each other because of me of course. But I didn't know they hung out too . . .

I take the opportunity to leave while both of them are engrossed in their conversation.

"What is *she* doing here? I thought everyone in your family was going out?" Aiden exclaims when he thinks I'm out of earshot.

"She decided to stay back. Why are *you* so bothered? I thought you guys were friends."

"I'm not bothered," he mutters. "Anyway, can you shut off the damn TV so that we can head to your basement and start with the x-box? I'm getting kind of restless here."

Darren lets out an audible sigh and turns off the TV. The house gets really quiet. I head back to my room and shut the door behind me. I can't help feeling slightly hurt. Aiden ignored me *yet again*. He refused to even look in my direction. And he's *clearly* frustrated regarding me being here.

The rest of the afternoon passes by agonizingly slow. I don't come across Aiden again. I go downstairs only once to grab something from the fridge and then return to my room.

When the afternoon heat finally makes way for cool evening air, I grab my Kindle and head out to the balcony. I'm so bored that I'm re-reading the Harry Potter series for the seventh time. Yes, you heard that right.

I hear laughter and chatter. I realize it's coming from below. I look down and see about a dozen people, some lounging near the pool, some swimming in it.

Seriously, when did they all come in? And I didn't even notice?

"Hey, isn't that Scarlett?" I hear someone remark. My head immediately snap in their direction. It's Damien. *God, he's here too?*

"Hey, why don't you join us?"

I don't think twice. I've been bored out of my mind since the past four hours. Being out in the pool surrounded by people would be a welcome change.

I slip on the bikini I'd brought along, in case I wanted a dip in Darren's pool.

I can hear them laughing and shouting when I arrive downstairs. They are creating such a ruckus, splashing water at each other. They turn to look at me as I arrive and wave. I wave back. They are all familiar faces, seniors mostly. But I don't know most of their names.

Aiden's still here. He looks smoking hot with his hair all wet and mussed up. I can't help ogling his bare chest, all toned and glistening with water.

So hot.

I feel my chest physically hurt.

A bunch of them are playing dodge ball on the shallow side of the pool. Who even does that? They beckon me to join them but I decide against it, and instead, sit down on one of the lounge chairs facing the pool. I soon regret my decision, seeing them having a lot of fun, dunking each other in the water, hitting each other with the ball, and having fun in general. So the next time someone begs me to join, I don't refuse.

I climb into the pool.

"Two people go in the middle and the rest try to hit them. They have to avoid the ball, got it?" Darren explains.

I nod.

"Good, go stand in the center. Anyone like to join her?"

This girl with curly blonde hair—I think her name's Abigail—wades into the center of the pool.

The very next second the first ball is thrown our way. I succeed in ducking out of its way just in time; it whizzes past my head. The next few minutes are spent dodging the ball. I narrowly miss it every time.

Update: This game isn't as fun as it looks. It's brutal.

Twenty minutes later, I'm panting really hard, almost out of breath.

Now tired, Abigail excuses herself to lounge by the poolside, leaving me by myself again.

"Who wants to go in the center now?" someone asks.

I see Damien opening his mouth to volunteer but Aiden beats him to it. He quickly swims to the center. "I'll do it!"

I stare at him, wide eyed. He's been ignoring me for the past week, and now he suddenly wants to play alongside me?

The game resumes. I'm getting good at this but I also feel a little tired. This is fun though. We're all laughing and just having a good time in general, dodging and hitting.

The ball suddenly lands in Damien's hands. He grins. "I'm aiming for your butt Scarlett!" he announces, winking at me. Before I can so much as blink, the ball's coming my way. I let out a strangled gasp. I'm definitely going to get hit this time.

But I don't.

Aiden grabs it before it can hit me.

"Dude, you can't catch the ball!" Damien protests. "You just ruined my shot."

Aiden glares at him. "I don't care. Aim there again and I'll break your hands."

Damien raises his hands, exasperated. "Relax, why are you getting so worked up!? I swear to God, Aiden has no chill."

I gawk at Aiden. *That was . . . nice.*

We continue with the game, dodging balls expertly, and splashing water as we duck below the surface.

Update: This game is actually fun.

"Okay, now you're done for!" Darren shouts, triumphant. He aims his throw at me. I narrow my eyes at him.

"Bring it on!" I challenge.

He cracks his knuckles and throws the ball in my direction.

It's too fast, the ball. My limbs freeze. My mind is telling me to move but I can't.

Suddenly something wraps around my stomach, giving me goose bumps all over. It's a hand. *Aiden's* hand. His other hand follows suit. I gasp for air, knowing what's coming next. He pulls me under the water with him, the ball whizzes above our head and we successfully dodge the ball.

There's water everywhere. His hands are still wrapped around me. We're floating under water, our eyes staring into each other's. The moment doesn't last for more than a second or two, but it seems longer.

We both resurface, gasping for breath. Darren starts to curse.

"Damn you Aiden! Why do you keep helping her? You're disqualified!"

Aiden rolls his eyes. "Yeah whatever, I'm tired of this game anyway." With that, he wades to the edge of the pool, pulls himself up and then walks away.

I decide to excuse myself from the game too. I'm quite tired. I sit near the pool for a bit before heading back to my room.

The moments we shared during the game replay in my mind again and again. Aiden and I hadn't exchanged a single word, but somehow, I'd felt this weird connection, this partnership with him. It felt nice.

I really need to pee and the nearest bathroom is in the guest room. So that's where I go, lost in thoughts of him. Of course, if I'd not been so lost in my head I would have noticed someone was already in there.

I'm greeted by a wide-eyed Aiden, currently in the process of putting on clothes. I let out a scream and quickly turn around.

How embarrassing to have stumbled upon him like this. I realize how *not* clothed he is. The only thing covering him up is a white towel hanging low on his waist. A slight tug and it'll be down in the blink of an eye. I feel my cheeks heat up as that thought crosses my mind.

"W-what a-are y-you—what are you—damn it!" I stutter, embarrassed. "Shit, what are you doing here?!" I exclaim, sounding aghast.

"What am *I* doing here? This is my room!"

"No, this is the guest room!"

"And *I'm* the guest!"

He's staying over?!

There's a moment of painful silence, before I speak up.

"It's—it's not like I *knew* you'd be here when I walked in, you know?"

"Fine, whatever. Now *leave.*"

My eyes can't help notice how well built his body is, the toned abs, the smooth skin—all tight and just begging to be touched. Drops of water trickle from his hair, and down his chest, reaching the towel wrapped around his waist, and getting absorbed.

Breath Scarlett, breathe.

"You done checking me out?" Aiden's voice interrupts my ogle fest.

"W-what are you talking about? I wasn't checking you out!"

"Sure, you weren't." A cocky grin is plastered on his face. He looks so smug right now I want to punch him.

"Why don't you just—just wear something?!"

He simply chuckles, leaning against the wall. "Why? Don't you enjoy seeing me like this?"

I ignore his comment and start to walk away, when he suddenly speaks up.

"It's sad really."

"What is?"

"It's sad that you're with someone who doesn't take your breath away."

"How would *you* know he doesn't?"

"Because, you don't look at him the way you're looking at me right now."

"And how am I looking at you?" I challenge.

"Like you're stuck in a world of darkness, starving for light, and I'm your sun."

I'm at a loss for words. A short pause, then: "where'd you get that line from?" I scoff.

"It doesn't matter. I'm right, am I not?"

I don't respond, so he continues.

"You don't love William. I know you don't. What you have with him . . . that's not love, that's charity. You're just holding on to him because you don't want to hurt him!"

"That's not true!" I exclaim.

"You *know* it is." He stares deep into my eyes, challenging me to deny the truth.

"*So?* It doesn't change things." I snap. "It doesn't change what you did, or how you made me feel. You don't know how *inadequate* I felt. I wanted to be *everything* you could ever want. You don't know how much it hurt when I realized I could never be that. You don't know how it felt *every time* you chose her over me, how I got my hopes up high only to see them crash. It's no news that you broke my heart. And then you had to go ahead and throw away our friendship too, throw it away, like it meant *nothing* to you. You don't know how *less* I felt, like I wasn't . . . wasn't good enough."

I stare at the palm of my hands, trying *so* hard to get a grip on my emotions. I don't want to end up crying in front of him. But he affects me in the cruelest way possible. He's got his fingers wrapped around my heart, and every time he tugs, I bleed.

A stray tear plops on my hand.

I feel the palm of his hand rest on my wet cheeks, rubbing my tears away. He cups my face, tugging it up so that I'm forced to meet his eyes. My heart lurches in my chest.

"Listen. I never, *ever* wanted you to feel inadequate, feel less; feel like you're not good enough. Never. But I'm sorry that I did. That hadn't been my intention."

His eyes do not stray off mine as he continues. "Scarlett, you *are* good enough. In fact, you are *more* than good enough. You are perfect to me. *I'm* the one who doesn't deserve you. You are so smart, kind, and honest . . . selfless. Everything about you is so intense and over whelming. Sometimes I wonder what I did to get *you* in my life."

I stare at him, feeling a mixture of anxiousness, fear and desperation. I don't know if I should believe him.

Words, he's just good with words. And words are what I've always fallen for. What I *fell* for. But that one time he had the chance to *act* on his words, he didn't. He abandoned me. All those things he'd said about wanting me? He obviously didn't mean it. Why else would he leave me like that?

I don't trust you Aiden. I don't think I can.

So I don't acknowledge his words. Instead, I push him away, refusing to look at him. "Just stop Aiden. I don't want to talk to you." I walk out of the room.

And for the first I wish he doesn't come after me.

And like always, he doesn't.

Chapter Twenty-Eight

Scarlett

"Hello?" My phone had been ringing continuously the past three minutes. But I didn't want to pick up. I'd felt so tired after my conversation with Aiden last night, that after a light dinner, I'd gone straight to bed. I hadn't slept very well though; lots of tossing and turning was involved as my mind buzzed with thoughts. I finally fell into a tired sleep at 4 AM. It's twelve noon now and I've been lying on my bed, giving my phone the evil eye, trying to convince myself that it's okay if I don't pick up.

But as you can see, I eventually gave in to its desperate ring and answer it.

"Hello Scarlett? You alright?"

It's William. He sounds genuinely worried.

"Yeah, I'm okay."

"Oh, thank god. You weren't taking my calls. I got worried."

I glance at the screen and see five missed calls. Yikes!

"Oh I was . . . asleep."

If it was Aiden on the other side, he wouldn't be worried because I didn't answer his call. He *knows* how much I hate talking on the phones. He *knows me*.

"Oh, I'm sorry if I woke you up. Go back to sleep Scarlett."

"No, it's okay. I'm up now. What did you want to talk about?"

"Oh, nothing in particular. I just wanted to meet you. Thought we could hang out, you know? It's a nice day. What do you say?"

My natural urge is to say no flat out. It's such a nice day? Yes, a nice day to sit at home. But then I realize what staying in means. It means another uneventful day I'll spend thinking about Aiden and feeling sorry for myself. So I force myself to say yes to William and then get out of bed. My stomach grows. So after taking a quick shower, I run downstairs to stuff my face with food.

What I hadn't been expecting was to see Aiden sprawled across the couch next to Darren. They're watching TV.

"You're *still* here?!" I exclaim, feeling thoroughly annoyed. Geez! I can't even have my breakfast without having to see his face. This is *not* how I'd planned to start my day. Today was going to be an Aiden-free day, without his presence tainting my mood.

Guess that was too much to ask.

"Yeah, I'm chilling with my friend *Darren*, what is it to you?" Aiden retorts.

I ignore him and head to the kitchen. Five minutes later, I plop down on the couch, on Darren's other side.

"So, can I um, borrow your car? I need to go somewhere," I ask him.

"Go *where*?" Darren responds, sounding extremely curious.

"Just someplace," I mutter.

". . . And that someplace is?"

I let out an exasperated sigh. "Fine! If you must know, I'm going out with William. So, are you going to lend me your car or nah?"

"Absolutely not."

"But Darren!"

"I *need* my car. Band practice, remember? But Aiden here can give you a ride. He's going home anyway, aren't you Aiden?"

I see Aiden tense up. He's as reluctant to share a car ride with me as I am with him. After last night, it's going to be absolutely torturous sitting next to him. No, I just can't.

Darren takes my silence as a form of acceptance. "Good, that's settled then!"

"But why can't you—" I begin to protest. But Aiden cuts me off.

"Sure, I'll do it."

I gape at him.

This day just keeps getting better and better.

"Alright, I'll just go and get dressed." I return to my room to get ready. Now that my stomach is full, I can focus on getting dressed. But honestly, I just feel ten times more reluctant to go now. I could have asked William to pick me up; he would have. But I didn't want him coming all the way here just for me. But Aiden giving me a lift is so much worse!

I'm not exactly sure what William has planned for us today, but we're going to a park. So I wear something cute yet casual—dark blue skinny jeans, a faded flannel shirt, and my good ol' black converse.

Once I return to the living room, Aiden grabs his car keys and starts towards the door.

Darren turns to me and says in the most serious tone ever: "Keep it PG-13."

"Darren!" I exclaim, abhorred. "That was definitely *not* on the agenda for today."

"Okay, okay, but use protection alright?"

I direct my best glare at him before walking out of the room, leaving a laughing Darren behind me. Aiden is quick to follow.

Soon we're on the road. I'm sitting shotgun and trying my best to look at anywhere but him. The stereo is playing some of Aiden's favorite songs (mostly loud rock music, peppered with some mainstream pop numbers) but even that isn't succeeding in reducing the awkwardness.

I feel a twinge of sadness as I comprehend the current state of our relationship. We used to be *best friends*. We'd literally never shut up when we were together. My stomach would always hurt so much because *that's* how much he made me laugh. But now we're barely speaking.

I can't help thinking this is my fault. *I'm* the one who started this. *I* decided it was okay to fall in love with my best friend. *I* messed it all up. I know I did.

But even as I think these thoughts, I know for a fact that it's not my fault, at least not entirely. He played a part in this too, a *big* part. I can't let myself take all the blame. We *both* screwed up, and now we've lost something special.

I realize with a start that the car has stopped. We're outside the city park. I, all but jump out of the car; pushing the door open almost immediately and stepping out. "Uh . . . thanks for the ride Aiden."

He nods in reply, choosing not to say anything. Instead, he's looking at something behind me, his expression solemn, with a hint of anger. I turn around to see what he's looking at.

Should've guessed. It's William.

He looks super cute, dressed up in a pair of jeans and—wait for it—a flannel shirt! It's going to look so weird when we hang out today. We'll look like those pretentious couples who try to match their outfits. William's carrying a big picnic basket in his hands, and a huge guitar bag is hanging down his back.

I should have known . . .

We're going on a picnic.

It's all so cute, and straight out of a romance novel, that I feel myself momentarily forget Aiden is right next to me and let out a girly squeal.

William starts walking over, and I run up to him, almost tackling him as I wrap my arms around him to give him a hug.

"Are we really going to have a picnic?" I ask, sounding super excited.

"Yup! *And* we're going to feed the ducks. I have this whole afternoon planned. I've made a list of all the boring things I want to tell you."

William's like . . . boyfriend goals. He organizes perfect picnic dates and sings custom love songs he's penned down just for you. He cooks delicious food and takes genuine interest in me. We don't have this incredible chemistry or connection, but he makes me happy, however twisted that sounds. When I'm around him I worry a little less and I'm at ease.

"There's this place by the lake, under this cherry tree. It is my *absolute* favorite. I usually go there when I want to sit by myself and pen a song or two. I don't know, there's just something about that place," he tells me. "You're the second girl I've brought here."

I don't know if I should feel special that I'm the second girl he has brought here or bothered that I'm not the only one. Either way, that's *not* something you should say to your girlfriend.

"Who was the first?" I ask.

"Angelina, my best friend."

I nod. "Well, I can't wait to see it."

"Yeah let's go, shall we?"

"Yeah just a second, let me just—" I turn around to thank Aiden for the ride, and tell him he can go now, but he's already left

* * *

William stops the car right outside Darren's house. He shuts off the engine, turns down the radio and suddenly we're shrouded in silence.

"I had fun today," I tell William, smiling at him. "I'll see you at school on Monday, okay? Goodnight." I smile at him, then proceed to leave.

"Wait!" I hear him say. His hand clasps around my own.

"What is it?" I turn around, confused.

"I just realized, we both spent the whole day together. But not once did we kiss."

My eyes widen as I realize what William said is true. We spent about ten hours together today. William's supposedly my boyfriend. But not once, not even *once*, did the thought of kissing him cross my mind.

I suddenly feel guilty.

"Stay a little. Don't go just yet." He requests. I'm a little too embarrassed to say no, so I get back in the car.

"You know, I've wanted to do this the whole day. But I guess, now's a good time as ever." With that, he slowly leans forward. I feel his hand encircle my waist, stopping on the small of my back. I feel trapped, trapped in the blue of his eyes. He A second later, I feel his lips on mine.

I wait for the butterflies to swarm my belly, wait for my heart to flutter in my chest, for my lungs to forget to inhale.

Nothing happens.

He knots his fingers through my hair and pulls me closer. It starts getting heated. Within minutes, his mouth is trailing down my neck, and his hands slowly inching *upwards*. All the while, I feel like someone's slowly choking me.

I can't. I can't.

I gently push him off, abruptly cutting off our kiss.

"It's getting late, I should go," I murmur casually, as if I didn't just act like I wasn't interested in making out with my boyfriend.

He nods. "Of course. I'll walk you to the door."

I want to refuse, but I'm tired of speaking. So I just let him follow me as I walk towards the house. I ring the bell two minutes later. I can feel William's gaze locked on me. He probably feels confused. I don't care. I'm too tired to explain this. All of this.

Almost a minute later, the door is flung open by a slightly disheveled Aiden glaring at us, looking extremely annoyed.

"Do you know what time it is?!" he bellows.

"What are *you* still doing here?! I thought you left this morning?"

"I had to come back. I forgot something," he mutters.

I get a strong feeling that he's lying.

"Anyway, why haven't you been returning your calls?! Do you know how worried I—uhm, *Darren* was for you?!"

"My phone died. We were out in the park, I couldn't recharge it. But honestly, why would *he* be worried? I was with William—"

"Exactly! Because you were with *him*. You've been gone for hours, not returning any of our calls. Honestly young lady, how can you be so irresponsible?"

"Ew Aiden, don't call me 'young lady', you sound just like my father!" I grumble, stepping inside the house.

Aiden glares at me then turns to William. "And you! What is your problem, huh? You've been by her side throughout the day, you know? Why aren't you leaving? Are you a leech or something?!" Before William can so much as say a word, Aiden slams the door on his face.

I gasp. "Aiden! God, what *is* your problem? That was *so* rude! I want you to go outside *right now* and apologize to him!"

"Please, I'm not doing that." He rolls his eyes. "Darren, tell her how worried you were!" Aiden turns to him.

I do the same. "Darren, were you worried?!"

He looks up from the TV screen (honestly, how much TV can a person watch?)

"Uh . . . I guess?" he replies, then turns back to look at the screen.

Aiden looks at me pointedly.

"You know what? I don't care. I'm going upstairs." I'm so annoyed right now, I could punch a wall. "Leave me alone, both of you!"

They don't. Actually, *he* doesn't.

I can hear the sound of his foot slapping against the wooden staircase as he follows me upstairs and right into my room.

"Didn't you get the memo? Leave. Me. Alone."

"Not before you explain *that*." Aiden points at me.

"What?"

"That." He points again. I look at him quizzically. He grabs my finger and plops it down on a spot near my collarbone. "There. It's a hickey. And your hair is all messed up. Your clothes are wrinkled. What happened today?" The way he's looking at me, it's like he's accusing me of doing something I shouldn't have.

I never realized William had given me a love bite back there. My cheeks heat up with embarrassment. "What do *you* think happened?" I quip, folding my arms.

"So you slept with him? Seriously?! Now he's finally got that *one* thing he wanted."

I ignore how he jumped at the most extreme conclusion possible and focus on the latter part of his statement.

"What do you mean 'he finally got that one thing he wanted'?! Are you implying he's with me just so he can—"

"Of course! He just wants to get in your pants. Are you really that *naïve*?!"

My mouth drops open. "Really Aiden, I didn't think you could stoop *this* low. You don't even know him. How can you accuse him of something like this?"

"Because I'm not *blinded* by his beauty or whatever."

I laugh out loud. "I'm not blinded by—"

And then it hits me—

"Are you . . . are you jealous?!" I snort.

His eyes widen. He suddenly looks flustered.

"What?! N-no. W-why would I be jealous? Pfft!"

"So that explains it. That explains why you've been acting like a total douche bag this whole time. Honestly, I don't know why I didn't realize it earlier. It's so obvious."

"I'm not *jealous*!"

I smirk. "Sure you aren't."

I bet he's getting a taste of his own medicine now. Now he knows how it feels.

"But I'm not! I just don't trust him—" He protests.

"Are you done? Because I've had a *really* long day, and I just want to settle down in my bed and relax a bit. You mind?"

"No, of course I don't. I was leaving anyway. Goodbye." He glares at me one last time before turning to leave.

I plop down on my bed and start checking the notifications on my phone. I'm distracted a minute later by a loud thud that causes me to look up.

Aiden's still here.

"Why haven't you left yet?" I ask, annoyed.

"Because this stupid door won't budge! I'm pretty sure it was wide open when I walked in a few minutes ago."

"Maybe it's stuck. Are you sure you didn't shut it accidently?"

"Of *course* I'm sure. Do you take me for a fool? Wait, don't answer that."

I roll my eyes. "Here, step aside. Let me try." I walk to the door and start to push. It doesn't move, not even a little. It's like it's locked.

"Hey, is that pizza?!" I hear Aiden exclaim.

I turn to look at him, wondering what he's going on about. But sure enough, there *is* pizza. A large one, kept nicely inside a pizza box in the corner of the room, with a bottle of cola and a box of Garlic Bread.

What the hell is going on!?

"There's a note stuck on the box," Aiden murmurs, taking it off.

"Here, let me see." I take it from him and read it out aloud:

Scarlett and Aiden,

You both obviously need to sort out your issues. Well, now you can. I'll return from band practice in a couple of hours. I expect you to kiss and makeup by then. (But not actually kiss and makeup, if you know what I mean.) And if not, well, what are another few hours locked up in a room together? Have fun!

Darren

"Oh he's going to get it!" I search Darren's contact on my phone and hit dial. He picks up almost immediately.

"Darren's phone!"

"You come back *right now* and open up this door before I break it!"

"Good luck trying!"

"This isn't funny. I'm *serious* Darren, come back."

"But I'm serious too! And anyway, I'm almost at my friend's place. I'm not turning back *now*. So you both fix this, and I'll set you free once I return. Bye!" He hangs up.

"Well, what did he say?" Aiden asks me, once I get off the call.

I shake my head.

I guess we just got locked in together.

Chapter Twenty-Nine

Scarlett

"So . . . now what?" he asks.

I shrug. "Darren's gone, but I suppose he'll come back in 2 to 3 hours. Till then, we must try our best to maintain a peaceful atmosphere in this room by staying *the hell away* from each other."

He stares at me incredulously.

Bad things happen when Aiden and I are left alone. Bad things like us kissing each other when we *definitely* shouldn't, and us having unpleasant arguments because we keep getting on each other's nerves. Just *being* around him makes my heart want to leap out of my chest. If I am to survive the next few hours, I must pretend he's not here.

"Shouldn't be too difficult. We'll sit in silence, minding our own business, and wait for this torture to end." I instruct. "Till then, *this* side of the room will be mine." I draw an invisible line going through the middle, "and *that* side of the room, will be yours. Capiche?"

"What? No! What, are we ten-year-olds? What if I—what if I want to go to the bathroom? That's on *your* side of the room." He protests.

Ugh, he's right.

"Well, in *that* case, you'll need to get my permission first."

"I'm not getting your permission to go to the bathroom!"

"Yes, you are."

"And, where will I sit? On the floor? Since the bed is, oh-so-conveniently, on *your* side of the room."

"Why not?"

"You know, that's really not fair."

"No, what's not fair is *me* being locked up in my room with *you,* because you decided to act like a jealous prick instead of a civil human being. If you had not over reacted back there, Darren wouldn't have thought he needed to lock us here. So yeah, it's *your* fault."

I take out my kindle from my bag and get busy reading a book. If I have to distract myself and pretend Aiden isn't in the room, reading a book is my best option.

He sighs. "I wasn't jealous," he mutters. "I was just trying to look out for you."

I stare at him pointedly.

"And okay, I *was* a little jealous." He confesses, raising his arms up in surrender.

"Good." I turn back to my kindle.

"How can I not be? It feels like I've been replaced."

You can never be replaced Aiden.

"Good. So now you know how it feels," I reply, surprising even myself. This is the first time I'm openly talking about how Hailey's presence in his life affected me.

"Don't be silly Scar. Nobody can take your place in my life," he says, looking up at me from his place on the floor.

"Of course, how *can* they, when there's no place to take? You basically kicked me out of your life."

"I fucked up, okay? I'm sorry."

Shit, we're doing exactly what I hadn't wanted us to— we're talking. But I can't seem to stop.

"Why did you do it Aiden? Why? You told me you had feelings for me. You had a *girlfriend* yet you made me feel like I meant something to you. And when things started heating up, you pretended you'd never said the words you had, never did the things you did, and you left. You led me on and you *left*."

"I'm sorry, okay? I'm really, really sorry. If there's one thing I regret doing, it's that I ever left you. And I know my saying sorry doesn't make things okay; it doesn't erase what I made you go through. But I deeply regret what I did. I just need you to give me another chance. I can't take it anymore, this hate from you. It kills me every time. So just tell me what I can do to make it up to you and I swear I'll do it—anything to turn you back into the Scarlett you used to be: the Scarlett who didn't hate me, who laughed at my lame jokes, who was my only friend."

He looks really ashamed, and slightly uncomfortable. Good. I want him to squirm. I want him to feel guilty. I want him to face what he's done, and admit he acted like a hoebag.

After this, we both silently divide the pizza and coke among ourselves and retire to two different corners of the room. We've both engaged in some really intense conversation yesterday and today. We need a break from this. We need a break from each other.

* * *

I glance at the time on my phone. It's been three hours since Darren left, and he *still* hasn't returned. Aiden tried to call him half an hour ago, but it just kept ringing. Darren did not answer. I hope the reason he didn't pick up his phone was because he was driving back here.

"I don't think he's coming back tonight Scarlett," Aiden says from across the room. This is the first time he's spoken to me after that conversation we had.

"He *has* to. He promised! He can't lock us up here all night. Call him again."

"I did. He's not picking up."

"Well, try again in a few minutes."

He tries again sometime later. I do too. But it's futile. Darren is just not responding to our calls. We have no option left. We'll have to sleep in together.

We both—in one tiny bed.

And just *one* blanket!

Oh God help us.

It's not the most ideal situation. Yes, I'd thought of this moment plenty of times before. I'd wondered how it'd feel to finally lie down next to my crush, to see his head resting on the pillow adjacent to mine, and his chest rising and falling as he fell into slumber.

This was *completely* different.

For starters, I can't sleep. And by the looks of it, neither can he. I don't blame him, really. I feel equally weird and uncomfortable. Darren has no idea how much I hate him right now. *He's* the reason we're in this mess right now. Why couldn't he mind his own business and leave us be?

* * *

There's something about the dark. When you're alone, it scares you. But when you're with someone, lying on a bed, cocooned in a blanket, you feel safe. You also feel lighter, freer, as if the dark void is slowly draining your pain, your fears, your inhibitions.

And maybe that's why, despite being so hateful to Aiden earlier, I decided to talk to him.

"Can we talk?" I ask him. I can't see him. I can only feel him lying next to me in the dark and hear him as he inhales and exhales.

If he'd ignored me or angrily refused, I wouldn't have been surprised. I hadn't been very nice to him these past two days.

"Yes, yes we can."

Phew!

"So . . . I was thinking about what you said and . . ."

"And?"

"I'm tired of fighting, Aiden. And I know things might never get back to the way they were but I don't care. I just want this to stop."

"So . . . so you're saying we should stop fighting?"

"Yes."

"So does that mean we're friends now?"

"I don't know. But we can try to be civil to each other at least."

"Yeah, we can." He sounds a little disappointed.

It's pretty clear by now that we're nowhere near falling asleep. But we're too lazy to get up and switch on the lights. Or get off the bed, for that matter.

"So how's everything going, Scar?" He continues, trying to fill the dark silence.

My heart flutters a little when I hear that nickname roll off his tongue.

"Good. It's been going good."

"So, tell me *everything* I missed while I was gone."

"You didn't miss much."

You just missed me missing you.

"Ha-ha, to be honest, you didn't miss much either. It's like my life hit a standstill while you were gone. I can't even remember what happened. All I remember is us not talking to each other."

I want to tell him that's all I remember too. All I remember is sitting and thinking about being with him. But I don't say that. He doesn't need to know how much power he has over me, how vulnerable he makes me feel.

"But, I *did* miss something—you and William getting together."

Here we go again . . .

"I never asked. How did that happen?"

"We met at that party remember?"

"Uh, yeah." He pauses, and I'm pretty sure he's remembering how aggressively he'd acted back then. "And then he asked you out, and you said yes?"

I nod. Then I remember it's still dark and he can't see me. So I say yes.

"So, you like him, huh?"

"Yeah, he's . . . he's a good person. I love talking to him."

"Talking? Talking?! What's special about that? You love talking to me too."

"Do I?"

"You do," he states adamantly. A hint of self-doubt creeps into his voice anyway.

I chuckle.

The room is suddenly illuminated. I squint. Aiden switched on the bedside lamp. He's wide awake, sitting up on the bed, his dark brown eyes sparkling in the dark.

"W-what are you doing? Turn off the lights."

"No. Now tell me, what else do you like about William?"

I glare at Aiden. I honestly think he's lost it. He sounds like a gossip-hungry school girl. It's ridiculous. I roll my eyes at him.

"I . . . like his personality?" My answer sounds like a question even to my own ears.

Aiden's giving me that look, that look he gives me whenever I tell him I'm staying at home during the weekends and reading a book instead of going out. He pities me.

"Seriously? C'mon, you can do better than that! Give me details. *What* do you like about his personality? What do you talk about? Tell me something you like doing as a couple."

"Like what?"

"Like kissing! Do you like kissing him?"

I get a flashback of this afternoon: how I spent the whole day with William, and not once, not even once thought of kissing him. "Uh . . . I—Yes, I like kissing him. It's nice."

He shakes his head as if he's disappointed in me. "I *hate* that word. There are so many words out there, that you can use to describe it. Yet you choose 'nice.' Nice is the adjective you use to describe the ugly dress your grandma buys for you, or the disgusting pudding your neighbor asks you to taste. Kissing shouldn't just be *nice*. It should be breath-taking, bone-chilling, heart-stopping, mind-numbing, intoxicating, flawless, perfect."

I stare at him incredulously. "Oh yeah? And have *you* experienced a kiss like that? It's easy to say. But when you get down to it—"

"As a matter of fact, I *have*."

Shit. Now I'll have to hear him describe how he played tonsil hockey with some girl. Perfect, just perfect.

"There was this girl I kissed at the beach. I've never experienced anything like it."

Some girl at the beach, huh? Wait, *we* kissed at the beach . . . But then, that doesn't mean anything. He must have kissed lots of girls at lots of beaches.

"I was a little tipsy, but I remember that night as vividly as the back of my hand. She made me feel . . . *alive*. Some experiences can be described. The really great ones, can be described using the words I'd mentioned. But then there are others: all the words, in all the languages all over the world, aren't sufficient to describe them. And that kiss, was exactly like that."

That's it. I just can't. I cannot hear him talking about this oh-so-special kiss he had with this oh-so-special girl.

"You know what? I think I'm going to go sleep now. I'm really tired." I pretend to yawn. "Good night!" I close my eyes and turn away.

"No! You can't sleep yet. We just started talking. Do you sleep so early at all your sleepovers?"

"*This* isn't a sleepover."

"It isn't? We ate pizza, talked some, and then we'll sleep together in one room, after talking all night. Isn't that how a sleepover works?"

"Well . . . yeah, but I don't care, okay? I need to sleep."

"Oh c'mon! How many times do you think we'll get a chance like this? To talk? Just you and me, without being interrupted by *anyone*. You can't sleep just yet. I'm not going to let you."

It's crazy how smoothly we've transitioned back into being friends. From the way we're talking, you would never guess we'd spent the last few weeks angry at each other.

"So where was I? Yeah so, that kiss with that girl—I think about it a lot."

"She must have been one hell of a kisser then."

"Maybe, but I think it had more to do with how *I* felt for *her*."

"She must have been really special, to be able to make you feel that way," I reply dejectedly.

"Oh, she was! I mean, she *is*. She's really, really special." He's looking straight at me, his eyes glinting under the lamp light as an amused smile plays on his lips.

And suddenly it hits me, the girl he's talking about . . . is me.

A blush hits my face full force. I silently thank my stars that the room is still quite dark, otherwise Aiden would have easily noticed how red my face had suddenly gotten.

"So, have you been kissed like that?"

Seeing that I've only ever kissed two boys in my whole life, it's pretty surprising to realize that yes, I *have* experienced a kiss like that.

I nod. "Yeah, I have. I actually kissed this guy at the beach. It was unlike anything I'd ever experienced. It was like . . . like someone had plucked all the stars from the night sky and laid it on my tongue. There was so much spark, so much heat. But anyway, he was kinda drunk. I'm sure he wouldn't have kissed me if he was sober."

"You're wrong. He still would have kissed you. He really wanted to."

"Which is *really* weird, because he had a girlfriend. Why would he want to kiss me?"

"Because there's just something about you. When he's near you, he can't breathe. His mind stops working and he forgets everything you could possibly forget. Nothing makes sense when he's with you. All he's sure of is the way you make him feel. You're everywhere, and nothing else matters."

I stare at him in awe, my heart fluttering in my chest. I'm not sure he's talking about himself anymore. Because everything he said describes *exactly* the way I feel when I'm with him.

Could it be, could it *really* be that he feels the same way after all? And not just the same way, but *in* the same way. Do I affect him the same way he affects me?

"And if he could, he'd turn back time, and do it all over again. But maybe a little differently. He knows he has hurt you. And you have no idea how much he hates himself for it. He hopes that one day you'll find it in your heart to forgive him, to *truly* forgive him. All he wants now is for you to be happy. Even if it's not with him."

He wants me to be happy, even if it's not with him.

I'm touched. It's the closest he's come to making me feel that maybe, just maybe, he feels what I do; feels it with the same intensity, wants it with the same desperation. For the first time, he sounds selfless.

I wrap my arms around his body and pull him into a hug. I hold him as tightly as I can, making the most of this moment—hold him like I never want to let him go. "I'm so sick of fighting. I'm so sick of not being with you, of not talking to you. I just can't do this anymore. I'm sorry Aiden. I'm sorry for being so harsh, so distant. Please forgive me."

"There's nothing to forgive. I deserved it. I deserved every bit of it and even more. *You* need to forgive *me*. I'm sorry."

"I know you are. You're forgiven."

He pulls me closer, our chests touching. I nuzzle my head in the crook of his neck, tears blurring my vision. I've missed this so much. I've missed him so much.

"I missed you," he says, gently pressing his lips onto my forehead.

I feel the butterflies dance in my chest. "I missed you too."

We hold each other for a long time. I'm not sure for how long. Some things can't be described—the way I felt right there and then, is one of them.

Chapter Thirty

Scarlett

I wake up in the morning feeling extremely fresh and warm. I'm nuzzling my head into a warm, albeit hard pillow. I snuggle closer to it, enjoying how amazing it feels. I can't remember the last time I'd slept so comfortably. I run my finger down the pillow, only to realize it didn't feel like a pillow at all!

My eyes pop open with a start. I realize I wasn't hugging a pillow. I was snuggled against Aiden.

Okay Scarlett, calm down, everything is going to be okay. Don't start hyperventilating right now.

Our legs are all tangled up. His right arm is wrapped around my body, clutching it close to his, with my head resting on his chest.

I've never felt so embarrassed in my whole life.

The door to the room suddenly bangs open, startling both Aiden and me. Aiden wakes up, his heart racing in his chest. "What the hell?!" he gasps out loud, bewildered.

Guess who stands at the door?

"Good. You're both alive. I thought you would have murdered each other by now," Darren says. He *actually* looks relieved.

"Oh don't worry; we were too busy plotting *your* murder. Killing each other didn't even cross our minds," I reply, smiling at him.

He ignores my threat. "So did it work?"

"If by that you mean whether if we decided to stop fighting and become friends again, then yeah, it did work," Aiden responds, sitting up.

"But seriously, next time, you *tell us* to talk things out instead of locking us in a room and forgetting all about it."

"I didn't forget, okay? I just drank a bit last night, and my friends wouldn't let me drive back here. So I had to spend the night there. However, based on how you two were snuggled together on the bed, I don't think it could have been *that* bad, am I right?"

I feel my cheeks heat up, and I'm sure Aiden looks equally flustered. We both make it a point to ignore Darren's comment.

Even though I'm still kind of annoyed that he locked us in together, forcing us into such an awkward situation, I can't help feeling a little thankful. If it hadn't been for him, Aiden and I wouldn't be talking right now.

* * *

"So your friend Susan is dating Adam now?" Aiden clarifies. I nod in response. "Wasn't he your date to the carnival?"

"Uh . . . yeah. We weren't really compatible, so I suggested he go out with her instead." I lie.

"Wow, girls are weird," he mutters.

"What? Don't tell me guys don't do this."

"No, we don't. We've got to uphold the bro code."

"We have the girl code too! But this is completely different. Adam and I just went out *once*. I never really liked him, so it's okay."

And it was. Susan was actually happy. After much thinking, Susan had finally agreed to go out with Adam. They'd gone to the mall, eaten some junk food, and watched a movie maybe—nothing over the top. They obviously had fun despite how reluctant Susan had been at first. I mean, they've hung out three times since then, and it's just been just a little over a week!

I remember how nervous she'd been on the day he was taking her out for the first time.

"Is it weird that I'm nervous right now?" Susan had pondered. "It's not like this is the first time I'm going on a date with someone."

I'd squeezed her shoulders reassuringly. "It's going to be great. Adam's an *amazing* guy. As your best friend, I wholeheartedly approve."

"Well, I hope the date is as amazing as he is." Susan had sounded *so* nervous.

I didn't care what she said, I knew for a fact that she liked Adam, a little if not a lot. She wouldn't have been a nervous wreck if she didn't.

"Well, better her than you. I didn't like Adam anyway."

"You never like any guy I hang out with, not that there are a lot…but still."

"I like *myself*," he replies cheekily. "Don't you?"

We've finally reached our destination. We continue talking as we unlock our respective lockers and gather our books for the next few lessons.

"But you don't count."

"Why not?"

"Because…you're you. And we're just friends."

"We don't have to be."

I stare at him. Trying to understand what he's getting at.

"Don't we?"

"Y—"

A loud clang disrupts our conversation. We both look up at the source of noise, momentarily distracted.

Standing a few feet away is Hailey. She's hitting a locker, presumably hers, with her fist. It looks like she's trying to bang it open.

I'm not surprised when Aiden heads over to her to help her out. Almost reluctantly, I drag myself after him.

For the two weeks we've been friends again, I haven't seen Aiden with Hailey once. I admit it was kind of weird, and I'd found myself wondering about the same on more than one occasion. He even spent most of his lunch hours with me if I'm not sitting with William. I'd assumed he was making up for all the lost time and hung out with Hailey when I wasn't with him. I hadn't had the chance to ask him what Hailey thought of us becoming friends again. Did it bother her? Did she want him to stop talking to me again?

It has been ages since the three of us—Aiden, Hailey, and I—have been in the same place, at the same time. I don't like it one bit. I'll never get used to seeing him with her. I'd rather not deal with this.

Hailey completely ignores me. She looks slightly surprised to see Aiden though. She tells him her locker's jammed, and she really needs to get her assignment inside. She needs to submit it today.

"Don't worry, I got this." Aiden starts putting pressure on the locker at different locations of its door. It doesn't seem like he's doing this for the first time. He looks like a 'jammed locker-opening' expert.

After several minutes, he succeeds. The locker door swings open. Hailey claps her hand in delight. "Thank you *so* much!" she chirps.

He chuckles. "Oh it's alright. C'mon, grab your assignment quick. You need to submit it, don't you? Lunch's almost over, and I think your class is all over the other side of the school, in Hallway B-21."

She nods. "You remember my class schedule?"

"Of course, I do. I used to walk you to them, remember?" he replies, all smiles.

Ugh. Next thing you know, they'll be kissing. And I'll be forced to watch. No thanks.

So I quietly excuse myself, saying I need to get going and leave. Aiden calls after me, asking me to wait. I pretend I don't hear.

After everything that's been said and done, we're back to square one. Aiden's still with Hailey, and I'm the third wheel, the jealous, unwanted best friend. I don't need this kind of stress in my life.

I'm distracted, lost in thoughts, which is why I end up crashing against someone head on. "Ow!" I rub my head vigorously. I literally walked into someone, a tall someone, causing my head to smack against his hard chest.

I look up, ready to apologize, feeling really embarrassed.

It's Damien.

"Oh, it's you. I'm sorry . . . I didn't see you."

"Well, that's obvious."

"Sorry again," I mumble. "I better get going. I'm going to be late for class." I start walking away.

"Hey! Don't you have math right now?"

"Uh . . . yeah. Why?"

"Just wondering, since you're going the wrong way. Our class is *that* way," he says, pointing in the other direction.

"Oh."

He chuckles.

I was in such a rush to get away from Hailey and Aiden, I started heading the wrong way. Maybe that's why Aiden was calling me out, to tell me I was going in the opposite direction.

How embarrassing.

"C'mon, let's go together. I have math too."

I nod, quietly walking beside him.

"Whoa! I didn't know they were still talking," he exclaims all of a sudden. He's looking at Aiden and Hailey.

I roll my eyes, then suddenly freeze when I realize what Damien just said. I turn to him.

"Why wouldn't they be talking? What's so surprising about that?" I ask.

"Well, it's no news that they broke up. I'm surprised they're still on speaking terms."

I stop walking, not able to believe what I just heard.

"They . . . they broke up?" Damien nods.

Is that why Aiden befriended me again?

"Who ended it? Who broke up with whom?"

"I think it was…Hailey. Yeah, I think *she* was the one who dumped him."

I should have known.

He didn't dump her. *She* broke up with him. He didn't leave her. He didn't want to. She ended it, for some reason. Does he still like her?

And he . . . did he . . . is he talking to me again because he's single again? Is that it? I've always been his back-up, his second option. So is that why he suddenly decided to talk to me? Because Hailey left him and he was bored?

"How long has it been since they broke up?"

"Almost a month, I think."

A month.

That means they'd already broken up when he came to apologize to me. Is *this* why he apologized? Did he genuinely want to be a part of my life again, or did he apologize because Hailey left him, and he had no one else to jump to?

But no, that can't be right. He's *Aiden* for god's sake! He always has some girl lined up. He's not one to wait.

But why didn't he tell me they broke up?

For the next two hours, I'm deep in thought, and quite distracted. I want to confront Aiden, but at the same time I need to gather my thoughts before I do. I wish I could move past all of this. We're friends again, and that's all that matters now. Why am I so weird? Why can't I just let things go instead of holding onto everything so fiercely?

At the end of my last class, I ask Sharon to get her car out of the parking lot while I take a trip to the washroom. I really needed to pee. Thankfully, the bathroom stalls are empty when I walk in. Dirty lipstick-stained tissue papers litter the sink. Someone missed the waste basket, so their dirty sanitary napkin is lying on the floor.

I scrunch my nose in disgust. Who says girls are always neat and tidy? This bathroom's filthy.

Without wasting much time, I finish my business and proceed to wash my hands before I leave. I'm shaking my hands to dry off the water when the washroom door is pushed open, and in steps none other than Hailey.

For a few awkward seconds, I stand there frozen, gaping at her.

Time to get out of here, I think.

She pays me no mind and heads over to the sink. I turn around to leave. But something stops me. This is only awkward because I'm making this awkward. Besides, this is the perfect chance to talk to her, to clarify all the doubts that have been plaguing me since morning.

So I stop. And instead of leaving, I turn back around.

"Hailey? I need to ask you something." I say in a matter-of-fact tone. She will *have* to talk to me. I'm not going to let her ignore me.

She doesn't respond, but I go on anyway. "Why did you break up with Aiden?"

She stares at me pointedly, then turns back to face the bathroom mirror and starts brushing her hair. I'm losing my patience real quick. I start speaking again when she cuts me off.

"I realized we just weren't right for each other; we weren't what the other wanted."

I snort.

"And you couldn't come to that conclusion a few months earlier? Before ruining Aiden and my friendship?"

She rolls her eyes and turns away.

"What? You don't have a response to that? It's a genuine question. Couldn't you have realized this earlier instead of forcing Aiden to choose between us and ending our friendship? Which by the way, existed *way* before *you* came into his life."

"Hold on, hold on. What the hell are you talking about? I didn't make him choose *anything*."

"Um, yes you did? Don't lie."

"Uh no, I didn't?"

"Oh, so you're denying that you ever said that he needs to choose between us?"

"Well, of course I told him to get his shit together, to stop messing up with my mind. But no, I didn't give him an ultimatum. So I have absolutely *no* idea what you're talking about. If he stopped talking to you that was *his* decision."

Her words are like a slap to my face.

I think the hurt and confusion I feel is obvious on my face because she looks at me sympathetically.

"Look." She begins softly. "I think you should talk to him, okay?"

I nod silently and then rush out of there.

Chapter Thirty-One

Scarlett

The next few weeks pass by in a blur. William and I continue to date. I hadn't been sure we'd last this long. Initially, it had really been a struggle. I kept thinking I was lying to myself, to everyone. I was with one person, but my heart was with another.

I got over that mindset though. I eventually relaxed into what William and I had. I stopped comparing him to Aiden. I just focused on him. So what if it didn't feel the same when we kissed, or when we held hands? It's not bad; it's just different. Being with him is different. We talk about different things and he gets me in a way Aiden probably wouldn't. We talk about deep concepts, have occasional heart-to-hearts. We're both poetic souls.

Aiden and I? We're still friends. I've started seeing a lot less of him though. It's just something I had to do. I needed that space. If I didn't do it, I'd never be able to get over him.

Am I over him though? Not really. But it doesn't seem so hopeless now. I know that if I try, if I *really* try, I'll be able to get him out of my heart. And that's what I need to do.

So yes, there has been an improvement. I might just be on the righteous path of moving on. Sure, I still can't help smiling when Aiden's around and every once in a while, I get butterflies but my heart doesn't race anymore when I think of him. Actually, I *don't* think of him, period. Hours pass without even one Aiden-related thought entering my mind. That's a big achievement in itself.

Christmas is around the corner and we have our Winter Ball in a couple of hours. I've bought a silver gown for this very occasion. It's a beautiful slip-on with a plunging neckline. I've also seen about hundreds of hair and makeup tutorials on YouTube. My girlfriends and I are currently in my bedroom, getting ready together for the event.

Kayla is curling Sharon's hair. Andrea is perched in front of the vanity mirror, touching up her makeup. A beautiful black strapless gown adorns her body. Her lustrous brown hair is styled into a sophisticated updo. If there's one thing I'm jealous of Andrea it is her hair. It has just the right texture and luster to make it look perfect.

Today is one of those rare occasions when we all have dates. I'm obviously going with William. Sharon is going with this guy in our chemistry class who is a total sweetheart. His name is Kevin. Andrea and Kayla are going out with the Jamison twins. They are one of the few twin guys in our school and are really hot. We're all *so* excited.

Tonight's going to be *magical.*

After an hour or two of applying makeup, doing each other's hair and nails, and discussing our boy problems, we decide to get going. We're meeting the boys at the destination itself. Andrea's driving us. It's dark when we all huddle up inside her Chevrolet, picking up our gowns so that they don't get dirty. It doesn't take us long to reach the school. Within half an hour, we've already reached the school, parked the car and are on our way to the gymnasium.

The gym looks breathtaking like it always does during a dance. The decoration committee has done a good job. Streamers and balloons cover the walls, a stage with a mike and a podium is set up in the front. The refreshment tables are on the side. Circular tables with chairs are arranged at the back, where students can sit and talk. The tables even have a bunch of white roses stacked up in the center, to give it a dash of elegance. The area right in front of the stage has been left bare so that the students can dance there. The DJ is currently playing song dedications.

I notice William and his gang hanging around the refreshment tables. I temporarily bid my friends goodbye and walk over to him. He notices me when I'm a few feet away from him. His face immediately lights up with a smile. As is customary now, he pulls me closer and kisses me hard. I greet his friends after that.

We're standing there talking among ourselves, when I see Aiden. He has his arms around a gorgeous African American girl. A long slit on the side of her dress exposing her long, shapely legs. I see her lean towards him and whisper something in his ear. He smirks.

I *know* that smirk. It's Aiden's 'I know you can't get enough of me' smirk. I can't help glaring at him, even though he's not looking in my direction.

He suddenly turns, catching me glaring at him. I look away, embarrassed.

Please don't come here. Please don't come here.

They start heading towards us.

Damn it.

He wraps his arms tightly around her waist, pulling her against him. He whispers something in her ear, making her giggle. I look away.

Well, two can play at that game.

"Hey Scarlett." He smiles at me. "Hello *Wilbert*," he utters his name with pure contempt. William is polite enough to ignore it. "You guys having fun?"

"Yes, yes we are," I reply immediately. "Aren't we baby?" I turn to William.

He nods. "Yeah, the night has only begun though."

"You guys haven't met Madison, have you? She's my date for tonight." He gestures towards the girl standing next to him.

She *completely* ignores me and smiles at William instead, looking dreamy-eyed. Typical. "Hi!" she chirps at him. He politely replies. I roll my eyes.

I wrap my arm around William's. "Do you want to dance?" I ask him. He nods, flashing me his superb smile, and we both head towards the dance floor.

* * *

Aiden

Humph. If she thinks I'm giving up so easily, she's wrong. I grab Madison's hand and practically drag her to the dance floor. She is the captain of the girls' volleyball team. She can act a little ditsy sometimes, but her looks and attitude make up for it. She practically begged me to take her to the dance.

Okay, *I* begged *her*.

We spend the next couple of minutes slow dancing to sappy love songs. My thoughts obviously take me back to Scarlett and my dance.

Things have changed so much now.

I see them, standing just a few feet away. He's holding her in his arms as they gently sway to the music. It hurts. I don't even want to look at them; that's how much it hurts. It's like there's this heavy pain in my chest that refuses to go away.

Scarlett's gaze meets mine. I wait for her to look away.

She doesn't.

Something passes between us. We're not even standing close. I'm here, across the room but I can feel it. It's like the sky before a storm—intense and electric.

We continue to look into each other's eyes for the next few minutes. One love song follows another, the same old sappy themes. They apply to us. But she's in someone else's arms and I'm holding another. Not the best love story, eh?

But our eyes are having a conversation of their own. The rest of the world lays forgotten. Maybe it's just me, but I think I spot a hint of yearning in her eyes—a raw, unconcealed desire.

The ache in my chest intensifies.

She's spilling sad poetry through her eyes; I'm left breathless.

* * *

Scarlett

The music suddenly stops. I blink. It's like I've been awakened from a trance.

What just happened?

It was surreal, almost like a dream.

My heart throbs. It's an actual, physical embodiment of all the emotions I feel in that moment. And there are so many, so many that I almost feel overwhelmed.

I feel angry. There's so much anger that it surges inside me like a tsunami. He does this. He *always* does this. Without even doing anything he does it. He doesn't even have to try.

It's like he has me by a chord: a thick, invisible chord that cannot be detached. It's wrapped tightly around my heart at one end; the other is in his hands. Every time I try to leave, he loosens his grip. He never drops it though, no. He loosens it, loosens it just enough to give me the illusion that I can walk away. And when I'm at the edge, just a few steps away from freedom, he pulls me back. It's so sudden, so unpredictable. You'll never see it coming. But it'll happen. And just like that, you'll be back to square one. I'm always dangling in the middle.

He doesn't want to hold me, but he doesn't want to let me go either.

A strange sense of longing grips me. Everything feels wrong. I shouldn't be here, with William. I should be there. He should be holding *me* in his arms, not that girl Madison.

"And now, it's time to announce the Winter King and Queen!"

Everybody starts gathering around the stage. The King and Queen are the best dressed boy and girl at the ball, decided by the committee of students who helped organize the dance. William and I stay where we are, ending up at the back of the crowd.

I'm not even excited. It's literally the same people who win every year, or at least have been winning for the past three years I've been here.

A girl walks onto the stage with a crown and a tiara on a cushion. Another follows her, carrying two sashes in her hands.

The speaker begins to announce the winners. The spotlight goes haywire, dancing around the room, pumping up the anticipation.

"And the Winter King is William Hayden!"

Nope, not surprised.

The bright spotlight blinds me. William raises his arms up in victory, almost mechanically. He doesn't even look excited. I smile at him, hugging him before he starts walking towards the stage.

"And the Winter Queen is Angelina Russo!"

No surprise there either. She actually *is* the best-dressed girl here. She is, *every damn year*. She's wearing a sapphire blue velvet gown with a plunging neckline. She looks tall and majestic like a real queen. Her makeup is *so* on point—smoky black eyes with nude pink lips. Not to mention the contour and highlight that are making her face look so sculpted.

They both walk up on the stage to accept their crown and sashes. I feel someone sidle up to me, arms brushing against my own.

"I'd be offended that *I* haven't won this yet if this wasn't so damn lame," Aiden remarks.

Sigh.

"William's hot. The whole school knows that. Maybe next year, when he's graduated."

"Have you had a good look at this face?" he says, pointing to himself. "I'm hot."

"William's hotter."

There's a *very* tiny shift in his expression, and I just know I hit him where it hurts. I quickly try to cover the damage. "I-I mean, he's hot in the conventional sort of way. Tall and lean, blonde hair, blue- eyes, charming smile. Plus he's got really good features, an aristocratic nose, and a sharp jaw. He's got the typical prince charming look working for him. You're . . . a different kind of hot, the more rugged, messy kind. You get what I mean?"

He's not entirely convinced but he seems satisfied enough.

I want to tell him that personally, I think he's much better looking. But that'll go straight to his head, so I don't. Instead, I turn to the stage.

The crowning ceremony is over, and they both are holding each other now. They are going to do the special King and Queen dance after which the rest of the student body will join them.

The DJ plays another love song (seriously, *how many love songs are there?*) and William and Angelina begin to dance. You would think that doing the same thing year after year would've probably gotten old by now. But not for them. Not this part at least.

I see them dancing and I'm transported back in time. Transported back to when I saw them dancing together for the first time as a freshman. It was magical; there's no other way to describe it.

I mean, they didn't do anything special. It was a normal slow dance to a normal love song. No, what made it so magical was the way they were looking at each other. It wasn't just looking—it was *gazing*. It wasn't just cute or romantic. It was real. And I wanted it.

It was still real.

There was something about the way they were looking at each other . . . something I couldn't quite put my finger on. It was just *more*, more than a stare or a look. There's something so familiar about it, and not just in their context.

"Can I have a dance with the most beautiful girl in the room?" Aiden's familiar voice whispers in my ear. My heart lurches in my chest. A chill runs down my spine. My body tingles all over.

Oh, he's so good at this, at smooth talking.

He has this way of making you feel special and keeping you on your toes all at the same time. You never get used to it. You never get used to *him*.

I gently take his hand in mine and walk a little closer to the stage, where many other couples have started dancing. I lock my fingers in his, letting my other hand rest on his shoulder. His arm wraps around my waist. I feel like we're two perfectly fitting puzzle pieces, finally coming together.

And right when we begin dancing, it hits me. I finally realize why that look between William and Angelina is so familiar. It's the same one Aiden's giving me right now.

* * *

"So, who's this girl Diana? You guys going out?" I ask him. I'd promised myself I wouldn't bring it up, but I couldn't help it.

"Why? You jealous?"

I roll my eyes at him. "Just answer the question Aiden. Are you going out with her now that you and Hailey broke up?"

"No, of course not. She's just my date for this dance. It's nothing."

"Why didn't you tell me you and Hailey ended things? I had to find out from other people."

"I thought you already knew. It was common knowledge."

"You know that's not the point. You're my best friend. I expect you to tell me if something happens in your life."

"Look, I didn't think it mattered. It wouldn't change anything, would it?"

I'm tempted to ask him what he means by 'anything', but I drop it.

"You know what? I thought it didn't matter either. I was wrong. Enjoy the rest of the night."

I walk away from Aiden. I don't want to talk to him any longer. I'm going to go find William and see if we can leave this party, go somewhere else. It's getting really boring real quick.

William's not on or near the stage with Angelina anymore. Neither is he anywhere near the food stalls. Where did he even go?

"Oh hey Scarlett, are you looking for William?" Joshua, his friend, comes up to me.

"Uh . . . yeah. Have you seen him?"

"I think he went out of the gym. He's probably in the hallway outside," Joshua says, gesturing towards the direction he went.

"Oh okay, thank you!"

I push my way through the crowd and exit the gymnasium, stepping into the empty hallway outside.

What I see makes me immediately regret my decision. There's William and Angelina. And they are kissing.

Chapter Thirty-Two

Scarlett

You've probably seen movies, right? Especially drama movies, preferably about teenagers. Maybe you've even come across the scene where the girl finds out her boyfriend is cheating on her. It's dramatic and super messy. It's like the world comes to a standstill, yet everything seems to be slipping out of your hands, like quicksand. It's intense, emotional, and even a little pathetic.

That's not how it was with me.

My mind just went kind of "*oh*, so this is happening." I'm not going to say I didn't get a nasty shock out of it. I mean when I stepped through the door, seeing my boyfriend kissing another girl was the *last* thing I'd expected.

What I hadn't expected was my own reaction to it being so calm.

One second, they're kissing. He's standing against the locker, she's leaning over him; her hands wrapped around his neck, his lips on her lips. The very next second, he stiffens and pushes her away. He notices me at the same time.

The panic is evident on his face when he comes after me.

"Scarlett listen to me. Look—"

I *don't* listen to him. I simply turn back around and vanish through the doors. I can hear him coming after me, so I hide. I don't want to talk to him, not right now. I don't want to listen to his excuses or his explanation, or whatever it is. The smarter thing would be to confront him, to ask him why he was doing what he was doing. But I can't. Not right now. I don't trust myself right now. It could get really messy. I feel numb right now, but I know it's only the calm before the storm. Any minute now, this dam could burst.

I don't realize I'm crying until I feel wetness trickle down my cheek. More tears follow. I feel embarrassed and humiliated, wondering what people will think when they notice me crying. I start looking for Andrea. I need to go home and I don't have a ride. Maybe she could lend me her car.

But I come across Aiden first. He's alone with a glass of punch in his hands. It's horrible, the moment he notices my tear-stained face. Concern flits across his countenance, he immediately drops the glass on a table nearby and walks up to me.

"Scarlett, what happened?" He sounds terrified.

"Aiden please, take me away from here. *Please.*" Maybe it is the desperation in my voice, or maybe it is how I'm literally begging him to take me away. He doesn't ask any questions; he doesn't ask why or where. He simply nods, looking grim. He grabs my hands, and we exit the gymnasium.

He glances at me, just once. He's worried. He's confused, he wants an explanation.

William spots me just as we're leaving the gym. He wastes no time coming over. "Scarlett please, just listen to me."

I feel so angry; I don't even want to look at him. One look at my face and Aiden knows that William did something. He stops mid stride.

"Aiden please, let's just go." I protest. I just want to get the hell out of here. Aiden has other plans.

He turns around to face William.

Oh god no

"I don't know what you did, but this is for making her cry." He forms his fingers into a fist, pulls back his arm and then throws a punch at William. The action is followed by a disgusting *thwack*.

Ouch.

I feel a little sorry for William, just a little. But I don't wait to see if he's okay. I head towards the parking lot with Aiden in tow.

"You know, that was *completely* unnecessary."

"Maybe, but I wanted to do it anyway."

Even though I feel really tired, and really sad, I laugh. Our feet slap against the granite pavement as we head towards his car. Once we're sitting inside his Mercedes, he starts the engine, and we're off.

"Take me to my house." I instruct him. He simply nods in response.

Twenty minutes later, he stops the car on the corner of my block. Then he slowly turns to look at me.

"Do you want to talk about it?"

"No, I just have to be left alone right now."

"Nobody should have to be alone when they're hurting. And Scarlett, you *are* hurting. So talk to me. I'm here for you." He gently rests his hands atop mine, giving them a gentle squeeze. "What did he do?"

"He cheated on me."

Aiden

I freeze.

My immediate reaction is anger—intense, uncontrollable. But then I just feel ashamed. I've got no right to be angry at him. I did the exact same thing to Hailey.

Only now am I realizing the gravity of my actions.

"I saw him kissing Angelina. And the worst part is, I'm not even surprised. And it's not because I expected this from William, no. I'm not surprised because I expected this to happen to *me*."

"Whoa, why would you expect it?"

"Because . . . that's what happens with me. I'm never anybody's first choice. I'm never *enough*. I'm not the one people fight for; I'm the one they settle for. I'm the other girl, the second in line. The invisible nobody who suddenly gets seen. That's who I am, and this is how things are."

For once, I'm at a loss for words. I never thought about it this way. I never thought she felt like this. I feel horrible.

"You'd know all about it of course, seeing you chose the exact same way—me as your backup girl, your ego-inflating side chick who you could flirt with when you were bored. That was me, wasn't it?"

"That's not true!" I protest.

She just laughs. "Oh you know it is." I try not to get mad at her for thinking this way. It's just her grief speaking.

"No. You hear me? *No*. That's *not* true. You weren't some . . . aren't some . . . *side chick*, someone who I keep around to inflate my ego. I wanted you in my life because you made me happy."

"…by inflating your ego."

"No! What's wrong with you!? Why would you even think that? Just . . . just keep it out of this. This is about William and what *he* has done. Don't twist and assume things when you don't know how it is."

"It's not *just* about William, okay? It's everything; it's just everything." She sounds so empty, so hopelessly broken that it makes my heart ache.

"I know Hailey didn't force you to make a decision," she says suddenly. "I talked to her. You *lied*. You stopped talking to me on your *own*. Do you know how horrible I felt when I found out about that?"

"So we're back to that again?" I ask, frustrated. "Are we ever going to get past it?"

"Probably never! We can't get past something that isn't completely out in the open, can we? You know, earlier I had at least this one reassurance, that the only reason you gave up on me is because she forced you to. But I was so, so fucking stupid. Nobody *made* you do it. You left because *you* wanted to. You cut me out of your life because you wanted to."

"I did it because at that time it felt like the right thing for us."

"For us?! Or for *you*? You don't get to make such decisions on your own, Aiden. You're not allowed to be that selfish."

"Look—"

"Save it. I don't want to listen to your explanations or his. You're all the same. You make loads of mistakes and then you come back with your apologies and your excuses. I'm done."

She gets out of the car, shutting the door behind her.

I quickly roll down the window to call out after her. "Scarlett wait—"

She completely ignores me and steps inside her house, leaving me all by myself.

* * *

"Hello? Aiden?" Hailey finally answers her phone.

"Um hi."

"Wow, you were the last person I was expecting to call me. What's up? Why are you calling me?"

"The reason I called you is selfish, really. I mean I hadn't even expected you pick up the call, but I just really needed to talk to someone. I usually go to Scarlett but since I can't...Just hear me out, okay?"

"Oh God, what have you done now?"

"Why do you always assume I'm the one who has done something?"

"Because it *is* always you, Aiden. So tell me, how did you screw things up this time?"

"Okay, I'll tell you. But this isn't something I've done, alright? It's personal so don't mention it to anyone. Scarlett just found out that William was cheating on her."

"No way!"

"Yes. It was horrible."

"It *is* horrible." She genuinely sounds sad about it.

"I am sorry, Hailes. I just realized it. I know that I apologized before. But today's the day I realized the gravity of my action, what it meant, what it did to you. I mean I saw Scarlett sitting on the passenger seat, crying her eyes out—her self-esteem destroyed, her confidence *completely* shattered. I don't want to give myself too much importance but maybe, probably, I did something similar to you. Worse even. It's just, I'm sorry. I never really thought about it.

I guess that's the worst part about me. I never think things through. I just do them. And I don't realize it until things are utterly screwed and there's no way of mending them. I'm *so* sorry. I'm sorry if I ever made you feel less, like you were not enough, or inadequate, or anything. Because you're not any of those things.

I'm sorry for all the times I hurt you. You deserved *so much* better Hailey. You still do. It's just, I really understand now. And I know I can't change things, but I just want you to know that I realize I was an asshole."

She completely ignores my apology. "Yeah, whatever. So, you said there was problem. What is it?"

"Why are you even hearing me out? I don't even deserve that."

"We're just talking Aiden, go on. What did you do?"

"Did . . . did Scarlett talk to you?"

"Actually yes, she did. Which reminds me, what the fuck have you been telling her Aiden?! That I *forced* you to not be friends with her? Okay like obviously that would have been the ideal situation. But at the same time, I knew I couldn't do that to you. So *you* break off your friendship with her and then tell her that *I* made you do it? That's a new low even for you Aiden."

"I wasn't thinking, okay? In fact, I didn't even say it. She just assumed! I just didn't correct her."

"And that's supposed to make it any better?! Look, I'm not that vindictive or manipulative, okay? But that's how you portrayed me."

"I didn't mean to, I *swear.*"

"Whatever Aiden, I'm done caring." She pauses. "So you've messed things up with Scarlett again."

"Yes, and she's *really* angry with me. She's not talking to me again. And I mean, it has happened before. But this time it's bad like *really* bad. I'm scared. I can't lose her again."

"Look Aiden, sometimes I just don't get you. What the fuck is stopping you?! Like really, why haven't you confessed your feelings to her already!? I think I have a fair idea of what all you've told her, and let's just say, you've never been completely honest."

"I just . . . I don't think there's a point, you know? She's with William. I mean, she was but . . ."

"Look, not everything needs to have a point, alright? You know what's selfish? Loving someone and expecting them to love you back. That's selfish! *You* don't get to make that decision. You don't get to demand someone to love you back. It's their choice. If you love someone, you just love them, because loving them completes you, it makes you happy. You don't expect things in return. It's not give and take. It's a commitment. So if you love Scarlett and think she owes something to you in return, then you just need to stop *right now*. If you're not doing what needs to be done because you don't think it'll lead anywhere, then you're stupid.

Just . . . just stop holding back, okay? I mean the only reason we're all even at this point is because you've been holding back; you haven't been completely honest, haven't been completely real. So I need you to get out there and tell her how you feel. Because she needs to know, and you need to get it out of your system. And I'm not saying it'll all work out and everything will be perfect. But it'll definitely be better than how it is now."

"Wow, you're right."

"God, you're so dumb Aiden. I can't believe I ever dated you."

"Hey, I'm not dumb!"

"Right. Anyway, it's late so I'll go sleep now. Night!"

I spend some time thinking about what Hailey said. As I do, a plan slowly starts to form in my head. It's nothing extraordinary, but it could work. I *need* to make it work.

Scarlett's birthday is coming next week. I'm going to throw her a surprise birthday party. And finally, *finally* I'm going to tell her everything. All of it. I can't delay it any longer.

I took one last look at Scarlett's house, particularly at the window on the floor above—Scarlett's room. The lights are on and I can see her silhouette moving around the room, until finally she turns the lights off.

I'm going to make it up to you Scarlett, I promise, I think to myself as I drive away.

* * *

Scarlett

If you've ever been hurt, you will know how much strength it takes to face the very person responsible. And right now, it's taking me every bit of my will power not to turn around and leave.

I woke up this morning to about thirty missed calls, and about half the amount of texts from William. How I slept so soundlessly last night, I don't know. I guess I was really tired.

I'm in school now. Aiden's with me. I got really mad at him last night. And okay, it wasn't completely irrational. But seeing that we promised not to fight anymore, going off on him like that wasn't really a good move. I've decided to let his actions slide for now. I'm much more concerned with what William did at the moment.

First period begins in half an hour. I'm out in the garden area, and William has just arrived. He's not alone though. He has Angelina with him. His nose is a little bruised. I cringe as I remember Aiden punching him last night.

"Are you here to apologize to her?" Aiden ask him. "Because bringing the girl you were kissing behind her back last night is not a very smart move."

"I've come to explain." For the first time, I see this anger burning in William's eyes. I've never seen him look like this before. He's not here to mess around, and Aiden realizes that.

"What *is* there to explain, huh? As far as I see it, you were kissing someone you shouldn't have. And I probably wouldn't have found out about it if I hadn't walked in on it." I huff.

He sighs. "Just listen." He pleads. "Tell her Angelina." He addresses her angrily. She looks really troubled.

"Go on, *tell her.*" Guilt and hurt crosses her features. She stares down at the ground, not able to meet my eyes.

"What you saw the night before was a lie—a well-planned lie." She begins, sounding really nervous. "I planned it, all of it. After the Winter King and Queen Dance, I told him I wasn't feeling very well, and requested him to take me out for a bit. Joshua helped me. When he saw you looking for William, he told you where we were. When I heard your footsteps, I-I started kissing William. And then you saw us and you thought what I wanted you to think. You thought that William was cheating on you. It worked. I am *so* sorry," she says all this in one breath. By the time she stops speaking, she's all breathless. Unshed tears well in her eyes.

"I am so, *so* sorry. You didn't deserve that. *William* didn't deserve that. And I take the blame—all of it; it was entirely my mistake. I shouldn't have done this. I am *so* sorry. Please forgive him—please! I beg you, just take him back. And I promise I won't do any such thing ever again. In fact, I'll stay far, far away from both of you."

I don't think twice. I don't ask her *why* she did what she did. I don't get mad at her. I head straight to William and jump into his arms.

"Is what she saying true?" I ask him.

He nods. "All of it."

And then I hug him tightly. My arms go round his back and I pull him closer. "I'm *so* sorry for not listening to you."

"Don't be sorry, you were only reacting to what you saw. I would have done the same. Plus my reputation doesn't really help my case, does it?"

"No, *I* should have known you would never do anything like this. I'm really sorry."

A couple of more apologies and tears follow; a little bit of hugging and kissing too, before we both fully forgive each other—whatever for. Never did I think this issue would get resolved so easily, so simply.

Of course, I get so busy with William, I never notice Aiden turn around and leave.

Chapter Thirty-Three

Aiden

I look around the crowded living room. Scarlett's house is big, but it's not big enough to comfortably hide forty-eight people in the living room. This is insane. *Oh why did I think it was smart to invite so many people over for Scarlett's surprise birthday party?*

I usher at least thirteen people up the stairs, telling them to sit down on the steps. A dozen and a few crawl behind the couches. Most of them stand near the walls though. A few of them duck behind the dining table that has Scarlett's birthday cake atop it. Mostly, we just stand there in plain sight, among balloons and streamers and fairy lights.

"Okay, so Darren has just texted me. They are almost here. Now listen carefully. I'm going to turn off the lights and we're going to stay here in silence. When you hear the front door open, get ready. As soon as Darren switches on the light, you all need to shout out a 'Happy Birthday', got it!? In complete coordination, just like we've been practicing for the past half an hour." A murmur of agreement goes through the crowd. "Well now that that's settled, take your positions and get ready."

I quickly turn off the light and stand next to the table. I can feel William standing next to me. Yes, you heard that right; William's here. How would Scarlett's surprise birthday party be complete if her beloved boyfriend wasn't here to celebrate it with her? No matter how much I despise this guy, I need to acknowledge that he's important to her.

I spend the next few minutes in the dark thinking about everything that has brought us to this moment. I'd always wanted to do something like this for Scarlett, and the recent events inspired me to do so.

This party . . . I'm hoping that this party would set things right. Tonight is very important to me, because tonight, I'm finally going to do something I should've done long ago.

Tonight I'm going to fix things.

* * *

I hear the door open, hear the footsteps patter down the room, see the lights switch on, and then suddenly everyone's shouting "Happy Birthday Scarlett!"

Through the crowd I spot her, standing a few feet away at the door, her hands covering her mouth, her mouth that has dropped open in shock. She looks absolutely stunned, and even a little confused. My heart leaps in my chest almost in reflex.

She is smiling now at Darren and her friends as she slowly makes her way through the crowd and towards the table. It takes her almost ten minutes to come over, as she has to stop every few seconds to talk to people who are wishing her. With every minute that passes, the beat of my heart increases.

It has been ages since *I've* made her happy. And here she is, with that beautiful smile adorning her face. She looks genuinely happy. And I can proudly say it's because of me.

How she feels is nothing compared to what I do though. She is happy, but I am elated.

Scarlett

"HAPPY BIRTHDAY SCARLETT!" I am greeted by dozens of people shouting as soon as the lights switch on.

I almost get a heart attack.

What. The. Fuck.

For a few confusing minutes, I have no idea what the hell was going on. I even feel like running away. What are so many people doing here?

Then it sinks in. I just realized what they'd shouted out. This is my surprise birthday party, and they are here for me.

This is insane.

I walk through the crowd, being greeted by people every few seconds. I awkwardly talk to them for a few seconds before moving on. There are so many people here, it's freaking me out.

Sometimes being an introvert sucks.

My eyes fall on the dining table at the far end of the room. Humph, that wasn't here before. Did they actually drag it all the way from the kitchen?

I spot Aiden and William standing side by side. My heart flip flops in my chest, and for one insane minute, I can't figure out *who* made it do that: my best friend or my boyfriend?

I spot the cake only a second later. It's a big, square-shaped, 3-tier black forest cake encrusted with cherries. The cake looks delicious. It's decorated with pretty little candles that burn brightly, their flames flickering every now and then.

I walk further, moving closer to the spot they are standing at. Butterflies flit in my stomach. I feel nauseous. I *clearly* don't do well around so many people.

Standing beside William is Sharon. Then there's Adam and Susan. Aiden is standing next to her. Kayla and Andrea are beside him. My girlfriends send a brilliant smile my way. "Happy birthday girl!" they cheer, enveloping me in a bone-crushing group hug. Adam gives me a tight hug too, whispering a happy birthday in my ear. Oh I'm so happy to see him here, and that too with Susan. It's perfect!

Once they're done hugging me, I turn to Aiden, hug him too, and then quickly turn to William.

"Happy birthday babe," William greets me, pressing a gentle kiss against my lips.

"TIME TO CUT THE CAKE!" Sharon shouts out, handing me a knife with a pretty blue ribbon tied around its handle. People hurriedly gather around me, my closest friends in the front. I lean towards the cake to blow the candles.

"Make a wish!" Susan urges me. I shut my eyes, wishing for the first thing that pops into my mind.

Answers. Give me all the answers I need.

Everybody starts cheering, immediately following it up with the 'Happy Birthday' song. I blow the candles. Then, for the next few seconds, I stare around blankly, not knowing who to look at. This is the most awkward part of any birthday celebration— when everybody's singing the song and you have no idea who to look at or what to do. Do you just stand there stiffly and wait for the end of the song, or do you smile at random people and join in singing? It's been seventeen years now and I still have no clue.

Once I'm done cutting the cake, I eat the first piece in front of everyone (and feel like a fat little pig while doing so.) Everybody around me cheers again and William quickly wraps his arms around me to give me a nice hug.

Wow . . . okay, I need a little space to process all this.

"Um I'll just uhm, go freshen up a bit," I announce to no one in general and start heading away from the crowd.

I hope I don't appear rude. It's just . . . this is so overwhelming. I appreciate what my friends have done, I really do. But I'm not good with surprises; especially surprises that include so many people. I just need five minutes to myself, and then I'll be okay.

I'm walking by when two girls catch hold of me. I think I know them...they're in my chemistry class.

"Happy birthday Scarlett!" They wish me enthusiastically. I smile shyly at them.

"Thank you so much guys. And thanks for coming, means a lot." They nod, still smiling at me. I'm walking away when hearing my own name in their conversation makes me stop. I stop, stealthily listening to what they are saying.

"Oh my god Scarlett is *so* lucky to have someone like him in her life."

"I know right!? He put so much hard work in planning all this. I wish I knew a guy who'd do this for me. But I don't."

"*Seriously*. And have you seen the way he looks at her? Man, if that's not relationship goals, I don't know what is. I'd *die* if someone ever looked at me like that."

"Seriously, they're perfect together! Ah, I'm so jealous."
Whoa.

So *he* did this. All this, it was William's idea. *Wow.*

I turn to look at him. He's standing right where I left him, talking to Sharon. They're laughing. I'm suddenly filled with this deep sense of gratitude. *What did I do to deserve him?*

Not able to help myself, I run back to him and embrace him in a tight hug. I can't believe anyone would think of doing something like this for *me*. I feel so special.

"Thank you . . . for today," I murmur, looking up at him. "I'm so happy."

He smiles down at me. "And I'm happy that you're happy." He cups my face in his and plants a kiss on my lips. His hands encircle my waist and he pulls me closer, not breaking the kiss. We're standing chest to chest now. His lips move slowly, savoring our kiss.

Aiden

Once Scarlett cuts the cake, she excuses herself and walks away. Darren wastes no time and heads straight to me. "So? Are you ready?" he asks. "Everything's prepared. Just give me the signal when you're ready and I'll do it."

"I-I don't know man. I don't know if I shou—"

"Shut up. We went through this, remember? You *need* to do this. And you need to do this *today*. It's now or never."

"But—" I shut up. Scarlett's back. She's hugging William now, and saying something to him; I don't know what.

I feel that familiar pang in my chest.

They are kissing now.

I look away. It's like a reflex. Whenever I see them together, I automatically look away.

Darren notices the pained expression on my face. He opens his mouth, probably to make me feel better, to ask me to not pay attention to it or something like that.

But I can't *not* pay attention to it. This just confirmed all my doubts about what I'd been planning to do.

It was a bad idea. I *knew* it was a bad idea.

Seriously, what's the point? She's happy with him. We've just become friends again. What's the point of complicating things again? *Ugh, I can't do this anymore.*

But somebody tell that to Darren. He's just not letting it go.

"Don't give up man. If you don't do it today—"

"Enough! I'm done. I'm out back, in case anyone needs me. See you later." I walk away before he can protest.

Scarlett

I step away from William, trying hard to ignore all the stares we're getting. I'm not used to this.

He smiles at me.

"Thanks for this party William, I love it. This means a lot."

I really need him to know how much I appreciate this gesture.

His smile immediately vanishes. He looks guilty (of what?) He even looks embarrassed.

"Uh . . . I didn't do all this. This wasn't my idea."

Wait.

"Truth be told, I didn't even know your birthday was this week. I'm *so* sorry. Aiden called me two days ago and invited me to the party."

Those girls . . . they were talking about Aiden, not William. Aiden did all this.

"I did get you something though." William rummages inside his jacket's pocket and extracts a tiny package. I take it, not even bothering to open it up. I'm too busy coming to terms with the fact that this, all this, was Aiden's work.

Scarlett is so lucky to have someone like him in her life.

Have you seen the way he looks at her?

Oh no.

I turn to look at Aiden, who had been standing just a few feet away. He's not here anymore. Instead of him I see Darren, shaking his head at me. He obviously witnessed everything that went down between William and me.

I quickly walk over to him.

"Aiden did this, not William." Darren looks disappointed in me.

"I messed up, didn't I?" I ask, already knowing the answer.

He shakes his head. "Honestly Scarlett, what are you even trying to do? I don't get it." He glances at William. "I don't get why you're with *him*."

"Just . . . just tell me where Aiden went."

"He went out back."

I waste no time. I push past all the people crowding the door, not stopping to talk to them. I push the door open and step out in the cool night time air. Everything's dark out here.

He's sitting on a lounge chair near the pool. It's so dark; all I can see is his silhouette. I take in a deep breath, and then walk over to him.

He looks up at me when I approach him but doesn't say anything. I silently sit down next to him. A few seconds pass; neither of us speak. Then:

"Happy Birthday, Scarlett," he whispers.

I rest my hand on his, giving it a gentle squeeze. "Thank you." A pause. "I know *you* did all this. I love it. Thank you so much Aiden."

He shakes his head dismissively. "It's nothing. It's the least you deserve on your special day."

"No, shut up. It really means a lot. Nobody has done anything like this for me before. So thank you, Aiden."

"Mhmm."

"C'mon, let's go back inside. I don't want you sitting here all by yourself. Let's enjoy the party *you've* worked so hard on."

"You go Scarlett. I want to be alone for a while."

"No!"

He doesn't respond.

"What's wrong? You're being awfully quiet. I'm not used to this. I want to see the old Aiden, the one who never shuts up."

"I-I can't talk to you right now Scar." He sounds like he's in pain. I suddenly feel scared. I've never seen Aiden behave like this before.

"Why? What's wrong? Hey, look at me." I grab his face and make him look me in the eye. "Talk to me. We're best friends, remember?"

"Are we Scarlett, are we really?"

I immediately retract my hands, as if they're on fire.

"I can't talk to you right now Scarlett, so just go."

"But why not?!" I explode.

"*Because* . . . because there are things I need to say; things that I *really* need to get out of my system right now. Things that I shouldn't say, that I *don't* want to say. Every time I open my mouth, those words choke me, begging to be let out."

My heart starts racing in my chest.

"Then . . . then let them out," I whisper.

He starts shaking his head.

Suddenly, he's bathed in bright light, and so am I. In fact, the whole backyard is. Thousands of tiny lights are illuminating the backyard. Fairy lights, so many fairy lights. It's stunning.

The lights are wrapped around the branches of all the trees. They are encircling the trunks too and are casually scattered around the bushes as well. The lights also form a border around the pool.

Soft jazz music starts playing out of *nowhere*. I look around, bewildered. What the fuck is going on!?

I turn to Aiden.

"Scarlett..." He runs his finger through his hair, nervously.

Nervously.

Wait a second . . .

Flushed face? Check.

That strain in his voice? Check.

Him running his fingers through his hair? Check.

Oh no. Aiden never gets nervous. Not unless he's—

"I'm in love with you Scarlett."

Chapter Thirty-Four

Scarlett

My head starts to spin. My heart lurches to a stop inside my chest. I'm forced to rest my hand on the chair for support. I'm shaken.

Aiden shift closer to me, resting his hand atop mine. His deep brown eyes look intensely into mine. "I need to say this today. If I don't—"

He's interrupted by a series of high-pitched notes from the music being played in the background. He presses his eyes shut in exasperation, then lets out an angry growl. He gets up and shouts to no one in particular: "HEY YO! CAN YOU SHUT THE MUSIC OFF?!"

The music abruptly dies two seconds later.

"So where were we?" He continues, sitting back. "Oh yeah, so . . . so, I-I just, I really needed to say it today. Darren was right. If I didn't say it today, I'd never be able to do it and—"

"Wait, Darren *knew* about this!?"

"Who else do you think help me put all these lights? Who else do you think was playing that music?"

"*You* did all this?!" I shrieked, gesturing towards, well, everything.

"No, the backyard lighted itself up for no reason. *Of course* I did this! You can be really, really dumb sometimes Scar."

"Uh . . . sorry," I mumble sheepishly.

"This . . . this was supposed to go a little differently. I was going to take you here, and then I'd sit you down and calmly talk about my feelings for you while you enjoyed the jazz music and the beautiful lights. I messed up. I wasn't supposed to bombard you with all this. It wasn't supposed to go like this. But fuck if I care! I just need to tell you how much I love you."

I regard him with bewilderment, my body frozen still.

"It's ridiculous how I figured it out only recently. And it's been killing me ever since. Every moment I spent knowing that you had no knowledge of how I felt, was unbearable agony."

"Like most people out there, I wanted to experience true love. As you know, I've been with a lot of girls. And it's not that I can't commit; I can. It's just, it never felt right, you know? I got with different girls but nobody made me feel the way; nobody makes me feel . . . nobody made me feel alive. There was just something missing. So I'd break it off and end up looking like an insensitive asshole. But really, what I'd be trying to do is end things before it got too intense for the other person. What's the point if it's not real? I *wanted* something real. And I'd promised myself I wouldn't stop until I found it."

"And so I searched, and searched, when all along, the real thing was standing *right* in front of me. Maybe I knew it all along. Maybe I was in denial, too scared to admit it to myself. But it just . . . it became too hard, too intense to ignore after a point. So here I am, telling you exactly how I feel. I prepared this whole speech and everything because I know how much words mean to you. So hear me out, okay?"

"You're the one who makes me feel alive. When I'm with you, it's like . . . like the blood in my veins evaporates, replaced by this all-consuming fire: this pure, unadulterated heat. When we touch, it's like fireworks. My heart doesn't just beat, it *jumps*. It threatens to explode in my chest. I don't know about you but that's how it is for me. It's like every inch of my skin is ablaze."

"And when I look at you, I forget everything, and I mean *everything*. I forget myself. Heck, I even forget to breathe sometimes. It's just you. Everything *becomes* you."

"And when you're sad, *I* feel sad. Which is so ironic because if it wasn't for me you probably wouldn't *be* so sad. *I'm* the one who keeps hurting you. But God damn if I don't feel it too! Seeing you in pain, it's almost like someone's twisting this knife in my chest. I *feel* your pain. And I'd do *anything* to put an end to it, even if it means that I don't get to be a part of your life. Ask me and I'll do it. It'll probably kill me but I'll do it anyway because you're the only one that really matters."

"And when you're happy, it's like . . . like my whole world is bathed in shades of gold. When you smile . . . oh the things I'd do to see you smile—everything gets a hundred times better. It's almost like I'm able to breathe easier knowing that you're happy. It's weird, really. I get all choked up with this deep, all-encompassing warmth that radiates through everything in my life. *You* make that happen. You make my *life* better."

"But most of all, and I've realized this now, I'm not me when I'm not *with* you. Without you, I'm someone else: half-alive, a stranger who rarely smiles, who rarely *feels*. It's all emptiness without you. The shades of gold vanish and my world is drenched in grey. "

"I love you because when I'm with you, I'm my best version. You bring out the best in me. Hell, you bring out the parts of me that I didn't even know existed. The good parts."

"I mean, I probably sound pathetic when I say this but I can't imagine my life without you in it. I can't imagine *myself* without *you*. It's that simple. I don't know how it happened. I don't know *when* it happened. But it did. And now it's too late to go back, to pretend I can be anything but in love with you. Because I can't. I really fucking can't."

"This is the truth, and it continues to be: I'm in love with you Scarlett Stevenson, and nothing, absolutely nothing can change the fact that I want to be a part of your life today, tomorrow, and for all the days to come. I *need* you like I've never needed anyone before."

Okay, can someone people get me a packet of oxygen? Because I CANNOT breathe.

"I'm *so* sorry for screwing everything up. If I had taken the right decisions at the right time, if I wasn't such a coward, maybe all this wouldn't have happened. You know, I'd made up my mind about leaving Hailey before you'd even given me an answer. I *was* going to leave her. But then I didn't. I got scared. I realized this was as real as it gets and what if *I* screw up? What if I ruin a perfectly good friendship? I realized I'd rather have you in bits and pieces, than not have you at all."

"But then, I guess I ended up losing you anyway. Yes, Hailey didn't force me to stop talking to you. She didn't force me to *not* talk to you. It was all my doing. You see, I wasn't planning to *end* our friendship. I just needed some space. I figured if I stayed away from you for a while, I'd get over you, I'd get back in control of my feelings and things would be normal again."

"But I was wrong, so, so wrong. I wish I'd taken the plunge. It just didn't feel right with her. She wasn't *you.*"

Wow.

Holy shit.

Can someone get me a packet of oxygen? Because I cannot breathe!

"I-I-I don't . . . I don't know what to say," I stammer.

"Telling me you love me back might be a good start."

I open my mouth to say those exact words—I *want* to say those exact words. But they get stuck in my throat.

"I—"

I want to spit them out—spit out those three words—but flashes of everything that has happened till now runs through my head.

And then I do what I always do.

"I-I need to go."

I run.

The tears are quick to fall, running down my face as soon as I turn away from him. He tries to stop me but I'm too quick for him.

God I hate myself! I hate myself! I hate myself!

I'm so sick of being like this, of being so self-destructive. I constantly throw away every good thing that comes my way. I think, I think, I think. I think *too* much. *Too much.* My mind just ruins everything for me.

I hate being this way. I hate the fact that I let my mind make all my decisions. Where has that reckless Scarlett gone? The one who saw how happy Aiden made her, who was fearless enough to embrace her feelings and take the fall. *Where has she gone?!*

I know that Aiden hurt me, that things were never really smooth between us. But he's here now, isn't he? He loves me. He's *in love* with me. That's all that matters! Then why—?!

Why do I run? I don't know. What is wrong with me!? He *literally* just confessed his feelings for me, said everything I had ever wanted to hear. Yet here I am, not able to open up my heart even now. Here I am scared, so, *so* scared. *When will I stop being scared?!*

This . . . all of this was so sudden; he's suddenly here, expressing everything he's ever felt; saying all the things I would have already known had I not been in denial, not been so completely dense.

I'd *just* started getting used to the idea of not being with him. How can I suddenly jump into this thing? Forget all that has happened and just get with him?

Forget? Ha! I cannot forget. No, all I can do, can't help doing, is remembering—remembering all those sleepless nights, remembering my tear-stained pillow and that throbbing ache in my chest that refused to leave. All I can remember is this voice in my head, continuously chanting: "You're not good enough. You're not good enough. You're not good enough."

All I can remember is believing it.

Maybe I *still* believe it.

I don't want to believe it. I don't. I'm so sick of feeling so insecure, so replaceable. I'm just so sick of feeling afraid, afraid that he'll change his mind again. I was so bold and strong once, not afraid of taking the plunge. But I took it. I let myself fall. And fall I did. I fell *so* hard, that I never really got back up. That fall shattered me, and I'm still broken. I don't want to be broken. I know I don't *need* to be broken. I know if I really try, I'll recover.

But what if I come together only to fall apart again? What if? I survived it the first time. But I don't think I can survive this again.

I'm scared. I don't want to be, but I am . . . so scared.

Chapter Thirty-Five

Scarlett

"Scarlett, c'mon wake up!" I groan, turning away from the source of the noise. I bury my head under the blankets, wishing my mom would go away.

"Nuh-uh, that's not going to work today. You've already missed school three days in a row. I'm not going to call them today and make some excuse for you. You've *got* to get up."

"But Mom—"

"Shush! Get ready and come downstairs in half an hour, I'll go prepare your breakfast. Get up *now*." She leaves, slamming the door behind her.

"Fine!" I huff, throwing the blanket off me. I resist the urge to just go back to sleep. But I have to go someday anyway . . .

Might as well go now.

I've been avoiding going to school for reasons. Reasons that have nothing to do with me hating school and everything to do with Aiden.

I just don't know how to face him. He poured his soul out to me, showed me his most vulnerable, most fragile side. And what did I do? I ran. How can I possibly face him? And worse, *what* will I say when I finally do? I still don't know. I'm still not sure.

I'm still a little scared.

* * *

Dad lent me his car today, since I was getting a little late. I spent the car ride listening to sad indie music, my mind on one thing and one thing alone: Aiden.

So what if you're in love with him too? You need to break up with William first. Sweet, sweet William who has been nothing but nice to you. You'll need to end things with him first.

How?

I cut off the engine, stop the music, and then park the car. I stare at the imposing brick building in front of me. I really don't want to go inside. Somewhere in there is Aiden right now, rushing to first period.

Let me spend some more time here. I'll go when class's about to start so that I don't have to talk to anyone.

* * *

I wake up with a start. I softly massage my neck, trying to soothe the dull ache coursing through it. I can't believe I fell asleep while waiting in the car! I *knew* I shouldn't have stayed up late reading fan fiction! *When will I learn!?*

I quickly take out my phone to check the time. Twenty minutes have passed since first period started. Shit, I'm *so* late.

I start getting out of the car when I hear something that makes me stop.

Someone's crying.

Now alert, I try to locate the source of this noise.

A few seconds later I realize it's coming from the car parked right next to mine. A boy is sitting in the driver's seat. There's this girl resting her head on his shoulder. It's obvious that she's crying.

I feel like I'm witnessing a very private moment. I feel ashamed. But I can't just open the car door and walk out, they'll notice the commotion and realize I was here all along. It'll be *so* awkward then.

So I don't leave. Instead, I roll down my window and try to figure out who she is.

"He'll never talk to me again, never," she cries, her shoulders shaking.

"Of course he will. You're best friends. He'll forgive you," the guy comforts her.

"No he *won't*. He hates me. It's over—all of it!"

I cringe in my seat, feeling guilty for listening to their private conversation.

You're a bad, bad person Scarlett. Stop eavesdropping!

But the next part of their conversation immediately grabs my attention.

"He loves Scarlett. Yes, he does!" My ears perk up when I hear my name. "I'm *sure* he does. That's why I did what I did—so that they'd break up and things wouldn't go further. Any now he *hates* me!"

Holy shit.

"Angelina shh, he doesn't hate you." Joshua comforts her.

"But he does! He's stopped talking to me. He doesn't even look at me." She sniffles. "I love him *so* much, but he's completely oblivious. My heart is aching for him and he's in love with *her*. It's not fair!" She starts crying harder. "And . . . and after what I've done, he's never going to forgive me. God, I miss him *so* much."

Joshua runs his finger through her hair, soothing her. "It'll get better Lina, don't worry. He'll come to his senses sooner or later."

"What if he doesn't? What if he never stops hating me?"

"He doesn't hate you. He could *never* hate you. You're best friends!"

"Are we? I don't know anymore. As long as *she's* in the picture, he'll always love her and I'll be forced to witness it." She turns to look at him, and I catch a glimpse of her face. It's all blotchy and red, her dark auburn hair sticking to her forehead. She looks so sordid, there's an air of misery about her. "It hurts *so* much. I'm so tired of feeling this way. I just want this to be over."

I can't listen anymore. I shove my earphones in my ear and hit shuffle. I can't listen to her crying for her best friend.

It's too real. It's too *me.*

A sick feeling starts making its way through my stomach. My head throbs; I can feel a headache coming on. I spend the rest of the hour locked up in my car, trying really hard to muffle out her crying. Somewhere along the way, I start crying too. I have no idea why.

Maybe it's because I can understand what she's going through. Maybe because when I see her crying, I don't really see *her*, I see myself.

I see another Scarlett. I see the Scarlett who cried because her best friend Aiden was in love with someone else. She cried because she knew there was no way in hell that he'd ever feel the same way about her. She cried because she was so scared of losing him.

How stupid was I not to realize what was going on. Why didn't I stop and think why Angelina tried to end my relationship with William like that? How could I be so dense?! Me, who has gone through the same situation. How could I be so blind?

Angelina's not my boyfriend's manipulative best friend. She's the girl who is secretly in love with him. She is me. And I'm not just William's girlfriend. I am thE girl who came between two best friends. I'm...I'm Hailey.

This right here is a moment of clarity for me. I now realize why hating Hailey was so wrong. I'd hated her simply because she was with Aiden. I'd hated her for coming between two best friends. And now, *I've* done what she did. It wasn't intentional, just like it wasn't intentional for her. We just didn't know. We just didn't see.

Angelina and Joshua leave after the second period bell rings. I leave a few minutes later, once I'm sure they are gone for good.

It's so obvious what I have to do now. There's no alternative. None of us are happy. Aiden's hurting, Angelina's heartbroken, I'm unhappy, and William . . . he deserves better. *So* much better. He deserves someone who will dedicate HER heart and soul to him; someone who will love him with everything they've got. Someone like Angelina.

I can't continue being so selfish. I need to let him go.

* * *

"Why are you doing this Scarlett? Tell me, what went wrong? Why do you have to do this!?" William asks me.

I sigh. There's no easy way to do this.

"William, the memories I made with you, are some of the best I have. I met you at a time when I was really sad, really broken. I'd completely shut my heart. If it hadn't been for you, I'd still be that way. You saw me. I'd always felt invisible but you saw me. You made me feel special. You treated me like an absolute queen. You made me who I am right now—a less broken, more confident person—and for that, I can't thank you enough.

But I can't continue living this lie. Admit it William, you're not happy. *We're* not happy. This isn't how it should be. We should be happier, but we're not. This relationship isn't going where we wanted it to and you know it. You deserve someone who takes it there, who makes you happy."

"*You* make me happy!"

"Not as much as I should! I need to do this William for both of us. We can't hold on to each other, to this imperfect relationship and let better people pass us by. We owe it to ourselves to end this while we can, so that we can make way for something more beautiful, more meaningful. I know this hurts you. It's hurting me too. But we have to do this. It's the right thing to do."

He sighs. He looks really, really sad. I wish there could have been a less painful way of doing this. But there isn't.

"What can I say to make you stay? You've already made up your mind."

And I had. He knew it. I knew it.

He let out a shaky breath, his defenses crumbling. He leaned in and pressed his lips against my forehead.

"I'm going to miss you so much."

"It doesn't have to be this way. We can still be friends."

"I'm not sure I can do that, but thanks."

I'm not angry. I understand.

After one last hug, I finally let him go.

Chapter Thirty-Six

Scarlett

"I'm sorry."

Hailey blinks at me, confusion prominent on her face, now more than ever.

"Weird. Suddenly everyone's apologizing to me," she murmurs to herself.

After ending things with William, this was the one last thing I needed to do before I contacted Aiden: talk to his ex-girlfriend and well, my ex-nemesis. So I asked her to meet me.

"I know how much you loved Aiden. And your relationship with him could have been something really beautiful and satisfying. But I ruined it. I know I'm not the only one to blame. Aiden screwed up a lot too. But I should've understood...should've *tried* to understand, at least. Instead, I was consumed by this irrational hate for you. I did some things I shouldn't have. I just want you to know that I'm ashamed and sorry for what I did. I wish I could say I want to take it all back, that I wish it never happened. But I can't. I just really love him."

Hailey regards me with curiosity, probably trying to figure out if I really mean what I said.

"Can you forgive me?" I ask her.

"Honestly? It was a very painful experience for me. It hurt me a lot and it was emotionally draining. But I'm okay now. I'm not so sad about it anymore. I've stopped thinking of the what ifs and maybes. Sure, I still wish things hadn't gotten so messy. But I'm over it now. So it's okay. I forgive you."

Then Hailey does something I hadn't expected her to do—she smiles.

"Still, I mean, like you said, it was so painful. And you and Aiden had this great thing going on and—"

"Yes, it was great. But it wasn't what it should have been. He wasn't right for me. He was that mistake girls make once in their life, and I'm saying once because we never make that mistake again, not after this."

"And what mistake is that?"

"Some guys—they are unattainable. And they aren't unattainable because they are too cool for you, no. They are just . . . they are never really with you *with you*, you understand? You can capture their attention, but never their heart. Aiden was just like that. When *I* got the chance to be with him, I took it. I thought I was different. I thought I could change him for the better. We all make that mistake. I wanted to be the girl that finally made him stay.

But when I got with him I realized I didn't have to change his mind about *anything*. He *was* ready to stay. He was just waiting for the right girl. And the right girl had been with him all along; he had no idea. And when I realized that, I was like God damn! What am I doing here? Where do I fit in this equation?

I realized I was just lying to myself, that I was wasting my own time. This wasn't helping anyone. I mean, *I* wasn't happy,

Aiden wasn't happy, and neither were you. Someone had to leave. And it obviously had to be me. But now that I *have* left, you two dumbasses *still* haven't sorted everything out."

"Actually, Aiden uhm told me he is in love with me." I feel rather awkward telling her this. She said she has let go, but has she really?

"About time that he did! *Please* tell me you told him you loved him back."

"Uh no, about that—"

"Damn it Scarlett, what is wrong with you?! You finally have all you wanted, right in front of you, within reach. And you're still pushing it away? I just don't get it." She genuinely looks disappointed in me.

I lose it. I lose my cool. Everyone I know thinks I'm an idiot for walking away from Aiden that day. But they don't get it. Nobody does.

"I'm scared, okay? That's what I've been all along: scared. I started so fearlessly. I didn't care about the consequences. I didn't worry about how it'd end. I just dived head first. I wanted this *so* bad. I might not have expressed my feelings, but I *did* open up my heart. I left it vulnerable. I dared to *hope*.

And hope is a treacherous thing. It can make you or break you. And in my case, all it did was break me. Not once, not twice, but *every time*. It wasn't just one big rejection, one hope dashed, no. It was like a domino effect. One hope crushed after another. Until all I was left with nothing. *I* was nothing.

So I'm sorry if I didn't run into his arms and profess my undying love for him when he confessed his feelings. I tried to do that before. It didn't work out very well, did it? And a few words won't erase that.

Aiden's *always* been good with words. And I've *always* been good at falling recklessly in love with them. So no, when he said *exactly* what I wanted to hear, I went against everything my heart wanted me to do. I was done being reckless. Done taking risks."

She doesn't say anything in response. Maybe because, in some messed up way, she relates. So we just sit there in silence for a while.

"Do you know when I realized he was in love with you?" Hailey suddenly speaks. "It's when I saw you both dancing together for the first time. One of my friends took me to the practice hall so that I could see you both together. She was convinced that it was something I needed to see. So we silently spied on you both as you danced. I wasn't even paying attention at first. There was nothing wrong with this. You both were just dancing. Aiden had told me all about the project. But then I stopped, froze, more like it. Because suddenly I was seeing what my friend was seeing. The way he was looking at you . . .

We girls have this radar. We just *know*. So when I saw you both looking into each other's eyes, I *knew*. I knew it was so much more than what I'd thought it was. It was bigger and brighter than anything I'd ever witnessed. For those few seconds, I felt completely helpless. Then of course, I brushed it off and pretended it was nothing. I was in denial, you see. The truth was too painful for me to accept. What Aiden and I had, in a way, was over before it had even started. I just didn't want to accept it."

I shake my head, confused. "But I don't understand. This is so long ago. Aiden and you had just gotten together. You can't possibly mean to say he's been in love with me all along."

"But of course he has! That's what I've been trying to tell you."

I'm still not convinced. "Everyone always talks about how Aiden looks at me. But I don't see it. I mean, when we three—you, me, and Aiden—would be together, his eyes were *always* on you. I felt so neglected. It was like he couldn't even see me."

"That's not true. He only paid attention to me when I was saying something or doing something. I had to work *hard* to get that attention. I had to keep the conversation going, had to keep touching him or doing something." Hailey explains. "You, on the other hand? You didn't even have to try. You'd be staring off into space or be laughing about something and he'd be looking at you, with this stupid smile on his face. I can't even say it was disgusting or annoying. There was something so genuine, so pure about it. It was difficult to find fault with it. I felt betrayed when he looked at you like that. But what could I possibly say? Don't look at her like you're hopelessly in love with her? And I've seen the way *you* look at him too. It's so obvious. How could you both be so blind? And now, that everything is finally falling into place, you're running away again. I just don't get it."

"I'm scared of getting hurt again. He's changed his mind about me so many times already. What if he changes his mind *again*? I mean this time it would be so much worse because we might actually even give this a chance, you know? And what if he realizes later on that he was wrong about me? That I'm not the one? He'll leave, and I'll be the one left hanging. Because I'm *always* the one left hanging, the one who gets too attached too soon and isn't able to let things go, the one who overthinks everything, who feels too much. I'll be the one left broken. The one left to pick up the pieces and mend myself." I argue.

"It *could* happen." I continue. "I mean, I don't even know if Aiden and I are right for each other. We're *so* different. The only thing we have going on for us is that we make each other happy. Hailey, you said it yourself. We girls make this mistake only once, thinking we can change the guy, that we can make him stay. And I've *already* made that mistake. I've *already* failed. Dare I make that mistake again?"

"You *have to* Scarlett. You have to risk it. You have to take the leap. You cannot fly before you fall. You have to do it! There's no other way. You can either fight for that one thing that has actually ever felt real to you, or you can run away like a coward. You need to make a decision. I mean, *I* thought what Aiden and I had was real. So I fought for it. I fought because I believed in us, even if it wasn't meant to be. But you, you have the real thing, and you're still hesitating? I think it's time for you to stop thinking and start doing. Because if you don't, then one day you'll realize you made a terrible mistake. But by that time, it'll be too late."

I see her point now. I *can't* be scared. Nobody said it would be easy. It certainly hasn't been easy. But when I think of all the good, happy moments—all the times that I *did* allow myself to feel, I realize how amazing it was, how amazing it could really be.

And it's worth it. *He's* worth it.

And nobody knows the future. Nobody can guarantee that it will last. But if it does? It'll be the best damn thing.

Is it too late already? I hope not.

I get up, suddenly ready to go. I've delayed enough. I can't wait anymore.

I turn to Hailey. "Thank you, thank you *so* much. It was good talking to you."

She just shrugs in response, like it's no big deal. I suddenly wrap her in a bone-crushing hug, taking even myself by surprise. "Thank you. I needed this."

She awkwardly pats my back. She clearly didn't see this coming. "Go on now, you've waited long enough."

And she's right. I've waited long enough.

Chapter Thirty-Seven

Scarlett

Susan opens the door to her house and lets me in. She has this dopey smile on her face, and her eyes are locked on the screen of her cell phone.

I smirk. "Is that Adam you're texting?" She blushes in response.

"I see it's going well."

She nods. "Yeah, we're planning to go out again this weekend. I'm *so* excited. I've selected some outfits. You need to help me choose."

"Aye, aye captain!"

I follow her upstairs to her room, plopping down on the bed as soon as I get there.

"What took you so long? I was expecting you over an hour ago."

"I'm sorry, I got busy talking to Hailey."

She looks over at me, confused; I don't blame her.

"Tell me *everything*." She demands.

And so I do. There's not a lot to say, really. Just that I've finally decided that I'm going to end this mess, that I'm going to give Aiden and me a chance. I'm done running.

Yes, I'm still scared. But maybe that's the whole point you know? We're human and we'll always be a little scared. But that doesn't mean we stop striving for the things that make us happy.

"Then why don't you call him? *Right now.* I want to *hear.*" She pouts pleading.

I shake my head. "No, I don't want to do this over the phone. I have so much to say. What if I mess up?" I groan. "I wish I could just write it or something—"

Susan suddenly jumps up, clapping her hands. "Oh my god, that's brilliant!"

I look at her, perplexed. "Huh?"

"I have *just* the thing! You just wait."

She walks to the nearest drawer. She returns a minute later with a pen drive in her hand.

I look at it, confused. "What am I supposed to do with that?"

She stares blankly at me. She looks *so* done with me right now.

"You did not just ask me that."

"What?" She glares at me. "I really don't know what you me—oh." It suddenly hits me.

She smirks. "Yes."

"No."

"YES."

I shake my head immediately. "No way! I'm not doing *that.*"

"Why not?! It's perfect."

And it is. It *is* kind of perfect. But it's also so, *so* terrifying.

What she's referring to here, is a file that is stored in this pen drive. But it's not just *any* file. It's a word document, 392 pages long. It has 113, 233 words, all of which are written in Times New Roman font size fourteen. It's a book, a book that *I* wrote.

I started writing it sometime after Hailey and Aiden got together. I wasn't really planning on writing a full-fledged novel or anything. I just wanted to express what I was feeling, just wanted to make sense of what was happening to me.

And so it began. Initially, it was just a bunch of journal-like entries. But as I started writing more and more, I could see a structure forming. I tweaked and refined that structure and consciously started writing a novel, a novel about *everything* I felt for him.

I'd hit a massive writer's block a few weeks back and wasn't sure how to continue this book anymore. *What could I possibly write?* This book had begun as something that was about Aiden and me. Then everything had spiraled out of control, ultimately reaching a point where there *was* no Aiden and me. Somewhere down the road, our flirtationship or whatever that had been had vanished. And this book, it couldn't be about someone else. It had to be about him.

And so, I'd given this to Susan.

"Help me come up with an ending. A happy ending. I don't know what to write anymore. I couldn't get what I wanted in real life, but I'll make myself get it in fiction. So help me figure out what happens next."

I'd completely forgotten I'd given her this until today.

And now she wants me to give this to Aiden. To let him *read* it. The very idea terrified me.

I bite my lip nervously. "I'm . . . I'm not sure if I'm ready to do that yet," I murmur.

How could I let him read this? It wasn't just a string of words; it was a collection of memories, frozen between pages of electronic ink. It was pages after pages of unspoken feelings recorded so diligently during the dark hours of the night—everything I'd felt at every instance yet remained unspoken. It was here. It was all here. So tell me, how could I let him read this? How could I expose the deepest sections of my soul so recklessly, so completely?

Susan grips my hand tightly, looking me straight in the eye.

"It's now or never Scarlett, now or never." She urges me. "Three words can never do justice to what you've felt for him, *how much* you've felt for him. Do it."

"But it's not finished."

"Then what are you waiting for? Finish it and send it to him."

She lends me her laptop, then leaves me alone for the next few hours so that I can write the remaining few chapters. I'm not sure what I should put in them. So I document all that has happened till now, and then decide to end it with a cliff hanger.

Well that's that then. It all depends on you now Aiden.

I remember everything he said to me at the night of the party. I let his words wash over me. He's screwed up more than any other person I know, yet he had the courage to put himself out there once more. And now it's my turn.

I start typing a text to him:

Three words are just not enough. This is how much I love you.

Then I attach the file: A Flirtationship.pdf

And now we wait.

Chapter Thirty-Eight

Aiden

My phone lights up. My heart soars in my chest for one tiny second, but I put it to rest.

It's not her Aiden. Stop getting your hopes up. It's not Scarlett.

But it was. It *was* her. Imagine my surprise when I looked at the notification bar to see that I've just received a text from her—a text after she's been ignoring me for the past four days?

I don't wait. I *can't* wait. I quickly open it and there's the text:

Three words are just not enough. This is how much I love you.

Stop.

My heart stops. I forget to breathe. For a few moments, it feels like time itself has stopped.

I love you.

I keep staring at that phrase with my heart in my throat. Is this reality or a dream?

I notice that she's also sent me a PDF file. I waste no time and quickly download it.

It's a book. It's some sort of book. At least that's what the number of pages suggests. A quick scroll confirms it. There are actual chapters here. By now, I'm thoroughly confused. I'm pretty sure she sent me the wrong file or something. I'm about to close it when I read something that makes me stop. I read my own name then hers.

What is this?

Feeling utterly confused, I scroll back up and start from the beginning.

> Some things never change. My best friend Aiden Walkers barging into my room every Friday night to urge me to go to some stupid high school party is one of them.

Whoa.

My eyes are glued to the screen. I continue to read, devouring the words.

> Today is no different. I am pretty sure he'll be making an appearance tonight. *Especially* tonight. School is over, and summer has officially begun...which is why I'm not wearing my favorite tee.

As I continue to read, it hits me that this, all of this, is written by Scarlett. And it's definitely not fiction. It's like I'm inside her mind, witnessing everything that has happened between us.

> *Think about it Scarlett, would it really be so bad for you two to kiss?*

> I shake my head in refusal, trying to convince myself. I can't just . . . kiss him. I can't.

Oh c'mon. Don't be a chicken. Go back in there and do it. You know you want to.

I freeze. I can't believe it! She'd wanted to kiss me back that night?! Damn it. That's the night I met Hailey. I pull my hair, frustrated. God, I wish I'd waited. I wish I'd I waited like I'd said I would. None of this would have happened if I'd just waited for her instead of rushing off to some other girl.

I continue reading, my curiosity piqued. Everything that's written here is depicted exactly the way it happened. Except, I'm also able to get inside Scarlett's head. As I read further, I realize Scarlett had always had some feelings for me.

The part when we both got assigned the dance project comes up. I hungrily read on, curious to know her thoughts.

Somehow, the scene of Aiden and I pressed up against each other chest to chest, hand in hand keeps entering my mind. I don't want to get excited but somehow even thinking about all this sends a thrill up my spine. I can't believe I'm actually excited about this.

Whoa, so she actually *wanted* us to dance together. She was as thrilled about it as I was. Wow, I had no idea.

I read further, reaching the part where I'd been messing with her over texts.

Me: Well go and talk to her if you miss her.
Why waste your time chatting with me?
Him: I'm already talking to her.
Me: Good. I won't disturb you then. Goodbye.

Ah yes, I remember this. I can't believe Scarlett didn't realize I'd been talking about her and not Hailey. God, this girl is so dense. I see I really pissed her off that night.

I continue to read:

"I like him," I say. It feels strange to finally admit this to someone, even if it is through the phone. I hear my best friend Susan gasp.

Wait, it's chapter five and she says she likes me *already*? Nothing has even happened yet. Wait, so she liked me all along, huh?

Wow.

I continue to read, flying through the chapters. I've *never* read anything so swiftly and with so much interest. I reach the chapter where she describes the library incident:

I want him to cover that teeny-tiny distance between us desperately. But at the same time I know I can do that too. But I don't. It's like I've frozen and my senses are all jumbled up. I can't even form coherent thoughts.

So, she'd wanted to kiss me too. So it wasn't just me who'd been caught up in the moment. There really *was* something there. I continue reading ahead, reaching the part where she comes over to my house for practice:

My eyes widen as I take in the scene before me. Disbelief washes over me and my stomach tightens. Hailey and Aiden are on the bed, kissing each other fervently, making out.

I cringe. Oh boy, so she *had* come for the practice that day. I'd thought she'd ditched me because of what had happened in the library. I can't believe she walked in on us like that. I genuinely feel bad for her and mentally punch my past self. Again, why couldn't I have met with Hailey later!?

I continue reading, reaching the part where Hailey confronts Scarlett in the washroom:

> "Now you listen to me Scarlett and listen carefully—because I won't repeat myself. Aiden is mine. He is my boyfriend."
>
> "I know that—"
>
> "Do you? Do you really? Don't act all innocent. I saw how you were holding his hand in the car this morning. And don't think I haven't noticed how you stare at him from afar. But by all means, you can stare at him the whole fucking day, as long as you remember that it's the only thing you can do—stare."

I gape at the screen. Wow, I had no idea that this had happened. *Why didn't Scarlett ever tell me?* I re-read the conversation, feeling utterly shocked. Girls can be *so* brutal to each other. There I was trying so hard to make these two get along, but *this* was happening behind my back.

Girls.

I keep reading. The next chapter is the one where we went to that carnival on a double date. The more I read, the more surprised I become.

She was only pretending to date Adam!? To make me jealous? What?! And *Hailey* had deliberately started the fight with her!? And the balloon fight hadn't been about the teddy bear, but about *me?* Geez.

I read ahead, seeing her perspective of the time she spent with Adam. Towards the end she says:

"Adam, I don't think we'll be able to make Aiden jealous. Let's just drop this idea. It's not going to work. I'm just glad you stuck with me, otherwise I would have felt like the third wheel, and this day would have been disastrous."

Oh Scarlett, you have no idea that you actually succeeded in making me jealous.

Then I get to the part I'd been anticipating for a while—our first kiss:

The only thing I can feel are his lips. Everything else vanishes. His hands run down my back and land on my hips, leaving a trail of blazing fire, igniting my skin. My thoughts don't make sense anymore. Nothing makes sense. I *can't* think. He has taken over my body, soul and mind. I feel euphoric.

Then comes the part I'd been dreading: me calling our kiss a "mistake." Just reading about it makes me want to kick myself. *I'd been such an asshole!* I don't deserve her. She's too good for me. I don't know why she still likes me, but I'm glad she does.

I resume my reading, eating up all the words that come my way. *Boy is this addictive!*

Our "date" arrives—when we went to the movies and hung out at the beach. I'm taken aback when I read what all I'd done after getting drunk.

"Stop making me want you." He leans in, brushing his lips against my neck, making me tremble. I remain quiet, not knowing what to say. The gravity of the situation is slowly dawning upon me, the grave realization of just what we've done.

"I like you Scarlett, be my girlfriend."

Oh my god.

I smack my forehead, feeling extremely embarrassed. I can't believe I'd gotten so desperate and clingy; not to mention I momentarily forgot all about Hailey and asked Scarlett to be my girlfriend.

I read further, getting at the part where I'd asked Scarlett to meet me after the match and tell me how she feels. She never came. In fact, she'd started ignoring me. So I'm very curious to know what had been going on in her mind. I mean now it's obvious she'd liked me. Then why didn't she come forward? What happened?

> With butterflies still fluttering in my stomach, I take slow, hesitant steps towards him. I almost reach out to touch his back.
>
> But then I don't.
>
> I see Hailey running into his arms, enveloping him in a tight hug.

Oh no. Oh shit. No, no, no, no. Shit. *She had come that day.* Fuck. She needs to know I hadn't meant to kiss Hailey. Hailey had just come out of nowhere as soon as the match ended and started kissing *me*. Damn it. I slowly massage my temple. How messed up is this? Every time we came even remotely close to confessing our feelings, something would mess it up.

I grimace, knowing what's coming next—me ending our friendship. I'm not sure I want to read further. Will I be able to handle it? Handle the shame I'll feel? The hate I feel for myself already?

> "But this can't go on. *This* has to stop. I don't know what we have—what we *had*—but it's *got to* stop. This—this . . . flirtationship. It needs to end *right now.*"

I remember saying these words and it's like a stab to my chest. I was *such* a coward!

> I blink the tears away. I won't cry here, not in front of him. He doesn't need to know how much I love him.
> Love him.
> *Wow, I love him.*
> This sudden awareness about the true extent of my feelings makes this even worse. Why did I have to realize how I truly feel in the midst of this heartbreak? Why did I have to realize it at all? I was better off ignorant. I was better off unaware of the fact that Aiden was like the air I needed to breathe.

Shit. I slam my hands on the table, frustrated. I'm so unbelievably angry at myself. It's one thing to know I messed up. But to read about it in such vivid detail and *exactly* knowing when and where I went wrong...it's horrible. I wish I'd just listened to my heart, gone with my instincts. I wish I hadn't been a coward.

When I read about how she sat on the swing for hours, crying in the rain, my heart aches. I made her go through this. Me. No wonder she didn't want to forgive me after that. I don't deserve forgiveness.

I close the PDF file, lying back against the chair. I need a break. I can't read this any further. I put down my phone. I've been reading for hours now. I should take a nap. I don't know if I'll be able to though. There's so much going on in my head.

* * *

I wake up three hours later and resume reading. My head feels relatively lighter.

The next bit is completely new to me. I'm not in it. This is the period when Scarlett and I didn't interact much. I read about the party. She describes how she met William, and how I'd acted like an ass to him—I'm not sorry about that though. She's too good for him. She's too good for everyone.

I keep on reading, reaching the part where we perform our dance in front of the class. That day, dancing with her...the feeling I'd gotten was ethereal. I can see that she'd felt it too.

It's like I'm in a trance. Everything's within my reach but I can't grab it. In that moment I am nothing, nothing but scattered fragments of my whole, floating away in the wind. I am not a solid, rigid being, but a fluid soul, melting in the arms of the one I love. In that moment I'm too much and too less. Too empty, too hollow but completely full at the same time. In that moment, I am nothing and everything.

And I have a feeling that I'll never get to feel this again, something so intense, so powerful. It's enrapturing, maddening, overwhelming, all-consuming. It's perfect. And I'll never get to experience this again.

I read further, remembering how I'd walked in on Scarlett and William kissing. I'm surprised to read that she'd actually been looking for me, and that William had caught her by surprise. I realize I'd overreacted. Again.

I'm forced to read about William worming his way into her heart. I read about her dates with Williams, their personal moments, their kisses. I'm not particularly excited about it. It kind of hurts, but I bear with it. The fact that she keeps comparing him to me makes me happy though.

The next major appearance I make is the day William and Scarlett became exclusive, the day I got shit drunk. I read about my ridiculous antics, how we both almost died, and how she took me home. My heart warms up seeing how she took care of me even though I was being such a pain in the ass.

Hmm…she should add a scene here describing how and why I got drunk.

Then comes the day I came over to hang out with Darren. I read Scarlett describing everything that happened. I smirk when she describes how she had felt seeing me half-naked. *Well, I don't blame her. I'm hot.*

The chapters that come after are the ones that don't bring many surprises. Scarlett and I had made up and I was aware of everything that was going on with her. However, things get interesting when I reach the part where she describes her birthday, and my confession. My heart flutters in my chest. This here will provide me answers. I'll finally know why she walked away, how she really feels.

> I'm so sick of feeling so insecure, so replaceable. I'm just so sick of feeling afraid, afraid that he'll change his mind again. I was so bold and strong once, not afraid of taking the plunge. But I took it. I let myself fall. And fall I did. I fell *so* hard, that I never really got back up. That fall shattered me, and I'm still broken. I don't want to be

broken. I know I don't *need* to be broken. I know if I really try, I'll recover. But what if I come together only to fall apart again? What if? I survived it the first time. But I don't think I can survive this again.

I'm scared. I don't want to be, but I am so scared.

I sigh. Now it makes sense. She'd been afraid. Of course, she'd been afraid. Why wouldn't she be? I'd always been so inconsistent with her, leaving her right when she was about to embrace her feelings.

I rush through the next couple of pages. I'm completely clueless about everything that has happened with her since. I'm floored when I read that she broke up with William after she found out that Angelina had feelings for him. Wow, I hadn't seen *that* coming.

I'm shook when I read she went and talked to Hailey, and bless her soul, Hailey actually *encouraged* her to tell me.

Tell me what?

Scarlett's email floats in my head:

Three words are just not enough. This is how much I love you.

She loves me. It's true, it's true she does. She always has.

My heart soars in my chest. I look at the total number of pages, wondering how much is left. One page. My eyebrows crease. What more could she have written? I scroll down:

After emailing Aiden, I head back home. I need to finish my packing. I have a flight to catch tonight. So much has happened. I just really need to clear my head, you know? I've told him everything I needed to. Now I can leave in peace.

THE END

Wait.

Wait. Wait. Wait.

This can't be right. She's leaving? Tonight? Leaving for where? What is she doing?! What?! My gaze falls on the wall clock. It's 7 PM.

I jump up.

Oh shit, *please tell me she hasn't left already?!*

Oh no, oh no, oh no. I need to hurry.

Chapter Thirty-Nine

Scarlett

I groan, burying my face in my pillow.

I can't focus on anything. All I keep thinking about is Aiden reading what I've written. He's going to judge me *so* bad. The book has every teeny tiny detail of how I felt, when I felt it. It's too . . . personal.

I know I have to open up my heart if I really want him. But this is so much more. It's not just opening my heart; it's like giving him a big chunk of it.

It's terrifying.

I have *no* idea what will go through his mind once he reads it. It's like . . . stepping out of my clothes and standing in front of him stark naked. Except the only thing being exposed here is my soul. It's so scary.

I turn up the music. I don't want to hear my thoughts. I just want to sleep. This sucks. I have so much to do but all I can think about is—

Knock! Knock!

"Coming!" I answer, feeling slightly irritated. I don't want to get off my bed. I don't want to talk to anyone.

I unlock the door to my room.

And almost die.

It's Aiden. *Aiden's* here. *Here!* In my room. Oh my god.

And suddenly that feeling returns—the cringe-inducing, embarrassing feeling of being completely exposed. Except this time, there's nowhere to run. I need to finally face him.

I resist the urge to run back to my bed and bury my head in the pillow.

"Oh thank god you're here!" he exclaims. Then before I know what's happening, he pulls me towards him and wraps his arms around me in a hug.

God, he smells good!

"What was that for?" I ask, when he finally lets me go. Butterflies swarm my belly. Their wings don't just flap, they thunder. My chest starts to ache as my heartbeat doubles up.

"I thought you'd left. I literally freaked out!"

"Left? Left where? I don't understand."

"I thought you wouldn't be here."

"And why wouldn't I be here?" I ask, confused.

"In the book you sent me, after you sent—I mean Scarlett, the character, sent me—I mean, she sent Aiden the character— ugh, this is confusing as hell! Basically, after Scarlett sends Aiden the book she's written about him in *your* book, she leaves the city. I just thought—"

I burst out laughing. "Oh my god! You thought I'd actually *left!?* Like *really* left?!"

"Uh yes?! I thought I wouldn't get to see you for God knows how long. Do you know how scared I was?! But obviously, I see that at least *that* bit was fiction," he says, noticing I'm wearing my favorite t-shirt and pajamas, not planning to go anywhere.

I can't stop laughing. I double up, clutching my stomach as tears of laughter stream down my cheeks.

"Aiden, you're *so* stupid!"

"What? Everything else in the book was exactly how it happened and I just thought—"

I shake my head. "Nah, I just wrote that because I didn't know how to end it. And I kind of wanted to mess with your head so you'd come meet me. Truth is, the ending hasn't happened yet Aiden. *You* get to decide how this ends."

I suddenly grow serious. I lean towards him, our lips almost touching. I look him straight in the eye and say, "so tell me Aiden Walkers, how does this end? Do we get a happy ending?"

A slow smile blooms on his face. My heart skips a beat. "Yes we do. *Of course* we do." Then he leans in, takes my face in his hands and gives me the longest, most mind-numbing kiss ever.

I take in a huge breath of air, when he finally lets me go. My head's spinning. I swear if I shut my eyes, I'll be able to see stars.

"Wow…that was nice," I murmur, shyly.

"Nice? Just nice?"

"Oh come here, you!" I grab him by his collar and push him against the wall, claiming his mouth. Our lips move against each other's in a fevered frenzy. His hands run down my back, gently grab my butt as he pulls me closer. I knot my fingers in his hair, as a soft moan escapes my lips.

I gently step away from him a few minutes later.

"God, you have no idea how much I've been aching to do this," I murmur.

"Me too, love. Me too."

He leans in, pressing his lips against my forehead, then on the tip of my nose, then a gentle peck on my lips. I smile against his lips, feeling warmth and relief seep through my bones. Being here like this with him, it feels like home.

We lay down on my bed, side by side, staring at the blank white ceiling, with our fingers intertwined.

I turn to look at him. I feel happiness surge through me. It's like drinking a cup of hot chocolate after a tiring day.

"I love you Aiden Walkers. So much."

"And I love *you*, Scarlett Stevenson. So much."

I just look at him. I don't say anything. I just look at the brown of his eyes, with those tiny gold flecks that are almost never visible. I look at his face, all the sharp angles, those high cheekbones, that firm nose. I look at the way his hair is falling on his face. Lying here like this, it almost feels like we've woken up from a long nap.

He's so close to me, I can touch him without it feeling all wrong, without that voice in my head telling me I need to stop. He's so close to me and he's so beautiful. I almost forget to breathe. Is this even real?

"You're really mine now, aren't you?" I murmur, not able to believe it. I've secretly always dreamed of this day. But now that it's finally here, I can't wrap my head around it.

"Yes. Just yours. Always."

I reach for his face, caressing his beautiful cheeks. God, I'll never get used to this.

"I love you." *God, it feels so good to finally say it out loud.* "Thank you for coming into my life. You showed me that it was possible to feel something so pure, so intense, so beautiful. And if some months from now, you change your mind about me, about us, then at least, I'll always have this one moment to hold on to."

He shakes his head in refusal. "I'm not going to change my mind, Scar. I can't. I'm too far gone to do that now." He brings my hand to his lips, kissing each of my knuckles. "From here on, we only go forward. There's no looking back."

"Really?"

He nods, pressing his lips against mine one more time.

"Now about that book you wrote . . ."

Epilogue

All we want, all we ever really want, is for someone to see us. To *truly* see us. We all feel invisible sometimes, and sometimes, all it takes is one person to change everything.

Aiden was that someone for me.

Now here I am today in front of the school steps, entering the school gates on the first day of my senior year. There are so many faces. There are groups of young scared-looking kids, terrified of entering this hell hole. The seniors are easy to spot, standing in front of the main gate, chatting in loud voices, looking excited. This is *their* year.

This is *our* year.

Most of the seniors graduated before the summer and are successfully starting college. I heard William got into Julliard (wow) and Angelina successfully got into an Ivy League university. A few months back, I'd heard that William had started dating her. I don't know if they are still together though. I hope they are.

Meanwhile here Hailey and I are good friends. Not best friends who tell each other everything, but we're friendly and every once in a while we hang out. Shocking, right? I know. Susan and Adam are still going strong. *Why do I get the feeling they are going to last?* Aiden and I go out on double dates with them sometimes. But they are so damn cheesy, it's borderline irritating.

Sharon's semester project about generating awareness on ecological issues inspired her to work with local NGOs. She also researched and came up with a sustainable and eco-friendly factory model. Topped with extra credits and tons of AP classes, she graduated early. She's currently taking a gap year, travelling across Europe on a grant. School's a little lonely without Sharon. I miss her, but we text each other almost every day.

And then there's Aiden and me. I'd dismissed the book I'd written as just something I'd done to cope with my emotions. But Aiden urged me to edit it. He even insisted there should be some chapters with *his* point-of-view in it. He's currently helping me write them.

As for us, we're really happy together. All this time that we've spent together has only strengthened our relationship and now we understand each other a lot more. We're growing up, we all are. And I don't know where we'll be a year from now, but I hope it'll be someplace nice. They say your high school years are the most memorable years of your life, especially the senior year, and I'm looking forward to what's coming.

I'm standing near the lockers with Kayla and Andrea right now. We're gossiping about the usual things. Everybody's sharing what they did during the summer. As we stand there talking, I think some things never change and these are the memories I'll cherish when I'll leave school.

"Oh look, your boyfriend's here," Kayla exclaims. Butterflies fill my belly almost instantly. Will I ever get used to the idea that Aiden, my best friend, is now my boyfriend as well? I turn around, coming face to face with him, trying my best to calm my heart.

I can't help looking at his handsome features—his chiseled cheekbones, the curve of his nose, his bright brown eyes and before I know it, I'm running up to him, wrapping my arms tightly around him as he lifts me up and spins me round before dipping me down in front of everyone and claiming my lips.

His lips evoke a beautiful, inexplicable sensation through my body. There are sparks, tingles, and butterflies all at once. My fingers lock through the strands of his hair as his hands wraps tightly around my waist, pulling me closer to him. I stifle a moan as his lips start moving even more furiously than before. "If we weren't in school, I'd take you right here, right now," he murmurs against my skin, causing me to tremble. A deep red blush colors my cheek almost instantly and I look away, not able to meet his eyes.

"Get a room you two!" Kayla exclaims.

"What do you say we take her advice and get a room?" He smirks.

"Aiden, we're in school!" I exclaim, shocked.

"Yeah, but we have half an hour before homeroom starts. I don't think there's any harm in making out a bit."

I narrow my eyes at him before laughing and let him guide me. We're heading towards the roof. I realize how perfect it feels—his hand holding mine, his fingers fitting in the spaces between mine so perfectly. And as we walk hand in hand through the crowded hallway, I stare at him with awe and adoration. We've come so far from what we used to be.

Reaching the roof, I realize we've come full circle. It all started here. *This* is where I realized what I felt for him for the first time. I also realize that it's started to rain.

I feel fat drops of water fall on my face. I look up at the sky.

"You don't mind getting a little wet, do you?" Aiden asks me.

"Uh no, why?"

"Because we're going to kiss in the rain now."

I start laughing. I know he's not kidding. I'm *glad* he's not kidding.

As the world transforms around us, the grass and leaves turning greener, the sky a bleak grey, we kiss. We kiss till the first bell rings. We kiss even after that. We kiss till we're soaked beyond belief.

Once done, he grabs my hands and leads me down the stairs. He looks up at me as he does, smiling his beautiful smile. And in that moment, I fall in love with him all over again.

THE END

Can't get enough of Aiden and Scarlett?
Make sure you sign up for the author's blog
to find out more about them!

Get these two bonus chapters and more
freebies when you sign up at
shreya-pandey.awesomeauthors.org

Here is a sample from another story you may enjoy:

Prologue

Let me just say that I absolutely *loathe* those goody-two-shoes. I have nothing personally against them, really. It's just that if they ever catch fire and I happen to have the last glass of water known to all humanity, I would rather use it to water the beautiful, glorious weeds behind me. They act all innocent and all wonderfully smart, teacher's pet and all. They are always seen, or portrayed, as the innocent ones, and then the "Queen Bees" or the head cheerleaders are always the main antagonists, trying to claim the guy and ruin the good girl's perfect humble life.

But hey, let me get this straight. When you read a story in the goody-two-shoes's point of view, it is pretty obvious that they want you to think that the good girl is the hero of the story, the protagonist. After all, it is an unsaid rule that the winners get to tell the story. Yet, have you ever wondered *perhaps* why those Queen Bees want to attack those girls so much?

Imagine this: You and your lovely handsome boyfriend have been in a relationship for three years now, ever since you were fourteen. *Young,* I know. You two practically have known each other since birth and are the typical clichés of "loving the best friend." The both of you rule the school undoubtedly; the perfect golden couple that is well-liked by everyone who has ever crossed your path. But then a goody-two-shoes suddenly comes in, snatches your best friend and boyfriend away from you, and practically tries to put you in a negative light. How would you feel?

Sadly, my friends, I was placed in that situation at the end of junior year. I grew up with my best friend, Blake Ryder, and we were practically "joined at the hip." Along the way, we had a few other close mutual friends here and there who completed our perfect little entourage. Times changed; those friends left, and Blake grew up to be the most glorious man I have ever met in my entire existence, and it didn't help that I was already hopelessly in love with him during my younger years. He would be what you guys call a typical bad boy. He, like I mentioned before, had the physical appearance that would put a Greek god to shame. He had that don't-really-care attitude, and—I must admit—was quite rude to the teachers and principals and practically everyone else in the school.

Sure, he was a big bad meanie, but he had a heart of gold. He was my best friend, and we stuck with other through thick and thin. When my parents got divorced, he was there almost immediately upon hearing the news and arrived with tubs of my favorite ice cream and chick flick movies. He was there when I had my first ballet recital, and he was also there when I had gotten my first bike. No, not a bicycle, a *motorcycle*.

Like I said, he had a heart of gold, and he cared for everyone that he held dear to his heart. However, he had a wall of stone that surrounded his heart, and if you didn't crack down that wall, he would appear to have a heart of pure ice.

He was everything to me, and when he jokingly asked if I would be his girlfriend when I turned fourteen, I agreed. I didn't know back then that he was serious and was surprised in the best way possible when he had really asked me out on my fourteenth birthday. Needless to say, that was the best birthday of my life.

But then came my seventeenth birthday.

I would like to believe that I was a pretty generous person, not the typical plastic Barbie. I didn't talk behind anyone's back, and I tried to participate in as many charity events as possible. Sure, I was the head cheerleader, but that *didn't* mean that I was mean or rude. I was not even a natural platinum blonde, for heaven's sake!

So like I was saying, it was my seventeenth birthday, and I had invited the whole school over to my house for a party. And yes, that included the smart people and the wallflowers, though I wasn't quite sure they would turn up. That's the thing; I made the mistake of inviting everyone. I had unknowingly invited my future enemy, Charlotte Brooke.

Charlotte would be your typical good girl. She had perfect grades and strict yet loving parents who held respectable jobs, and she only lurked in the shadows of Crescent Grove High. She never tried to make herself known throughout school, and some of my cheerleaders bugged her out.

Cliché enough for you?

On my birthday, however, she had to make herself known. She and her best friend, Miranda Hastings, had always worn baggy clothes to hide and blend in with the crowd. Sure, Miranda was more outgoing compared to Charlotte, but that didn't mean she was *that* outgoing. They had to choose my night—*my night*—to wear the skimpiest clothing and get all the attention.

When they stepped into the room, I was stepping down the long stairs. Their entrance looked like Cinderella's big reveal, and I looked like her mice friend trailing behind. Needless to say, I was absolutely *humiliated*. The worst part in all of this? Blake had the audacity to ask her for the first dance of the fairytale ball themed party. My party was trashed, and ever since that day, I made it a point to make her life miserable.

See, I had a reason. Okay, maybe I did take this a bit too personally.

Without any other warning, Blake had gotten close to her, and soon, some rumors of me cheating on Blake spread throughout the whole school like a wildfire, and I was known as a *whore*. I felt cheap, walking the hallways and having people stare at me as if I were in an issue of *Playboy*. Blake broke up with me exactly two weeks after my birthday and went after Charlotte because of this.

I had hit my all-time low and lost everything then. My best friend, my confidence, my cheer head status. Everything.

In time, my close friend and cheerleading comrade, Summer, dragged me out of that ditch, and I got my confidence back.

However, I wasn't going to be the head cheerleader anymore since it was obviously not enough for Blake.

Nope. I was going to be the bad girl.

And he'd *better* watch his back.

If you enjoyed this sample then look for
<u>Bad Girls</u>
on Amazon!

Other books you might enjoy:

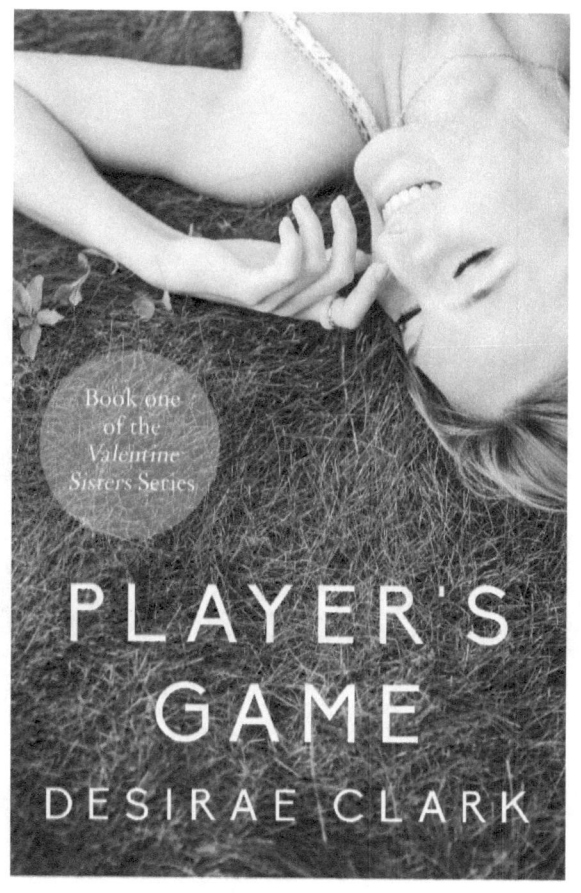

Player's Game
Desirae Clark

Available on Amazon!

Other books you might enjoy

Outcasts
B.D. Fresquez

Available on Amazon!

Introducing the Characters Magazine App

Download the app to get the free issues of interviews from famous fiction characters and find your next favorite book!

iTunes: bit.ly/CharactersApple
Google Play: bit.ly/CharactersAndroid

Acknowledgements

A big thank you to all my Wattpad readers. Without you, this book wouldn't have been possible. I always wanted to experiment with the cliché teen fiction tropes, giving them my own twists. Wattpad gave me the space to do exactly that. And you, my readers, supported me every step of the way. When the writer in me felt like giving up, I'd go back and read all your wonderful, supportive messages that moved me to tears. You might not be the reason I started this book, but you are the reason I finished it. Seeing so many of you relating to Scarlett, engaging with this book, laughing and crying as you read it, made me complete Aiden and Scarlett's story. All your comments and feedback helped me shape this book from its disastrous and messy first draft to what it is today. Thank you so much.

Thank you to my favorite person ever, my best friend, Snigdha Chopra. You spent hours brainstorming with me, giving me constructive feedback and pushing me to write. Thank you for always believing in me and urging me to have faith in myself. You were there when no one was. I love you.

Thank you too, to my friends and family for their enthusiastic support and unending love. Thank you also, to BLVNP Incorporated for recognizing my talent, believing in my book, and bestowing me the opportunity to publish it. I am truly grateful.

A last series of thank yous to the strangest sources of inspiration in my life. Thank you to Taylor Swift. She not only inspired me with her music, but her consistent use of her own experiences to create art made me want to do the same. Thank you to all the people in my life, there are pieces of you strewn across this book. And lastly, thank you to the boy who broke my heart. You ignited a flame in me, only to extinguish it. But if you hadn't, I would have never written this book in the first place.

Author's Note

Hey there!

Thank you so much for reading A Flirtationship! I can't express how grateful I am for reading something that was once just a thought inside my head.

I'd love to hear from you! Please feel free to email me at shreya_pandey@awesomeauthors.org and sign up at shreya-pandey.awesomeauthors.org for freebies!

One last thing: I'd love to hear your thoughts on the book. Please leave a review on Amazon or Goodreads because I just love reading your comments and getting to know YOU!

Whether that review is good or bad, I'd still love to hear it!

Can't wait to hear from you!

Shreya Pandey

About the Author

Shreya Pandey is an upcoming Teen Fiction and Romance author. She started writing her first serious novel *A Flirtationship* on the social reading and writing platform Wattpad, deemed the "Youtube of books" when she was just fifteen. Today it has over 11 Million hits and is one of the most popular Teen Fiction novels there. She is also a Top Writer on popular question-and-answer website Quora.

Shreya is sassy, passionate and intense. In her free time, she embarks on the quest for new music and reads literature. She has a special affinity with thunderstorms, dark skies, city lights and the color blue. She takes inspiration from the people and the world around her, creating characters that are undeniably human and stories that are unforgettable.

Shreya has recently graduated from Ambedkar University Delhi with a Bachelor of Arts in English.